One Morning Like a Bird

ONE
MORNING
LIKE A
BIRD
ANDREW MILLER

SCEPTRE

First published in Great Britain in 2008 by Sceptre
An imprint of Hodder & Stoughton
An Hachette Livre UK company

1

A CIP catalogue record for this title is available from the British Library

Hardback ISBN 978 0 340 82514 3
Trade Paperback ISBN 978 0 340 95215 3

Typeset in Hiroshige by Hewer Text UK Ltd, Edinburgh
Printed and bound by Mackays of Chatham, Chatham, Kent

Hodder & Stoughton policy is to use papers that are natural, renewable
and recyclable products and made from wood grown in sustainable
forests. The logging and manufacturing processes are expected to
conform to the environmental regulations of the country of origin.

Hodder & Stoughton Ltd
338 Euston Road
London NW1 3BH
www.hodder.co.uk

For Frieda

PART ONE

Fire Dreams

I may live on until
I long for this time
In which I am so unhappy,
And remember it fondly.

Fujiwara No Kiyosuke

1

He is squatting in his room in the High City, an open book in one hand, the fingers of the other hand stretched towards the glazed blue belly of a brazier. The room is small, the old sewing room, only four and a half mats, and made even smaller by the clothes that hang from the beading along the walls, by the piled books, by the bedding still unrolled from the previous night, though it is already past seven o'clock and pitch dark outside, this last evening of the year.

It has been his room ever since he was sent to sleep there on his return from Uncle Kensuke's after the Great Earthquake. The first room he ever slept in on his own and where, in his twenty-first year – the eleventh of the Showa Era – he wrote, between the February coup attempt and the end-of-the-summer cicadas, all the poems in *Electric Dragonfly*, a miraculous season, but one that has never returned . . .

He sighs, withdraws the hand he was warming, turns the page of his book, transfers the book to the warmed hand and holds out the other to the charcoal. He is reading in French – not his beloved

Rimbaud, but a tale by André Gide he read in Professor Komada's class at Nihon – a strange romance he did not quite understand then, and which now, for entirely different reasons, he is failing to understand for a second time. For how is he to concentrate on the adventures of Gérard Lacase when so many other matters – matters that cannot simply be pushed aside – turn the words on the page into marks as meaningless as the light reflected in the panels of the drying-platform door beside him? So the young hero (who confesses to knowing *nothing* of life except through books) must set out again and again for the château of la Quartfourche while Yuji examines from every futile angle the latest and most pressing of his difficulties, the matter of his allowance, of its cessation, announced to him by Father in the garden study three days ago, no warning, no warming up, everything delivered in a kind of distracted aside, Yuji by the door, Father at his writing table, smoking and peering at the end of a bookshelf . . . Apparently, the allowance had become a burden on the household economy. There was a need to make changes, to curtail expenses. It was the new circumstances, etc. An unfortunate but necessary measure, though at twenty-five he was surely old enough, etc. He was thanked for his understanding. It was understood, of course, that he understood.

'With immediate effect?'

'From the New Year.'

'Ah.'

So now he must find ways of making up the difference, the difference being almost everything. He will have to rely on people like old Horikawa, on Hideo Makiyama, a future of hackwork like the copy he wrote in November for the West Japan Shipping Corporation. (The newest ships! The fastest routes! Niigata docks are truly a gateway to the world!) Is this how a life goes wrong? How ambition is cut off and talent thwarted, so the fishmonger can be paid?

In the street below, too narrow for much in the way of traffic, a car is creeping towards the house. It stops beneath his window. A minute later the front entrance slides open and a voice, the sort that might emerge from the throat of a speaking bear, calls, 'Is this a house of ghosts? Where are you all?'

Yuji drops the book onto his bedding, shrugs off the blanket he has been wearing round his shoulders, stands and descends – careful on the polished wood – the steep, unlit L of the stairs.

'Grandfather!'

'Grandson!'

Yuji bows. Miyo takes the old man's cape. It's almost too heavy for her, like some huge, dark moth she has captured. Under the cape, Grandfather is wearing a kimono of slate-blue silk, an inch or two of saffron at the sleeves. Father comes in from the study. He greets Grandfather – an exchange of the slightest, most stubborn nods – then the three of them go through the Western room to the Japanese room, where, with Grandfather in the honour place, the alcove behind him, they settle onto sitting cushions. The brazier here is the largest in the house yet seems to warm only the tips of their noses, their knees and fingertips. For most of the winter the room is unused, but the Western room, with its comfortable furniture, its electric heater, would not be quite proper at New Year.

'A good trip over?' asks Father.

'A driver I've had before. He knows his way around.'

'He'll collect you later? You know you are welcome to stay . . .'

'These days I prefer to wake in my own house.'

'Mmm. I understand. And how is your health?'

'Better than yours, I expect. Books will cripple a man faster than digging in his garden ever will. Look at you. You can't even sit with a straight back.'

'Well, I shall have more time for the garden now.'

'And Noriko?'

'Noriko?'

'She's joining us?'

'I'm afraid not.'

'No? A pity.'

'Yes. A pity.'

Grandfather frowns. Father frowns and stares at the matting. On each visit the same question about Mother. On each visit the same reply. A ritual neither seems able to abandon.

The front entrance again. A voice calling its greeting.

'That'll be Kushida,' says Father, standing and going to receive him.

Yuji, left alone with Grandfather, wonders if there might be some way of hinting at the matter of his allowance, of its cessation etc, the difficulty it will cause, the sheer unfairness of it, but the old man, with his wide, wind-burnt face, looks as if he is stirring an enjoyable anger somewhere in his depths. It is not perhaps the moment.

'You haven't been out to see me for a while,' says Grandfather.

'Please excuse me . . . I've been meaning to.'

'I've made some interesting additions to the model.'

'Yes? I'll come soon.'

'You should. I'll be dead one of these days, you know.'

Father leads Dr Kushida into the room. The doctor is chaffing his hands. 'The snow at last,' he says, bowing to Grandfather.

'Started just as I was passing the botanical gardens. One minute nothing, the next . . .'

'I could smell it as I set out,' says Grandfather. 'Like iron.'

Miyo brings in a tray of red and gold cups, red and gold flasks, the festival set. Father and the doctor light cigarettes. Yuji coughs. The scroll in the alcove is a Chinese painting of two figures with packs on their backs labouring up a hill where the pine trees are bent almost double by the weight of the snow. On the shelves beside the alcove is Father's collection of antique incense burners.

'I have a new patient at the clinic,' says the doctor, combing his moustache with the tips of his fingers. 'Came in at the beginning of the week. Name of Amano. He was' – turning to Father – 'at Imperial the same time as us or, at least, there was an overlap – 1911, I think.'

'Is his case serious?' asks Father.

'I'm afraid so.'

'Mmm.'

For several minutes they discuss him, this Amano, or someone who, in 1911, might have been Amano. Was he in the rowing team? Was he the one whose elder brother died of blowfish poisoning? Or was that Maruyama?

Grandfather holds out his cup for Miyo to fill. He stares impassively through the smoky air. He does not think highly of the doctor, once describing him – to Father! – as having the looks of a Meiji petty bureaucrat, the type he'd had to deal with at the mayor's office in the days he was selling his transport interests to the city. And what can 'university talk' mean to one who was earning his rice in the wards of the Low City by the time he was twelve? The life at Imperial, the high ideas and the in-fighting, must be as strange to him as the dancing of cranes.

Haruyo appears, informs them the bath is ready. As their guest, Kushida has the fresh water, then Grandfather, Father, Yuji and finally – as Mother and Haruyo bathed in the morning – the little serving girl, Miyo. The bathroom is on the ground floor, opposite the panelled wall of the stairs where the telephone (one of three private lines in the street) is mounted. At one time the water was heated with coal, but five years ago, when everything in Father's world suggested only serene progress towards an honourable retirement, a new system was installed to heat the water electric-ally, a method everyone praised as clean and modern (and long overdue) but that has somehow never worked as well as the coal.

Crouching in the tepid steam, Yuji washes at the bucket, then lowers himself into the water on thin white arms. The bath is a wooden oval bound with hoops of steel, a little land-locked boat. Whenever Kushida bathes at the house, whenever Yuji has to use his water, he is sure he can smell Lysol disinfectant in the steam, just as he is sure he can smell it on his clothes for several hours after he has been up to the clinic to collect Mother's drugs. He rests his chin on the tension of the water and finds himself thinking of Amano, of poor Amano in his metal-frame bed listening to the horns of the New Year traffic, to the nurses scuffing along the polished corridors in their paper shoes. It was Monsieur Feneon, one French Club night at his house in Kanda – the discussion taking an unusually serious turn – who said that while everyone understood that everyone must die, no one was able to imagine his own death. Imagination, he told them, baulked at that. But could this be true of Amano now? Must he not, as gravely ill as the doctor suggested, imagine his own end constantly? And what does he picture? His wife and children standing around him weeping or bored, and then, at last, the white cloth, which someone has been carrying carefully folded for just this purpose, floating down to cover his face? Or is he beyond anything so obvious, so literal, and sees instead his death figured in a sequence of memory, something mysteriously retained and played like ten frames of film in a relentless loop against the inner skin of his eyelids?

Yuji slides beneath the water, lies there in a foetal hunch. Because his chest is weak, he cannot hold his breath for long. He listens to the world played through the water, to the muffled drumming of his heart. A poet, even one who has not written in almost two years (who poetry has abandoned as mysteriously, as abruptly, as it arrived), has a duty to imagine what imagination baulks at, but the best he can achieve before the air in his lungs starts to burn is something indistinct and swirling, a patch of brightness disappearing into the general dark, like a coin sinking to the bottom of a pond, or the moon through blown clouds, or a head, a face white as a mask, peering through smoke . . .

He surfaces. Whoops for breath.

After the baths, more sake. Grandfather has brought with him a bottle tapped from the cask he receives each year from a business associate who retired up in Iwate. Miyo and Haruyo bring through trays of food – clear soup, steamed yellowtail, deep-fried tofu, pickles and rice. At half past eleven the dishes are cleared, and everyone, with the exception of Mother who goes nowhere, and Haruyo, who goes nowhere with her, prepares to leave for the shrine.

Of the men, only Grandfather is wearing a kimono. Father and the doctor are identical in suits, sack coats and homburgs. Yuji is in a woollen jacket, and a coat that looks, from a distance, as if it might be made of camel hair, like Monsieur Feneon's. Miyo, thin as young bamboo, has on her usual kimono of dark blue stripes on grey, a black jacket, a grey shawl, colours appropriate to her station, and ones that will not offend those guardians, official and unofficial, of the new austerity, among whom Haruyo it seems now numbers herself, for she has already made the girl wipe off the smear of lipstick she had put on, and would have forced her to remove the comb from her hair, the tortoiseshell one with moonstones Mother gave her last summer for her fourteenth birthday, if Father had not spoken up for her. ('No one will notice such a trifle.')

In the front garden, those five yards between the porch and the street, the snow is already ankle-deep. It lies like laundry in the arms of the persimmon tree outside Mother's window, and like a perfect scoop of sugar on the saddle of Yuji's bicycle, which he has left propped against the fence. They gather in the street, adjust hats and scarves, put up their umbrellas. On the gate of the neighbouring house a lantern is burning beside the coil of sacred rope, and on the pavement below two sets of footprints are filling with fresh snow.

Grandfather gestures to the flag that drifts and snaps from a nail in the pillar of the gate. 'Is that a decoration,' he asks, 'or is the boy still away?'

'Saburo?' asks Yuji. 'He's not expected back for months.'

'So the wife lives alone with the old woman? That can't be much fun for her.'

'Three more flags in this street alone since the fighting at Changsha,' says Father. 'Half the city must be over there by now.'

'Well,' says Kushida, buttoning a glove, 'not every young man needs to worry about that.' He glances at Yuji. Yuji bobs his head.

Father mutters something. Grandfather grunts but says nothing. They start to walk.

Halfway to the shrine, they hear the first bell, the first deep note of the hundred and eight. Moments later the air is a solemn confusion of bell answering bell across the widths of the city.

A voice cries, 'The Year of the Dragon!' Neighbours flit past – Mr and Mrs Itaki, Kiyama the wedding photographer, the Ozonos. Then out of the veils of snow directly in front of them appears Father's old assistant, Tozaburo Segoshi, with his wife and two gangling teenage daughters at his side, the same Segoshi who rose through the law department at Imperial by clinging to Father's bootlaces, who has made a career for himself by filling out the margins of Father's work. Seeing Father, he stops mid-stride, emits a mew of embarrassment, and hurries off at such a pace his women, hobbled by the tight skirts of their kimonos, can barely keep up with him. Even a year ago he would have stopped and bowed profoundly. He would have waited for Father to pass. He would have been honoured.

At the shrine, they join the back of the crowd and shuffle through the churned snow between big yellow lanterns. Ahead of them, muffled handclaps summon the *kami*. The snow is lighter now, and as the last flakes fall the air turns sweet with the steam from the hot sake the priests and shrine-virgins are ladling from cauldrons big as baths. Grandfather gives Miyo a pair of coins to make her offering and buy herself a trinket at one of the stalls lining the path. Yuji waits, considering whether he too might be given something. And then the thought strikes him – if Father one day mused aloud, however obscurely, about the difficulty of managing without his salary from the university, of living on his savings, could it even have been *Grandfather* who suggested the allowance be scrapped?

He hangs back, slips away, climbs onto a stone by one of the vermilion gates and looks out over army caps and student caps, over shawls and scarves and the bright lacquer of women's hair. He is hoping for a moment of casual good fortune, and that out of all this crowd he will spy Kyoko Kitamura, whose footprints were one of the sets leading through the snow from the neighbours' gate. His plan – a plan that never varies – is to catch her attention without, at the same time, being discovered by the old woman. If he succeeds, then Kyoko, supposing she is in an indulgent mood (and why should she not be on New Year's Eve?), might find some way to join him for a minute, perhaps share a baked sweet potato with him in the shadow of a camphor tree. But if the old woman sees him, then the game is up, and not out of any unusual zeal on her part to keep her grandson's wife guarded, but because she cannot forgive Yuji for living a safe and idle life while Saburo, only child of her only son, risks everything. She has a photograph of Saburo, a big one she keeps beside the god-shelf and which, one morning, she invited Yuji to admire and be shamed by. A picture taken in a studio in Nanking, Saburo in a winter coat with fur collar (non-standard issue), his left shoulder turned to the camera to show off his acting corporal's chevron. A handsome soldier, the sort schoolgirls develop squints knitting mittens for. And should something happen to him – a not unlikely prospect, as everyone knows the casualty lists are far longer than those names inscribed each year in the Yaskuni shrine – then it seems certain the old woman, in her grief, her rage, will denounce Yuji as a coward, accuse him in front of Itaki the tobacconist, Otaki the noodle-seller, Ozono the brush-maker, in front of the whole street. For what would restrain her? Is it not true that these days the Takano family can be insulted at will?

Someone is calling him. He turns, scans, sees at last, in the light of a kite stall, the Miyazaki brothers, Taro and Junzo, waving to him. He waves back, pushes through to them. They exchange their New Year greetings, first in their own tongue, then, more quietly, as fellow members of the club, in French.

'Your people here?' asks Taro.

'Somewhere,' says Yuji.

'Ours too,' says Taro. 'Somewhere.'

'Have you noticed,' says Junzo, leaning and speaking in a stage whisper, 'how the priests all look a bit Chinese this year? And there's a definite smell of garlic about the place. Shouldn't we, as respectable citizens, report them to the *Tokko*?'

Taro punches his brother's shoulder. He's grinning but there's no amusement in his eyes. 'Little brother's had a few,' he says.

Yuji nods, looks from one to the other – from Junzo, with his hair poking in tufts from under his student cap, a yellow scarf wound round his neck and trailing almost to the ground, to Taro, who, in his new hat, his new coat (a ministry pin on the lapel like a drop of spilt silver), is as neat as the menswear poster outside the Shirokiya department store. There's a second of silence between them, then, as though to cover an unexpected awkwardness, they start, in hurried voices, to speak about the French Club's year-forgetting party at the Feneons', and laugh, all three genuinely amused this time, at the recollection of Junzo's barking competition with Feneon's pug, and how at the end of it, Alissa Feneon awarded Junzo the prize, a mock diploma torn from the back page of a newspaper, an advertisement – aimed, presumably, at the families of military men – for a kind of indestructable Rayon sock.

When the laughter stops, Yuji says, 'I've had some bad news.'

'Your father?' begins Taro, cautiously.

'No, no . . .'

'You mean,' says Junzo, 'someone's given you a job?'

'I mean I shall need to find one now.'

'So, it's the allowance,' says Taro.

Yuji nods.

'A cut?'

'Worse.'

'All of it?'

Yuji nods again, then finds, suddenly, he does not want to discuss the matter at all, that there's a tightness in his throat, a bubble that threatens to swell into a sob. If he was to stand in front of the Miyazakis blubbing, the shame of it would burn for months . . .

He is saved by drums, by lights. The priests and their assistants, illuminated by the brilliant-white cones of two searchlights, are processing up the steps of the hall of worship. Afterwards, the 'Navy March' is played through speakers slung from wires between the trees. The friends agree to meet at Watanabe's bathhouse as soon as the holidays are over, then Yuji enters the crowd again, moves through its shifting labyrinth until Mrs Sakaguchi, mad for gossip about his embarrassing parents, tugs at his sleeve as he passes the purification trough. He backs away from her, apologising and bowing, then follows a side path out of the shrine precincts and onto the road to the cemetery.

He has given up the hunt for Kyoko (did he really expect to find her?) but is in no mood to be at home, sitting in the cold and perhaps having to listen to more reminiscences about the old days at Imperial. In a few minutes he is alone, walking through the lanes of a neighbourhood almost untouched by earthquake and fire – or as untouched as anywhere in this city of disasters. A secretive place where the mouth of an alley, a pair of wooden sandals propped on a verandah, the snow-covered slats of a dog-fence, float uncertainly in the light from tightly latticed windows. At night almost anyone can become lost in such a neighbourhood, but Yuji, preoccupied by an unhappiness almost indistinguishable from a certain type of boredom, navigates with an unconsidered sureness of step until a subtle chilling of the air warns him he is only a turn or two from the cemetery. He does not believe in ghosts and yet, somehow, this does not stop him from being afraid of them. He slows his pace, imagining them roused by drums and gongs, gathering at the cemetery gates (rustling together like the wings of insects) and waiting for some foolish young emissary of the living to pass close by.

And it is then, just as he is considering turning back towards the holiday crowds, that he sees two figures appear, palely, from the dark at the end of the street. He steps under the eaves of the nearest house, presses himself against the shutters, but already he can tell that the figures are men, not spirits, and pale only because, other than for loincloths and headbands, they are both naked. They are running, hopping over the snow, though their progress is pitifully slow. As they come closer, he hears their little yelps of pain and self-encouragement, and as they draw level with him, he sees how their skin glitters with ice like fish scales. Shrine runners. Middle-aged penitents hoping to earn a year of better luck by dousing themselves with buckets of bitter-cold water at every shrine they stagger into. Clenched teeth, clenched buttocks, they do not even glance at Yuji as they pass, though he is no longer hiding from them. If Junzo and Taro were with him, he might have found the scene absurd, would, perhaps, have slyly laughed, but on his own he simply watches them as they disappear into the bend of the street, stares after them, enviously, as if these men had found a form (forget how mad it looks) that answered whatever urgencies provoked them. If he was to strip now and bundle his clothes, would they object to him hopping over the snow at their backs? It would almost certainly kill him, but no one – not Father or even the old woman – would dare to call him frivolous. How amazed they would be to see him return to the shrine in nothing but his underwear! To hear him hollering to the *kami* as the well water broke over his head!

It's two o'clock before he is in his own neighbourhood again, cold and hungry. He would like to warm himself with a bowl of steaming noodles, and wonders if Otaki, in festival humour, might still be open, but the shop is shut and shuttered, a tongue of snowless pavement outside where the dregs of the broth have been poured away. On the Kitamura Gate the flame is out. He watches a while, his ears stinging with the cold, then goes into his own house, slides the door and stands on the beaten earth of the vestibule listening for voices. A glow in the panel above the doors to Mother's room is enough for him to see Father's boots beside the vestibule step, and the shadow of Miyo asleep under her quilt on the mats at the bottom of the stairs, an arrow charm from the shrine next to her pillow.

He goes to the kitchen, eats a mouthful of congealing rice, washes it down with a cup of water. When he's finished, he steps over Miyo and climbs towards his room. At the turn of the stairs, his toes touch the shaped hard edge of something, and though the turn is the darkest place he knows, as he reaches down, that it's the old talisman of the seven gods that Mother leaves out – with her own hands or Haruyo's – for him to slip beneath his bolster and so enter the New Year with propitious dreams of eagles, sacred mountains . . .

He carries it to his room, pulls off his jacket and tie but nothing else, then gropes his way into the bedding, curls up and lies gazing at the blue snow-light in the glass of the drying-platform door. The shrine runners run through his head, feebly glittering figures always a step or two from disappearing into the night. In reverie they gain strange identities. Father and Dr Kushida. Junzo and Taro. Himself and Ryuichi. Himself and Saburo. Staggering over the snow, hopping over the snow . . .

Then out of the small-hours hush he hears, faintly from some neighbouring house, the sound of piano music on a wireless. The Schumann piece, perhaps, everyone pretends to like so much. Then it ends, or the dial is turned, and something else begins, the simple notes of a koto playing a song he remembers from earliest boyhood, 'The Boatman's Song', a sentimental, empty-headed little ditty, and to his own cold fingertips he starts to whisper the old words: 'I am dead grass on the riverbank. You are dead grass too.'

2

Despite the seven gods his sleep is dreamless. He lies in to some unseemly hour (as young boys, he and Ryuichi were always up at dawn on New Year's Day), and in the afternoon plays flower cards with Miyo in the Western room, now and then looking up to watch Father in the garden brushing snow from the delicate plants, unburdening them. Miyo, who excels at flower cards, wins fifty sen and insists on being paid immediately. He pays her, wondering if she has a little purse hidden somewhere, a purse of little coins, perhaps under the house.

At twilight he goes upstairs and onto the platform. With his back to one of the drying posts he gazes over snow-heaped roofs to where a red neon sign for Jintan Pills winks blearily from its gantry in the Low City. He likes sometimes to imagine it's sending him a message, a warning, an invitation, something meaningful, but today it is simply, 'Jintan Pills, Jintan Pills, Jintan Pills . . .'

From the gardens he hears the collar bell of Kyoko's cat. He leans over the parapet and sees its shadow spring from the fence and glide under the bare branches of the gingko tree. The animal is pregnant and seems to have made a nest for herself in the bamboo that grows in a screen round the garden privy. No way of knowing, of course, which of the local toms has been with her.

3

On the second day of the holiday he does what he calls his accounts. The reckoning is very simple. After paying Miyo, he has eleven yen and fifty sen left in the world. He owes two yen to Taro, one to Shozo and three at the noodle shop. This leaves the almost useless sum of five yen and fifty sen. On the credit side, there are ten yen owing to him for the Niigata Docks copy, another ten for translating, for the Fukuhara Toothpaste Company, a document entitled '*Gingivite – Le Grand Défi de Notre Époque?*' The rest is all hope, ambition, speculation. No sign yet of any New Year gift money. No one decently to borrow from. Little chance of credit.

He turns over the paper and on the other side starts to make a list of people who might help him. He puts Grandfather at the top. Even if the old man was involved in the decision to stop the allowance – *especially* if he was involved – would he not agree to a small loan? There have been several in the past (some of them repaid). But with Grandfather there is always the difficulty of knowing what he has anymore, whether he has given all his money away to shrines (a new carved roof for the shrine at Mita, a god-car for the shrine at Kitazawa), to family spinsters in the country, to former employees on hard times, or whether it is still lying in bars of jade and bolts of silk in a fireproof godown somewhere by the river.

Horikawa (of Horikawa and Son, Horikawa Trading Inc., the Horikawa Talent Bureau) can usually be counted on, but only for scraps . . .

And Makiyama? Whatever one thinks of him, whatever one cannot avoid thinking, it must be admitted he has the necessary connections. He took the John Ford essay last summer, placed it with *Eastern Review*, and might, if Yuji can find him sober, be persuaded to take something else, something on Fritz Lang, or the stories of Akutagawa, or even – why not? – on Arthur Rimbaud. For *that* he would need only the books that lie around in his room. He could write it in a week, in two days, though he would have to find some contemporary relevance, some angle to make a dead French poet enticing to a modern Japanese readership . . .

There is a way, of course, a way he has thought of countless times. Monsieur Feneon must be persuaded to show him the letter, the one he mentioned (and so casually!) that spring afternoon in Professor Komada's rooms, but which, in the years since, nobody in the club has succeeded in gaining so much as a glimpse of, all requests met with the same enigmatic smile, the same flutter of the hand. But a story based on the letter, an essay that linked the names of Rimbaud, Feneon and Yuji Takano, a literary detective story, a kind of séance, it could even make a news story, something for the human-interest pages in the *Yomiuri*, a respite from reports of battlefield sacrifice, or some village in Shikoku where they have vowed to give up sleep so

they can plant more rice. With the letter in his hand, would he need Makiyama?

Out in the garden the crows are squabbling. In the Western room the clock is chiming the hour. He puts down his pen. Today, perhaps, he will see Mother. Today is one of the usual days, one of those appointed to such meetings. He combs his hair, goes downstairs to find Haruyo. She is in the kitchen squatting by the half-open door to the passage along the side of the house, a heavy shawl across her shoulders, her long-stemmed pipe in her mouth. Without looking at him, she says that Mother is too tired to see anyone, that she is resting. Resting? She nods. He wonders if she also forbids Father, this nurse-servant who has become Mother's warder. He wonders, too, how a person can be tired when they do nothing, when they have done nothing for seventeen years, when every day they are resting, resting.

Back in his room, he picks up the little sheet of accounts, stares at it, then takes his fountain pen and writes across the bottom, in the neat, cursive script he first learnt at middle school, '*Ô saisons, Ô château, quelle âme est sans défauts?*' Then he rips the page in two, drops the halves into the brazier. Black-ringed holes appear. Finally, a flame.

4

Early on the morning of the last day of the holiday, Uncle Kensuke rings. Yuji, still in bed, knows it must be Uncle calling because Father, who has answered the phone, is asking about the snow in the mountains. 'Has there been much yet? Hmm. I see. That must be difficult for you . . . Yes. Here too, a few inches.'

Sometimes Uncle Kensuke and Auntie Sawa come to Tokyo for the holiday, but this year they will not be coming until the Festival of Lanterns, the Festival of the Dead. Father asks about the children, Hiroshi and Asako, and Asako's husband, who everyone says is doing so well with Mitsubishi. 'And Sawa? Her back? Hmm.'

Now it's Uncle's turn to ask questions. 'Oh, much the same,' says Father, though Yuji cannot tell if he is speaking of himself or Mother, or everything. 'This year will be better, perhaps. I might try my luck at a little farming, like you. I could buy some chickens, keep a pig.' He laughs. 'If we have food shortages, I can make my fortune.'

There is a long pause while Uncle speaks. He is the younger brother and not, therefore, not strictly, the one to be proffering advice to the head of the family, but Yuji hopes that is exactly what he is doing. If Father has the subtler brain, the one best suited to the play of abstracts, the framing of elegant questions, the exegesis of documents whose difficulty is like a glass surface thick as a fist, it's Uncle Kensuke who has inherited Grandfather's common sense.

'Well,' says Father, 'well, we'll see.' Then he laughs the same unhappy laugh at what is evidently a question about Grandfather. 'The model? Oh, yes, it still goes on, I believe.'

That night Yuji wakes out of a dream. Not one of the fire dreams – he's been spared those for almost half a year – but some troubling dream whose details disperse in the instant of waking, leaving only an atmosphere, a sense of ominous approach, of struggle. And what comes to comfort him as he lies in the frigid small-hours stillness of his room is the memory of Uncle Kensuke's farmhouse above Kyoto, and of Uncle himself, always more artist than farmer, hoisting sheets of silk and linen from the vats in the floor of the dyeing barn, where all through the cold season the indigo leaves lie steeping in a brew of wood ash and lime and sake. Men's urine, too, if Hiroshi is to be believed.

It is so many years now since that summer – the invalid nephew sent to get clean air in his lungs, to become a proper boy with a boy's vigour – it still surprises him how much he has kept of it, that it was not all swept from his mind the moment he returned to Tokyo and saw Father pushing through the tattered crowd at the station, ash on his shoes, ash on the cuffs of his trousers. Instead, it has survived, like something improbably fragile salvaged from the chaos of a ruined house, though time has coloured it with a thin wash, a binding glaze, so that the shadows under the pine trees and the smoke from the saucer of smouldering chrysanthemums, the black of Asako's hair, the grey of storm clouds, are all faintly indigo now. Even the moon of that summer, westering over mountain villages and lonely farmhouses has, in memory, some blush of indigo, as if it, too, once hung dripping over the vats in the barn.

5

Two days later he rises from his bedding an hour before first light, breakfasts in the kitchen on a handful of yesterday's rice, a mouthful of cold tea, then steps over the sleeping Miyo, puts on his boots, scarf and 'peach-bloom' trilby, slides the front door to the width of his shoulders, and posts himself, quietly as he can, into the dark of the front garden.

Most of the snow has melted but the air is cold as pond water colder now than when the snow was there. He hurries to the end of the street, pushes up the sleeve of his coat to check the luminous dial of his watch, then turns onto the main road, the north–south that runs in front of Imperial and on towards Kanda. When he has walked some two hundred yards, he stops and slowly retraces his steps. A one-yen taxi passes, a woman in the back, her powdered face lit for an instant by the flare of her cigarette. Then an old man goes by, hauling a white cow on a length of rope, muttering to it his complaints about the world while the beast pours steam through its nostrils. At last, coming towards him, he hears the quick scuff and tap of the footfall he has been listening for. A shadow appears, hesitates at the sight of him, then comes closer.

'So it's you, is it?' Her breath touches his face. He nods, then tells her – with what he hopes is an appealing listlessness – that he has been out most of the night, walking and thinking.

'Out drinking on the Ginza, you mean.'

'I'm not one of those,' he says. 'In fact, I have a lot on my mind right now.'

This, she must know, is not unlikely (though whose mind these days does not carry its burden?). Her voice softens a little. 'Even so,' she says, 'I don't have time to talk to you now.'

'You're going to work?' he asks, as if the idea has just occurred to him, though he could, if called on, write down her hours as accurately as any of her supervisors at the railway company. Kyoko Kitamura, reporting to Tokyo Central Station at six o'clock for the seven fifteen express to Shimonoseki. If he was to unbutton her winter coat, he would find beneath it the black dress and black stockings of her uniform. Her cap and apron – washed and starched – will be in the canvas bag over her shoulder, next, perhaps, to a lunch box, a pack of cigarettes, a magazine or two.

'As we've run into each other,' he says, wondering at how easily these half-lies come to him, if he should be troubled by such a facility, 'why don't I see you to the station? There's no sense my trying to sleep now.'

At first she refuses, then seeing he will not be easily shaken off, and seeing too how well the darkness covers them, she agrees he can walk her the five hundred yards to the tram-stop. He talks to her about the New Year holiday, how nice it was, how boring. He tells her he looked for her at the shrine.

'We didn't stay for long,' she says. 'Grandmother's chilblains are bad this winter. The cold is painful for her. I have to bind her feet at night.'

'And Mr Kitamura? Did the New Year mail get through?'

There was, she says, a card with a printed New Year message, to which Saburo had added a line of his own.

'A line? Well,' says Yuji, 'there can't be much time out there for writing.'

'There's plenty of time,' she says. 'He's just not the sort to write much.' She doesn't add 'as you know' or 'you know how he is', and again Yuji wonders what, and how much, Saburo has ever told her about the two of them. Would he have reminisced, with a bark of indulgent laughter, about his days at middle school, when it was Yuji, skinny little Yuji with no elder brother to protect him any more, who did much of his writing for him? Would he have recalled for her the fact that, though he was indeed expert at making water-bombs or cracking people over the head with a shinai, in calligraphy class he barely knew which end of the brush to hold? Has he, then, with a frown of amazement, tried to explain to her his long alliance with Yuji, a bond between two kinds of weakness, revived at the outset of each new term with a leisurely beating and certain simple though effective acts of humiliation, such as forcing open Yuji's mouth and spitting into it. Or is it *his* task to explain to Kyoko that her husband – heroic young veteran of the Kwangtung Army – was, for some years, his private bully? Not, it should be said, that they ever truly hated each other, not then. On the contrary, they were drawn together by mutual loneliness, a precocious knowledge of loss (Saburo's mother a victim of the influenza in Taisho 8, his father dead from cirrhosis of the liver the first year of Showa), so that even as one brought down his fist and the other grunted with pain, it was a type of friendship, and one that lasted, in its own mysterious fashion, until the marriage two years ago, or until that spring afternoon three weeks after the wedding when Yuji, outside Otaki's, watched the couple returning to the old woman's house arm in arm under the shade of a parasol, petals in Kyoko's hair from blossom-viewing in the park, and on the groom's face, a look of imbecilic happiness, even a kind of innocence, as if, five minutes earlier, he had suddenly imagined himself a man of boundless virtue, and immediately, without the slightest struggle or doubt, had started to believe it. It was then that Yuji should have rushed across the street and flung himself on Saburo's back. When would he own such invincible rage again? Instead, he had watched them turn in at the old woman's gate, heard the street mutter its approval of such a handsome pair, and without so much as a shrug retreated to his own house, climbed to the drying platform, and stared, an idiotic sneer on his face, across the fence to the neighbours' garden.

To be forgotten by someone like Saburo Kitamura! To be thrown aside like a broken sandal so that the present moment could be enjoyed without the inconvenience of remembering anything as unpleasant as spitting into a boy's mouth. It was an insult both painful and shaming. Also, perhaps, a judgement, a moment of revelation that exposed him, if only to himself, as the kind of man even thugs and dullards could leave behind them in their dust . . .

At the tram-stop, a dozen men and women are huddled, half-asleep, in their coats. 'Stay here,' says Kyoko, peering to see who among them might recognise her. 'That's far enough. Go home.'

He does not wish to anger her – he's seen her temper flash out more than once when he's been slow to follow her direction. He lets her go, retreats a little, then crosses to the gateway of a school on the far side of the road, where he waits until the tram rattles into view, collects its load, and rattles off, its single headlamp throwing a limp yellow beam onto the track ahead.

She will be gone for two days, sleep most of the third, be back on shift by the fifth. Five trips a month, Tokyo to the deep south, waiting tables in a swaying box as the country flashes by the window (a glimpse of mountains, a glimpse of the sea, towns and cities half known, half anonymous).

Does Saburo approve, or is he just relieved not to have to send more money home? Even with his promotion, there won't be much to spare after buying fur collars for himself and paying for studio portraits. The old woman takes in sewing, of course, in the season, but so do half the wives and widows in the city, there's no money in it. It's Kyoko who makes ends meet in that house, Kyoko with her cap and apron, her strong legs of a farmer's daughter from Saitama Prefecture.

He leaves the gateway and turns for home, feeling something awkward, something more difficult than his usual sly pleasure in harming an absent enemy, the usual uncomplicated interest he takes in that tight, sturdy body under the winter coat. But it's not until he's passing the university library, where a lone light burns feebly against the brightening sky, that he realises he has started to respect her. It startles him. He cannot believe he ever really intended to fall in love with her, this wife of a man he has never stopped being frightened of. And yet how interesting it is, how poetic, to think that he *might*!

6

When Yuji arrives at the office – a rented room above a bicycle repair shop in the Hibiya district – Horikawa is sitting at his desk speaking on the telephone. He is also doing calculations on the *sorobon*, smoking a cigarette (Airship brand), picking at his breakfast rice, glancing at the racing pages of the paper and waggling a finger to welcome his visitor. His feet are hidden by the clutter under the desk but Yuji wonders if he might be doing other things with his toes, a little typing perhaps, some filing. No one else he has ever met can perform as many tasks simultaneously, and perform them well, for the calculations will all be correct, no rice will be spilt and the good horses will be sorted from the bad. So remarkable is this talent it's generally agreed that he would, by now, have his own building in the Marunouchi were it not for certain bad stars that gave him a son, Yuji's age, who staggers through the house moaning and drooling, a wife, a third the husband's size, with a taste for brandy, and in his chest a swollen heart that now and then lingers between beats, so that – terrifying to those who have witnessed it – he sometimes halts mid-stride in the street, suspended between two worlds, the living and the dead.

He points to the bench by the door. Yuji sits. On the wall opposite the bench, a wall that on his last visit still had a framed photograph of Tokyo Central on it (a view from Nihombashi before the earthquake, the station's dome and towers on the far side of the tracks that separated it from the Low City), there is now a map of Japan, like the ones they used to have at school. Red dots and red circles for the towns and cities, the country the colour of flypaper, the sea an unbroken blue. One of the pins holding the bottom of the map has fallen out and the paper has rolled upwards, giving the country a curled tail like a smoked fish. While Horikawa talks, and the wooden beads of the *sorobon* click, Yuji counts off the dots and circles he has been to outside of Tokyo: Kyoto and Nara on visits to Uncle Kensuke; Snowy Akita on trips to Grandfather Yakumo and Aunt Togashi, both long dead now; Yokohama – which hardly merits inclusion on such a list – to look at the foreigners, to look at the liners, to make (once) an outing to a certain place behind the docks, an afternoon he would prefer to forget about; and Kamakura, where on family holidays they used to rent a villa in the hills and spend two weeks of the summer, holidays whose heat and flavour are now just a clutch of mental postcards – Father on the beach with a towel round his head, reading a newspaper, Mother in a polka-dot swimsuit, Ryuichi eating watermelon, the juice running off his chin.

As for anywhere beyond the black lines marking the coasts of the islands, there is nothing. Father, at his age, or a little older, was preparing to set sail for Marseille, the beginning of a six-month tour of British and European universities – Mother, who now travels only to the bathroom or, on rare occasions, into the garden, lived a whole year in Korea when Grandfather Yakumo was teaching at the Christian college in Seoul. But for himself, he finds it hard to believe he will ever do more than add a red circle or two to his collection. And anyway, these days leaving Japan means leaving in a uniform on your way to China . . .

When Horikawa puts down the telephone he pays Yuji out of the petty-cash tin, then lights the spirit burner in the corner of the room and makes them both some coffee. The morning is bright. Despite the cold, they sit at the open window watching trains cross the railway bridge. Horikawa knows them all, each engine's destination, and points them out for Yuji with the tip of his cigarette, speaking of them as if they were old friends leaving for the country but whose return was promised.

To Yuji's question about more work he answers with a grimace. The West Japan Shipping piece, he says, was well received. The vice president's assistant had his secretary call to say how pleased they were. But business almost everywhere was slow. It was the time of year. It was the international situation. War was always good fortune for someone – a skilled worker in heavy industry could get all the overtime he wanted – but for others . . . 'Take your Monsieur Feneon, for example. Silk brokers like him can't rely on the old markets any more. How much Japanese silk will there be on the catwalks of Paris this spring? These days—' He stops, leans to the window. 'Ah, engine two hundred and seventy-one. She's for Nagoya. These days you need to know someone in the government. Someone who can hand out a nice fat contract. If I was in Feneon's line, I'd go to the War Ministry and talk about parachutes.'

'Parachutes?'

'They're made of silk, aren't they? Even with our airmen's indomitable spirit I expect they still like to take off with a parachute on their backs.'

Yuji, who has long wished to be of service to Feneon, to repay his many kindnesses and show that he is not only a loyal friend but someone whose thinking can have practical as well as merely intellectual outcomes, is immediately struck by the brilliance of the idea.

'Should I suggest it?' he asks. 'Do you know someone who could help?'

'I was . . .' says Horikawa widening his eyes, '. . . I mean, do you really think the government would employ a Frenchman to make parachutes for us?' He starts to giggle. 'We might, while we're at it, ask the Americans to make our gun sights.'

'But we're not at war with France. Or with America for that matter.'

'Well, it's true . . .'

'And Monsieur Feneon's been here for years! Everyone knows him. *You* know him. His daughter walks around in kimonos. She takes classes in classical dance.'

'The lame girl?' At this, Horikawa begins to wheeze. He presses a hand to his chest, then tugs from his jacket pocket a large handkerchief and carefully, starting at the brow and working down to his throat, wipes the shine from his face. Horikawa sweats winter and summer, an oozing that carries the not unpleasant smell of the preparations he takes for his heart, those bitter teas of roots and fungi harvested in remote mountain forests. 'Perhaps she really thinks she is Japanese, but it will take more than kimonos and being able to dance Flowers of the Four Seasons to persuade the gentlemen at the ministry. But don't worry.

Feneon's an old hand. He'll use his contacts in Indochina. Move back into tobacco or rubber. He'll know what to do.'

He asks Yuji to stay and play a game of *shogi* with him, but Yuji, who has not enjoyed being laughed at, invents a vague appointment, excuses himself, and leaves the office. In the repair shop below, the mechanic in his oil-grimed leggings is squatting on the floor with a bicycle wheel in his hands, holding it up like a type of old-fashioned sun-sight. He nods to Yuji, calls out a tradesman's bright good morning. Yuji nods back, takes in, in a single glance, the cluttered workshop, and walks towards the palace moat thinking how hard it is not to become at last like everyone else, not to lose, as one grows older, all delicacy of response. Horikawa, for example, is a clever man, but he is too cynical, too interested in money, too sunk in the narrow ambitions of commerce. Feneon, of course, is also interested in money, but Feneon knows literature, knows art, while Horikawa knows – what? Trains, racehorses. Is that how you protect yourself? By reading? By listening to music? Or does the world exert an ineluctable force that only the most exceptional can resist? And is he one of them? Is *he* exceptional?

He stops by the bank of the moat opposite the boat-rental pier and looks down at his reflection, an outline that could be almost anyone's. Between the drifting willow leaves, bubbles break the water's surface. Something is down there, some bony fish or other, dull in its own dull kingdom. He turns away, and to protect himself a little from his own interest in money, to distract himself from the nagging fear he may not be quite as exceptional as he once believed, he conjures up the spirit of Arthur Rimbaud striding along a country road to Paris, crazy grey eyes, his pockets stuffed with paper, a poetry so pure everyone will either fall in love with him or want to murder him . . .

At home, lunch is ground beef and grated yam. Father has carried his food out to the garden study to continue, undisturbed, his reading in those volumes of archaeology that are his new obsession. The Jomon Era, the Yayoi, the far edge of history. Cultures that have to be imagined from shell-mounds, fragments of terra-cotta. Yuji eats with Miyo in the Western room. After lunch she shows him a beauty magazine she has borrowed from one of the other serving girls in the neighbourhood. In an article called 'Please Be Proud of Your Japanese Skin' there is a character she cannot read. It is, he says, the character for 'fate' or 'the path you are obliged to follow' or 'the unrefusable way' or, to put it plainly, 'the unavoidable', 'the inevitable'. Also, perhaps, 'submission'. She thanks him, then hearing Haruyo slide open the door of Mother's room, she hurriedly rolls the magazine and thrusts it inside her kimono, between her little breasts.

7

Rain, then sleet. Yuji hurries through the door of the bath-house, stows his umbrella, picks at the knots in his laces, tugs off his boots, examines the fringes of wet sock where his boots have leaked, puts the boots into an open locker, and greets Mrs Watanabe, who bows and tells him that his friend, that *nice* young man, arrived ten minutes ago, something Yuji already knows, having just seen Taro's leather brogues drying in the locker above his own.

In the next room, he strips, takes his towels and slides open the door to the baths. The bathhouse has been here since before the Great Earthquake (the boast is that they only closed for a week), a shadowy place, slightly shabby and not, perhaps, as clean as it should be, but for its customers its dereliction is its charm. They would go nowhere else.

There are only six or seven this side of the screen, and on the other side, to judge from the light voices that float under the ceiling on steam clouds, a few more. Taro is perched on an upturned bucket, a towel round his neck. Yuji joins him, scrubs Taro's back.

Taro scrubs Yuji's. Clean, they climb into one of the baths (not the hottest, nor the one with the swaying bag of medicinal herbs). They shut their eyes and sigh.

'Junzo?' asks Yuji.

'Mmm?'

'Junzo?'

'Supposed to be here.'

'Ah.'

'Mmm.'

It's twenty minutes before Junzo arrives. Yuji, with one ear cocked to the cooing and chattering of the women – he knows Kyoko sometimes comes to Watanabe's – watches him washing at the tap and thinks how easy it would be, through the steam, like looking through the fine linen of a mosquito net, to take him for a boy of thirteen or fourteen, though only two months ago they celebrated his twenty-first birthday at the billiard parlour on the Ginza, a raucous and beer-drenched occasion, half the philosophy class from Imperial there, singing or spewing . . . He has rarely traded schooldays stories with Junzo but can imagine well enough how things might have been. Did he too have to marry himself to a creature like Saburo, or did brains and little-dog fearlessness and having Taro at his back keep him safe? For so much better made is the elder brother than the younger – who seems, by comparison, to have been stitched together from whatever was left over, the trimmings – even big-fisted Saburo would think twice before taking him on. When Taro was called up for his year of service (it was 1935 and still, despite the best efforts of the military, a time of peace), he was barely out of basic training before they were using *him* to put some muscle on the city limbs of the new intakes. Barracks judo champion, a sprinter, a notable swimmer, he never even had to leave Tokyo. Just the type the army is always hungry for, the sort who makes them look the way they like to imagine themselves – virile, graceful, natural conquerors.

A different story when they are faced with material like Yuji or Junzo. Then they feel offended, and something wild comes into their eyes. Captain Mori, the officer who, in the July of Yuji's twentieth year, examined him in the gymnasium of a high school in Hongo, had particularly expressive eyes, and for three minutes, as Yuji stood in his underwear in front of the desk, the captain had stared at him with such a concentration of contempt it was as if all the oxygen was being sucked out of the room. Between them, on the gymnasium floor, was a sixteen-kilo burlap sack of rice. The captain ordered Yuji to lift it over his head. Yuji, bending, gripping two burlap ears, dragged the sack to his waist, swung it towards his chest, and for a second seemed to have it there safely, before some lapse of will, some failure of technique, sent it plunging to the floor again, where it landed with such a thud it startled into flight a pair of horseflies mating on the tip of the captain's swagger stick. He was made to try twice more. The last time, he could hoist the sack no higher than his thighs, and at this, this failure, this *sickening display*, the captain sprang from behind his desk. Despite the heat, he began to demonstrate a callisthenics routine, performing the moves as if tearing to shreds an invisible mattress. Black moons appeared beneath the arms of his field shirt. After a minute he stopped (he was not so fit himself), snorted, mopped his face, and informed Yuji that the army would rather have a schoolgirl than him, it would rather have a *Korean*, it would rather have . . . Yuji, head bowed, kept his gaze on the desk. In the open file he could see Dr Kushida's letter, typed on clinic stationery, a large military stamp on the top left corner. Approved? Not approved? The captain sat down, rocked on the rear legs of his chair and lit a cigarette. To his NCO he said (no longer shouting, no longer interested), 'Mark this hero down Class F. Health grounds. Case to be reviewed in twelve months . . .'

He has never been recalled. Nor – as long as Kushida could be relied upon to send his annual letter – did he think it likely he ever would be. Why should the Emperor burn such crooked timber as Yuji Takano or Junzo Miyazaki – for Junzo, along with his student deferment, has a Class D – when each year another half-million boys turn twenty and repopulate the empty parade grounds? But this was before the fighting at the Khalka river, the fighting at Changsha, the casualties at Changsha, the defeat at Changsha, the calls for a new offensive, an invincible tide of fighting men to sweep away the nation's enemies once and for all. Would half a million be enough for that? A million? Last month Ozono's son, who can barely see across the street without his glasses, received his red paper. How long, then, before everyone was equally suitable, and some functionary at the War Ministry placed quite a different stamp at the top of the doctor's letter?

Pink from the heat of the baths, they retire to the matted room upstairs, a little mah-jong hall old Watanabe, in a brief and long-since dissipated mood of entrepreneurial ambition, took over on the death of the previous owner. The maid brings the young men beer and salt crackers. As they start to drink, Junzo, to explain his late arrival and the green bruise on his cheek the water has brought out, tells the others about the book fight in the corridor of the philosophy building, the Hegel gang versus the Schopen-hauer gang. His bruise was *The World as Will and Idea* glancing off his cheekbone, a blow he repaid with volume three of *The Science of Logic* that split open his opponent's lip.

'So you were in the Hegel gang,' says Yuji. 'For the beauty of his dialectics?'

Junzo shrugs. 'Schopenhauer hated women,' he says.

Taro grins at Yuji. 'Little brother's in love,' he says, 'but it seems he has sworn never to reveal her name.'

'Could it be Mrs Watanabe?' whispers Yuji, for which he is shot with a star-shaped cracker that ricochets off his chin and lands in his beer. He fires back but misses.

Mr Watanabe, presiding over a mah-jong game on the far side of the room, scolds them. They are, apparently, disturbing the concentration of the players, four bathhouse regulars slamming down the little tiles as though to shatter them. Taro apologises, then looks at his brother and Yuji with a quick frown as if to say that he, a government employee, cannot any longer conduct himself so carelessly, that something more and better is expected of him. It's a look Yuji sees on his face more frequently these days.

For a minute, sipping at their beers, scratching their chins, inspecting fingernails, they are silent. Then Yuji, under cover of the game's clatter, calls to order a meeting of the club.

'Any business?'

'*J'ai vu* Alissa,' begins Junzo, 'in Kyobashi with one of her piano students. She said her father has agreed to a film evening, the first Sunday of next month. She asked me to suggest a film.'

'You?'

'Why not?'

'I hope you didn't ask for *Cyrano de Bergerac* again,' says Taro. 'Why don't we have *The Thief of Baghdad* or *Iron Horse*?'

'My vote,' says Yuji, 'is for *The Blue Angel*. Or maybe *Flesh and the Devil*.'

'It doesn't matter what you want,' says Junzo. 'She asked me and I said we'd be happy with anything by Chaplin. Any objections?'

There are no objections.

'That's enough French,' says Taro, flicking his eyes towards another bather, a sharp-featured man, who, nursing his beer, has, perhaps, been taking an interest in them, this foreign babble between them. They lean away from each other, sit on their heels again.

'But you're really making progress,' says Yuji, softly, in Japanese, to Junzo, and though he says no more, not wanting to cause embarrassment or a swollen head, he considers Junzo's progress in the language to be nothing less than remarkable. For himself, for Taro, there were the years with Professor Komada. They could even count Monsieur Feneon as one of their teachers, for everyone made good progress once the professor persuaded him to take the short walk from his house each month in order that the senior class might come to know for the first time an actual Frenchman. The other members of the club, Shozo and Oki, have all the resources of the language school at Keio. Only Junzo (who in his first term at Imperial successfully pestered his brother to show him this club where Japanese and foreigners mingled so informally) has had to rely on his own efforts, on the occasional class from Taro, some prompting from Yuji. Alissa, of course, is always patient with him, untangling his grammar, making him study her lips as she pronounces some phrase the Japanese mouth seems hardly framed for.

Across the room, the mah-jong ends with shouts, accusations. Two of the players walk out, the other two growl like street dogs.

Mr Watanabe, with an expression of high disdain, totters away to the kitchen and the rattan armchair beside the hot-air flue, a snug corner for drinking shochu and smoking homemade cigarettes, and where, once or twice a year, sleep hitting him like a wave, he sets fire to himself and wakes to the sound of his own shrieking.

Hungry, suddenly bored of the old bathhouse, the three friends put on still-damp shoes and coats and march through the cold to eat sushi at Kawashima's. They arrive as three others are leaving and take their places along the counter on three warmed stools. Behind them, the tables have their usual mix of diners, the casual, and those of a more serious character, for though the most dedicated of the *tsu* will not eat sushi later than midday, fearing for its freshness, even at night there are men who lean over their food like scholars, who eat without speaking, who know everything . . .

Yuji has squid and tuna belly, mackerel, kuruma prawn. The little plates mount up. He becomes morose at the thought of the expense. Kawashima's is far from cheap, and once he has paid Taro what he owes him, he will have spent a week's money in an evening – a perfect example of the recklessness he can no longer afford. But as his mood blackens so his appetite grows perversely sharper. He tries the blue-fin, the scallop, the Pacific saury.

'I thought you were out of cash,' says Junzo. 'The allowance?'

'Exactly,' says Yuji.

'That's tough,' says Taro.

'On the positive side,' says Junzo, dipping the tip of a little finger into the Murasaki sauce, 'perhaps your need will inspire you.'

'To leap into the Sumida?'

'Ah, but are you the type?'

'Seriously,' asks Taro, 'what will you do now?'

'Shave my head and squat in the subway with a begging bowl.'

'You could still take the Civil Service exams . . .'

'I'm too old. It would look odd. Like I had failed at something else.'

'There's always school teaching,' says Junzo. 'Couldn't you bear it for a year or two?'

'Just the smell of a classroom makes me want to throw up.'

'Well, there'll be something for you,' says Taro. 'A man of your talent. *Something* will come along.'

Yuji thanks him, but in that moment all three fall silent as if struck by the same thought, the same vision of what, one day soon, might come along for them. Their silence catches the sushi-master's attention. He glances up – three young men scowling at the polished wood of the counter – but his hands go on with their work. There is no discernible pause in the movement of his blade.

8

Out of the throng at the Kanda bookstalls, boss-eyed Ooka taps the shoulder of Yuji's greatcoat and tells him he's seen a copy of *Electric Dragonfly* on sale, good as new, not a crease or a thumbprint, nothing, in fact, to suggest that anyone has even held it, yet alone read it. It was on Yoshimasu's stall but maybe it's gone now.

'I expect some pretty girl has bought it. Pretty girls like poetry, don't they?' He laughs, and Yuji laughs, too, then comes straight home and shuts himself in his room.

How many others are there out there, untouched, unread, not even a crease or a thumbprint, no tea ring, no ink splash? Is there anything sadder or more useless in the world than a book of poems nobody wants?

9

Though Grandfather's home lies within the thirty-five wards of the city, reaching it is like going on a trip to the country. Tram, subway, train, then a forty-minute walk past new homes, building plots, fields of tea, rice paddies, even a pair of thatched farmhouses like Uncle Kensuke's.

From the garden gates a gravel pathway curves between persimmon and plum trees, jujube, maples. Then after a hundred steps the ground on one side is suddenly clear, and there, beneath a dreaming pine, is the old rickshaw, its leather hood bright with moss, its painted spokes woven with long grasses. It is not *the* rickshaw, of course, the one in which, in the time of the Meiji Emperor (or so the story is told), the eighteen-year-old grandfather – already known among his fellow runners as 'Iron Thighs' – pulled some eccentric actor the 230 miles from Tokyo to Kyoto to attend a moon-viewing party in a villa above the Daisen Temple. This one, used now by the hens as a roost, is only a souvenir bought for a few yen from a scrap merchant in Honjo, but each time Yuji passes, he is tempted to lift its shafts out of the grass, to lean his weight against the chest bar, to rock it a little. Has he inherited any of the old man's skill or strength? How far would he get, even with hens for passengers? As far as the station? As far as the road?

Another hundred steps and the house appears, low and weathered under a heavy roof of blue tiles. Grandfather's housekeeper, Sonoko, is outside, leaning over a starching board she has propped against one of the verandah corner posts. Hearing Yuji, she straightens and wipes her brow with the back of her hand, like a countrywoman looking up from harvesting. She's forty, forty-five. Dark-skinned, a few freckles across her cheeks, broad hips swelling the lines of her kimono. Pretty in a rustic, old-world way, and with some unusual quality of stillness, of inner poise, that makes Yuji think how pleasant it would be to lie with his head on her lap and sleep for an hour, as he assumes – as everyone assumes – Grandfather sometimes does.

'He's in the model room,' she says.

He thanks her, though he would have looked nowhere else on a winter's day at such an hour, just as, arriving on a summer's morning, he would look first in the vegetable garden, or in autumn, in the shade of the trellis outside the kitchen where the pickling barrels are kept.

He pulls off his boots, crosses the eight-mat room, and announces himself at the doors to the twelve-mat, the model room. After a few moments he receives an invitation to enter.

'I need your young eyes,' says Grandfather, who is kneeling at the far end of the room, his head almost touching the mat as he peers under the shin-high table that carries the model. 'There's a boat down here somewhere. I must have caught it on my sleeve.'

Yuji kneels beside him. After half a minute he finds the boat in the shadow of a table leg. He lifts it, carefully, as though lifting a little singing insect, a *kusa-hibari*, perhaps, and places it in the palm of Grandfather's hand.

'I need stronger lights in here,' says Grandfather. 'Or,' tapping an arm of his glasses, 'a stronger pair of these.'

The boat, he explains, is a sweet-seller's boat, the kind that used to be common enough on summer evenings in the old days, advertising its presence with the beating of a drum and carrying such delights as 'moss in a stream' and 'the beautiful Bay of Tango'. He smiles to himself, smiles at his modern, half-Westernised grandson (a creature he should, perhaps, disapprove of, but never has, treating him always with a shrewd generosity of judgement which the boy's father – the professor, the travelled man! – seems incapable of), then he takes a pair of bamboo tweezers and sets the boat down on the Sumida, that length of curving blue satin he cut from one of his wife's obi the year she died, the year the model began.

'So,' he says, brushing a hand over the stubble on his skull, 'I told you I had some interesting new pieces. Think you can find them?'

Pausing now and then to crouch and look more keenly, Yuji, in a sideways shuffle, slowly moves the length of the room where, on a table that leaves only the narrowest of corridors, the Low City, from Tsukiji to Umaya Bridge, has been rebuilt out of paper and pins, out of memory and street maps and stories. Hundreds of cardboard roofs, bicycles made from fuse wire, trees whose foliage is skeins of coloured wool. The sides of trams are cut from tins of soya oil. Utility wires are black thread from Sonoko's sewing box. Those dogs coupling outside the fish market are chewed paper and

Chinese ink, their tails a pair of bristles from a writing brush. The Low City, as it might have appeared the last day of August 1923. Still hours to go before anyone will notice a light bulb start to swing or see ripples in the surface of his tea.

'These are new, I think,' says Yuji, pointing to two geisha, tall as thimbles outside a tea house in the Yanagibashi district.

'Shall we see where they're going?' asks Grandfather. He holds back the sleeve of his kimono and lifts off the roof of the tea house. Below – and Yuji half expects to see their faces turned up in horror – the tea-house guests are gathered in matted, discreetly screened rooms, while maids and brightly painted geisha dance attendance. Some twelve or fifteen of Grandfather's buildings have been treated this way, including, below its roof garden, the top floor of the old Mitsukoshi, where Mother was shopping with Mrs Hatanaka when the first shocks hit the city, and where, escaping over the glass of the shattered display cases, she cut her feet so badly.

At midday, Sonoko calls them to eat. They sit around the table-stove. An iron pot is simmering on a stone tile. Sonoko, her hand wrapped in a piece of scorched linen, takes off the lid. Steam pours out, a scent of braised onions, the earthy scent of turnips and something else, something ripe and sweet and bloody.

'Mountain whale?' asks Yuji, using Grandfather's name for the wild boar.

'I thought we would have something special today,' says Grandfather, 'as your visits are rather infrequent.'

'I apologise,' says Yuji, 'I would come more . . .'

'Have I,' says Grandfather, 'told you how, one winter, when I was out at Shizuoka, we hunted the young boars?'

'Hunting . . .' says Yuji, who has heard the story many times. 'At Shizuoka?'

'All they could find to eat at such a season was yam. They dug them up, ate them until they were stuffed. As soon as we had shot one, we opened its belly, hauled out the guts. Ready-made yam sausages! Cooked them over the embers of a fire. Ate them with the snow falling on our shoulders . . . Ah, a feast like that and you're ready for the Mongol hordes!'

Yuji waits to see if he will start to sing. He often, under the press of such nostalgia, lets his voice roll from a growl into the wavering line of some old song, but today the stew is too tempting. They grin at each other, three at three, take up their chopsticks, lean towards the pot.

As they eat, Yuji tries to imagine what will happen when the model is finished – what will happen to the model and what will happen to Grandfather. The moment cannot be far away now, no more than another winter, two at most. Will he build an extension onto the house, turn the twelve mats into twenty, let the model grow north to Asakusa? Or will the end of the table be the end of his labours, his memorial to the last of Edo, to the spirit of his eldest grandson, to a thousand streets shaken to firewood then burnt to red ashes?

He has never said what he intends, only that the last piece will be a rickshaw and its runner hurrying past the Bank of Japan. And though he likes to announce this with a solemn, emphatic nod, Sonoko, in her gentle voice, teases him – 'You were still pulling rickshaws in '23? Was it your hobby, perhaps?' – knowing perfectly well that in '23 Grandfather was a valued customer at the bank, a rickshaw passenger, perhaps, but not for twenty years the man sweating between the poles. The teasing doesn't offend. Grandfather knows she understands, and Yuji too. The model is a kind of poem, and in a poem time can be folded many different ways.

When they have eaten, when the lid is back on the pot, the pickle dish is empty and the rice tub returned to its winter wrap of plaited straw, Grandfather excuses himself, and with a quick wave, retreats to the back of the house for his afternoon nap.

Yuji goes with Sonoko onto the verandah. He puts on his boots. A breeze is ringing the little iron bell that hangs from the eaves (and how cold the sound is, like the tinkling of ice). When he is ready, and his coat is buttoned, she hands him a sheet of writing paper wrapped round a pair of ten-yen banknotes.

'Grandfather understands your difficulty,' she says, 'but hopes you will learn soon what needs to be done.' She bows to him. He pushes the money into his coat pocket and sets off down the path, his boots crunching over a lattice of winter shadows.

10

From the drying platform he watches Kyoko at the edge of the pond crumbling dried silkworm for her carp. He whistles to her – a soft, low whistle. She turns her head, but before she can find him the old woman rolls out of the house on her chilblained feet and immediately looks up to the platform. Startled, he steps back, hides behind the quilt airing over the drying poles. He wonders if his legs are still on view. He wonders if the old woman is possessed.

That afternoon he rings Makiyama's office. Ito, one of his assistants, answers the phone. Makiyama isn't there. Ito has nothing intelligent to say. Yuji hangs up. To find Makiyama he will have to hunt him, bar by bar, along the Ginza. But not today.

For supper they eat seven-herb stew. Dr Kushida is their guest. He informs Father that their colleague from Imperial, Mr Amano, has died of a brain seizure. Father nods, puffs on his cigarette. Yuji, touched by the sake, almost asks, 'But is it serious?'

Night. On stockinged feet he comes down the stairs to fetch water from the kitchen. He steps over Miyo, who's sighing in a dream as though some lover was with her, the soy-seller's son perhaps, tampering with her virginity. In the Western room, a thin light spills over the rug as far as the circular dining table. He steps inside. The screens to the Japanese room are open and the light is coming from the box-lamp beside the alcove. Father is there, sitting cross-legged, surrounded by his collection of incense burners. He is cleaning them, wiping each one carefully with a cloth. On the dresser (next to the photograph of Father and Mother, stiff as dolls, outside the shrine on their wedding day), the hands of the clock stand at twenty to two, Thursday morning.

11

O n the fourth day of the second month, the day of the Season-changing Festival, Yuji cycles through a dusk of lightly falling snow to the year's first full meeting of the French Club. Arriving, he leans his bicycle against a drainpipe, unwinds the scarf from about his face, and rings the bell, a brass bell, round and scalloped like a flower.

He likes this ritual of ringing and waiting on the step. The house is a little fortress sealed off by red-brick walls, by the black panels of a stout wooden door. Unlike his own home – unlike almost any Japanese home – the inquisitive world cannot simply announce itself with a cry then get halfway in and crane its neck to see round a screen. It's true, of course, there are windows, large ones, but those on the street are usually shuttered, while those on the upper floor give little away beyond a reflection of roofs and sky, or at night a thread of light between the curtains. It is, he believes, the sort of house the heroes and heroines (not the grandest, of course) of the novels he has read might live in, in Paris or London, or, more particularly, in Moscow or St Petersburg, for the house was built by a Russian in the year after the Nicholai Cathedral was finished. A foreign outpost in the hills of Kanda, a house – despite the new spirit in Japan, that disinterred hostility to the world beyond the black lines of the coasts – he is proud to be seen going into, and which, in the privacy of his own thoughts, he calls *my house of life*.

He is expecting Hanako, Feneon's maid, to answer the bell, but it's Feneon himself, tall, grey-eyed and dressed in an ankle-length smoking jacket of goose-grey silk, who ushers Yuji inside, the pug, Beatrice, peeping from between his slippers.

As he has hoped, Yuji is the first to arrive. He shakes off his boots and follows Feneon through the hall to the salon, where, in the centre of the room, Hanako is on her knees by the stove, grimacing and crimson-faced as she thrusts a poker into its mouth. The stove is a relict of the house's original owner, a cask of black iron forged in a Russian foundry for Russian winters and decorated on its sides with a frieze of wild animals, birch trees, iron stars.

Alissa is sitting at the end of the sofa next to a lamp, an open book on her lap. There is no kimono tonight. Instead, she is wearing a black woollen dress, black stockings, a little red jacket fastened with a row of black buttons. Her hair, which at the year-forgetting party was arranged Shimada-style, is now in a simple glossy plait secured by a black ribbon. Her stick is propped against the rolled leather of the sofa's arm.

'Not much like spring, is it?' she says, glancing behind her to the garden window, where snow flickers in the house light and lies along the grey limbs of the magnolia tree. To answer her, Yuji explains that the official opening of spring is not intended to indicate any imminent improvement in the weather but is connected to the yearly cycle of agriculture, the advent of a new planting season, the need for the community to purify itself through rituals such as the scattering of beans and the lighting of sacred fires. He knows, of course, she knows all this, knows it as well as he does himself, but she has spoken to him in Japanese and he wishes to rebuke her for it. On club nights he expects her to speak French. It is, in fact, a rule.

'To warm you up a little,' says Feneon, handing Yuji a dainty glass in which a mouthful of eau de vie is trembling. He gives a second glass to his daughter, then returns to the drinks table behind the piano for his own glass.

'And what shall our toast be?' he asks. 'Health and happiness?'

'An end to stupid wars,' says Alissa.

'Or at least,' says Yuji, who here, in a borrowed language, has the dizzying sense he can say those things it would be most unwise to say anywhere else, 'at least, perhaps, an end to conscription?'

Feneon rests a hand on his shoulder. Yuji hardly dares to breathe. They raise their glasses, sip, swallow. The doorbell rings. Beatrice leaps from the sofa and pursues Hanako into the hall.

'Things will work out,' says Feneon. 'They usually do, somehow.'

'The Emperor will come to his senses,' says Alissa. 'He'll deal with the warmongers.'

'The Emperor?' says Feneon. 'It seems to me we know very little about him. I'm not sure we should depend on him doing anything decisive.'

'And in Europe,' asks Yuji, wishing to remove the name of His Sacred Majesty from the conversation before they are intruded upon, 'what can people depend on there?'

'Oh,' says Feneon, shaking his head, 'on France making lots of speeches, being brave but at the same time utterly incompetent. On England making treaties, then looking after nothing but her own interests. On the Germans being good at catching trains and reducing everything to rubble. On the Russians . . . well, who can tell what our friends the Russians will do?'

'Arrive in Tokyo,' says Alissa, 'if the army keeps provoking them. It's not 1904 any more. There's Zhukov's tanks to deal with this time.'

Taro, Junzo, Shozo and Oki enter the room, laughing together and rubbing their hands. They bow to Feneon then make a half-circle round the stove. At Junzo's feet the dog dances on her hind legs. Junzo takes a square of chocolate from his pocket, reaches down and lets her, with her soft muzzle, her little tongue, eat from his hand.

'Junzo's the kindest of you,' says Alissa.

'Because he gives chocolate to an animal?' asks Oki.

'Animal!' says Feneon. 'Beatrice is a beautiful woman bewitched on the road by a goblin. If one of you would just agree to kiss her, I'm sure she'd change back to her old form. Don't any of you want to get married?'

The young men, gazing at the dog, colour slightly and say nothing. Feneon, smiling to himself, goes to the table and fills more of the dainty glasses. They drink, give back the glasses, then file past the carved oak door into Feneon's study. On the desk the projector is raised on a plinth of books (*A Cochin Almanac*, *Warren's Encyclopaedia of Industry*, a volume of Darwin, of Malthus), its brass-bound lens aimed at a linen tablecloth stretched and pegged over the bookshelves. Alissa, with the pug in her lap, sits on the swivel-chair behind the desk, while the others take their places on the rug. Feneon, with the cuff of his smoking jacket, gives the lens a last polish. When he's satisfied, he nods to Hanako, who pushes up the switch on the wall by the door. There's a second of utter darkness, then the whirr of the projector's motor, the ticking of spools, a cone of white light, the pulsing of numbers on the cloth and finally, appearing out of the broken grey like something surfacing at sea, the film's title: *Pay Day*.

They've seen it before, of course, three or four times, but that's expected, it doesn't matter. Nor does it matter that the film is old, because that too is expected: all the films in Feneon's collection date from before 1929, the year his little unofficial cinema in Saigon (that amusement for the ladies and gentlemen of the Foreign Section) caught fire during the second reel of *Fool's Paradise*. What matters is the ritual of being there, the occasion's innocence, like an echo of those childhoods they have so recently left behind them.

Yuji, his back against the side of the desk, looks between Junzo's head and Shozo's, chuckles at the Little Tramp's antics, then – so familiar is it all, so comfortably familiar – lets his eyes stray from the tablecloth to the gilded spines of Feneon's library, the silk scrolls on the wall, the Khmer masks, the rack of dragon pipes above the door, the glinting brass lamps from Laos, the Thai Buddha spectral and serene in the weird moonlight of the projector, and plays his usual guessing game as to where amid this clutter, this haul of an adventurer's life, the letter from Rimbaud is lying, lost or hidden.

Out of the Frenchman's hearing, the club is divided on the subject. Oki, with a wave of his cigarette, with that old man's cynicism he affects, says it's all a tease, a game of the sort foreigners often play, and which only a simple-minded Japanese would take seriously.

Taro asks them to consider the facts. Wasn't Feneon's father trading in the Arabian Gulf at the same time as Rimbaud? Doesn't his family come from Sézanne, no more than a short ride from Rimbaud's Charleville? And why would he make up such a thing, this man who, to the best of their knowledge, is scrupulous in all his dealings?

Shozo agrees, but argues that the letter never left France, or if it did, has long since vanished, blown away on a breeze or rolled into a taper to light someone's evening pipe in any of a dozen cities from Pondicherry to Yokohama where Feneon has lived and done business.

As for Junzo, he is predictably stubborn. For him, the letter is somewhere in the house, somewhere near at hand, and for no better reason than because Alissa Feneon has told him so. She even claimed to have read it, though was, apparently, as evasive as her father when it came to speaking of the contents.

And Yuji? He does not know, not any more. Letters are rather fragile objects. By this winter of 1940 it would be more than fifty years old. Shozo, perhaps, is right. The letter is just a family legend now, like Grandfather's journey to Kyoto. But he cannot, not yet, give up the delightful fantasy of one day catching sight of it, a ragged envelope left as a bookmark in some long ago put-aside novel, or forgotten in a drawer of tradesmen's receipts or carelessly left among the sun-yellowed piles of *Le Figaro* under the study window. And inside, in ink paled to ochre – what? Ten lines of a lost poem? Some theory of poetics to set the professors on their heels? Or even something like advice, a hint on how to live, how to write, how to live as a poet, how to be brave enough for that.

*   *   *

When the film is over, they troop back to the salon. On the table between the sofa and the armchairs Hanako has put out plates and glasses and a cake of fresh eggs and French chocolate, baked by Alissa in honour of the year's inaugural meeting. Only Feneon and Alissa drink wine – it would take too long, says Feneon, to educate the young men's palates. For them there is beer in bottles that have been plugged for an hour into the snow of the garden.

Holding up his wine to the lamplight, tilting the glass, Feneon smiles lugubriously and says, in a low voice to Yuji at his side, that this time drinking red wine will be his only contribution to the defence of his country, his only patriotic act. Yuji nods, frowns, and thinks of the photograph in the study, the one that shows what Feneon did *last* time, the picture of the young soldier with his blond beard leaning with one of his comrades against the tracked, man-high wheel of an artillery piece. He longs to ask him how it was, what it was like to be a soldier, whether he was scared, scared all the time, but Junzo is doing his Chaplin walk, Beatrice is leaping at his heels, Alissa is helpless with laughter, and the moment is lost.

When they have devoured the cake, they sit around the stove for the evening's discussion. It's Shozo's turn to choose the subject. He removes his glasses, blinks, puts the glasses on again, and with great seriousness, in good French, tells them that the question for debate is 'Which of all the arts should be accounted the most sublime?'

'Well,' says Feneon, reaching for the wine bottle, 'that should keep us busy.'

Having proposed the question, Shozo begins a defence of folk art, in particular those ancient dances still seen at country fairs and which, in his opinion, represent an unbroken tradition stretching back to the very origins of . . .

Oki rolls his eyes. Folk dances might be all right for peasant farmers in Tohoku, but for everyone else . . . 'What about architecture? The Chrysler Building, the Bauhaus . . . why can't we build like that in Tokyo? Why doesn't Tokyo look like New York? Maybe we need another earthquake.' He turns and quickly, in Japanese, apologises to Yuji, who excuses him with a blink and starts on his own small speech, arguing not for poetry but for what he assumes would have been Feneon's choice. Cinema, he says, is where the arts are brought together. All the most interesting artists now are film-makers. Isn't Jean Renoir even greater than his father, Auguste? And who in Japan deserves more attention than Yasujiro Ozu or Mikio Naruse?

He's warming to it, beginning to enjoy himself, the sound of himself, the accent he has worked so hard at, when Alissa cuts across him. Theatre, she says, is superior to cinema because a live performance is always superior to a recorded one. However many times a play is put on, however familiar the actors are with their parts, each performance is unique.

This, thinks Yuji, is an absurd objection. (And should a nineteen-year-old girl in the company of men, all of them, with the exception of Oki, at least a *little* older than her, express herself in such a forthright manner? Even for a foreign girl it is surely slightly improper.) He does not look at her, but assumes the tone of a professor whose lecture has been needlessly interrupted by one of his students. All performances, he says, regardless of whether they are filmed, have, at the moment of their enactment, the self-same quality of the unique. Celluloid is but a method of preserving this, which means therefore it remains, permanently, or at least in a practical, but also perhaps in an ontological sense, even at the thousandth time of showing—

'I'm not sure,' says Alissa, 'anyone understands what you're saying.'

'My opinion,' says Junzo, 'is that in debates of this type one should always side with the person who knows how to make chocolate cake.'

'Aren't we forgetting music?' asks Feneon.

'In the West you have music,' says Oki. 'Here we have twanging.'

'I'd rather have the music of the *shamisen*,' says Alissa, sharply, 'than almost anything. I'm bored to death with Schumann and Beethoven.'

'But you play the *lieder* so sweetly,' says Feneon. 'I was lying in bed this morning listening to you.'

'I play them very badly,' she says, smiling at her father.

'Won't you play something now?' asks Taro, the peacemaker. 'Then we can settle this matter at once and give the prize to music.'

She shakes her head. She's not in the mood, she's unprepared, she does not give impromptu recitals, but Taro persists and the others join him, until, taking her stick, she gets up from the sofa, and goes to the piano. It's an English make, Collard & Collard, an odd and lovely object that must have travelled half the world crated in the hold of some wallowing cargo vessel. She settles herself on the stool, looks put out, irritated, flicks through some pages of manuscript on the music stand, then shuts her eyes, opens them, and leans her whole body into the first soft chords. She plays for five, six minutes, no more, her head tilted to the side, an expression of intense listening on her face. The music spreads in ripples, its rhythms simple as a lullaby, light as spring rain. The debate, with its mixture of earnestness and nonsense, is forgotten. When she finishes, and the echo of the last deep note has faded, there's a hush in which only the murmuring of the embers in the stove can be heard. They applaud. She blushes, stands, limps back to the sofa.

'That was beautiful,' says Yuji quietly, the words out of his mouth before he has considered them.

'Chopin,' she says, turning to him, her blush briefly deepening. '"*Grande Polonaise*". I'm glad you liked it.'

12

An earth-tremor at three in the afternoon. Yuji is in the garden, talking through the fence with Kyoko. The old woman and Haruyo are in the street haggling with the boiled-bean-seller. There's a sudden breeze, the bamboo rustles. Under their fingers, the fence vibrates, under their feet, the earth. They wait, breathlessly, three, four seconds. Then everything resumes, everything is normal again.

In 1923, Kyoko was a small child in her home village in Saitama Prefecture. She thinks Yuji was in Tokyo. He has not chosen to correct her, and Saburo, he assumes, has simply forgotten, as Saburo forgets so much. He grins at her. She grins back. For a while they hold the fence as though, without their gripping it, it would fly into the air and be lost.

13

On Mother's birthday, to please her, or rather, to honour her as one honours on certain auspicious dates the family ancestors, Yuji spends the day being as useful as he can. He tidies his room, puts his bedding to air, returns various cups and dishes to the kitchen. He helps Father in the garden weeding and pruning, and after lunch pays Otaki the money he owes. In his room again, he sews a button onto a suit, reads a dozen pages of *Isabelle*, learns a new French idiom (*entre chien et loup*). Then, a few minutes before five, the little parcel with its wrapping of dark red paper in his hands, he goes downstairs and slides open the doors to Mother's room. Haruyo is there, hunched beside a brazier on which a small copper kettle is beginning to steam. She dips her head to him. He walks past her, past the folding screen, and kneels opposite Mother. He bows, and wishes her a happy birthday.

There is only a single lamp for the whole room, and not a bright one, so it's difficult to tell if becoming fifty-one has made much difference to her. He can see no threads of grey in her hair, and the skin of her face – a little blue under the eyes – shows, in this light, barely a wrinkle. Of her body, wrapped in an unpatterned kimono and darker shawl, he has only the sense of something immensely fragile.

She says how nice it is to see him. He thanks her. Round their knees the shadows lie like pools of water. She smiles drowsily as though she has recently woken from a sleep or will shortly need one. Has he, she asks, lost some weight? He says it is unlikely. In the holidays everybody ate a great deal. 'You know how you get in the winter,' she says. He says he knows. 'I pray for you,' she says. He says he knows. He thanks her. 'You must listen to Dr Kushida,' she says. 'He will advise you. He has been a good friend to the Takano family.'

Behind her head, Ryuichi, school uniform buttoned to the throat, school cap clasped in white-gloved hands, examines Yuji with a gaze he can only endure for a few seconds, such is the weight of judgement in those twelve-year-old eyes. Above the photograph is the slender cross of ivory tipped with iron presented to Grandfather Yakumo when he left the college in Seoul, and on the table below, a stick of incense, a flickering nightlight, an offering of mandarins.

He passes his mother her birthday present, a box of taorizakura cakes from the shop by Ueno Station. She thanks him. She says she hopes he hasn't spent too much money on her. He assures her he hasn't.

'Really?' she says, unwrapping her gift, 'but it looks so expensive.'

'Just something small . . .'

'You've been too generous.'

'Not at all.'

'Still . . .'

Haruyo brings them tea, then retires to the far side of the screen. Though he would admit it to no one, Yuji is frightened of Haruyo, her slab face, the unseemly vivid bulk of her, afraid of her ever since the night – the second after his return from Uncle Kensuke's – he crept down the stairs from his new room hoping to find comfort in Mother's bed and found instead Haruyo, motionless by the side of a lantern whose flame splashed her shadow over the walls, big as a net. Nothing was said, but she looked at him then as no adult had looked at him before, certainly no adult he knew, no adult who lived in his *home*.

'What is your news?' asks Mother. 'Let me hear your news.'

He tells her what seems appropriate, harmless. A few remarks about his friends, about what he's been reading. He does not, of course, mention the matter of the allowance. Nothing of that nature can even be hinted at. They are silent for a minute. Yuji looks at his tea but does not pick it up.

'Your father . . .' she says.

'Yes?'

'How hard it is for him now.'

Yuji drops his chin in what he hopes will be taken for a gesture of reflection. How long has he been in the room? Fifteen minutes? Half an hour?

'There's blossom on the plum tree,' he says.

'At the bottom of the garden?'

'Yes.'

'That was always the first.'

'Shall I bring you some?'

'Thank you,' she says, 'though sometimes I prefer just to picture it in my mind. It seems more perfect.'

He tells her – the clever boy lecturing his mother – how the old poets used to cover their windows on the night of the full moon so they could imagine its beauty rather than be distracted by anything so obvious as the thing itself.

She smiles. 'My son,' she says, 'a poet . . .' And for a few seconds it looks as if she might hold out one of her long, white hands to him, as if the spell might break. But then she shivers and looks down. Behind the screen, Haruyo stirs in her fabrics, clears her throat. Yuji rises to his feet, his movements, in this strange room, soft as incense smoke.

That evening after supper he opens the doors of the storage cupboards that stand on the landing between his room and Father's. The cupboards are so solid, so mysteriously large, he has no idea how they were brought into the house. Lowered through the roof? Carried up the stairs plank by plank and assembled there by a carpenter? For all the years of his life (and for years before that) the cupboards have been the dark and mothballed repositories of whatever was finished with but could not be thrown away. Bamboo fencing swords, school satchels, carp banners, kites, foreign hats long out of fashion. There are even parcels of baby clothes preserved by meticulous hands for some imagined continuation of the Takano line.

He wants to find Ryuichi's gloves. Each boy had two pairs, white, with three rows of raised stitching on the back and a single mother-of-pearl button at the wrist. One pair of Ryuichi's was, presumably, reduced to a powder of ashes, but the other . . . He looks, does not find them, neither Ryuichi's nor his own. Instead, behind a box of Shunkei lacquer, on which the remains of a large insect are lying, he discovers a pile of jazz records from the 1920s – Jimmy Harada, Noriko Awaya, King Oliver's Creole Jazz Band. One by one he slips them from their paper covers, runs the light over the shellac grooves, blows away grains of dust. There was music in this house once. Music and tapping feet, the wail of trumpets, voices, flippant or heartbroken, singing of love, the city, the future . . .

He goes to his room, opens the door to the drying platform, steps up into the night air. He drags his bedding from the poles and carries it inside. It's too early to sleep but too late to do much else. He spreads the bedding on the mats, then, still on hands and knees, recites to himself, like some manner of talking dog, the ghost poem from *Electric Dragonfly*.

> *Do ghosts get bored of being ghosts?*
> *At night they burn like candle flames*
> *But the days must be difficult –*
> *Hearing children on the way to school,*
> *Hearing the thrum of kite strings.*
> *At the song of the red-hot-pepper vendor*
> *Even a dead tongue burns.*

There he stops, for though the poem has another four lines, there are tears falling onto the backs of his hands. He can no longer speak.

14

He finds Makiyama in a bar by Shibuya Station drinking beer with his assistants, Ito and Kiyooka. It's four in the afternoon. At six they move to Sukiyabashi and start on the sake, then to the Black Pearl on the Ginza and finally through the stained-glass doors of the Don Juan, where they take one of the booths by the dance floor and Makiyama buys a bottle of whisky. A tango band is playing. The singer, in his white tuxedo, sighs into the microphone. Between the pillars, clouds of cigarette smoke shift in the breeze from a ceiling fan.

Sweating from the drink, Makiyama undoes the top button of his shirt, hangs his hat on his knee, and pulls the cork from the bottle. He's thirty-five or thirty-six, dressed in a new suit of lime-green serge, a pair of tan and cream spats on his feet. In his jacket lapel he has a pin, a curious pin with a head of red glass, perhaps even a ruby. Does it mean something?

A waitress takes the seat beside him and starts to feed him peanuts, sweet-bean paste. On the other side of the booth, Ito and Kiyooka are watching the dancing, their heads moving in unison like a pair of Siamese cats in the window of a hair-dresser's shop.

Yuji hasn't drunk like this for months. Beer, sake, whisky. The effort of keeping up, of being congenial, of remembering why he's there at all, is starting to exhaust him. He has extracted no promises, nothing but a few vague and lordly assurances that may already have been forgotten. He sips from his glass and listens to Makiyama trying to impress the waitress with his wealth of connections, though it's obvious she has never heard of any of them. Only when he mentions the pulp writer Kaoru Ishihara does she show any genuine interest.

'Ishihara, eh?'

'An old friend of mine. You could even call me a kind of mentor.'

'Really! But it must be nice,' she says, dropping another peanut into his mouth, 'to know someone like Ishihara.'

He grins at her, then pushes her away and turns to Yuji. He has, he says, grinding the nut between his large yellow teeth, just had another of his celebrated intuitions. 'Come closer,' he says. 'Lean closer.'

Hideo Makiyama's story is a Low City story, his success a Low City success. No one seems quite sure of where he comes from – Honjo, perhaps, or Asakusa, or even somewhere out of town, some unlikely little place only the slow trains stop at. Has he attended university? Has he attended much *high school*? He seems to Yuji a man who would struggle to write a thank-you letter, and no more of an intellectual than Miyo. His talent – if talent is the right word – is of a different order entirely, simpler, much more lucrative, for behind the shine of his brow, his slick moustache, he possesses a gift of insight into the appetites of the crowd, their vanities, their fears, the strange fastidiousness of their obsessions, their fickleness, their love of novelty. He would have done as well in the dry-goods sector, or selling cars, or women's fashion, except that literature offered a certain status, a certain respectability, though one that did not at all prohibit him from passing the working day in a Ginza beer hall. He has no prejudices. High art or low, he doesn't care. Nor is he burdened by tradition, for he knows nothing of it. His questions are so simple, so childlike, so unapologetic, some of the older writers (who thought their reputations safe) live in terror of him. Will it sell? How many? To whom? What will the margins be? The percentages? The profit share? You cannot catch him out. His memory for numbers – monthly circulations, print runs – is unfailing. He knows (for example) that only thirty-seven copies of *Electric Dragonfly* were ever sold and this, at five per cent of two yen per copy, represented an income of three yen and seventy sen, a contemptible sum even by the miserable standards of the genre. A head for numbers is starting to make him wealthy. Numbers, and a snout like those dogs one sees foraging in the spilt bins behind restaurants.

At midnight the band starts to pack away their instruments. The dancers-for-hire sit down and rub their aching calves. The waitresses are tired too. They move from booth to booth collecting bills, their sandals scuffing the wooden floor. Startling from a short sleep, Makiyama drops a banknote on the table, crams his hat on his head, and strides down to the Ginza Crossing, where he stops a one-yen taxi by stepping in front of it and spreading his arms. They squeeze, all four of them, into the back. Makiyama calls an address to the driver, who seems to know it. They jolt forwards, cruise awhile under the lights of the Ginza, then turn up towards the park and into the darker, emptier streets around the government buildings.

As they travel, and the wind stirs the litter from the night-stalls, Makiyama starts to sing. It's the lovers-parting-in-the-dawn-mist song from a new musical he's invested in at the Moulin Rouge in Shinjuku. Then he breaks off and says it's a shame, a damned shame what they did to your father. Writing a few lines about the Emperor – what was it? Fifteen years ago? – really came back to kick him in the teeth, eh? It was tough. It was damned tough. But certain things just couldn't be allowed any more, and if the people at the top didn't set an example, what could you expect from the riff-raff? It wasn't personal. Just a question of discipline, of being ready for what was coming, of showing the world that Japan meant business. Even so, yes, he was sorry for what had happened, genuinely sorry for the Takano family's misfortune.

Yuji, trapped against the car door, bows as best he can. The speech has surprised him. He is also surprised at how grateful he feels, though it's inconceivable that Makiyama has ever read the 482 pages of *Democratic Principles and the Japanese Constitution*, or has the slightest real grasp of Father's arguments. The same, of course, could be said about most of the others, those whose muttering – or in some cases shrieking, hysterical shrieking – made, in the end, Father's situation intolerable. And now that they have pulled him down, they will, perhaps, like Makiyama, begin to pity him, so that in a few years it will appear he fell through something as natural and implacable as bad luck, his enemies nothing more than bystanders, innocent witnesses to an event they could not possibly have altered the outcome of.

They stop at the mouth of a stone-paved alley somewhere in Sanbancho. The neighbourhood is poorly lit. The houses have their eaves pulled low, like caps. The alley is so narrow they have to go in single file. At the end, there is a little shrine to the fox god. A woman is praying there, but hearing the men, she lifts the hems of her kimono and hurries, on wooden soles, through a doorway where a lantern marked with the characters for falling leaves swings its crimson light in the wind.

They follow her inside. Makiyama shouts for service. The hostess of the house appears, trotting out of her booth and calling a welcome. Recognising Makiyama, telling him how well he's looking, how prosperous, she leads them up the stairs and along a corridor to a room at the back of the house. From the tobacco haze, the smell of fish, it's evident the room has only recently been vacated. A maid appears and straightens out the sitting cushions, polishes the table. Yuji slips the catch on the window. There's a courtyard below with a few shrubs, a line of sake kegs outside the open doorway of the kitchen. On the far side of the courtyard, where shadows blur and focus behind the paper windows, a girl's voice is singing to the accompaniment of a *shamisen*: 'Yes, I am in love. They were talking about me before daylight . . . though I began to love without knowing it . . .'

The maid brings in a tray of tea and sweets, then a tray with sake flasks and sake cups. Yuji shuts the window and joins the others at the table. The hostess is telling them the local scandals – affairs, jealous lovers, who's in money trouble, who's disgraced. After twenty minutes the doors slide open. Two girls are kneeling in the corridor. They chant their greeting and enter. One of them Yuji recognises as the waitress from the Don Juan. The other is perhaps also a waitress, though with her purple kimono, the ribbons of raw silk in her hair, she could pass for a certain grade of geisha. She is not as pretty as the girl from the Don Juan but when she starts to talk it's obvious she's a natural storyteller, an excellent mimic. Soon she's the favourite, and takes her place beside the sprawling Makiyama. The other girl, seeing that Ito and Kiyooka can have no interest in her, kneels in front of Yuji, picks a flask from the table, and fills his cup. She asks him if he likes to drink, if he likes the Ginza, if he likes tango or prefers some other kind of music. Does he ever go skiing in the winter? For herself, she has never skied, though sometimes she thinks she would like to try. How cold it is these last days. Cold as anything.

Every minute or two (though minutes are no longer evenly divided but float like globs of fat in water) Yuji holds out his cup and watches her replenish it. Now and then she lets him fill a cup for her. He wants to make her drunk – as drunk as he is himself. Then they will be helpless as children, and the worst that could happen is they wake in a pile on the mat together, daylight streaming through the window. He doesn't mind that. What worries him is that she's been given orders – by the hostess, by Makiyama even – to *do* something with him (or whichever of the men shows a taste for her). He steals glances at her while she pours for him, and sees, with inebriated clarity, that what is natural in her, her youth – she's several years younger than him – her laboured, youthful interest in him, is not yet entirely sunk in artifice or the fatigue of her trade. She has little in common, then – little beyond the obvious – with the woman in the room behind Yokohama Docks, but it's *her* he starts to think of now, of the hour he spent with her after the negotiations with Momoyo's family had failed and in his anger, in the violence of his disappointment, he had set out to prove that love was an itch any man could satisfy by spending a few yen.

The place he chose, a street of unlicensed women, he had heard about from a student bragging at the university, and though it meant a train ride it also offered anonymity, for in Tokyo, a city where one is always running into the same people, where coincidences grow like bindweed (read Kafu), who knew who might, at the wrong moment, look out of a restaurant window, a passing taxi . . .

The room he finally entered – he had walked the length of that street a dozen times, building his resolve – had nothing but a narrow mattress on the floor, and walls so thin any passing sailor could have punched a hole and watched the woman laugh at him, his ignorance. She called him, as she unbuttoned his shirt, her 'little virgin', and when, hotly, he protested this, telling her how his mother's friend Mrs Sasaki, under the guise of giving him some of her deceased husband's good clothes, had, shortly after his nine-teenth birthday, made him 'a man who knows women', she applauded with her fingertips, crying, 'So you've done it once! With one of Mama's friends! Congratulations!' And with *this* woman, with her gold teeth, her tongue like a stick, he let himself be intimate, had lain on her, gasping and writhing as though swimming through sewage.

The hostess is at the door. She is so sorry to disturb them, but she wishes the gentlemen to know that the bath is ready. She bows, withdraws. The girl with the ribbons hauls Makiyama to his feet. Yuji, an unlit cigarette between his fingers (who gave it to him? If he smoked it, he'd choke), hears himself talking – passionately, insistently – about Momoyo, his dear Momoyo, with whom he shared a thousand silent glances of innocent devotion. If they had married, he would by now – it can be taken for granted – be established in some reputable university or publishing house or newspaper office or *something*. Certainly he would not be living in a former sewing room. He would not be writing about toothpaste. They would have an old house in the High City, a verandah, tangled with flowers. And then a child, a grandchild for Mother, a little boy who, as the first-born, could even be called Ryuichi.

'But how nice,' says the waitress, quickly hiding her yawn. 'So you're definitely going to marry her?'

'Who?'

'Miss Momoyo?'

'But this was years ago. Don't you get it? Her family refused to permit the match. They sent a letter to my father. "Momoyo is, regretfully, too young for such a momentous step." It was a stupid lie, of course. The truth was, they could never let their daughter marry into a family in which the mother had not left the house in a decade. It would be even easier for them, today. Today we would not even dare to ask.'

The waitress looks confused, then sorry for him. He knows that he should ask her something now, should flirt with her, make jokes, even if they're bad ones, but he needs, quite urgently, to find the toilets, to be privately in the darkness, to press his forehead against something cool.

He puts down his cup, then climbs a rope of air until he's standing. Somehow he gets clear of the room. The corridor is bright, bare. No one's about. He cannot remember where the stairs are. He takes a few steps in one direction, a few in the other. Through the walls and doors of the rooms on either side of him come murmurings, muffled laughter. He hears what sounds like a woman weeping. He wishes it would stop. He wants to leave now. He must leave . . .

At his shoulder, a door slides back, half the width of a face at first, then wider. The girl with the ribbons is there, undressed to her under-kimono, which is bound so loosely it looks as if at any sudden movement it must slip to the floor. Below her throat he can see the place where her make-up ends and the rose of unpowdered skin begins.

'Your boss is snoring,' she whispers, 'and now I have no one to wash my back.' She pouts at him, widens her eyes.

He asks her where the toilets are.

'Downstairs,' she says, and points. 'Shall I wait for you?' she asks.

'Please do,' he says. 'Yes.'

She bows. He backs away, finds the stairs, finds the stalls, vomits, spits into the stinking hole, then sits on the step in the foyer putting on his boots. He has, in a way he cannot begin to comprehend, lost one of his socks. The sight of his naked foot moves him almost to tears. He is touching it, stroking it as if it was some poor hairless cat, when a movement in the mirror beside the door makes him glance up. The hostess is standing behind him at the bottom of the stairs. There is nothing kind in that face and he does not dare to turn. He thrusts his feet, the bare and the dressed, into his boots, ties the laces, snatches his coat, and plunges into the alley, racing headlong through Sanbancho, a runner matched against himself.

15

Twenty-four hours after reaching home from the House of Falling Leaves, his winter illness begins. It announces itself with the usual prefatory dream, a fire dream in which he stumbles through dense smoke across a field of charred grass in search of the boy with the shutter.

He has had these dreams so many years now it is hard to know where history ends and the invention of his dreams begins. Certain things, of course, he has no need to question, for they are facts known to everyone. He has not simply dreamt the thirty thousand who burnt to death in the grounds of the old army-clothing depot on the east bank and whose charred bones and blackened teeth are still uncovered by builders, by anglers digging for bait, by ghoulish children. But the rest of it – the boy, the shutter, the miraculous escape – where did he hear all this? Did Father tell him? Grandfather? Someone at school? Or was it one of those newspaper accounts, those 'My Story' columns that ran for months after the earthquake, tales of improbable survival that began with lines such as 'I was sitting quietly a home . . .' or, 'Just as I turned into Okura Dori . . .'

The boy – for this is what Yuji remembers of it, what he *believes* he remembers, what he would set down as an account, more or less accurate, of the actual events – was from the Low City and not perhaps the eleven- or twelve-year-old he is in the dreams but a teenager or even a young man of sixteen or seventeen who, once the fires started soon after the first shocks at midday (shocks so violent the seismographs at the Central Weather Bureau were immediately rendered useless), would have been a link in those disciplined chains of neighbours who went on passing water from the wells until, unable to keep their faces to such a terrible heat, they dropped their buckets and fled. Some then returned to their homes to rescue a roll of cash, a tethered dog, a household shrine. Of these, most were never seen again. The rest, the boy and his family among them, retreated through blazing streets towards the river, only to find the bridges were also burning. Overwhelmed by exhaustion, tormented by heat and smoke, hundreds leapt into the water where, in the days that followed, their swollen corpses, face down, jostled each other in the currents. Those who still had the strength for it fought their way along the bank until they found a bridge intact, then streamed across it, lifted now by the wild hope of saving themselves on the far side.

From somewhere – the ruins of his own house or the debris in the street – the boy had picked up a wooden shutter to protect himself from the rain of sparks and cinders that grew heavier with every moment. With this held over his head, he waited, one of the thirty thousand, in the grounds of the old depot.

By the middle of the afternoon, observers in the hills of the High City could see a number of fire storms, swirling columns of fire hundreds of feet high, collecting over the surface of the river. People took photographs, but these, in their stillness and silence, record only great areas of darkness, a blurring, like collapsed sky. Of the fire's shrieking, its unpredictable movement, the quality of intention it possessed, no means existed to convey such horror. Whatever the storms touched – a boat, the piers of a bridge, the shady honeycomb of a waterside pleasure house – it was consumed in an instant as though by a force infinitely more destructive than fire. At last, at four in the afternoon – the moment recorded precisely on the heat-shocked faces of countless wristwatches – the largest of the storms discovered the crowd in the grounds of the depot, and having nothing left to burn, and ravenous for fuel, it fell on them. In an instant, the field became a furnace. Men and women, who seconds before had wept or prayed, were suddenly welded into tangled house-high sculptures of blackened limbs. But as the fire raced forwards (more like a great body of water now, a death-wave), it sent ahead a violent wind that surged beneath the boy's shutter and flung him upwards with such force and speed the flames, quick as they were, could only roll and boil beneath him as he flew.

How high did he go? As high as the wind? As high as the black pall that had formed over the city and later doused the embers with a rain black as tar? He was found on the afternoon of 2 September, lying completely naked in the Yasuda Gardens, the shutter wedged in the boughs of a nearby tree. The soles of his feet were scorched and all the hair had been singed from his body, but he was otherwise unharmed. On waking he remembered nothing.

Later, he recalled seeing birds, vast flocks of them, flying across the face of the sun.

Of the dreams, no two are quite the same, but in all of them Yuji must cross the grounds and find the boy before the storm falls. He must crawl under the shutter with him. He must cling on and brace himself for the fire, wind and flight that follow. Sometimes he comes within a dozen strides of the boy; at others he can see nothing but the tormented crowd. This time, this dream, he is close enough to glimpse the boy's bare legs under the smoking wood of the shutter, and he is fighting his way forward, fighting with a desperate strength, when suddenly he sees, in ordinary daylight, Miyo with a basket of washing in her arms looking at him quizzically from the step of the drying platform. She puts down the washing and hurries off. A few minutes later Father is there, kneeling beside the mattress and smelling faintly of ink and cigarettes. He puts a hand on Yuji's brow. He says something. Yuji hears himself reply, a voice that blossoms out of the air between them and says the strangest things. Father goes. Miyo comes back. She has a bowl, some medicinal broth, its steam acrid as smoke. She holds it to his lips and when, a minute later, he brings it up again, she cleans him.

He knows his body is suffering. He observes the familiar symptoms, the signs both sides of the skin that he is in for an unpleasant ride, perhaps a dangerous one, but his mind is buoyant, gently exhilarated, and sits on his flesh like a butterfly on a statue. His neck aches a little, his mouth is dry, but it doesn't matter. February sunlight is pouring through the panes of the drying-platform door and everything, the piles of books, the backs of his own pale hands, the light itself, seems precious and extraordinary. He would, he thinks, be quite content to die like this, to leave the world with this accelerated sense of things. First, of course, like the old poets, like Basho taken ill on the road outside Osaka, he must compose his death poem, but the lines that come to him, far from being solemn, wistful, somewhat wry, are all exclamatory and pathetic, like the lines a stage lover cries before he swallows poison. And who would he dictate it to, this death poem? To Father? To Miyo, dabbing his face with a cloth? He squints at her. She smiles. He wonders what she would do if, under the guise of sickness, of a fidgety delirium, he reached a hand inside her kimono. Would she run away? Or would she loosen her obi, keep her gaze on the wall? He shuts his eyes. A dying poet should not spend his last hours stroking, in his imagination, the thighs of a housemaid. (And wasn't he offered far more than this in the House of Falling Leaves? An offer he fled from like a frightened boy.)

When he opens his eyes again, Dr Kushida is in the room, black bag in hand, his face quite expressionless, the way, perhaps, he had once looked at poor Amano. From the bag he takes a syringe, loads it from a glass ampoule, pulls down the quilt, rolls Yuji onto his side, and injects him in the muscles of the right buttock. The injection is bizarrely painful. Yuji groans, though in a voice so small it's like the voice of a mosquito. The doctor shines a light in his eyes, then presses the ivory horn of his stethoscope so hard against the flushed skin of Yuji's chest it leaves behind a pattern of raw circles.

On later visits he burns, in leisurely fashion, little balls of moxa on Yuji's back. There are more injections – neuronal, trional, camphor. And as Yuji coughs phlegm into a bowl or lies prostrate (all lightness has passed now, his body is wet earth, a sack of wet earth), Kushida, in a low voice, a confidential purr, talks to him about the cases he has at the clinic, and in particular the venereal cases. Gonorrhoea, syphilis, sores that never heal, or seem to heal only to break open again months later. He never speaks of such things when Father is present. With a half-smile he offers Yuji advice, telling him that if he goes with a woman he suspects is unclean ('and so many are, so many'), afterwards he should wash his genitals in his own urine. Is this what Mother meant when she told Yuji to listen to Dr Kushida, that the doctor was a good friend of the Takano family?

His fever builds, breaks in a drench of sweating. In the days that follow he passes hours gazing at the old language of cracks on the ceiling. Questions appear – the sort that lethargy incites but cannot answer. He longs to be left alone, to be wretched alone, but the hours are punctuated by visits – Father, Miyo, Kushida, even, one afternoon, Haruyo, who stands above him like a wall and recites the message from Mother, her expression of concern, her wishes for his recovery.

And then, from no observable cause other than the slow accretion of new strength, he wakes out of a deep sleep, seventeen days after falling ill, and listens, with simple curiosity, to the noises of the street – the tofu-seller's bugle, the play of wind chimes, the chattering of sewing machines and radios. He sits up. When the dizziness passes he drinks the water by his bed and washes the taste of medicine from his mouth. He dips two fingers into the glass and wipes his brow, his eyelids. He is setting the glass down again when he sees the marks on his hand, the scatter of ink scratches over the muscle at the base of his left thumb. He angles his hand to the light, then turns it so that his fingers point towards his chest. Is . . . hi . . . ha . . .

Ishihara.

Ishihara!

It is a full minute before he can explain it to himself, can draw to the top of his mind the memory of Hideo Makiyama leaning across to him, pen in hand, under the slowly turning blades of the ceiling fan in the Don Juan. The intuition. The wonderful idea. He did not want Fritz Lang, or that troublesome neurasthenic Akutagawa. He certainly did not want Arthur Rimbaud (Arthur who?), with or without the mysterious letter. What was needed, what was long overdue, what he – and therefore the public – had a raging thirst for, was a comprehensive study of the young star of modern Japanese writing, the author whose books were read even by those who, strictly speaking, could not be called readers at all, who did not give a damn about 'literature' or the values of so-called educated people and who could only be spoken to by a man with a genius for simplicity. And this was his offer, *this* he would allow Yuji to attempt. And to seal the matter, to make some manner of contract between them, he had clutched Yuji's fingers between his own and written, with a few quick darts of his pen, Ishihara's name, an act so pointless, so entirely ludicrous, Yuji, his head already throbbing from the drink, had let the moment fall like spilt ash to the dark of the bar's floor.

Cautiously, he stands up from the mattress. He puts a jacket round his shoulders and goes onto the platform. A fine rain is falling, and further off, in columns of blue shadow, a heavier rain is falling over the Low City. There is no one in the Kitamura Garden. In his own garden, Miyo is hurrying back from the privy, sheltering herself under an umbrella painted with irises. He holds out his hands. On his palms he feels each raindrop's soft arrival. He should, he knows, attempt to be like rain, to have the same indifference and generosity. He also knows that by tomorrow he will have quite forgotten the wisdom of this.

16

Downstairs for the first time in three weeks, he sits in the calm of the Japanese room, sipping tea and waiting for the bath to fill. In the alcove, the scroll has been changed. The snow, the bowed pine trees, the men ascending, have been replaced with a painting of bush warblers on a branch of plum blossom.

The bath is so hot his body becomes numb. He lies there, fingering the soft fringe of ragged hair at his chin, his sick-man's beard. The light of a spring day is slanting through the vent in the wall above him, a clear gold light that falls on the little bran sack Mother uses in place of soap. The season has moved on while he lay upstairs, the year has turned. He should be pleased, but the thought of going back, of starting again the struggle involved even in an existence like his . . . is he ready for that? It is almost a relief when, standing up from the bath, he is swept by a sensation of profound weakness, so that for several seconds, as the light flickers and the water drips from his skin, he can do nothing but stand there, wavering between the elements.

17

The last of the night sweats give way to nights of honest sleep. His face, smooth-shaven again, loses its shadows. In weak sunshine he takes strolls in the garden, little restorative circuits in which he breathes, as deeply as he can, the ripening air. He is out there one afternoon, reading on the stump of the old pine tree they cut down in Showa 10, when the phone rings and Miyo calls him from the verandah. When he takes the receiver and offers his tentative '*Moshi-moshi*' he cannot quite identify the woman's voice.

'But it's *me*,' she says, switching into French. 'Don't you know my voice yet?'

'You've never called me before,' he says.

'Do I sound so different on the telephone?'

'A little, perhaps.'

She speaks to him in Japanese again, the usual mix of Tokyo polite-style and something more direct, more blunt, more definitely Alissa Feneon. She tells him how Junzo came to the house with a book he had promised her ('one of those impossible volumes of philosophy he always has his nose in'), and how it seemed no one had seen Yuji or heard from him in weeks. Had his winter illness come?

'Yes,' says Yuji, 'it came.'

'But you have recovered now?'

'There has been an improvement.'

'You don't *sound* ill.'

'Would you like to hear me cough?'

'No,' she says. 'I don't want that, of course.'

There's a pause. He waits. He cannot begin to imagine why she has called him. He is not even sure where she found his telephone number. Could she have asked Junzo for it?

'I was going to mention something,' she says.

'Yes?'

'If you would like to go to the *kabuki*.'

'To the *kabuki*?'

'To see *Kasane*. Do you know it?'

'It's a ghost story,' he says. 'Everyone knows *Kasane*.'

She explains to him that Mrs Yamaguchi, her dance teacher, has been assisting a company of young actors who, though amateurs, are, in Mrs Yamaguchi's view, both talented and dedicated. Their speciality is the staging of performances in the old style, such as might have been seen in the days of the first Nakamura. They do not, for example, use any electric lighting.

'I see,' says Yuji, half fearful this is some sort of game. 'So it's *kabuki* in the old style.'

'Mrs Yamaguchi will be going. And she has given some tickets to her students. I have two.'

'Two?'

'Yes.'

'To *Kasane?*'

'Yes,' she says. 'Why do you keep repeating everything?'

'I'm sorry . . .'

'It doesn't matter,' she says. 'You've been ill. You probably haven't been speaking to people.'

'No.'

'So you'll come?'

'When?'

'Tomorrow.'

'Tomorrow!'

'We could meet at the house at five, then take a taxi. The theatre's in Tsukiji.'

'Ah, Tsukiji . . .'

'I thought you might find it amusing, especially as you've been unable to leave the house for so long. Aren't you bored to death?'

What, he wonders, what form of words, would make her understand that he would rather spend the evening grinding chalk between his teeth than go to a student performance of *kabuki*? Why has she chosen him? What does she want? It is highly irritating that she refuses to translate his hesitation into what it so obviously signifies.

'At five o'clock?'

'You could wear a kimono,' she says, 'if you think you remember how to.' And she laughs, a sound like someone throwing petals in his face. He hangs up. Miyo is eavesdropping in the Western room. Haruyo, he supposes, will have heard everything from Mother's room – Mother too, perhaps. He goes upstairs, lies on his mattress. Is she, perhaps, a little crazy? He has known her since she was sixteen, but other than Garbo, Dietrich, Bette Davis, Vivian Leigh, Danielle Darrieux and a few others, he has no one to compare her with. He has *seen* other foreign women, of course, has surreptitiously studied them, their height, their high colour, their colourful eyes, their interesting hair, but it is only Alissa he has had any dealings with, just as her father is the only foreign man he has ever spoken to. What is her interest in *kabuki*? What is her interest in classical dance – a form not even Japanese people take much notice of? Can she not be satisfied with Molière and waltzes?

Lying there, he is starting to feel pleasantly fatigued again. There is, he assures himself, plenty of time before tomorrow to think of some excuse, some unavoidable commitment he forgot somehow to mention to her. My sincere apologies . . . Most awkward . . . Most unfortunate . . . Another occasion, perhaps? She, who seems to so admire all things Japanese, and who doubtless subscribes to the curious Western theory of Oriental inscrutability, might enjoy a little demonstration of it. He will hide from her in language. He will conceal himself in a smoke of impeccable manners. It would, after all, require nothing more difficult than a passable imitation of Father.

18

He leaves for the house in Kanda a few minutes after four o'clock. He rides his usual route, but being ill has stripped him of a layer of skin so that the sudden flights of sparrows, the singing of tram cables, sunlight in a gutter, the whiff of, what? – spring mushrooms? – startles and amuses him, diluting a little the exasperated mood he has been in all day, the sense of having been burdened by a ridiculous commitment he has been too dull, too timorous to escape from. His hope now is simply to persuade her to give up the *kabuki* and come to the cinema instead. There's a Marcel Carné film at the Montparnasse in Asakusa. He could buy her a coffee, perhaps an ice cream, get her home by nine. If she becomes tedious, argumentative, starts to lecture him on the traditional arts of Japan, he can cough into his sleeve and let go a few deep sickbed sighs. Even Alissa must understand that.

He props his bicycle by the drainpipe, folds his raincoat over his arm, rings the bell. Hanako answers. 'The master isn't here,' she says.

'Ah . . . ? But Miss Feneon?' He would like to add, 'She called me.' He would like even Hanako to know he has not simply taken it upon himself to ring the bell without a proper invitation, but before he can speak she has stood aside to let him enter.

He follows her through the house to the kitchen door, the only door – some quirk of Russian architecture? – that gives onto the garden. She stands aside again, stares at him, then drops her gaze. Alissa is under the magnolia tree, reaching into its lower branches, apparently to inspect the buds that line the wood like so many creamy-white candles. For a moment he observes her in silence, her braided hair, her rose kimono tied with an obi of the deepest indigo. Then Beatrice barks and runs over the grass to greet him, sitting at his feet and gazing at him with moist, adoring eyes.

'She thinks you've got something for her,' says Alissa. 'She thinks you're Junzo.'

'I don't,' says Yuji, who thinks it not quite right that a dog should be fed sweets like a spoilt child.

'I'm sure she likes you anyway,' says Alissa, taking her stick from where she has hung it over a branch. 'She's very forgiving.'

'Monsieur Feneon isn't here?'

'No,' she says. 'I told you on the phone, didn't I? He's in Yokohama.'

'Yokohama?'

'He can't be here all the time.'

'Of course.'

'He has a business to attend to. I'm sorry if you are disappointed.'

He says he is not. They look at each other. Already, he thinks, it's started, the long evening of embarrassment, but when they go into the house to drink tea she starts to play the hostess, asking him, earnestly, about his health, gently scolding him for not wearing a kimono, and does it all so skilfully, in such a grown-up manner, he is, despite himself, put at ease. The stance he has imagined himself taking, the tone of vexed politeness, has no opening, no chance to emerge. When he tries to say something sarcastic about the failings of student theatricals, it comes out as a perfectly harmless enquiry, one she answers at length, with much enthusiasm.

From in front of the house the taxi sounds its horn. Yuji accepts his coat from Hanako and follows Alissa into the street. They settle into the back of the cab. The driver manoeuvres to the main road past a party of schoolgirls on bicycles, and what looks like a neighbourhood *shogi* competition, a dozen benches spilling into the middle of the street, young and old sitting astride them, leaning intently over the boards.

He settles back against the frayed leather of the seat, looks out drowsily at the traffic, at the sunlight slanting over the roofs, the evening air in which a golden dust seems to hang, suspended. And as they ride – so slowly they will surely be late – something begins in him, an emotion as sweet as it is painful, and that he cannot, in this perfectly ordinary Tokyo dusk, begin to account for. It is as if he was sitting at the side of a piano on which someone was sounding the same deep note again and again, louder and louder, more and more insistently, until his entire body, the blood itself, vibrated at the exact same pitch. If this is memory then it's memory as possession – but memory of *what*? He presses his fist to his lips. Alissa turns to him.

'I've been selfish,' she says. 'You are not well yet.'

'No,' he says. 'It's nothing serious.'

'Should we turn back?'

'There is really no need.'

'You're sure?'

'Quite sure.'

'It's not far now,' she says. 'You'll feel much better out in the air again.'

The theatre is on the corner of a street by the Tsukiji Canal, close enough to the market for a breeze from the bay to carry with it a small stink of fish and fish guts. Yuji, to give himself more time to recover, insists on paying the driver, then walks beside Alissa to the entrance of the theatre. It is not, despite the brightly painted banners over the doors, a place of any great promise, but once they have left their shoes with the attendant and stepped inside, he sees that it is larger than he had imagined, and has, with its scattering of old posters, the age-darkened wood of its beams, the slight confusion of its architecture, something homely and authentic which, despite himself, his mood, the sense of dislocation it has brought with it, touches him with its charm.

They find Mrs Yamaguchi surrounded by her students. She is wearing a kimono of Omeshi silk, and over it a formal coat marked with the crests of the school. To Yuji, though he is certainly no expert, she has the look of a retired geisha, a former O-ka-san, perhaps, from one of the older, stricter houses in Shimbashi or the Yoshiwara. Her eyebrows are razored, her hairline neat as if she still wore a wig, though her hair, with its delicate chain of red coral, is, as far as he can tell, her own. Alissa introduces him. The teacher smiles and says, 'So you are the poet? How wonderful.' If she laughed, he would not be surprised to find she had blackened her teeth, like the beauties of Grandmother's day.

The rhythmic wooden clapping of the *Ki* begins. The inner doors swing wide. They wish each other a pleasant experience, then join the queues filing into the auditorium. The only illumination comes from the pulsing of a half-dozen naked gas flares along the edge of the stage, an uncertain light that leaves large areas draped in shadow, but it does not take long for Yuji to realise that all the seating is in traditional matted stalls and that there is not a single Western-style chair in the whole room. Was Alissa warned of this? How could such a mistake have been made? He turns, stares back to where Mrs Yamaguchi and her students are already settling onto their knees, adjusting their collars, batting their fans. Are some of them watching him, slyly, waiting to see how the 'poet' will manage his little difficulty?

The flares are dimmed. The clapping builds to its crescendo. He leans towards Alissa, clears his throat – there is nothing for it but to guide her, as swiftly as possible, out to the foyer again – but she is speaking to him, saying, 'Here, in here,' and they shuffle sideways into an unoccupied stall between the aisle and the raised walkway of the *hanamichi*. She passes him the stick, then, without the slightest visible difficulty, gracefully even, as though easing herself into a hot bath, she kneels. He takes his place beside her. He is still holding her stick, the warm handle. After a moment he lays it carefully on the mat between them.

The last lights gutter, go out. For quarter of a minute the hall is in perfect darkness, then Yuji hears the sound of bodies turning (silk on skin) and turns himself to see, at the back of the auditorium, a candle flame moving in hesitant rhythms along the *hanamichi* towards the stage, and carrying on its tip the long white oval of an actor's face. It is not until the flame is almost level with where he is kneeling that Yuji sees how the candle is attached to a long pole and the pole carried by a figure in black who moves in the shadow beyond the candle's soft bloom of light, stepping back as the actor steps forwards, stopping when he stops. They reach the stage. The *shamisen* begins to play, a single string plucked with a kind of violence, a sound so sharp, so heavy with nostalgia, the audience lets go a soft collective sigh of grief and pleasure. And in that instant Yuji understands what it was that wrung his heart in the taxi – that his journey with Alissa has unburied the memory of another journey, eighteen, nineteen years ago, when he went with Mother to the Kabuki-za Theatre, just the two of them (Ryuichi must have been with Father or at one of his many school clubs) riding in a rickshaw over the pitted roads of the Low City, crossing Sakura Bridge, crossing Kamei Bridge. He cannot remember the tea house they stopped at. The Kikuoka? He cannot remember which of her kimonos Mother was wearing. He cannot even remember what plays they saw, but what has stayed, what has lain inert all these years waiting for the precise circumstance that would allow it to burn again, is the ecstasy of being pressed against her shoulder, the scent of her, the warmth, the rich serenity of being in exactly the place he wished, above all places, to be. So meagre is his store of such memories – material from the *time before* – he almost laughs out loud at the luck of coming across it like this on an evening he expected nothing from. It is a victory of sorts. A small defeat for that darkness time drags in its wake.

And in this state he starts attending to the play. He doesn't care that the theatre is chilly or that his knees are beginning to ache. How skilled the young actors are! How wise of Mrs Yamaguchi to assist them! The shrieks, the bursts of drumming, the sudden stillness, the buffoonery are no longer quaintly antique but a language profound and perfectly evolved. He gives himself up to it – Takao's murder, Tanizo's love for Kasane, her transforma-tion into a limping monster – and when the *onnagata* playing poor

Kasane strikes the gesture for pointing to the moon, Yuji is as excited as anyone, and had he known the actor's name, would have shouted it out along with the others.

It lasts an hour. The next act, following an interval, will be a dance piece, the one which Mrs Yamaguchi presumably has been helping with, but as Alissa stands, Yuji sees her face contort. She leans heavily on the stick, then, after a few seconds, straightens and smiles at him, an apologetic smile that is also sad and somehow coquettish.

'We could leave now,' he says.

'Don't you want to see the dancing?'

'Perhaps,' he says, 'I've had enough for today.'

In the foyer, they find Mrs Yamaguchi again, explain to her how, most unfortunately, they are unable to stay. The teacher nods, turns her eyes from Yuji to Alissa, back to Yuji. She and her students, she says, will be going to the new Chinese restaurant in Shimbashi, once the dancing has finished. Would Alissa and Yuji care to join them? Yuji opens his mouth to answer but Alissa, bowing swiftly, excuses them both. The girls, her fellow students, wave their neat goodbyes. 'How nice,' says Mrs Yamaguchi, smiling at Yuji from a face as stiff and white as those on the stage, 'to meet a friend of Miss Feneon's.'

They collect their shoes, step into the street. Yuji offers to find a taxi but Alissa says she needs to walk off the stiffness. 'You're sure you didn't mind leaving so soon?' she asks.

'I was ready to go.'

'I think I've converted you a little.'

'Yes,' he says, 'a little.'

It's a night more like mid-May than March. They walk beneath a half-moon, its light in shallow silver pools on the roof tiles of the houses. From the corner of his eye he watches her, wondering if she is still in pain. If she is, she hides it well. She is walking easily now, and with no more than the usual small adjustment to each stride, that slight roll as she settles onto her left foot. A block from the Matsuya, as though by unspoken agreement, they slow, then stop. She adjusts her obi; he glances at his watch.

'Do you have to go home now?' she asks. 'Are you hungry at all?'

He suggests one of the neighbourhood noodle bars, places he has been to at the end of an evening's drinking with Junzo and Taro, and where a dish of *yakisoba* costs no more than a tram ride.

'Or,' she says, speaking quickly, 'we could go to the Snow Goose.'

'The Snow Goose? But isn't that . . .'

'I have a new pupil,' she says, 'a financier of some kind who has fallen in love with Beethoven. He's twice as old as my other students and at least twice as rich so I charge him twice as much.'

'You're good at business,' says Yuji.

'I mean,' she says, 'it could be my treat. A way of apologising for making you sit through an hour of *kabuki*.'

Has someone spoken to her about the allowance? Is this financier of hers a fiction, a way of saving his blushes? Should he be offended? He must refuse her offer, of course, that seems clear, though he would, very much, like to go to the Snow Goose, a proper restaurant, an authentic Western-style restaurant he has passed by a hundred times without ever having stepped inside. And if he leaves now, brings the evening to an end, he will have to go and eat in Otaki's on his own, or take the risk of some icy encounter in the kitchen at home with Haruyo. He studies the toes of his shoes, frowns at the moon, performs in his head the tiresome mathematics of obligation and counter-obligation – though with a foreigner (even one in a rose kimono) the rules are surely different. More lax, more agreeable perhaps . . .

'It seems . . .' he mutters. 'I mean, I wonder if . . .'

'Good,' she says, turning from him and starting to walk again. 'That's settled, then.'

The Snow Goose is on the Ginza, opposite the billiard parlour where they celebrated Junzo's twenty-first birthday. On the front of the restaurant, on the frosted window, a flight of geese are picked out with pieces of golden glass. The doors are open. A doorman pulls back a curtain of red plush. It's noisy inside, and busy. They have to sit for half an hour on a velvet sofa, then a waiter – a waiter with a blond moustache! – escorts them to a small round table by the wall. He pulls out the table for Alissa, pulls back Yuji's chair. On the starched linen the cutlery glitters. In the skins of the wine glasses twenty different lights are trembling.

'I already know what I'm having,' says Alissa. 'Its called a Wiener schnitzel. Have you ever had it?'

'Is it new?'

'It's the speciality here. A bit like *tonkatsu*, though made with veal instead of pork. You should try it. It's delicious. And we should have a bottle of wine, too – unless you would rather drink something else?' She picks up the wine list, runs a varnished but unpainted fingernail down the page. 'I think . . . I think Papa might choose this one. A white from Alsace.'

'Alsace?'

'They sometimes think they're German but they're French really. We don't have to worry.'

'Your father said that drinking wine was his duty now. His patriotic duty.'

She nods. 'He fought the last time,' she says. 'He was wounded twice, the second time' – she touches her breast – 'a piece of shrapnel just missed his heart. Anyway, there's no one to fight yet. I mean, they haven't actually invaded or anything.'

'Perhaps it will stay like that.'

'Yes,' she says. 'I suppose it might. The truth is, I mean, between you and me. I worry more about what's happening on this side of the world.' She throws a glance to the end of the room where a dozen young officers are drinking together, a party Yuji has already noted, then carefully ignored, not wishing to lock eyes with some drunken lieutenant fresh from Shanghai or the Mongolian border. Other than the waiters the only men in the restaurant not in uniform are at least twenty years older than him.

Alissa orders the wine, the food. She is quite at ease in the Snow Goose, the elaborate etiquette of the place, and when the waiter pours a splash of golden wine into Yuji's glass she prompts him with her eyes.

'Oh, yes,' he says, hurriedly swallowing, 'it's quite nice' though he is perturbed that the wine does not really taste of grapes at all but has, instead, a somewhat surprising flavour of stones.

The waiter fills their glasses, sinks the bottle into an ice bucket, puts the bucket on a tripod next to the table, and with a nod of his blond head, withdraws.

'What shall we speak now,' asks Alissa, 'French, or Japanese?'

'Why not French for the first half of the bottle, then Japanese for the rest?'

She smiles, agrees, but having chosen a language, they sit in silence, looking at the points of their cutlery.

'Say something,' she says at last. 'Tell me something.'

'What shall I tell you?'

'Anything you like. It doesn't really matter.'

'Tonight,' he says, 'I remembered going on an outing.'

'Long ago?'

'I was, perhaps, seven years old. I was with Mother.'

'A happy memory?'

'Yes, I think so.'

'I don't even know her name.'

'Mother?'

'Yes.'

'Noriko.'

'And your father?'

'Kenji.' He laughs. Somehow it seems amusing to say Father's name here. Comically indelicate.

'Papa's is Emile.'

He nods.

'You knew?'

'It was written inside one of his books.'

'You're very fond of him, aren't you?'

Yuji feels himself reddening. *Bien aimer. Bien aimer quelqu'un.* 'He treats me, mm, almost as an equal? He does not assume that what I have to say will be wrong or foolish. He listens to me.'

'He would have liked to have had a son, I think.'

'Yes?'

'He could have shared more with a son.'

'His business?'

'That . . . and other things, too.'

'My father,' says Yuji, 'is not in the habit of sharing things.'

'It's rude of me,' she says, 'and please don't say anything if you'd rather not, but for a long time I've wanted to ask you what happened to your father. I know some of it, of course, but it's all second or third hand, and that's not much better than gossip. I mean, obviously he's completely innocent. But I'd like to know what the facts are.'

'The facts,' says Yuji, 'might not be as interesting as the gossip.' He takes another mouthful of wine, can feel it starting to work in him, to loosen his tongue. He leans towards her a little, his hands folded on the linen. 'When Father was in his thirties, he published a book, a very long and technical book, on democracy and the constitution. One section, just a few pages, was about the relationship' – he drops his voice – 'between the Emperor and the Diet. In Father's analysis the Emperor is simply another organ of the State. The Diet should take account of his wishes but it is not bound to follow them. Its decisions would be those of a freely elected body. In this way, I think, Father hoped the Emperor could be protected from those elements who might use his authority to justify extreme actions. The book was only read by a few specialists, people like Father. And the atmosphere was quite different then. The criticism didn't start until after the coup attempt in '36. They said he was tainted with Anglo-Saxon ideas, that he had failed to recognise the uniqueness of the Japanese situation, that he was a pacifist. I don't think he took the charges very seriously. He used to tell us they were a symptom of the times and would cease as the times changed. I suppose you could say he misread history, even that he suffered from a certain arrogance.'

'No,' she says, 'I wouldn't say that. I would say he was principled and courageous.'

'At the university he became a target for groups like the Black Dragons. His lectures were broken up, his office was ransacked. In the end almost no one would risk speaking up for him. He resigned to protect us, to protect his colleagues. He received no pension, though I suspect he would not have accepted one even if it had been offered.'

'There was *nothing* he could do? Nobody he could appeal to?'

'It's been worse for others,' says Yuji. 'And I, of course, had no position to lose.'

Their food arrives on big white plates, each plate with its piece of breaded meat crowned with a quartered lemon. In the centre of the table the waiter sets a silver dish of fried potatoes, a bowl of steamed rice. '*Bon appetit,*' he says, a quick smile at Alissa.

'And *your* father,' says Yuji, nervous she will want to go on speaking about his own, that he will be tempted, in this public place, into indiscretions, 'does he often stay in Yokohama?'

She shrugs. 'Once or twice a month. We lived there, remember, when we first came to Japan. We still have friends there . . . Miss Ogilvy, for example.'

'Miss Ogilvy?'

'An American. Actually, we knew her in Saigon. She has a house on the Bluff, with lots of cats.'

'I only know Americans from the films,' says Yuji.

'I don't think she's a typical American. I don't think she's a typical anything.'

'But your father stays in her house?'

'Sometimes. He doesn't always tell me where he's going and I don't always ask. We prefer it like that.'

She forks her lemon, twists the juice from it. They start to eat. To Yuji, though he has used Western cutlery before, the knife and fork feel almost unusably heavy, unusably large, more like weaponry than implements for feeding himself, but the food is good and he eats it gratefully.

'You must,' says Alissa, pouring wine for them both and taking them into the Japanese half of the bottle, 'have wondered about my mother.'

'I have,' says Yuji, though this is not exactly true. He has simply assumed that Madame Feneon belongs among the distant dead. There are no pictures of her in the parts of the house he has been in, no fond mementos.

'It's not a secret,' says Alissa. 'At least, there's no reason for it to be. Certainly there's nothing I need to be ashamed of.'

He nods vigorously, suddenly convinced she is about to tell him that the mysterious Miss Ogilvy is her mother. Instead, with a studied nonchalance, she says that she has never met her mother.

'I mean, I must have glimpsed her in the moments after I was born. At least, I suppose I did, though naturally I can't remember any of that. Does that count as meeting somebody?'

'It could, I suppose.'

'She wasn't married to Papa or anything like that. She was a sort of companion of his, in Saigon. Probably they met at a dance or something, I don't really know. There were always lots of parties. Anyway, one day she disappeared. No letter, no forwarding address. Just vanished. Seven months later an old woman came to the house carrying a basket with a baby inside. She gave the baby to one of the servants, a girl called Songlian. She said it was Suzette's – that was my mother's name – but that Suzette couldn't look after it. Papa tried everything to find her of course, but he couldn't even find the old woman. I stayed with Songlian. I slept with her in the servants' quarters, was fed by her. One night, in the middle of the night, Papa came and sat beside us. He fanned me with his hat, watched me sleeping.' She smiles. 'He says he fell in love with me then and decided he would raise me, openly, as his daughter, though it wasn't quite as easy as that. All sorts of people made their disapproval clear, the club people, the church people, but Saigon isn't like here. It's more chaotic, freer. Here, it would probably have been impossible.'

'When you were little,' says Yuji, struggling to make sense of her story, 'you must have thought the servant was your mother.'

'Don't they say a duckling will follow whatever it sees first, even if it's a dog or a monkey or the farmer's wife? Later I realised there was something strange about it, though when I asked questions – I spoke good Cantonese by the time I was three – Songlian would only say, "Speak to Papa," and when I asked him, it was always, "When you're older." I was eleven before he told me all this. He sat me down in the kitchen one night, cooked me *oeufs en cocotte* and poured me my first glass of wine.'

'You were shocked?'

'No, I don't think so. And Papa made it sound as though I was a little girl in a fairy tale, you know, arriving in a basket carried by an old woman who was obviously a sort of good witch. But later I went through a time of wanting, very desperately, to see her, Suzette, I mean. I would look at the women in the market, the ones with children my age, wonder if one of them was her, if she would look up and somehow recognise me. When we came to Japan, of course, that stopped. It was a relief, really . . .'

'And she was French?' asks Yuji.

'Not, perhaps, in quite the way Papa is.'

'No?' He waits.

'I have never,' she says, 'seen a photograph of her. I don't think there is one. Papa tells me she was very pretty, that she was tall, that she was a good dancer. My mirror tells me she was also probably mixed race. Don't you think so?'

She looks at him, her eyes wide with some mute appeal, some silent defiance, and for several seconds they stare at each other until Yuji drops his gaze to his glass. Is this the answer to the riddle of Alissa Feneon? A mixed-race girl? Cautiously, he raises his eyes again. She has turned a little in her seat, turned away as though to make it easier for him to study her. And suddenly he believes he can see it, as though over the bones of her skull she is wearing a score of faces, tissue-thin, and one of these – not the top or the one below or the one below that – but *one* of them is a face out of the East, an intrusion.

'I think I'd prefer it if you didn't tell the others,' she says. 'It's not as if it's important or anything.'

'No,' says Yuji, manoeuvring the remains of his Wiener schnitzel to the edge of his plate. 'No.'

At the end of the room, the young officers have started to sing. Just two or three at first, but soon the others join in and all of them beat time with their glasses. A glass shatters. Alissa asks Yuji to call for the bill. When it comes (on a little silver salver) she pays with a note from the purse she keeps inside a fold of her obi.

The waiter brings them their coats, helps Alissa into hers. '*Vous êtes Française?*' he asks.

'*De* Saigon,' she says. '*Et vous?*'

'Genève.' He grins at her, the permitted intimacy of a fellow foreigner, then nods to Yuji, holds back the red plush curtain and they leave the Snow Goose with a chorus of 'Oh! Our Manchuria!' ringing in their ears.

On the pavements of the Ginza, the mild air has brought out an evening crowd of strolling couples, office workers, street hawkers, mobile fortune-tellers. Outside a drinking shop (a place that used to be known as the Lenin), the doorman claps his hands for business, while across the street a gang of students are ragging each other noisily in the neon shadows of the billiard parlour.

Yuji has his usual trouble with the taxis, losing out to people who flagged them more aggressively or who, the moment they saw one approaching, sprinted recklessly into the middle of the road. When, at last, he succeeds in stopping one, he takes his place in the back beside Alissa. She gives the driver the address of the house in Kanda. From there – or so he assumes – he will collect his bicycle, make some remarks about how enjoyable the evening has been, about seeing each other at the next meeting of the club, then wave to her and ride home. But when they step down from the taxi and the taxi leaves, she tells him she has something she would like him to see. Would he mind coming inside for a few minutes?

Hanako, who does not live at the house, has long since left. Alissa uses her own key to open the door. In the salon, Beatrice snorts, shakes with excitement. Alissa put on a side-lamp, drapes her coat over the back of the sofa, excuses herself. Yuji waits by the piano. He lifts the lid and touches, but does not depress, a white key at the bass end of the keyboard, then closing the lid, he walks to the half-open door of Feneon's study.

Through the unshuttered window, moonlight picks out a pattern in the rug and lacquers the familiar edges of things – the book-shelves, the Buddha, the metal lock of the projector box. He glances over his shoulder, then steps inside, performs a quick circuit of the room, swivels the swivel-chair, and made bold by the dark, sits in the chair, resting his palms presidentially on the desk's broad surface, the thumb-deep slab of bolted mahogany, and decides that the West's ascendancy – that dominance the generals and admirals seem so personally humiliated by – comes, in part, from the solidity of the objects they surround themselves with, while the Japanese live among what is fragile and evanescent, in homes any man in a moderate rage could pull apart with his bare hands. Would they really, one day, have to fight these pragmatists who long ago put their faith in iron and steel and high explosives? What is this *inevitability* everyone seems to have agreed to believe in? This urge to lie down together in the fire?

When he hears Alissa, he moves hurriedly away the desk, from the impertinence of sitting where only Emile Feneon should sit. She pauses in the doorway, and before he can apologise to her, she says, 'I love the smell in here. Don't you? I'd like to have it in a little bottle so I could take it with me everywhere I go for the rest of my life.'

'Go? Where would you go?'

She shrugs. 'Nowhere unless we have to.'

'But your father has discussed it with you?'

'Of course.'

'I didn't know.'

'You must have assumed it.'

'You want to go to France?'

'It's far too late for that, don't you think? Back to Saigon. Perhaps Hong Kong. As I said, we won't go anywhere unless we have to. Japan is my home.'

'I'm sure,' he says, 'there will be no need for you to leave. I'm sure . . .' He tries to think of some phrase, in Japanese or French, that will reassure her, but she says, 'Let's not talk about it any more.' And then, 'Were you looking for something in here?'

'What would I be looking for?'

'I don't know. The letter perhaps?'

With the light behind her he cannot see her expression, but he recognises the tone of voice, the streak of silent amusement in it. 'It would,' he says stiffly, 'be unforgivable. It would—'

'I know,' she says. 'I didn't mean . . .'

'No.'

'Of course not.'

'But is it here?'

She laughs. 'Probably. Though it would take us all night to find it. It might even be in the attic. There are boxes and boxes up there.'

'You've really read it?'

'Years ago.'

'And you remember nothing about it?'

'He's your hero,' she says, 'not mine. I prefer Hitomaro.'

'Hitomaro!'

'"One morning like a bird she was gone in the white scarves of death. Now when the child whom she left in her memory cries and begs for her, all I can do is lift him and embrace him clumsily." Isn't it beautiful? But I was going to show you something,' she says, 'unless you'd rather stay here and start looking through the desk drawers?'

He follows her out of the study, then through the salon to the bottom of the stairs. He has never been to the top of the house before, nor, as far as he knows, has any other member of the club. Upstairs was '*interdit aux élèves*', and though he has been curious about it, has on occasion exercised his imagination on it, he has been content it should remain so, a place apart, a sanctum where the *kami* sleeps.

Beatrice patters behind them. Alissa sends her back to the salon, then leads Yuji up to the landing, a narrow carpeted corridor where two windows look over the road. On the walls between the windows there are paintings, watery landscapes, a view of a town with tightly winding grey-stone streets.

'This is Papa's room,' she says, opening the door wide enough for Yuji to see the brass bed-end, the big wardrobe, the vitreous gleam of the washstand. 'And this one,' she says, passing another door and going ahead to the end of the landing, 'is mine.'

It is smaller than her father's room, and almost half of it is taken up by a bed with a muslin canopy, a heaped quilt of ivory satin. At the far end of the room, under the window, is a dressing table littered with hairpins, perfume bottles, spools of ribbon. There are photographs there, too, in various decorative frames, and one of these she picks up, wipes carefully with her sleeve, and holds out to him. He crosses the room and takes it from her. It's a small, informal picture of a young woman holding in her arms an unsmiling black-haired baby. Behind them is a window, a slatted shutter, the bough of some flowering tree.

'Songlian,' she says. 'Songlian and me outside Papa's house in Saigon . . . I didn't want you to go home thinking I was one of those girls who makes things up about her life, you know, to make herself more interesting.'

He nods and gives the picture back to her. Did she honestly think he had not believed her, or is she showing him the picture so that he understands, fully, what she was trying to explain to him in the restaurant – that through her mother, through her mother's mixed blood, she is, in part, an Asian girl? A quarter, an eighth, some fraction of her, not from the grey-stone streets in the painting on the landing but a member of that Great Asian Family the radio keeps lecturing them about. Is this what she wants him to know, to believe? He finds it rather ridiculous, but then, to his amazement, as she turns to replace the picture on the dressing table, he sees his hand reaching up to the back of her head and touching the place where her hair sweeps in a black stream behind one of her ears.

She tenses, stiffens as if it was a gun or the blade of a knife he held to her neck, as if the slightest movement might destroy them both. Then she turns and stares at him, searches his face (for some mark of insincerity?), smiles, and sways towards him. They kiss, lightly at first, then more and more deeply.

'Help me,' she whispers. She is undoing the pearl-headed clasp of the cord round her obi. He helps her. They work in silence, pulling, tugging at the material. It unravels at their feet, a nest of coiled indigo. She loosens the under-sash. They avoid each other's eyes now, but she finds his hand and guides it through the crêpe of her under-kimono to where, under the cotton of her slip, her hip and upper thigh are joined.

'It's a defect of the joint,' she says. 'Probably from my mother's family. There are no scars, nothing that's ugly. Nothing to be afraid of. You can look if you like, if you don't trust your fingers.' She lifts the hem of her slip. And it's true. No scars, nothing ugly. Only the blushed white of her skin, the swell of her thigh.

There is a tautness to the moment Yuji finds almost unendurable. He watches his hand (though it hardly seems his) mechanically stroking her thigh. Her mouth is partly open, her long, black lashes lie against her cheeks. It is a face both childlike and lewd, tender, stupid with tenderness and trust. And then, on an impulse that comes from some place in him where violence and desire are equally mixed, he darts his hand to the shadow between her thighs, his whole hand clutching her there, seizing her, so that she folds against him with a sudden sharp cry.

At first he thinks it must be morning, but the light is just the lamp's flat electric shining, and the room, the house, the world beyond the curtains is wrapped still in some vagary of night, some secretive hour, immense and empty, the dawn's dawn perhaps. He gazes into the cloud of gathered muslin above the bed, and for a minute he rests at the half-woken ebb of himself and thinks of nothing. Then, when he can do it no more, when nothing starts to fill with remembering, he turns to look at her, her sleeping head on the pillow next to his, her slim bare arm in front of her face, as if to protect it. She is under the ivory quilt, and tried perhaps to get him beneath it too, until, finding it impossible, she dragged the rose kimono from the floor and covered him with that.

He slides out his feet, collects his clothes from different parts of the floor and goes onto the landing. Other than his watch, he is wearing nothing. It is five fifteen exactly. He puts on his clothes. Her stick is leaning against the wall by the bedroom door. He cannot recall her leaving it there. He goes down the stairs. He is afraid Beatrice will start to bark, or worse, far worse, that he will be confronted by Hanako, but the dog only blinks at him from the sofa and there is no sound of servant's bustle. He turns off the side-lamp, goes into the hall, puts on his coat, his boots. The saddle of his bicycle is wet from a rain shower, though the sky has cleared. He wipes the saddle, wheels the bicycle into the road. Whatever he was before, he is sober now, intensely so, a stark and comfortless sobriety in which the moment he raised his hand to touch Alissa Feneon's hair appears to him as the most foolish, the most reckless of his life. She tricked him of course, that much is obvious. *Kabuki* in the old style! But how can he go back, how can he stand in the salon warming his hands at the stove while *she* is there? And when her father learns of it – as assuredly he will – when he summons Yuji into his study, what then? What decent defence can he offer?

He, whose only wish has been to keep the world from throwing him off, a drop of water from a spinning ball, has now, through his weakness, through something as apparently innocent as curiosity, through the malevolence of fate, through the scheming of a mixed-race girl, undone the last good thing he had. He has betrayed Monsieur Feneon (who wanted a *son!*), he has scattered his friends; he has lost, irretrievably, his house of life. He peddles, a yell of silent outrage in his wake. Above him, the last stars are fading towards morning.

19

He considers writing Feneon a letter. Briefly, he considers writing one to Alissa. He has no idea what he could say to either of them. He is sorry? He is angry? He is miserable?

He stays in his room where now and then he laughs out loud, bitterly. He doesn't care who hears. He has long and elaborate daydreams about volunteering for the army, going to Kanda in his new uniform, saluting smartly at the door of Feneon's study, then turning on his heel and marching off to certain death. Two days pass, three days, a week. He does nothing. Nothing happens.

He follows old routines, bathes at the customary hour, eats with Father and Miyo, reads, walks in the neighbourhood, performs his few chores. He begins to tell himself he has over-reacted, that his reaction has, in fact, been somewhat hysterical. And why did he assume that Feneon would learn anything? Why should he? From whom? From Hanako? All Hanako could say is that they left for the theatre together in a taxi. Mrs Yamaguchi? She is Alissa's teacher but not, as far as he knows, an intimate of the family. The only person other than himself who could speak, who could tell everything, is Alissa, and why would she tell her father a story that threw on her such a shaming light?

As for his own part in the affair of that night, each gesture, each sequence and exchange revised in memory many times, it seems to him now he cannot, reasonably, be held responsible for any of it. It was the last of his fever. It was the excitement of recapturing, so unexpectedly, his boyhood outing with mother. It was the wine (the wine Feneon wisely forbids him). And above all, it was *her* – her wiles, her questionable blood. How many others has she invited upstairs to look at the photograph of her servant foster mother? Was he the first, the tenth, the fiftieth?

Forgetting is a hard art, he knows that (as hard as its apparent opposite) but he starts to fold the memory of that night like a sheet of paper into smaller and smaller squares, imagining, as he does so, Alissa, sitting on the ivory quilt in her room, engaged in the same dogged exercise of the will. And when each of them has folded the paper to its smallest measure, dense as a pellet, tiny enough to hold in a crease of the hand, in one of the fate lines, hidden, then, surely, it will be – almost be – as though none of it ever happened.

How long must he wait? A month? Two? Longer? It would be a mistake to try to go back too soon. But eventually, the end of the spring, say, the beginning of the June rains, he will stand on the step at Kanda and ring the bell, and Feneon, who will have had nothing to forget, nothing to fold, will greet him in the usual way. They will drink a glass of eau de vie. Yuji will explain his absence easily (his health, his mother's health, even, perhaps, that he has been writing). Then the club will sit on the study floor to watch a hundred shades of grey flicker soothingly over the sheet pegged to the bookshelf. She will be there, of course – she must be if things are to be normal – but she will know how to behave. She will behave impeccably. And after the film they will practise their French in some harmless discussion and the evening will end with laughter, with calls across the dusky street as the club cycles home. He has only to be patient, to be silent, to keep his nerve. The end of the spring, the start of the rains, the first big cloudburst to drum on the roof.

Could it be that nothing has been lost at all?

20

At Setagaya, he sits on the verandah with Grandfather and Sonoko making bags for the loquats. If the young fruits are not covered while they are still the size of a child's fingertip, weevils get in and suck out the juices. To make the bags they have on the wood between them a bowl of flour paste, a stack of magazines and newspapers. Sonoko is the most dilligent. Her pile of bags grows quickly, but Yuji's pile is smaller even than Grandfather's, for though his fingers are nimble, he is constantly stopping work to peer at a photograph or read a dozen lines of some story, weeks or months old.

One of the pages he pulls from a magazine, then pauses to read, is an account of a tour of Manchuria by a group of 'notable authors' invited to see first-hand the great strides made by the new administration in transforming such an antique place into a showcase of Asian modernity. At the bottom of the page, the authors are depicted standing in a line with certain representatives of the military. The most senior authors, the most notable, are in the middle of the line flanked by the highest-ranking officers. Ishihara is there (not in the centre but not at either extreme), dressed in a long leather coat like the one air ace von Rauffenstein wears in *La Grande Illusion*.

The faces of the writers are mostly smiling, as though the tour was a welcome break from the rigours of composition, the confines of their studies, but the officers' expressions, shadowed under the peaks of their caps, are set and somehow unamused. Below the picture the caption reads, 'Forward as one! The pen and the sword link arms.'

'You want the weevils to beat us?' asks Grandfather. He takes the page from Yuji's hand, tears it in two and dips his brush into the paste. 'Sonoko,' he says, 'it seems that Grandson wants the weevils to beat us!'

21

At home, the doors of the Japanese room are opened wide to the garden, the first time since the previous October. The mats and the woodwork are beaten and wiped. In a corner of the room where the air is touched by sunlight, an insect becomes a fleck of gold.

On the radio, daily bulletins plot the northward progress of the cherry blossom – Fukuoka, Hiroshima, Kyoto, Nagoya. There are also reports of the German advance into Norway, an action intended to protect the Norwegian people from the aggression of the British. Miyo, her hair tied up in a cloth, a duster in her hand, asks Yuji if Norway is close to Japan or as far away as Russia. He shows her the map in the morning paper. She stares at it, then laughs. She cannot explain why. 'Because . . .' she says, and shrugs and goes on with her work. Is she frightened? Or do the movements of armies, the fall of nations, genuinely amuse her?

22

A bright Saturday, the second week in April, he goes to the blossom viewing in Ueno Park. He has arranged to meet Junzo, Taro and Shozo under the clock at the subway terminus, but when he arrives there with Miyo, only Taro and Shozo are waiting.

'Little brother's sulking about something,' says Taro. 'His mystery girlfriend, I suppose.'

The park at ten o'clock is already crowded and it takes them half an hour to find a place for themselves, two yards of unoccupied grass between a group of middle-aged office workers and a circle of young mothers, drowsy, with drowsy babies on their knees. They spread their blankets. Above them, the blossom is so dense that when a breeze blows, the whole head of the tree moves like a single flower. Miyo opens the *bento* boxes. They eat, picking the food from the little wooden pockets. They have sake with them but after the first cup no one bothers to pour. They watch the passers-by, are watched in turn. Somewhere in the park a van with loudspeakers is broadcasting speeches. Miyo takes out her sewing. Shozo pulls his cap over his eyes. In a quiet voice to Yuji, Taro says, 'You've heard the rumours?'

'Rumours?' Yuji's heart begins to pound. 'What rumours?'

'Spies, saboteurs, traitors in high places . . . At the ministry it's all anyone talks about.'

'I've heard nothing,' says Yuji, hiding his relief in a frown. 'Is any of it true?'

'Some, I suppose. I don't know how much. Anyway, it's best to be watchful.'

'Of course.' Yuji picks a blade of grass. 'Though what is it exactly we should watch for?'

'Whatever is out of the ordinary. People who seem to have something to hide. Foreigners . . .'

'Foreigners? Like the Feneons?'

'Well, the Feneons, that's different.'

'If necessary,' says Yuji, 'we could speak up for them.'

'It would be more sensible,' says Taro, 'to be discreet.'

'Then we could speak up for them discreetly?'

'And who would we speak to? The *Tokko*?'

'Why not?'

'Now you're being stupid.'

'Monsieur Feneon's been here for ten years.'

'I know all that. But these days it's not how something *is*, it's how it *looks*. Think of your father's situation.'

'Father?'

'Even an important man like him was not protected.'

'I am aware of it.'

'And you are his son.'

'So?'

'Nobody is invisible.'

122

'It almost sounds like you're warning me.'

'I'm saying you should use your head.'

'And you?'

'Yes,' says Taro, nodding slowly. 'More than you perhaps.'

They sit together, silently, as though on the brink of some sharp exchange neither is quite ready for, not today, not here in the open. Yuji flicks the rolled blade of grass away and gets to his feet. 'I'm going to walk,' he says. 'You want to come?'

Taro shakes his head. 'I'll stay,' he says. 'Shut my eyes for a while.'

Alone, relieved to be alone, Yuji thinks first of heading towards the pond ('In the dream of a city poet, electric dragonflies over Shinobazu Pond.'), then finds it easier to simply fall in with the movement of those around him, the aimless swirling of boots and wooden sandals, silken sleeves, epaulettes, piled hair, cigarettes, parasols. Only a man in tattered leggings hunkered in the shade of a stripped windbreak, one of the hundred or more who sleep in the park, who scavenge in the bins and grow beards like Chinese sages, seems to Yuji independent of the crowd and the crowd's enormous slack mind. He watches him, admires the steadfast gaze, the immobility, then sees on the rising grass beyond him a woman's back wrapped tightly in unpatterned water-green silk. He grins, almost calls out to her, but stops himself and circles cautiously until he is sure the old woman is not about to descend.

'I hope you haven't been following me,' she says, as he walks up to her.

'How could I? I had no idea you were coming today.' He points to the tea tray in her hands, the two cups. 'Have you lost her?'

'I'm sure this is where I left her, though now it seems she has vanished.'

'She will have met a friend,' says Yuji, 'and the friend has taken her to meet another friend.'

'Someone with a lot of grandchildren, perhaps?'

'Lots of grandchildren and lots of interesting ailments.'

'So now I'm waiting for her like a servant,' says Kyoko, turning her smile into a pout. 'What a nice way to spend my day off.'

'Did you arrange a meeting place?'

'The usual,' she says.

'The statue? I could carry the tea for you.'

She bites her lip, throws him a hard glance, but lets him take the tray from her hands and follows him as he steps into the current of the crowd again. Soon he's making her laugh with his muttered commentary on the blossom-viewing parties, the over-ripe wives, the shrunken husbands, the red-faced children chasing each other bawdily between the trees. A holiday crowd more akin to the big-thighed clay manikins unearthed from Yayoi sites (grainy pictures of them in Father's books) than the race of 'warrior gods' the vans with the loudspeakers are shouting about in the distance, though this last thought, mindful of his talk with Taro, mindful too that he is in the company of the wife of an acting corporal in the Kwangtung Army, he keeps to himself.

'I heard you were ill,' she says.

'Who told you that?'

'Who do you think?'

'Who told her?'

'Who do you think?'

He nods. He would like to know what else Haruyo tells the old woman. That she heard him make arrangements to go to the *kabuki* with the foreign girl? That she heard the front door slide open at six the following morning?

'I'm well now,' he says.

'That's good.'

'Any news from over the water?'

'A photograph.'

'Another new coat?'

'A coat? No,' she says. 'It's not that sort of photograph.'

He waits for her to explain what kind it is but she doesn't. He has heard of soldiers sending pictures home of prisoners or even of the enemy dead. Some girls, it was said, carried such pictures as love tokens.

'What will you do now?' she asks.

'Now that I'm well?'

'Yes.'

'I have lots to do,' he says.

'You've found a job?'

'Not exactly a *job*.'

'Grandmother says that soon everyone will be forced to work. In factories, digging shelters . . .'

'Shelters? In Tokyo?'

'It might be good for you to do some digging. That kind of work can soothe the nerves.'

He glances across at her. Is that what she would like to see? Him wielding a mattock, excavating some great hole under the city, choking on the dust?

'As I told you,' he says, 'I've got plenty to do. You've heard of Kaoru Ishihara, I suppose?'

'*Mother Behind my Eyes?*'

'Yes. *Blood of Honour, The Last Stand.* I've been commissioned to write a piece on him. A critical essay for *Young Japan.*'

'On the train,' she says, 'I've seen some of the junior officers – the more serious ones – reading *Young Japan*.'

'It will be quite an important piece. Literary but also political. Different dimensions and so on.'

'You must be pleased,' she says. 'You could really make a name for yourself.'

'It's the sort of thing,' says Yuji, 'I'll be doing a lot more of now. I'm afraid the shelters will have to wait.'

'Of course.'

At the statue of Saigo Takamori there is, happily, no sign of Grandma Kitamura, though a dozen others are stood there, women and children mostly, looking out expectantly for some familiar face to blossom suddenly among the ranks of strangers.

'The tea will be cold,' says Yuji.

'It doesn't matter,' she says.

He turns and gazes up at the bronze samurai and his faithful dog. 'Did you know,' he says, 'that after the Great Earthquake people used this statue as a noticeboard? It was covered with the names of the missing. A name, the last known location, the address of the family, sometimes a photograph or a sketch. It was the same with the statue of Kusunoki Mosashige outside the palace.'

'I hadn't heard that,' she says, and he can see, as she joins her gaze to his, that she's imagining it, the way it must have looked with hundreds of little pieces of paper fluttering on its sides. He, too, of course, must imagine it, for by the time he returned from Uncle Kensuke's most of the notices were gone, though some, yellowing and torn, stayed up stubbornly for a month or more, until the autumn winds released them. Where Father posted Ryuichi's name he has no idea, but he points to a spot halfway up the plinth and tells her it was there.

'If it troubles you to wait here . . .' she says, a voice more tender, more intimate than any he has heard from her before.

'Thank you for your thoughtfulness,' he says, 'but I have been here many times. It no longer . . .'

'Anyway,' she says, 'might it be better if you left before Grandmother arrives?'

He nods, hands her the tea tray. 'It was nice to meet you today,' he says.

'I am glad you are well,' she says. 'Please have good luck with your new work.'

He thanks her again and leaves. He does not look back. He is afraid he will see a boy in a high-collared uniform, white gloves on his hands, crouching at the warriors' sandalled feet. He is afraid that if he turns the boy will leap down and pursue him through the park, enraged, swift as a fox.

23

As the embarrassment of doing the piece is now outweighed by the shame that would follow from not doing it, from being discovered as a liar, a fantasist, a person who should immediately be sent to dig shelters beneath the streets of Tokyo, he calls Makiyama's office and leaves a message with Kiyooka that he would, if it is still possible, if he has not left it too late, be grateful to accept Mr Makiyama's generous suggestion of a study of Kaoru Ishihara.

'By the way,' drawls Kiyooka, 'we have one of your socks here. Perhaps you would like to collect it?'

24

At the dining table in the Western room he reads an account of the German Army's capture of Copenhagen. This time there is no attempt to claim that the action was intended to protect the inhabitants from an aggressor. The Danes have simply been absorbed into the Reich. The audaciousness of the attack, the speed with which both the city and the country have been conquered by small forces of determined soldiers, is a lesson, so the author of the article suggests, the Japanese military will surely wish to profit from.

He folds the paper (which today has a special supplement on patriotic recipes) and looks into the garden at Miyo crouching on the path beside the bamboo. What is she doing there? The door onto the verandah is open. He goes outside and crouches beside her. She points into the heart of the bamboo, the little depression where the cat made its nest. He cannot see anything at first – the ground there is densely striped with shadow. Then he notices the death-shrunken form of a kitten, and nearby, partly buried under the pale leaves, a second.

'Did none survive?' he asks.

She puts a finger to her lips.

25

The day before the Emperor's birthday, Yuji cycles to the Kanda bookstalls to buy second-hand editions of Ishihara's novels. In warm streets under a faultless sky even Yuji with his old habits of self-care, his sick-boy's caution, is dressed for the good weather – open-neck shirt, flannel trousers, canvas shoes.

To find Ishihara's books will be easy enough. The people who read him are not collectors. When the story has been read the book is empty, used up. Those who can be bothered dispose of them for a few sen at the stalls. The rest leave them under their seats in the subway or on the luggage racks of trains, where they become part of the city's unofficial circulating library.

On Ooka's stall half a dozen of the books are on prominent display, but Yuji does not want to explain himself to Ooka, who will certainly try to make a joke about this new and unexpected interest. He slides past to Shinkichi's stall. Shinkichi is a sullen man who does not enter into conversation with his customers. He buys *Song of Death, The Last Assault, Tears of a Hero, Blood and Beauty, Mother Behind My Eyes*. Each of them has some wild illustration on the cover. A pair of schoolboys splashed in their own gore, gazing at each other passionately in the moment of death. A pair of samurai with gaping wounds, gazing at each other admiringly in the moment of death. A grieving mother kneeling under a rain of blood . . .

Shinkichi makes a parcel of the books. Yuji hangs the parcel from his handlebars. He has what he came for but cannot quite resist going the ten yards to Yoshimasu's stall to look there (under the guise of general browsing, of an idle and utterly carefree examination of the stock) for that unloved edition of *Electric Dragonfly*.

Has someone bought it? Has the pretty girl Ooka laughed about taken it home with her, where even now she is lying on the mats of her room reading it aloud to herself while a drop of tea slides from the rim of her cup to leave a perfectly neat little splash on the page? He rests the bicycle's crossbar against his belly, starts to flick through the piles. There are volumes here, armfuls of them by people he has never heard of, young poets who, no doubt, considered themselves on the cusp of a brilliant career, then found they could not fly again. What became of them? Where have they gone? What becomes of those who have ceased to promise?

Around him the day suddenly darkens, as if at the passing of some large and unpalatable truth, but the moment is fleeting, the sunlight falls on the back of his neck again, and when he finds *Electric Dragonfly* in its pristine cover (a line-drawn dragonfly, a lily pad) he silently greets it, lifts it deftly to the top of the pile, and turns away, wheeling his bicycle through the crooked corridor between the stalls.

At the end of the street, he hesitates, looks in both directions, then climbs into the saddle and rides towards the Russian Cathedral. It is not the way home, certainly not the most direct way, but the route will lead him past Feneon's house. The unwisdom of this, the untimeliness, is perfectly evident to him, but makes no difference. He brakes as the house comes into view, freewheels past the shut front door, his heart like a stone in his throat. What did he expect? That Feneon would be sitting on the doorstep looking out for him? Or Hanako waiting with a message – 'Everything is understood, everything is excused. Please come back'?

He stops outside the fan shop, looks over his shoulder. Should he ride past again, keep riding up and down until at last someone comes out? At his side, in the shade of the shop's awning, a little girl is playing with a doll. She tells Yuji the doll's name, holds it out to him, the grubby wood of its limbs, the painted blue eyes. He nods to her and rides away.

That night he has another fire dream, unforeseen, unseasonable. In the dream he finds Dr Kushida cross-legged on a pile of corpses, his skin flaking from him like the skin of a grilled fish. Miss Feneon, says the doctor, has a message for him. She is out there somewhere (he waves a ruined hand). Yuji must search for her before it is too late. 'Look at your watch,' says the doctor, then sighs and settles back on the corpses as the flames creep over him like red and blue vermin.

Yuji wakes. He gropes his way off the mattress, reaches up for the light. His watch is lying as a bookmark inside *Tears of a Hero*. He takes it out and squints at it. Ten to four! Ten minutes to find the boy. Ten minutes before the fire falls. Ten minutes to be ready.

And what message could she possibly have that should delay him?

PART TWO

The Drunken Boat

鳥

I drifted on a river I could not control,
No longer guided by the bargeman's ropes.

Arthur Rimbaud

1

Ishihara's house is in the southern suburb of Azabu. It is not easy to reach and for the last part of his journey Yuji has been forced to the expense of a taxi, the young driver taking several wrong turns before arriving on a tree-lined street, a place half rustic, half genteel, with nothing to disturb the singing of birds and insects except a small party of children playing soberly in the care of a servant.

Outside the gate, in the partial shade of a tree, is a large, brilliantly polished car, an Armstrong Siddeley (the new six-cylinder Merton model) with tan leather seats, walnut dashboard, headlights under peaks of chromed steel. Yuji tidies his hair in the glass of the car's rear window, then tries the garden gate. It's locked. He looks for a bell but finds instead a cabinet at the side of the gate with the end of a speaking tube inside. How does one begin with a speaking tube? He utters his name into the mouth-piece, listens to the hissing of air, closes the cabinet and waits. After several minutes a bolt is drawn and a man two or three years Yuji's senior stands in the gateway, the expression on his face suggesting he has been needlessly disturbed from important work. He is dressed in a finely cut lightweight suit. His hair is cropped like a soldier's and there's a small scar by his right eye but he's as pretty as an *onnagata*. In reply to Yuji's bow he says he is Ota, Ishihara's personal secretary, then, saying nothing more, he shuts the gate and leads Yuji around the side of the house – a two-storey building in a style not quite indigenous, not quite not – to the garden at the back. Here, the land slopes gently down to a pavilion in the shade of a purple-flowering sandalwood tree. All the pavilion's screens are open, and on the far verandah a man, stripped to the waist, is vigorously wiping his chest with a cloth. On the wood by his feet is a set of barbells.

'*Sensei!*' calls Ota. 'The journalist is here.'

'Who? Oh, he's not really a journalist,' says Ishihara, crossing the mats towards them and smiling at Yuji. 'I'm not sure I would have invited a mere journalist to join us today. Mr Takano is more of a . . . literary gentleman.' He laughs, still rubbing himself with the cloth. 'Won't you come inside?' To Ota he gives orders for tea to be brought out. 'I only drink Ceylon tea,' he says to Yuji, 'and in the English way, with lemon and a little sugar. I hope that suits you? I find it helps my concentration.'

Yuji takes off his shoes and steps into the pavilion. Ishihara picks up a silk shirt the colour of persimmon leaves, puts it on and begins, with slender fingers, to button it. He apologises for not being ready to receive a guest. Yuji apologises for disturbing him.

'You'll be staying for lunch, of course?' asks Ishihara.

'Lunch?'

'Just a few of us – Major Yamazaki from the War Ministry; Dick Amazawa, a director with the Shochiku film company; Ota; and you. And you needn't worry. I haven't invited our mutual friend, though he speaks rather highly of you. He was quite excited at the thought of your writing a really in-depth piece, quite persuasive.' His shirt is buttoned now. He lights a cigarette, exhales slowly. 'So, how shall we begin?'

'However you prefer,' says Yuji, who, as he crossed the city, had nothing more precise in mind than that he would scribble frantically into the pad he has in his pocket while Ishihara made some sort of speech about himself.

There is a playful grin on Ishihara's face. 'You're a writer,' he says. 'I'm sure you can read a man's character in the objects he surrounds himself with. This is where I work. It's what the Americans would call a "den". Feel free to explore. I shan't disturb you.' He turns and goes again to the far verandah with its view across the ample roofs of neighbouring houses, the heads of trees luminous in their fresh May foliage. For a few seconds Yuji stands regarding the other's back and wondering what exactly he is being tested on. His skill as a writer (if that is what he is)? Or something else, something less obvious?

He starts to look. The pavilion – the *den* – seems more a place for relaxation, for pleasure, than for the hard, anxious business of writing. At one end, there is a desk of glass and tubular steel, a chair of steel and leather, but the typewriter on the desk seems as ornamental as the vase of white lilacs beside it. There is not, in fact, any paper to be seen.

At the other end of the room, under a raised and tied mosquito net, is a divan upholstered in peach silk, and on the mats beside it a scattering of magazines – *Vogue*, *Jardin des Modes*.

Bookshelves (coloured glass) hold mainly copies of Ishihara's own works, though with some unexpected additions: volumes of history and economics, like Shigeo Iwanami's *Lectures on the*

Historical Development of Japanese Capitalism, the same edition Father keeps in the garden study. On the wall between the shelves is a large photograph of Ishihara with an older man, the pair of them muffled in winter coats and standing in front of a monument Yuji has seen before but cannot quite identify.

'The Brandenburg Gate,' says Ishihara, who has stepped quietly in from the verandah, 'Berlin. That's Kyushi Hiraizumi. It was my thirty-fifth birthday. I am, as you should know, almost exactly as old as the century.'

'So you've been to Europe?'

'Berlin, Paris, London, Vienna . . . even to the Eternal City.'

'The Eternal . . . ?'

'It is what they call Rome. Do you think you would like to see Rome?'

'Yes.'

'Perhaps you will.'

'I've hardly travelled at all.'

'You are still young.'

'But the way things are going, the international situation . . .'

'The way things are going will give many excellent opportunities to adventurous young men. You needn't worry about that. But is this what you want to talk about? The international situation? I suppose the author of *Electric Dragonfly* cannot have a very high opinion of my little efforts with the pen.'

'Not at all,' says Yuji, 'I was only . . .'

'"In the dream of a city poet, electric dragonflies over Shinobazu Pond. The lilies open like distant gunfire." Have I got it right? I hate to misquote.'

'Yes,' says Yuji, blushing and looking down at Ishihara's naked toes. 'It's correct.'

'The problem,' says Ishihara '– and you don't object, I hope, to our speaking freely? – is that people now prefer stronger flavours. Or to put it another way, it is the tastes and appetites of the popular classes that dominate our society, as they dominate societies all over the world. Your poetry, Takano, belongs to a more elegant age, the time, perhaps, of our grandfathers or great-grandfathers. It is over. It will not return.'

'So poetry is finished?'

'Have you ever stood outside a factory and seen the workers streaming out of the gates the moment the steam-whistle sounds? I recommend it if you want a view of the future. A featureless crowd, semi-educated, longing for some distraction from the harsh reality of their lives. By their mid-thirties they're exhausted. Do you think they read much poetry? Indeed, do you think they read at all?'

'Then what hope is there for your own . . . work?'

'None whatsoever.'

'So . . . ?'

'What shall we do?' He lights another cigarette, flicks, with a frown, a speck of ash that has settled on the cuff of his shirt. 'What else but side with history? With the future. I wonder if you know what that means.'

'Siding with the crowd?'

'I've heard,' says Ishihara, 'that you care for cinema.'

'Yes.'

'And your favourite film?'

'*La Grande Illusion.*'

'Shall I tell you mine? Ah, but here is our tea.'

Ota places the tray on the verandah, pours from a silver teapot, throws Yuji a glance of rich hostility, nods to his employer, and withdraws.

Ishihara hands Yuji a cup. 'Don't worry about Ota,' he says. 'He is somewhat possessive, that's all. Now, take a sip and tell me what you think.'

'It's very good,' says Yuji.

'Just the right degree of stimulation?'

'Yes,' says Yuji. 'But I think you were about to tell me the name of your favourite film?'

'It does not have a name. I saw it privately at General Sugiyama's house. It was filmed by one of the general's aides and lasts no more than a few minutes. It shows a battlefield in Shangtung Province. Hundreds, perhaps thousands of dead soldiers, ours, theirs, lying where they had fallen a few hours earlier. The beauty of it is . . . beyond my poor powers of description. Their gestures, their stillness, their wounds, their youth. I was filled with an emotion that goes far beyond patriotism or pity, or even terror. A voluptuous sensation, an ardour that no poem or novel or song could have inspired in me. I stood. I leaned towards the images on the screen. I *longed* to be there!'

'And this is what the masses want to see?'

'Oh, probably they do. In a diluted form at first, and dressed up a little. But that is not quite the point I am making.'

'If you are arguing that cinema is the pre-eminent form, the form of the future, I suppose I must agree.'

'But would you agree that the future is not simply the depiction of such scenes – a depiction that must indeed be cinematic – but the scenes themselves?'

'War?'

'Yes, war. But more than that.'

'More?'

142

'It is the imaginative aspect, the aesthetic aspect, even, dare I say, the religious aspect.'

'A worshipping of war?'

'Not exactly war,' he laughs, 'but you are getting close. Do you think you'll remember all this? Perhaps you have a little notebook in your pocket you could use. You see, I am putting myself into your hands. I hope I have not made a mistake?'

Lunch is in the house, an upstairs room where double doors of decorative glass open onto a balcony overlooking the garden. The lunch guests are already seated by the time Yuji and Ishihara join them. The table is as formal, as cluttered, as the tables at the Snow Goose. There are vases of flowers, bouquets arranged in the Western style, and on the walls four or five large paintings, black-and-white abstracts, some kind of Japanese constructivism. Ota is pouring glasses of Monopole champagne. Major Yamazaki is sketching thrusts and dispositions on the starched linen of the tablecloth with the handle of his fork: 'Naturally I accept the need for a showdown with the Soviets, but the country needs fuel oil – the navy's using four hundred tons of the stuff every day – and *that* means pushing to the south.'

Yuji is given a seat beside Dick Amazawa who, paying no attention to the major's lecture, is leaning heavily on his elbows in a crumpled suit of yellow and white striped linen. There is a woman with him in a short gingham dress who chain-smokes throughout the meal, the food on her plate untouched. To Yuji, Amazawa confides that he has not slept in two weeks. His doctor gives him pills to help him stay awake. He has been awake so long he's afraid to sleep now. 'Aren't you some sort of writer?' he asks.

'Well,' says Yuji, 'I suppose.'

'You're going to work in the Unit?'

'The unit?'

'He hasn't told you about the Unit?'

'No.'

'But you want to work in cinema?'

'Yes, perhaps.'

'Who do you like?'

'Renoir, Ford. Ozu . . .'

'Hitchcock?'

'*The Man who Knew Too Much.*'

'*Murder!*'

'*The Lady Vanishes.*'

'Imagine a film that's just a woman screaming. The whole film. Just that.'

'It's difficult to imagine.'

'That's because you sleep too much. Have some of these. I've got more than I can use. More even than she can use.'

The woman blinks, a lizard on a stone. Amazawa takes a handful of brownish-pinkish tablets from his pocket, eats one, and drops the rest in the pocket of Yuji's jacket. From across the table Ishihara is smiling at Yuji as though they alone understand that the afternoon is a kind of game, an elegant charade, something to divert themselves with until the serious business of welcoming the future becomes possible.

The houseboy serves the coffee. The major, face to the ceiling, is snoring in his seat, a piece of tomato from the cuttlefish '*à la française*' dangling from a corner of his moustache. Yuji excuses himself and stands.

'Ota will drive you,' says Ishihara.

'Really, there is no need,' says Yuji.

'What is the point in keeping a car,' smiles Ishihara, 'or even a personal secretary, if one doesn't use them?'

Bowing, Yuji begins to thank him. Ishihara cuts him off with a movement of his hand. 'Until next time,' he says. 'Until our next little meeting.'

Outside, the sun is dancing off the curves of the big car. Ota holds open the rear door, every gesture of servility carefully deranged to express its opposite. They drive in silence, the car rocks expensively on its springs. As they pass the Yasukuni shrine, Yuji, who certainly does not wish to arrive outside his house in such a car, to be seen by Father (to be seen by someone), asks to be dropped. He has, he says, some business in the area. Would it be convenient . . . ? Ota says nothing. The car rolls to a halt. Yuji gets out. The instant he has closed the heavy door, the car moves off. Yuji watches it, waits until it is out of sight, then unbuttons his collar and begins to walk. He wonders where the nearest tram-stop is. He wonders, too, whether, when he comes to write the article, he should mention the fact that all the men at the lunch had in their lapels the same ruby-headed pin he saw Makiyama wearing in the Don Juan.

2

Wisteria, azaleas, peonies. The first mosquitoes, the first bites . . .

On 10 May the radio announces that all stores will henceforth be prohibited from carrying non-essential merchandise. Zen monks, in recognition of the rice shortages, vow to live on nothing but fruit and vegetables. Citizens are ordered to sell their gold to the government. Soon there are stories of people hiding their gold watches and buying chrome ones to wear instead.

In China, the army suffers heavy casualties in its advance on the Nationalist capital at Chunking. The brush-maker puts up his shutters. His son is among the missing. In Europe, German tanks sweep into France. After four days the battle already looks lost, soldiers and civilians fleeing along clogged roads. (And what is Feneon doing? What is he thinking? Does this disaster not justify a visit? Does it not *require* it?)

The nineteenth is Yuji's birthday. He goes with Taro and Junzo to the Ginza. They visit the Black Pearl, but not the Don Juan, the billiard parlour, but not, of course, the Snow Goose. By midnight the question is what to do with Junzo. Yuji has never seen him like this, not even on his twenty-first, when he was babbling about 'spineless intellectuals' until he tripped down the steps to the toilet and had to be carried home by his brother. When he hears about Yuji's lunch with Ishihara, he immediately wants to take a taxi to the Azabu Hills. 'At least we can break a few windows, eh? At least we can do that.'

He pulls at Taro's arm. Taro shakes him off. 'What,' says Taro, 'do you suppose would happen if we were caught? You would be thrown out of Imperial, I would be finished at the ministry, and Yuji would lose any hope of finding a respectable job.'

'Perfect!' cries Junzo. 'Don't you see that's the best that could happen to us?'

A group their own age come into the hall, and though out of uniform it's obvious – the shaved skulls, the sediment of fatigue in their faces – they're all off-duty soldiers. Junzo leaps to attention, salutes them. They come over. Taro tries to calm things down while Yuji hustles Junzo through the back door into the yard. The door swings shut. Side by side they urinate against the bins, blue neon above, then stars.

'Let me congratulate you,' says Junzo.

'On becoming an old man?'

'I just hope you're not going to be an idiot.'

'Idiot? What about you? Those soldiers would have—'

'Just don't be an idiot,' says Junzo. 'And please take care of yourself. Please take care of—'

'Are you getting sentimental?'

'You're right,' says Junzo, buttoning his trousers. 'I should probably despise you, but somehow I can't. So instead, let me congratulate you. *Toutes mes félicitations! Au vainqueur, le gloire!*'

'*La gloire.*'

'*La gloire . . .*'

Taro comes out. 'Their friends have arrived. Now they want to show us how things are done across the water. Let's go.'

The door out of the yard is locked. They clamber over the wall, drop into the alley behind, then run past the shack-like backs of restaurants, past dog-fences and silent birdcages hanging from the eaves of unlit houses. They come to a railway line. Before they can cross it a bell starts clanking. They crouch, wait. The train lays down a bitter scent of coal, but when they run into the streets the other side, the air is fragrant with night flowers blooming on countless rooftop gardens. Are the soldiers after them still? There are no cries of pursuit, no hurrying feet. They hear water and walk onto a bridge over a canal. Below them, tethered boats shift in the current. They lean on the parapet. Taro lights a cigarette. Junzo seems to have sobered up, though Yuji doubts he was ever quite as drunk as he pretended to be (and what did he mean, '*au vainqueur?*' Did he know what he was saying?). They start to laugh about the soldiers, go on laughing even when the joke's exhausted. None of it matters now. They have had an adventure. They are unscathed. It is like old times. And suddenly it feels immensely pleasurable to be standing together on the warm stones of a bridge in the heart of the Low City, this Year of the Dragon, immensely pleasurable, immensely precious. Then Taro blows out a last lungful of smoke, flicks away his cigarette. The ember arcs over the water, an early firefly.

Then gone.

3

It is only because the front door is open that he manages it at all. If he had to ring the bell and stand there waiting, he would, he is sure, simply run away before the door was answered. He approaches slowly, creeping up behind the steadily falling rain. Hanako is in the hall wiping the tiles with a cloth. When she sees Yuji, she looks up, startled, then nods and gestures with the cloth towards the salon. Yuji shakes his umbrella, folds it, takes off his rubber boots, his raincoat.

In the salon, Feneon is alone. He is sitting on the piano stool in his shirtsleeves, his braces hanging down from the waistband buttons of his trousers. There is two or three days' growth of stubble on his face. His feet, by the piano's brass pedals, are bare.

'I can't play it,' he says. 'None of her talent could have come from me.' He sounds a note with the edge of finger, smiles, then turns and squints at Yuji as if they were much further away from each other than they are. 'I thought you two would have come together. I hope you haven't fallen out.'

'Fallen out?'

'Had a row.'

'Row?'

'A dispute.'

'But with whom?'

'With Junzo. He left ten minutes ago.'

'Junzo was here?'

'He plays the clown but underneath he takes it all terribly seriously, don't you think? You're a much more carefree fellow. It's all that German philosophy he studies. I can think of nothing more detrimental to a young man's health. Philosophy was invented by the Greeks as a guide to good living. Then the Germans got hold of it and made it joyless. Better off spending his time in a bordello. Women there can teach you a great deal. Live with their eyes open, not just their legs.' He chuckles to himself, shakes his head. 'Fancy a drink? Or don't you, in the morning?'

The urge to flee, to splutter some excuse and get out, is very strong. He has never seen Feneon like this before. He is drunk, of course, or almost drunk, but that would be tolerable – it might even be exciting – if the disarrangement of mind that made the first drink necessary was not so disturbingly plain. He clears his throat. He has a little speech prepared but when he starts (listening all the while for the opening or shutting of a door, the approach of footsteps), he finds himself quite unable to manage the language with his usual assurance.

'I am . . . I wish, monsieur . . . I wish to say how profoundly . . . how the unfortunate events . . . the suffering, naturally. And all those who revere a great culture, and I, who have been inspired. And you, monsieur, who, with great consideration, most generously, with the Japanese people—'

'My dear little Frenchman!' says Feneon, standing and clapping

Yuji's shoulders. 'My dear, dear little Frenchman. You're going to drink wine with me! Here, I'm going to start you off at the deep end. This is a Saint Emilion, and a pretty good one. Take your time with it. Give it a good sniff. Now, roll it over your tongue. Slowly, slowly . . . It's the last case. There won't be any more until the Boche go home, though what they can't drink they'll try to carry with them. There must be cellars the length and breadth of the Reich full of good French wine from the last time they visited.'

'France has not yet surrendered, monsieur.'

'You've seen the pictures in the paper. Storm troopers on the Champs-Élysées! Another week, two at most . . .'

He sits at the piano again and stares at the keys as though their surface is a riddle staring might solve. 'I've been dreaming,' he says, 'one I haven't had in years. A memory as much as a dream. Woods near Noirceur. A place we advanced and retreated through a dozen times in the summer of 1917. I was on my own one evening bringing up a sack of loaves for the company. Somehow, I lost the path and wandered into a small clearing where a soldier was sitting with his back against the trunk of a tree. He must have been there for months. There was no flesh on him. His uniform was so black with rot you couldn't even say which army he was from. What made me stop and take a closer look was his boot, just the one, standing in the grass beside him like a tombstone. My first thought was that he must have been taking off his boots when he was hit, that he had been marching all day dreaming of the moment he would sit down and let the air at his feet. It even seemed slightly amusing, the idea of him planning his little rest and suddenly starting a much longer one. Then I saw his rifle in the grass, the muzzle pointing towards him, and I realised the reason he had taken off his boot was so he could press the trigger with his toe.'

'And you dream of him?'

'He talks to me. Whispers things I would rather not hear.'

'I have dreams about fire,' says Yuji.

Feneon nods. 'You'll have more of those before this is over.'

In the garden, the leaves of the magnolia are trembling in the rain, the last of the white petals scattered in the grass. Is this the moment to take his leave? He has been fortunate, but how long before they are interrupted? He swallows a last large mouthful of wine (such a heavy, soporific drink) and is looking for somewhere to put the glass when Feneon begins to speak again.

'I try to imagine,' he says, 'how it is for her. She's never even been to France. It's just a story, a few pictures. What can it mean to her, a country she's never seen?' He shakes his head. 'I should have taken her, even only for a month or two. It would have helped her, I think. But somehow . . .' Once more he sounds a single note, waits as it melts into the air. 'I'm afraid if you were hoping to see her, you're out of luck. She went out a few minutes before Junzo arrived.'

'She could not have known.'

'What?'

'That I was coming here.'

'You might have a daughter yourself one day.'

'Me?'

'Or a son.'

'A son!'

'Well, why not? Didn't you tell me you almost got married once?'

'Yes. Once.'

'Life is full of the unexpected, Yuji. Anyone who thinks they know what's going to happen is a bloody fool. What's that saying you have? "When men talk of the future, devils laugh."'

152

Yuji nods. 'It is one of Grandfather's favourite sayings.'

'The great pickle-maker? I'd like to meet him one day. I always think you're more impressed by him than by your father.'

'Perhaps Father is not so impressed by me.'

'No? I never liked mine much either. Left France to get away. Tried to do a better job with Alissa, better than he did with me. It appears I might not have been as successful as I thought. The truth about being a parent is that it's completely impossible. Did you know that? When they're small they worship you. Later, secretly or openly, they judge you. The best you can hope for is that you live long enough for them to forgive you.'

'May I ask, monsieur, if you forgave your father?'

'To forgive someone, you need to stand in front of them. You need to look them in the eyes. You can't do it by post. When my old man died, I had not seen him for thirteen years.'

'He was Rimbaud's friend.'

'They weren't friends, not really. Neither had any gift for friendship.'

'Verlaine?'

'Rimbaud shot Verlaine.'

'Only a small wound.'

'Is that your definition of friendship? Fine to shoot them so long as you don't actually kill them? I shall have to warn the others.' He rubs his hands across his face, rasps the stubble. Beneath his breath he starts to sing. ' "*Quand Madelon vient nous servir à boire*" . . . I think,' he says. 'I shall go to bed with the rest of the Saint-Emilion. You don't mind, I hope?'

'No,' says Yuji. 'No, of course.' Then, speaking carefully as though stood before the examiner, he expresses again his regret over the fate of France.

'I don't hold you personally responsible,' says Feneon.

'Thank you,' says Yuji. He bows, steps back, turns, and retreats to the hall. Hanako has gone out, the door is shut. He pulls on his boots, takes his umbrella, opens the door. From the step, as he buttons his coat, he sees that someone is sheltering behind the pillar of the verandah across the street. The brim of a hat, the hem of a raincoat, the heel of a shoe. For a moment he can go neither forwards nor back. Then he puts up his umbrella and hurries to his bicycle, his boots splashing in the yellow mud of the road.

4

H e is sitting on the drying platform, his back to that part of the wooden wall that divides the platform from Father's room. The writing board is on his lap, and on the board a page of writing, the last of the Ishihara piece. He has found an entirely unexpected pleasure in the work, just as he found something disquietingly sympathetic about Ishihara himself. Even the novels, with their utter indifference to the genius of the language, their interminable dark combats between unblemished youth and corrupt old age, the page after page of impossible odds, flashing swords, terse farewells, the boy heroes with skin 'pale as a maiden's' or 'shining with the vitality of his seventeen years', have had unexpected virtues, have even, on occasion, *spoken* to him, to some inner and unattended condition of his heart, his spirit.

Is he not, then, quite what he thought he was? Not the observer standing at a distance, arms folded, a supercilious smile on his face, but nearer to one of those Ishihara spoke of as the future, pouring from the factory gates as the steam whistle shrieks? Can he imagine himself among them, brow grimy with sweat, eyes narrowed against the evening sun, not an individual any more but part of the animated destiny of the nation? 'A hundred million hearts beating as one!' 'Onward, Asian brothers, onward!' 'Work, work, for the sake of the country!' To say such slogans sincerely, to shout them out when everyone was shouting them out so that you cannot tell your own voice from your neighbour's, might that not be a little like falling in love?

He is crafting a sentence about Ishihara's manner of speech, its passionate sincerity (he wants, but cannot quite bring himself to write 'apparent') when Miyo puts her head out of the door and tells him he has a visitor.

'Someone to see me?'

She makes a face as if to say. 'Isn't that what a visitor is?', then slips away. He brings the board inside, buttons his shirt. He has not heard anyone arrive, no car pull up, no call from the vestibule. Who visits him in the middle of a Tuesday morning? An angry woman? A father demanding explanations? Or someone from the military clerk's office, a red envelope in his hand?

He goes downstairs. The doors of Mother's room are open. There are voices inside, the sighing sing-song of middle-aged women. Cautiously, he peers inside. 'Mother . . . ?'

The room is lighter than usual, morning sunlight filtering through the paper screens where the sharply etched shadows of leaves move almost imperceptibly.

'Here he is,' says Mother. 'Please sit with us, Yuji. Mrs Miyazaki is paying us a visit.'

He looks at the other woman, recognises her, though only just, for in all the time he has known Taro, the seven years since they first sat beside each other in Professor Komada's class, he has seen her no more than three or four times. A woman – today in a

156

pigeon-coloured kimono – in awe of her children, her children's confident friends. One of the old-style wives, content to kneel at the kitchen door waiting to be told when to bring the sake in. A life lived at the edge of the visible. Yet here she is, sitting on a cushion at the house of Professor Takano and his well-born wife, her hands in her lap, the little movements of her fingers suggesting an embarrassment that moment by moment threatens to crush her.

Yuji kneels beside Mother.

'Mrs Miyazaki was just telling me about her son,' she says. 'It appears that he has volunteered for the army.'

'Taro?'

'Junzo,' says Mrs Miyazaki. 'Junzo has gone.'

He gapes at her. 'Junzo?'

'He left the house four days ago. I have not seen him since.'

'*Junzo?* But he has exemption. He has his student deferment . . .'

'Mrs Miyazaki,' says Mother, 'was wondering if he had said anything to you.'

'About *this*? No. Nothing.'

Discreetly, Mrs Miyazaki begins to weep. Haruyo brings in the tea.

'He has not been himself for several weeks,' says Mrs Miyazaki, dabbing her powdery cheeks with a tissue. 'His elder brother thinks he might have made an attachment. One that has caused him some unhappiness. Please forgive my rudeness, but you are quite sure there is nothing you can tell me? You are his friend. He would not have done this without a reason, would he?'

For the first time, Yuji sees something of Junzo in her, something sharp and unexpectedly wilful in her gaze. He turns from her, exchanges a glance with Mother, then looks at Ryuichi, the candlelight playing palely over his face. He cannot take it in.

Junzo in the army? Junzo at boot camp? Junzo at the Front with the likes of Captain Mori and Corporal Kitamura? And what is this nonsense she wants him to tell her about? A mystery girlfriend he has never met?

They sit there in silence, their faces composed as though waiting, with some impatience, for a messenger to arrive. After a minute Yuji makes a sound in his throat, a grunt of irritation. (What is this pigeon-coloured woman doing here, tearing his day in two?) He tells her that he is, regrettably, unable to answer her question. Is it possible there has been a misunderstanding? That Junzo only *spoke* of volunteering without ever intending his words to be taken seriously? He will, however, attempt to investigate. He will try to discover the information he should already possess but somehow does not. He apologises, climbs to his feet.

'There,' says Mother, her voice like the careful folding of silk. 'I was sure Yuji would be able to help you.'

'Indeed,' says Mrs Miyazaki. 'He has been most kind.' And she begins again to weep, more loudly this time, crying up tears from her belly as though her second-born, her baby, her brilliant Junzo, was already lost to her. It is unlikely, thinks Yuji, as he slides the doors shut behind him, that such a disturbing sound will be permitted to remain much longer.

5

It takes three days to find Taro. When he has tried all the usual places he goes down to Tokyo Central, to a drinking house in the precincts of the station, a fifteen-seater that specialises in broiled eels and a clear soup of eel livers, and where he knows that some of the junior men from the government offices like to stop for an hour between work and the train ride to the suburbs. Taro is at a table in the corner with four others, all in shirtsleeves. The cook, fanning the charcoal, where a row of skewered eels is sizzling, sees Yuji and barks a welcome. Taro glances up. Yuji raises a hand. He hopes that Taro will leave the table and join him but Taro stays where he is. Yuji takes the seat opposite him. He is introduced. Everyone is perfectly civil but the mood is cool. *They* are from the ministry, servants of the minister, agents, in their humble way, of the Imperial will. He – whoever he is, whatever it is he does – is an outsider. Soon they politely ignore him. When one of them mentions a certain Mr Honda and the others immediately guffaw, no one troubles to explain why Mr Honda is so amusing. Yuji studies the tabletop. After twenty minutes two of the men, draping jackets over their arms, picking up their umbrellas and briefcases, leave for their train. A few minutes later the others go.

'You want to stay here?' asks Taro.

'Are you expecting more of your colleagues?'

'It's possible.'

'Mr Honda, perhaps?'

They move to a coffee shop in a side street near the station. There's a mural of a Roman temple along one of its walls, and on top of a glass cabinet of *kasutera* sponge cakes, there's a hand-tinted photograph of Mussolini greeting Hitler or Hitler greeting Mussolini.

They sit, order from a girl in a beret. Taro puts a pack of cigarettes and a lighter on the table in front of him. 'I suppose Mother has been to your place,' he says.

'Yes.'

'I hope she was not an inconvenience.'

'She told me about Junzo.'

'Of course.'

'So it's true?'

'Of course.'

'He volunteered?'

'Yes.'

'And his student deferment?'

'He *volunteered*.'

'He's Class D!'

'When someone volunteers,' says Taro, flatly, as though reading from a sheet of paper, some government prescript, 'it's supposed to be an occasion for rejoicing.'

'This is Junzo!'

'Why not Junzo? He has put the nation's needs before his own. In doing so, he has brought great honour on the family. Once

Mother has stopped looking for foolish explanations she will prepare his thousand-stitch belt, and when the moment comes we will go to the station to bid him farewell.' He stirs his coffee, lights a cigarette. He looks gaunt, exhausted. 'The country is at war,' he says.

'You believe Junzo could ever make a soldier?'

'In a soldier, spirit counts for more than stature.'

'So you won't try to stop him?'

'How can I?' He volunteered.'

'Isn't there someone you could speak to? Someone at the ministry?'

'I work in the education department, not the War Ministry.'

'Where is he now?'

'He has a room.'

'A room?'

'In Kagurazaka.'

'You've seen him?'

'I have respected his wishes.'

'And his wish is not to see you?'

'He is preparing himself.'

'Preparing?'

'Hardening himself. Visits from an elder brother will not help him.'

'You sound like a character in an Ishihara novel.'

'Far from criticising us,' says Taro, 'you might want to study his example. You might even want to imitate it.'

'Eh?'

'Wouldn't volunteering solve your allowance problem?'

'They would never take me.'

'They took Junzo.'

'Even so . . .'

'They don't throw any back these days.'

'My chest . . .'

'Your chest would benefit greatly from the exercise. That doctor of yours, what's his name?'

'Kushida.'

'He could write a new letter explaining that in his opinion you are now fit for active service.'

'So what's stopping *you* from going? You seem so eager for us all to be in uniform . . .'

'For now I have my work at the ministry. But as a reservist, I can, as you know, be called at any time. When the call comes, I will welcome it.' He stubs out his cigarette on a picture of Mount Vesuvius in the ashtray. 'It will be a great relief to me.'

They look past each other. On the gramophone there is a song in Italian, some swaying, lachrymose love song that the girl in the beret, drying cups, is silently mouthing the words to.

'I saw Feneon,' says Yuji.

'I suppose they will try to move now.'

'Where could they go?'

'Anywhere.'

'Anywhere? How unconcerned you sound.'

'Was Alissa there?'

'No.'

'I am not unconcerned.'

'Junzo was there before me.'

'He told me.'

'I wondered if Feneon might have said something to him.'

'Suggest he join the army? It's hardly likely, is it?' He glances at his watch, counts coins onto the table, pockets his cigarettes and lighter. As they cross the road, a few drops of rain begin to fall, each fat drop hitting the pavement with a noise like something snapping.

'Taking the train?' asks Taro.

Yuji shakes his head. 'I think I'll go to Asakusa. See a film.'

'Japanese or foreign?'

'I'll decide when I get there.'

'I couldn't have stopped him,' says Taro. 'You know how he is.'

'Yes.'

'Perhaps he's seen things more clearly than us.'

'And this "attachment"?'

'All of that sort of thing . . .' Taro shrugs.

'I know,' says Yuji. 'He's volunteered.'

'Yes.'

'The country's at war.'

'Yes. He will be angry with me, but if you want to see him so much . . .' He takes out a pen and writes an address on the back of a business card. 'Tell him that his family are thinking of him.'

'I will.'

'And don't take too seriously what I said about you doing the same. I don't want two of you to worry about.'

'I would not wish to burden you,' says Yuji. They grin at each other, shyly. 'Will we meet again soon?'

'Of course.'

'*Au revoir*, then.'

'Yes. *Au revoir*.'

They walk away from each other, but after twenty strides Yuji stops. Why not persuade Taro to come with him to the cinema? A good film, a bowl of noodles, some beer . . . They can still do that much, can't they? He turns and sees his friend crossing the concourse, his broad back, his big shoulders already starting to be rounded by desk work, but before he can follow or call out to him, the crowd opens one of its many doors, and Taro, without a pause, without a moment's hesitation, steps inside and is lost to sight.

6

He cannot, as he has intended, go straight to Kagura-zaka the next morning. Haruyo catches him as he crouches by the vestibule step tying the laces of his shoes, and tells him that Mother's medication needs collecting from the clinic. He cycles there. Kushida is out on a call but a nurse who recognises Yuji, takes him up to the dispensary on the first floor. 'Mrs Takano,' she mutters, 'Mrs Takano . . .' then lifts down a pair of grey canisters from the shelf and passes them to Yuji. She cocks her head. 'Anything for yourself?'

She is one of those ominously flirtatious older women who have an appetite for men ten or fifteen years their junior. She reminds him of Mother's friend, Mrs Sasaki, and of those farcical scenes at her house in Sendagi as she made him try on all the dead husband's jackets, adjusting the collars for him, smoothing the shoulders, the heavy perfume from the sleeves of her kimono making it difficult to breathe.

'This must be worth something,' says Yuji, nodding to the

well-stocked shelves, the bottles and boxes, many with their labels printed in German or English.

'Shall we go into business together?' asks the nurse, pulling the steel door shut behind them and double-locking it with a key from the bunch she carries in the pocket of her apron.

On the corridor, even in the middle of the morning, the overhead lights are burning as though shadow was a kind of pollution, something that might get into a wound. They pass Kushida's office. The door is open. 'Sensei?' coos the nurse, tapping softly on the wood, but there is no reply. On the desk under the window, a large bell jar is striped with the sunlight that falls through the slats of the venetian blind. Inside the jar, hanging in a colourless fluid, is an object about the size of one of the carp in Kyoko's pond. Yuji has a glimpse of an eye, immaculately shut, the splayed fingers of a miniature hand, a loosely flexed knee. 'Everyone,' says the nurse, ushering Yuji to the top of the stairs, 'must have a pastime, no?'

He leaves the canisters outside Mother's door, leaves his bicycle in the front garden, and walks to the tram-stop to catch a number 7 to Iidabashi. From there he crosses the main road, and keeping to the shadow side, the narrow strip of cool at the pavement's inner edge, enters Kagurazaka, a High City district, one of the old pleasure quarters, but now long since left behind by the steady westward flow of money and fashion.

Distracted by the shimmering blue line between sun and shade, he walks straight past the turning Taro spoke of and has to double-back until he finds it, an alley lined with boarding houses, Meiji or early Taisho firetraps, the way between them so narrow the little front gardens, growing wild in so much rain, have reached across to each other, tendril twisting round the tip of tendril.

Ahead of him, two arrow-headed dogs are sleeping in the dust but there is, at first, no sign of the residents, the inhabitants of these shuttered, blank, blind old buildings. Only when he enters the alley does he begin to see them, soft human forms squatting or lying wherever the shade is deepest. Do they watch him as he passes? He cannot tell, but halfway down the alley he becomes aware of light feet following him and he turns to find a girl of eight or ten, a sleeping infant on her back, some little brother or sister tied to her with a length of patterned cloth, the weight of it making her stoop like an old woman carrying firewood. She asks if he is lost. He tells her he is looking for his friend. 'That's good,' she says, she knows everyone in the alley, she even knows the names of all the cats and dogs. He gives her Junzo's name. 'He's not here,' she says, because she has never heard of him, but when Yuji describes him she nods. 'He doesn't have a name yet,' she says, 'He hasn't been here long enough.' She takes his hand and guides him to a house a degree more decrepit, more hopeless than the others. It is the house of an uncle of hers, she says, a sort of uncle. Inside, Yuji cannot see at all. He shuffles behind her, following the pull of her bony hand, the curdled-milk smell of the infant. They climb a tightly turning staircase. Now and then some partly open shutter or torn screen suddenly reveals the elaborate makeshift of the house's inner structure, and as they ascend, their heads press against a damp and thickening heat as if they are climbing into the base of a storm cloud.

At the top of the house, the girl sings out a greeting and slides open the tattered door. It is the attic room (what does one *pay* for such a room?), a space that can never have been intended for human habitation, its ceiling nothing but the steeply raked beams and tiles of the roof. Light comes from a hole you would have to lie on your belly to look through. There is a smell of birds, bird droppings, sour human sweat.

'He must have gone out,' says the girl. And then, as though the house, the whole alley, was truly another country, she adds, 'You have made a journey for nothing.'

On the wooden boards is an old but neatly rolled mattress, and next to it a shoulder bag and four or five books – *The Science of Logic Vol. IV*, a book of campcraft for boys, a Sino-Japanese dictionary. There is also a small picture frame, face down. On the girl's back, the infant whimpers in its sleep. The girl whispers to it, a language all their own, then asks Yuji if he wants some tea. Cold barley? Salty cherry blossom? If he wants some, she will run and fetch it. He shakes his head. He cannot possibly wait here. Alone in this room it would steal into him; he would breathe it in like bad luck. He brushes a mosquito from his cheek. He would like to leave something, some evidence of his having been there, and he rummages in his pockets but can find nothing more personal, more suitable, than the propelling pencil he carries for making notes (those insights and observations that have no purpose to them any more). He stretches into the room, places the pencil on top of the books, then follows the girl down, each of them brushing the stairwell wall with their fingers. In the alley, he gives her a coin. She puts it in a fold of the sash round her waist. 'He has to be fed now,' she says. 'Don't you think he's like a big insect?'

Next morning, reluctant to be there again, in that heat, that stink, he finds excuses to put off his return. He has the Ishihara piece to revise, and now that he knows where Junzo is staying, has been to the alley, the room, what urgency is there? If Junzo wants a taste of squalor, if he is 'hardening' himself, then that is up to Junzo. It is not *his* responsibility to drag him home. Taro will take care of it, or Mr Miyazaki, or even Mrs Miyazaki, who, in her own way, is evidently not without resources. He stays busy, lets the day pass, but on the second day, stricken with shame, he makes up a parcel – a tin of Mosquiton, a wooden-handled French-made clasp-knife, his much-prized, much-scribbled-into copy of Rimbaud's early poems (including 'The Open Road' – 'A week of walking has torn my boots to shreds'), and on the third morning he sets out again for the alley. He looks for the girl, then, not finding her, finds the house and goes up on his own. The attic door is open, the rolled mattress is there, but the books, the bag, the picture frame have gone. He comes back down. As he opens the screen to the verandah a man in a crumpled *yukata*, a lacework of pale scars around his eyes, shuffles from the shadows and bids Yuji good morning.

'Good morning,' says Yuji.

'You were looking for someone?' asks the man, not recognising Yuji's voice.

'The one who was in the attic,' says Yuji.

The man grunts, straightens his back, puts his stick across his shoulder. He swings an arm, marches on the spot in sandals soled with pieces of motorcycle tyre. 'I was an army man myself,' he calls, as Yuji, the parcel under his arm, walks away between the light and darker blues of morning glory. 'How do you think I lost these, eh?' – a finger jabbing towards his eyes, the broken stare – 'Sitting at home minding my own business?'

7

On the dance floor of the Don Juan – a floor at this mid-afternoon hour otherwise deserted – Dick Amazawa's mistress, Fumi Kihara, is dancing alone to the music of a gramophone. At the edge of the floor, in the same yellow-striped jacket he was wearing in the Azabu Hills, Amazawa is conducting the music with a matchstick the length and thickness of his arm. The match is a prop from a short film he has just completed, a Home Ministry commission in which – so he has just explained to Yuji – Fumi plays a bored young woman about to light a cigarette when a silver-haired gentleman in civil defence uniform leans through the window to ask, 'Do you need that more than he does?' At this, the camera spins to a trench – in fact, the corner lot of a studio in the suburbs – where a handsome sapper under heavy fire is searching frantically for a match to light the fuse of his bomb.

'It's simple,' says Amazawa, now holding the match like a *kendo* sword and softly tapping the top of Yuji's head, 'but simple takes some thinking about.'

Stretched the length of the bench opposite, Hideo Makiyama is reading Yuji's article. Now and then he clucks, pulls out a pen from the breast pocket of his shirt, and puts a line through a word or sometimes, imperiously – the movement setting Yuji's teeth on edge – through an entire sentence. The white light of the Ginza stabs the bar's permanent midnight each time a customer pushes through the swing doors. Waitresses from the early shift are coming down the stairs, while those for the late shift go up with their bags and parasols to the dressing room on the first floor. Yuji watches for the girl who poured for him at the House of Falling Leaves but does not see her. Nor does he see her friend, the girl with the ribbons he left waiting for him in the corridor.

'Too academic,' drawls Makiyama, sitting up and shuffling the sheets of paper together. 'Too much showing off. But other than that, not bad . . . not bad at all.'

'You think it will be suitable?'

'With some tidying up.'

'You'll be able to place it, then? In *Young Japan*?'

'I said so, didn't I? They're running a special on the key men of the new era, generals, politicians, sportsmen, writers. Ishihara will have three or four pages to himself. Lots of pictures, too, of course. Author at home, author at the Front, author contemplating the evening sky.'

'So it will come out?'

'In two weeks.'

'So soon?'

'They've been waiting for you.'

'If I had realised.'

'I told them not to be concerned.'

'I'm grateful for your confidence.'

'I look inside people,' says Makiyama, yawning and stretching himself on the bench again. 'I looked inside you.'

'Don't forget to pay him,' says Amazawa. 'And if you like it so much, shouldn't he have something extra?'

Still prone, Makiyama peels three ten-yen notes from a roll carried casually in a trouser pocket, then, after a second's teasing, peels off a fourth. 'Didn't you,' he says to Amazawa, 'have something you wanted to say to him? Some proposition?'

'A proposition? Yes.' He looks at Yuji with small bloodshot eyes, then hurriedly eats something out of the palm of his hand, swallowing it with a mouthful of beer. 'Ever tried writing a screenplay?'

Yuji shakes his head.

'There's not much to it.'

'No?'

'It's not really like writing a story. More like the blueprint for a machine.'

'I see.'

'You could try writing something for the Unit. You know the sort of thing.'

'Hmm. I wonder . . .'

'It was *his* idea.'

'Mr Makiyama's?'

'Ishihara, of course. He said he had spoken freely to you. That you understood.'

'A vision of the future, perhaps?'

'Perhaps.'

'Or like the film at General Sugiyama's?'

'Don't speak of that in here.'

'I'm sorry.'

'No one is ready for that yet.'

'I'm sorry.'

'You've read the Italian futurists? Marinetti, Balla?'

'I've heard of them . . .'

'Something exalted, something delirious . . .'

'I could try, I suppose.'

'By the way,' says Makiyama, 'you may find you have to break your connection with certain people.'

'You think so?'

'The front line,' says Amazawa, pressing the head of the match against Yuji's chest, 'runs through every heart.'

'I hadn't thought of it like that.'

'You can have that if you want,' says Amazawa. 'The front-line line. I'm giving it to you.'

'Thank you.'

Amazawa and Makiyama look at each other. They start to giggle, though to Yuji, Amazawa seems close to tears as if his emotions had a life of their own and cycled mechanically through their repertoire with little regard for what he was doing or thinking.

'You want to dance with her?'

'With . . . ?'

'With her.' He points the match at Fumi.

'You think she wants to dance?'

'She's on the dance floor, isn't she?'

'It's true.'

'Don't you like her?'

'She seems nice.'

'How old do you think she is?'

'I don't know. Twenty-four, twenty-five?'

'You're not even close,' he says. 'If you want to be a real artist, you'll have to learn how to tell such things at a glance.'

So Yuji dances with her. She lolls her head on his shoulder. She smells of sherbet and honey and cigarettes. They are moving, but much more slowly than the music. Talking into his chest, she says she used to be a taxi-dancer at a place called the Polar Bear Club in Shinjuku but that one night a girl jumped from the roof and after that business wasn't so good. People complained the place was haunted.

'You think it was?'

She shrugs, her shoulders like the delicate, useless stubs of wings. 'Are you going to work at the Unit?' she asks.

'I'm not sure what the Unit is.'

'It's whatever he wakes up thinking it is.'

'Ishihara?'

'The general.'

'The general?'

'I'm awfully tired,' she says. 'You won't let me fall, will you?'

He tells her he won't. He tightens his arm around the top of her waist. They sway, their feet scuffing the boards. He is, to his surprise, quite comfortable with her, and as they turn in slow motion across the rhythmic gloom of the dance floor, his mind goes out in a long exhalation . . . He finds himself thinking of a forest in France – Champagne? Compiègne? – where the French have signed the instrument of surrender (he has not dared to visit Feneon again); of the barracks near Yokohama where Junzo, who in a letter to Taro has confirmed his *unshakable resolve*, is starting basic training; of that trouble at the cinema yesterday afternoon (he had gone to watch Mizoguchi's *The Gorge Between Love and Hate*) when a man, slow to stand at the sight of the Emperor's black Mercedes on the Nihon News newsreel, was shouted at, threatened by a figure at the back of the auditorium, one of those new-style patriots who, it was said, carry billy clubs beneath their jackets; and of the morning paper, the *Yomiuri*, that had on its front page a photograph of schoolchildren carrying their classroom stove slung from a pole like a pig on its way to slaughter. They were delivering it to the War Ministry to be melted down and made into part of an aircraft or the barrel of a howitzer or whatever it is the nation needs more of to ensure its victory. How bright their faces were! And how merrily they seemed to march behind their teacher! It was affecting, a genuinely inspiring example, yet with something so pitiful in it Yuji, reading on the downtown tram, found himself wishing it was *he* who marched ahead of them, leading them – by some suitably circuitous route – back to their classroom where the stove could be fitted again and next winter they would have something more than the spirit of sacrifice to keep them warm.

In his arms, Fumi has fallen asleep or passed out. He is holding her entire weight, though fortunately she is thin, emaciated even, and only her head, pressed against his chest, seems to have any weight to it. Should he manoeuvre her, unobtrusively as possible, back to the booths, or keep swaying with her until she comes to? He looks across the top of her head, her not very clean hair, hoping to find Dick Amazawa and somehow signal to him, but the film-maker is over by the bar using his outsized match to putt an orange into the cupped hands of a kneeling waitress. He lines up the shot with the greatest care. A small crowd gathers. At the third attempt the orange rolls neatly into the waitress's hands. Everyone applauds, enthusiastically.

8

The rains are over. It's high summer now. The sewing room, uncomfortable by night, is, by the middle of the day, impossible. The coolest place is the garden privy. There, the shade of old wood, the breezes that lap through the open lattice at the base of the door, the scent of cedar boughs and black earth, give the feeling of sitting in the depths of a forest, and though the light is pale grey or brown or a soft green, it is, when the brilliance of the outer light is shaken off, just bright enough to read by, or even to write sketches for a screenplay, blueprints for a machine whose purpose he does not yet understand, visions of the future where the dead are admired as a kind of poetry.

He is in there one morning considering a fresh attempt (something of Hitchcock, something of Marinetti) when he decides instead to use the paper on his lap to write to Junzo. It is a short letter, boyish and full of trivia – 'Yesterday I was at Grandfather's and helped lay out the plums to dry for pickling . . . Mother and the serving girl are down with "B shortage" . . . My uncle, the one from the farm, will be coming for the Festival of the Dead. Will you have any leave? Will you be in Tokyo?'

Invisibly, at the side of this letter, another, much longer letter is being written, one that contains all that cannot now be raised between them. The unexplained remarks in the yard of the billiard parlour, the sudden decision to volunteer, the visit from Mrs Miyazaki, the room in Kagurazaka and the Feneons, of course, *père et fille*, about whom he has, anyway, no news.

In a drawer of the dresser in the Western room he finds an envelope, addresses it care of the Miyazaki house. Miyo is on a mattress on the floor of the Japanese room. When he asks her how she is feeling, she whispers that she is still too weak to move. 'B shortage' is a kind of annual holiday for her, an enervation vastly preferable to doing chores in the full heat of late July. It is Father who allows her this time (the half-deception of it), who sends Kushida to her with vitamin injections and sees that she has the same medicinal foods – the clam broths and twice-cooked brown-rice porridges – Mother has. Without his orders, Haruyu would drag the girl into the kitchen by her hair.

With the letter in his pocket, he cycles to the post office in Ueno, then on to the park, to Shinobazu Pond, where he looks, with strange pangs of regret, at the lilies. From a barrow he buys a slice of watermelon, finds an empty bench and begins to eat, spitting the glossy seeds into his fist. On the grass nearby, four teenage recruits are smoking, sharing two cigarettes between them. As they lift the cigarettes to their mouths, Yuji sees how the flesh of their hands is bruised, cut about, the knuckles swollen and raw. They show little interest in the world about them. Only when a girl goes by, some schoolgirl in a pleated skirt (the sort of girl who will one day soon dutifully wave them off from a station platform) do they glance up, as if out of habit, to watch her passing.

He looks at his own hands, feels for them a sudden anxious affection, then cleans his fingers on the grass, wheels his bicycle out of the park, and rides for home. On either side of the road, the screens of houses stand wide, dark mouths waiting for a breeze to swallow. On verandahs, on shadowed stoops, fans flicker like bird tails. The heat streams over his face, his throat. In this breath a taste of jasmine, in this, of drains. He crosses the dual shimmer of the tram lines, free-wheels into the end of his street, then pulls on the brakes with such sharp force the bicycle bucks and almost tips him off. Drawn up outside Itaki's tobacco store is the car he climbed out of (with such relief) by the Yasukuni shrine in May. There is no mistaking it, the glitter, the fulsome curves. Itaki's grandchildren are walking slowly round it, following their splayed reflections in the metal. The car door opens. The children jump back. Ota, in white high-waisted trousers, a dazzling white shirt, steps from the car's interior and watches, with mocking gaze, Yuji pushing the old bicycle towards him.

'You came to see me?' asks Yuji, flushed from his ride. He takes in the cufflinks, the ring, the gold-rimmed sunglasses hooked over the monogrammed breast pocket of the shirt. Everything this man is wearing has the character of an admirer's gift. 'Perhaps you would care to come into the house?'

Ota opens one of the car's heavy rear doors and from the stitched leather of the back seat he takes a magazine, also a small square package wrapped in black crêpe. He passes the magazine to Yuji. It is the new edition of *Young Japan*, on the cover a picture of Kaoru Ishihara, his groomed head in three-quarters profile as he stares, solemnly, into the undisclosed distance.

'It will not be on sale to the public until next week,' says Ota. 'But he thought you might care to see a copy in advance. He also wishes you to have this. A small expression of his gratitude for your efforts.' He holds out the package. It is clear to Yuji that Ota knows exactly what it contains and that it is, in his opinion, a wasted gift, one that Yuji will not know how to value.

'There is really no need,' says Yuji.

'He prizes loyalty,' says Ota.

'Loyalty?'

'Surely you understood that much?'

'Yes. Of course . . .'

'My arm,' says Ota, 'is growing tired.'

Yuji leans the bicycle against his thigh. He takes the package from Ota's outstretched hand and is reciting the formal expressions of gratitude when, from the opposite side of the street, a woman's voice rips the air with a yell of fury. Startled, they turn to find Grandma Kitamura hastening through the gate of her house while the postman, in his straw hat, retreats ahead of her, bowing compulsively and screwing up his face like a dog desperate to avoid a thrashing. Kyoko, her feet bare, her hair undressed, is tugging at the old woman's obi to slow her down and has almost brought her to a halt when they both catch sight of Yuji. They stop. Across the old woman's face spreads a light of savage triumph. She swings towards him, aims at him the crumpled telegram in her fist, points it at his head like a pistol. 'They're sending him home a cripple!' she roars. 'That will make you happy, won't it? But even a cripple is more use than you! Do the Takanos think they can leave others to do their suffering for them? You wait until he's back! You wait and see what he'll do with types like you!'

Behind Yuji, the Armstrong Siddeley's engine ignites, revs throatily. There's a blast from the horn, then the car accelerates away, Ota at the wheel, his face creased with silent laughter. Those who are left – the protagonists, the gang of neighbours, the casual audience of passers-by – stand in a little haze of gasoline and summer dust. Someone coughs. The postman makes his escape. The old woman, shoulders heaving, tears dripping stickily from the hairs of her chin, is guided by Kyoko back towards her house. At his own gate, Yuji is dimly aware of Haruyo, and behind her, peeping from the heavy shade of the vestibule, Miyo, risen from her bedding. A sudden hush descends. It seems that everyone is waiting for him to do something. He stares at the road, the drops of fresh oil like spoor, the tyre prints, then looks at the package in his hand. Is this the ending they require? To see what the dazzling stranger has brought him? He rolls the magazine, tucks it under his arm, and tears the black crêpe. Inside is a velvet-skinned box, and inside the box, lying in a crease of cream satin, a pin with a ruby head. He studies it awhile, then, with a fingernail, extracts the ribbon of folded paper from the lid of the box, unfurls it, and reads what, in passable calligraphy, is written there. 'What do the victims matter if the gesture be beautiful?'

'Yuji!'

Father is calling him in. Father is scowling magnificently. Yuji, clutching his gifts, crosses the street towards him.

9

In the little cemetery at Kotobuki the men are cleaning Grandmother Takano's grave. When they finish, they cross a path to Ryuichi's grave and start again, wiping and scraping away another year of lichen, of the city's soft fall of soot from the stacks across the river. Kensuke's daughter, Asako, sits with her child, three-year-old Akiko, in the shade of a gingko tree, and answers, as simply as she can, the little girl's questions about the world of the dead, the duties of the living. All across the cemetery, across the whole city, the smoke of incense uncoils in the shimmering heat of midday. The men step back, mop their faces. Their brows are shining. They stand in silence until the child, running from the shade, clutches Kensuke's hand and tugs it as though suddenly afraid for him. He lifts her up, sits her in his arms. Grandfather takes out his pocket watch. The lid flashes in the sunlight as he opens it. 'The taxis will be waiting,' he says. 'I don't like to make them wait in this heat.'

They go to a restaurant in the Hamacho quarter, owned by a Mr Kono, the adopted son of one of Grandfather's old employees.

Kono has kept the best table for them, in a private room that overlooks a small garden where the blooms of the pomegranates are so vivid they almost burn the eye. The meal begins with chilled bean curd. Later there are salads, persimmon leaf sushi, eel hamo-style. Yuji is kneeling beside Asako. When, yesterday, she arrived at the house with her father and daughter (Sawa, at the last minute, had decided her back was too painful for such a journey), she was wearing a skirt and blouse, but today, for the Festival of Lanterns, the Festival of the Dead, she is dressed more formally in a cream kimono with a pattern of tangling ivy. To Yuji, who has not seen her since her wedding in Showa 10, she appears to have lost all trace of the old mountain-child boisterousness that once so impressed him. Each speaks evasively about the present, the recent past, and starts to smile only when they reminisce about the long-ago summer at the farm – the waterfall, the berry-picking, the ill-tempered cockerel that pecked at Yuji's heels until she chased it off with clods of earth. As they talk, the little girl, shy, almost voiceless in this unfamiliar company, prods suspiciously at her food and every few seconds glances up intently at the side of her mother's face.

Across the table, Uncle Kensuke is showing Grandfather a photograph. Yuji has already seen it – Hiroshi stiff and gaunt in the uniform of a newly graduated pilot of the First Air Fleet.

'He should be with us today,' says Grandfather. 'He should be here.'

'He would have liked to,' says Uncle Kensuke, 'but it seems that their training is intensifying.'

'The same goes for your husband,' says Grandfather, looking over the table at Asako. 'You would think Mitsubishi could spare him for a day or two.'

'Minoru,' says Uncle Kensuke, 'is helping to build the planes Hiroshi will be flying. Skilled technicians are in short supply.'

'Like everything else,' says Grandfather. 'Well, at least they let my great-granddaughter come, eh? I must be grateful for that, I suppose.'

As the meal ends, Kono persuades them to take some little glasses of cognac. He joins them, and sits with Grandfather while the old man tells him tales about the city in the days of the first China war of '94, stories that falter into song, into sighing nasal elegies for the tea houses of the Yanagibashi, the night cherries of the Yoshiwara . . . Father and Uncle Kensuke move to the open screens, light cigarettes and peer out at the lengthening shadows of the garden. Yuji, his back to them as he shows the child for the fifth time, the sixth, the seventh, the only magic trick he knows (a ten-sen coin that 'sinks' through the skin of his hand to reappear behind one or other of her ears), listens to Uncle Kensuke talking, quietly and earnestly, about Father and Mother coming to the mountains.

'We've more than enough room since the children left. We grow much of what we eat, kill the occasional hen. And Noriko can be as quiet there as she is here. With all that has happenened it can hardly be comfortable for you staying in Tokyo. As for the future . . .'

'Things are not as bad as all that.'

'Really? That's not been my impression.'

'And what about Father?'

'I'd ask him too if I thought there was the slightest hope of his coming. At least out in Setagaya he's practically in the country-side. Things should be safer there.'

'Safer?'

'If there's bombing.'

'Bombing!'

'Look in the papers. The Germans are raiding English cities every day.'

'The comparison is a little misleading, isn't it? Where would these bombers come from? Chungking? Moscow?'

'You should talk to Hiroshi. He has told me things I do not dare to tell Sawa. She has trouble enough sleeping as it is.'

'I can't see Noriko making such an upheaval. You saw her this morning.'

'Better to make such a move now while there is still some normality.'

'I appreciate your generosity.'

'So you'll consider it?'

'There's the question of Yuji.'

'He, of course, is welcome too, but his situation . . . I doubt even your friend Kushida can keep him out of the army for good . . .'

Two butterflies, black as charred paper, blow into the room, flutter clumsily over the end of the table, then find their way back into the garden again.

'On a day like today,' says Father, 'the situation doesn't seem so serious. I don't want to act rashly.'

'I understand that,' says Uncle Kensuke, 'but if you don't act at all . . .'

For the three days before the visitors make their return journey, the child, with her small, determined face, follows Yuji around the house as though connected to him by a length of wire. When he slips away from her, she calls for him, hunts him down. He tells her, in an exasperated voice, that he is trying to write a film about the end of the world. She frowns, then squats on the mat in front of him and begins to wail. He gives in, takes the records out of the storage cupboard, lifts the gramophone from its long sleep beside the corner bookshelf in the Western room, and plays ragtime and jazz until the needles are blunt. He folds her birds out of paper, catches cicadas for her and shows her how, from her cupped hands, to free their clumsy bodies into the air again.

'She'll miss you,' says Uncle Kensuke, sitting down on the verandah beside Yuji, the last morning of the visit. In the garden, the girl, a straw hat tied under her chin, is chasing dragonflies, now and then pausing to be sure that Yuji is watching her.

'It must be the trick I showed her in the restaurant,' says Yuji.

'Who knows. Children choose the people they want.'

'I thought I might remind her of Minoru.'

'It's possible. Though you could hardly be more unlike him.'

'Is the taxi on its way?'

'Another half-hour.'

'I hope Auntie Sawa will be feeling better,' says Yuji.

'Yes. Let's hope so.'

'And please give my regards to Hiroshi.'

'When we see him. They don't give him much leave, and these days he often prefers something more exciting than a farm in the mountains and the company of two old people. You might see him in Tokyo one day.'

'Yes. If I'm here.'

'You want to go somewhere?'

'I'm not sure what I want. But probably it won't have anything to do with what I want.'

'You mean, if you get your papers?'

'Isn't it inevitable?'

'Tell me, are you writing these days?'

'Some journalism.' He shrugs. 'I wouldn't necessarily call it writing.'

'Your father said it was something on Ishihara. He said it was well written.'

'I didn't know he had seen it.'

Uncle Kensuke smiles. 'Apparently you left the magazine open on the table one morning.'

'And he said it was well written?'

'He doesn't much care for Ishihara, of course, or *Young Japan*, but he has always respected your ability.'

'My ability!'

'When Ryuichi died your father became rather cynical. Stubborn and cynical. He wasn't always so. When he was young he was full of enthusiasms. Quite a talker, even. You should not mistake his reticence for indifference.'

'Did he say anything else? About me?'

'Only that he was afraid he would not be able to protect you.'

'From whom?'

'He was not specific.'

'I thought it was Father who needed protecting.'

'All of us will need some protecting before the world is much older. But what about poetry?'

'It doesn't seem like a time for poetry.'

'No? I can't think of a better one. Isn't poetry just about paying attention to what is here? Two men, for example, sitting talking while a child runs in the garden. The quietness of that has a certain value, don't you think, in such a clamorous age?'

'I'm not sure many share your view, Uncle. People want other things now.'

'You might think it's not a time for something as trivial as dyeing cloth, but now I'm doing it more carefully than ever because indigo is my way of speaking. Which reminds me. I have something for you. It's in the suitcase. I'd almost forgotten . . .'

They go through the house to where two tan leather cases are waiting by the edge of the vestibule step. Kneeling, Uncle unbuckles the smaller case, pulls out a pair of folded *yukatas*, some Tokyo newspapers, then lifts out a square of folded silk and holds it up to Yuji.

'I remember the summer you stayed with us as a little boy you used to sit in the dyeing barn, sometimes for an hour or more, watching what I was doing. Hiroshi never had that sort of interest.'

Yuji takes the cloth, lets it fall open. It's a square of subtly dyed silk, the indigo darkening in diagonal waves from blue-black to a blue so pale it's like the blue of a vein on the inside of a child's wrist.

'It's just a test piece, too small to be of much use, but somehow I liked the way it came out. I thought you might like it too.'

Yuji thanks him, holds the cloth up to the light that comes through the open doors of the Western room. 'Do you also remember,' he says, 'how, that summer, you would often massage my chest in the evening before supper, and because the dye was on your hands it stained my skin? Even a month after I came home I could see it, though every day a little fainter.'

'Indigo has special properties. Wrap something in indigo and you preserve it.'

188

'Then,' says Yuji, carefully folding the material, 'I must find something precious to wrap in this.'

'I'm sure you will,' says Uncle Kensuke, absently, as he buckles the straps of the case.

In the garden the girl is calling Yuji's name. A repetitive little voice, shrill as an insect. 'Yuji! Yuji! Yujiii!'

10

The days that follow the visitors' departure bring the first rumours of Saburo's return. In the noodle bar, Sachiko, Otaki's wall-eyed sister, serving him a lunch of zaru soba, tells him she has heard from a regular customer, who has a nephew who drinks with an assistant at the military clerk's office in Ueno, that Saburo will be back before the beginning of the ninth month. The next afternoon, Mrs Itaki, wiping down the woodwork at the front of her shop, assures Yuji that her husband has been told by a soldier who saw Saburo in Dairen only two months ago that his ship, in all probability, will dock at Yokohama on 7 September. Even Miyo claims to know something, telling Yuji that their neighbour will return no earlier than the thirteenth but no later than the twentieth. Her informant is the soy-seller's son, who heard it from his father, who heard it from the wife of an official he delivers to up in Yanaka.

The first of September – the beginning of the typhoon season, the seventeenth anniversary of the Great Earthquake

– is a mournful day of sultry heat that feels neither like summer nor autumn. Yuji waits in his room and once an hour imagines he hears, rising above the cries of itinerant salesmen and the cooing of radio orchestras, the voice of his old friend, his enemy, calling to him.

On the seventh he waits again. Again on the eighth, on the ninth . . . There are no more rumours. People seem to have forgotten about Saburo. Is he coming back at all? Yuji has not seen Grandma Kitamura since the telegram (is she ill?). Kyoko, he has glimpsed several times in the garden, early mornings and dusks on those days she was not on the trains. On the last occasion he imagined he noticed a subtle alteration in her, a suggestive melancholy in the way she picked a leaf from the surface of the pond, then stood still as a horse in the shade of the plum tree . . . If a wound can get better, it can get worse too. Could the Kitamuras be waiting for a second telegram with darker, more conclusive news? Whatever the truth of it, he will listen to no more gossip from waitresses and serving girls.

On the thirteenth he cycles through a rising wind to meet Oki and Shozo at the bathhouse. As they wash at the taps, Oki says that he saw Junzo, two days after the Festival of the Dead, in a café in Jinbocho.

'Who was he with?'

'He was on his own.'

'What did he say?'

'Not much.'

'Not much?'

'It hardly seemed like him at all. After a few minutes I felt embarrassed and made up some appointment. In fact, I said I was meeting you.'

'Did he ask about me?'

'Just said I'd better go if I was meeting you.'

'That's it?'

'That's it.'

Upstairs, after the bath, they drink beer and watch through the room's only window the sky building with storm clouds. On the roof of the house opposite, a woman plucks streaming washing from a line, balls it in her arms, and hurries inside. 'We're in for a blow, all right,' says Watanabe, swaying by the young men's table on big splayed feet. 'There'll be roofs stripped by morning.' His wife shouts up the stairs, tells him to close the rain shutters. The light goes on, feebly, under a shade of insect-speckled glass.

'By the way,' asks Shozo, as the young men gather by the street entrance, buttoning coats and tying mufflers, 'is the French Club still going, or is that all over now?'

'Over?'

'I was just wondering. You know . . . With things as they are.'

Outside, they separate with hasty waves. Yuji, his trouser cuffs snapping at his ankles, wheels his bicycle into the teeth of the wind. The sky is turquoise, orange, bruise yellow. A warm rain begins, a swirling downpour that seems to fall from all sides at once. In less than a minute Yuji is as wet as when he sat in the baths. A man beckons to him from a doorway. Yuji shakes his head. There is not far to go, and this sudden violence – all of summer being torn to pieces – is exhilarating. He shouts out scraps of poetry: 'Cette idole, yeux noirs et crin jaune, sans parents ni cour!' The wind smears the words across his face, the rain dashes them away. A pot of flowers (the kind of big ceramic tub he would struggle to lift on his own) sails from a roof garden and explodes in a halo of earth and petals against the manically creaking sign of a leather-goods store. When he reaches home he'll carry the sake bottle up to the platform and stand there, captain of a doomed ship, reciting the whole of 'Le Bateau Ivre' to the thrashing gingko tree. What does it matter if it's bad for his health? With things as they are, isn't good health more of a threat to him than sickness? Good health could be the death of him.

By the time he arrives at the end of his own street the air stinks of sea wrack and flooded drains. He pauses beside the telegraph pole outside Otaki's to wipe the water from his face. Then shielding his eyes with his hands, he watches an umbrella of lacquered paper (some kind of dark flower painted on its top) weaving up the middle of the road towards him. It's hard at first to tell what's going on. There seem to be three, perhaps four people beneath it, and with the wind behind them they are having to fight hard to keep the umbrella from being snatched away and flung over the singing radio aerials. What a subject for a Hiroshige print! The driving rain, the gloom, the jumbled legs, the shimmering umbrella held so low it hides their faces completely. It looks like a crab, or some strange blind cuttlefish labouring across the bottom of the ocean. He would laugh if he didn't think the wind would scoop the air from his lungs. Could this be in the screenplay? An opening shot, comic-pathetic, an image redolent of struggle, absurdity . . .

As they come closer – now accelerating a little, now trying to anchor themselves against the force of the storm – he begins to make it out. A woman on one side, a woman the other and between them, rocking between them, a figure, a dark figure, a man, a three-legged man, a man with a crutch . . .

A *crutch*!

Dragging the bicycle with him, he presses himself against the pole. The umbrella comes to a halt fifteen yards away. A head appears – the old woman. She shoulders open her gate, then turns, and like some aged flunky from the court of Pu Yi, starts to shuffle backwards up the path, the umbrella gripped in both fists over the stooping man's head. Kyoko is left behind to shut the gate. She glances into the street, looks both ways, her hair whipping about her face, but if she sees Yuji, if she picks out his ragged shadow from all this shifting, melting world, she gives no sign of it, and in another moment, hauling the gate against the wind, she is gone.

It blows all night, and in his dreams the sound of the wind becomes the noise of the firestorms twisting over the surface of the Sumida. It is blowing still when, at first light, he wakes (who was that woman with her hair on fire, her hair burning up like grass?), but the wind's hard edge has gone and the rain has become a fine mist, a haze of saturated air. Cautiously, stealthily, he kneels on the wood of the platform and peers into the neighbours' garden. The surface of the pond is thick with leaves but there is no one out there, and the house, what he can see of it through the dripping trees, looks as hushed and empty as a house abandoned.

He dresses, goes downstairs, drinks tea with Miyo (though tells her nothing), then puts on a beetle-coloured coat of oiled silk, puts on his old student cap, and taking the long way round, not passing the old woman's house, sets off for Setagaya. Beads of rain drizzle from the peak of his cap. Before he has finished the walk from the station, past the building plots and the tea fields to the gates of Grandfather's garden, the damp has permeated the silk of the coat and covered his skin with a blood-warm slick of atomised Pacific. The concertina roof of the old rickshaw is a vivid green slime. Between the wheels, a cockerel, its feathers dark with water, shifts its weight from foot to foot, and with a single hostile eye, watches Yuji on the path.

Grandfather greets him with a shout of laughter. 'Look what the wind blew in!'

Fortunately, the bath is still hot from Grandfather's morning ablutions. Yuji wallows in it, safe here, and almost sung to sleep by the mosquitoes in the coiling steam above him. Afterwards, he dresses in one of Grandfather's *yukatas* and drinks tea with him, Sonoko sitting behind them with her sewing.

'The neighbour's back,' says Yuji. 'The old woman's grandson.'

Grandfather nods. 'I always thought he was half-witted.'

'Perhaps.'

Later, there is the usual tour of the model ('That temple bell comes from a child's rattle. The real one, iron, and high as a man, melted like wax.'), then a lunch of bean curd and baked seaweed.

In the afternoon the sun appears, and with the help of a neighbour – the genial Mr Fujitomi – they disentangle an old pine tree from where it has fallen across the canes and netting of the fruit garden. Yuji is back in his dried clothes. He offers to start sawing the tree up, and for two hours, until his fingers blister, he cuts clumsily through the pale wood while seeing, from the corner of his eye, Grandfather and Sonoko repairing the beds, bending and straightening like a pair of wading birds on the mudflats.

He is invited to stay the night. He telephones Father. 'Saburo's back,' says Father.

'Yes,' says Yuji.

'You knew?'

'Yes.'

'It might,' says Father, 'be wise to pay a call when you come home.'

Grandfather goes to bed at ten. Yuji has a mattress in the eight-mat room. He has hoped that his work with the saw, the good air he has breathed, might bring him an early sleep, but he sits up on his own by the light of a Blanchard lamp, a bowl of tea cooling on the mat beside him, and looks past the part-open screens to where beams of blue moonlight are falling through the darker blue of the trees. For a while he is troubled by visions of the umbrella lurching towards him through the storm, of that stooped figure probing the ground with his crutch. Then – some effect of the moonlight, the stillness, the hour – his mind quietens, his thoughts descend like water into the earth, and when it seems he is quite empty (his body a presence loosely wrapped around his breath), he feels it again – distinctly, though less intensely – the same sweet unhappiness he knew that evening in the taxi beside Alissa. What is it this time? Another memory? Of what? Mother again? No, not Mother. Who, then? He stares at the weave of the matting by his knees, brings before his mental gaze a dozen different faces, Momoyo to Junzo, tests them, then gives it up, sips his tea, and immediately, in its fragrance, the faint bitterness of its savour, finds the answer . . .

Love. A love of *this*. The room, the light, the shadows, the singing of the insects, the tea, the rain-scoured air. A love of his country. Or if not that exactly – the phrase is too often in the mouths of the worst people – then love for a place he has always known, always, even in its convulsions, understood perfectly, a place he could never abandon without ceasing, in some way, to be Yuji Takano. Yet tonight it is almost as though he is experiencing it for the last time, gazing back at it from the stern of a boat, the line of the coast melting into the horizon . . .

Is he, at twenty-six, falling into that cast of mind – regretful, elegiac – better suited to a man twice or three times his age, a man of Grandfather's years? It is easy to affect such things, to wear them insincerely. But tonight he *does* feel old, as old as one of those broken pots Father pores over illustrations of in the garden study. Hiroshi in his airman's uniform, Junzo no longer like himself, Taro bent with anxious labour, Oki, Shozo . . . How many of them will see thirty? How many will be left when it's over? Next month, by government decree, all the dance halls in Japan will close their doors for the duration of the struggle. The Harlem, The Tokyo Follies, The Big Ben, The Eastern Empire . . . Piece by piece, life is being put away. To make more room for death? So that death can tour Japan in a black Mercedes, waving a gloved hand to the people lining the streets, their necks stretched out in readiness?

And what if he refuses it? What if he is the nail that cannot be hammered in? How, in this world he has been given but never asked for, does one make plans to survive?

For a week he manages to avoid paying his visit to the Kitamura house, and might, had he not sat so unguardedly on the verandah for half an hour flicking through his latest find at the Kanda bookstalls (a tattered but serviceable copy of *Ciné-Journal*, Sarah Bernhardt on the cover), have put off the meeting a few days more.

He is reading a review of Pathé's *Le Coupable* when he hears a whistle – short, low, and of such shocking familiarity he immediately feels a violent contraction of his heart that for two seconds dims the daylight around him. He closes the magazine, rolls it, and goes to the gap in the fence. Saburo – a face-wide strip of him – is waiting there, one hand holding a young black cat against his chest. The other hand, though not in view, is presumably clenched round the cross-strut of a crutch.

'Welcome home,' says Yuji. 'I am sorry you have suffered a misfortune.'

'Misfortune? I've lost half my foot, but now I can lie back and watch the others sweat. I'm going to enjoy it.' He is smiling, an eager, open smile, but the face is no longer the one in the picture the old woman sighed over. Something has happened to Saburo, something that cannot be explained by the mutilation of a foot.

'I was coming to see you,' says Yuji.

'Everybody else has already been.'

'I was at Grandfather's, and then . . .'

'Granny says your father's friends are keeping you out of the army.'

'My chest . . .'

'Ah! The famous chest!'

'It's probably only a matter of time.'

'Probably? I'd say definitely.'

'You made it to corporal, then?'

'You know, I've only been back a week and already I'm sick of the prattling of women. Though sometimes Granny has interesting things to say. Surprising things, in fact.'

'You heard about Ozono?'

'No one to take over the brush business now.'

'No.'

'I bet the box they got back was empty. They usually are.'

'The box?'

'Of ashes. Most of them are empty.'

'I didn't know.'

'What were you reading? Show me.'

Yuji, unrolling the magazine, holds it up. Saburo frowns at it. 'You could get into trouble with something like that,' he says.

'It's just about films.'

'It's not Japanese, though, is it?'

'No.'

'You've got your father's disease.'

'Father doesn't have a disease.'

'I don't mean a real disease.'

'I know what you mean.'

'How touchy you are!'

'I'm sorry.'

'Would it surprise you to know I often thought of you over there?'

'You did?'

'We could have had some fun, you and me. I could have shown you things.'

'What sort of things?'

'Oh, I'd have to whisper them to you. You'd have to push your head through the fence.'

'It was kind of you to think of me.'

'I can't really talk to the women in there. But I can't escape from them either. Not with this.' He tilts his head to indicate the crutch, the cut limb. Yuji nods. Despite what he sees in the other's eyes, he pities him. 'I'm going to have a special boot made. The front half will be filled with wood. There's a place in Sendagi. A workshop that makes wooden parts for soldiers.'

'A special boot would be good, I suppose.'

'Lucky I got married before, eh? What kind of a wife do you think I'd get like this? Women don't want a man with a piece missing. Not unless he's rich.'

'Is that cat one of the litter?'

'The only one to survive. I had to give Kyoko a bit of a dressing-down, army style, when I found that out.'

'It might have been difficult to have helped the others.'

'You're sticking up for her?'

'The cat could have gone somewhere secret to have the kittens.'

'What do you know about cats?'

'I'm not an expert.'

'That's right. You're not an expert.'

'It's good that one survived.'

'It needs a name though, don't you think?'

'Doesn't it have one already?'

'It's my cat. I'm the only one who can give it a name.'

'Have you chosen one?'

'Mmm, I'm not sure. I thought' – he furrows his brow in a clumsy mime of consideration – 'I thought "Foreign Girl" might be good.'

'A strange name for a cat.'

'I told you Granny had been telling me interesting things.'

'Some of them might not be quite accurate.'

'Then why are you blushing?'

'I'm not.'

'You're red as a cherry.'

'Let's forget about it.'

'And what if I don't want to forget about it?'

200

'I'm only saying we could talk about something else.'

'Then let's talk about how grateful you are for my sacrifice. About how you're going to show your gratitude.'

'We're all grateful.'

'Look at you with your stupid magazine! You talk like you're somebody and I'm nobody.'

'No,' says Yuji, quietly. 'I'm nobody. You're a war hero.'

'That's right. A returning hero.'

'Yes. A returning hero.'

'A veteran.'

'Yes.'

'Tried and tested.'

'Yes.'

'Think you can tell me what to do?'

'No.'

'So who gives the orders?'

'You. Of course.'

'I'm just pleased to see you again, Takano.'

'I'm pleased to see you.'

'You were my right-hand man when we were kids. You could be that again if you wanted.'

'I remember it,' says Yuji.

'Wouldn't it be wonderful to be kids again? Even for a day?'

'Yes. I suppose.'

'We were free then. Not a care in the world. And now . . .' He lifts the cat, nuzzling its head with the point of his chin. The animal mews, drowsily. 'Time for Foreign Girl to have some milk,' he says. 'Though not any cream. Cream's bad for their livers. You can kill a cat with cream.'

'Yes?'

They look at each other, intimate as criminals, as lovers.

'It's you and me against the rest,' says Saburo, starting, with little precarious movements, little grunts of effort, to turn himself round. 'You and me against the *women* . . .'

11

On Father's birthday, Yuji presents him with an envelope containing a dozen steel needles for the gramophone.

'If you were concerned about disturbing anyone, you could listen in the garden study.'

'Listen to jazz?'

'Wouldn't you like to hear King Oliver again?'

'Hmm. The New Orleans sound. You played it for the child, didn't you?'

'Yes. She was quite a good dancer.'

'A child's spirit is light. Jazz needs a light spirit. Dancing too, of course.'

'You told me once that Mother was a good dancer.'

'It's true. We used to go to clubs in the Low City, even after Ryuichi was born. Dancing was one thing that did not seem to fatigue her.' He smiles. 'And we too had light spirits then.'

In the evening, Kushida comes for supper. He is wearing a field cap and a civil defence jacket, though the jacket, unlike most of the others Yuji has seen, has a neat and tailored appearance, more staff officer than front-line soldier. He apologises for it, feigns embarrassment, and explains that he had to attend a meeting of his local neighbourhood association – new directives on fire-fighting. As one of the senior people, he was, unfortunately, required to stay until the end. It had gone on so long he had not had time to return home and change.

Miyo brings in the sake flasks from the brass heater in the kitchen. They are sitting at the table in the Western room. The doors are part open to the muggy air. On a corner of the dresser, a coil of acrid-smelling mosquito repellent burns in a saucer. The birthday menu has been chosen by Mother (another of those household traditions that feel, somehow, spectral). This year it is a dish of chicken and garlic that she must, in the remote past, have instructed Haruyo how to make to an acceptable standard.

'I suppose we should be drinking wine with it,' says Father, 'but I thought you'd prefer sake.'

'You are quite right,' says Kushida. 'I imagine Yuji has more experience in drinking wine than either of us old men.'

'Not really,' says Yuji.

'No?'

'Not really.'

Though it is Haruyo who has prepared the food, Yuji manages to persuade himself that what is on his plate comes directly from Mother's hands, and he eats it, the slightly stringy chicken, with good appetite. He wishes he was alone with Father, or that Grandfather was there, Grandfather and Uncle Kensuke. He wishes they were talking about jazz, that they were drinking wine. (Red or white with chicken? Sweet? Dry?) When he remembers the wine he drank at the Snow Goose, the bottle divided between two languages, he is surprised – startled, even – to discover that the memory now provokes only pleasure, and has, through some unobserved activity of time, completely lost its residue of high anxiety.

At the end of the table, Kushida and Father are at their usual game, sifting names out of the ashes of the past, out of the class of 1911, and holding them up to desultory inspection. Nakiyama has published his study of Clausewitz. Tamura is on Prince Konoe's new political order committee. Kuroda's son is making his fortune in Tientsin, the construction business, army contracts mostly. Ayukawa, for reasons that remain obscure, is divorcing his wife.

Listening to them, watching them as he finishes his food, Yuji tries (again) to guess at Father's true feelings for the doctor. If they did not have Imperial, what would they talk about? There is nothing in their manner together to suggest any deep regard, any affinity beyond the historical coincidence of going up to the university together thirty years ago. Are they really such good friends? Or is possible that Father has kept up the alliance for the sake of Mother, for the foreign medicines in the clinic dispensary and, later, for those headed letters to the War Ministry, one of which found its way into Captain Mori's folder? If there was no *need* for Dr Kushida, would he be here at all?

A rumble of thunder. A gust of wind blows the doors wide. Yuji gets up and pushes them shut. A minute later it starts to rain, heavily.

'There was a mudslide at a village in Shikoku,' says Kushida. 'A whole family buried alive. Did you read about it?'

'You'll need a car to get home,' says Father. He sends Miyo to call the garage. She hurries off. The phone excites her. (She would, she has confided to Yuji, like to work at the Central Telephone Exchange – she is already old enough – and demonstrated for him, in a voice she had found who knows where, how she would ask the caller, 'What number do you wish to be connected to?')

'Is it true your neighbour is back?' asks Kushida.

'Yes,' says Father. 'He was unfortunate enough to suffer an injury. A blister that became infected. They had to remove part of his foot.'

'An amputation?'

'Yes.'

'One can never really be safe as a soldier. Not out there, certainly.'

When the taxi sounds its horn, Kushida extinguishes his cigarette and pulls on the khaki jacket. 'Could Yuji take an umbrella out for me? If I use my own, it will drip in the car and the driver will grumble. They don't need much encouragement.'

Yuji selects an umbrella from among the dozen in the square pot in the vestibule, then waits under the porch roof for the doctor to finish his goodbyes to Father. When he comes out, they hurry across the garden, through the gate. The taxi's headlights are two converging cones of rain. At the door of the car, Kushida turns and says, 'A pity about your Frenchman.'

'My Frenchman?'

'Yes. What's his name? Fabien?'

'Feneon?'

'Feneon, of course.'

'Has something happened?'

'A little visit from the authorities.'

'What sort of visit?'

'Oh, I don't have the details. It was the Higher Police, I think, the *Tokko*. A colleague at the hospital in Kanda mentioned it. I thought you might be interested.' He opens the door, lowers himself onto the seat. 'I noticed tonight how much healthier you are looking. The way you ate your food was hardly like an invalid, was it?'

He shuts the door. His shadow leans towards the driver, then the car moves off, cautiously, into the dark.

12

When Feneon opens the door, he looks, thinks Yuji, like a man who has sat up all night reading some weighty, some impenetrable volume, something that exhausts both eyes and brain. He scans the street, then reaches out, takes Yuji's arm, and draws him inside, shutting the door behind them.

'You should not be here,' he says. 'It is perfectly likely they have someone watching the house.'

'If so,' says Yuji, 'it must already be too late.'

'Who did you hear from?'

'An acquaintance of Father's. A man called Kushida.'

'Kushida? I don't think I know him. Though I am remembering now what I was perhaps foolish to forget. I mean how visible I am. Any foreigner.' He is speaking French to Yuji but uses the Japanese word for foreigner – *gaijin* – filling both its syllables with a still-raw anger. Then he shuts his eyes, breathes, opens his eyes, and leads Yuji to the doorway of the salon, pausing there for him to take in the room's chaos.

'It's the same all over the house. Thank God Alissa was away.'

'She's away?'

'Yes. Somewhere safe.'

'But she knows?'

He shakes his head. 'It was only two days ago. And with things as they are it might be better if she remains in ignorance.'

He goes through to the study. Yuji follows, unable for the moment to tell if he is relieved to find Alissa absent again or disappointed.

'I made a start in here. Put the desk drawers back, began to collect the papers they scattered, but after a few minutes I felt like poor Sisyphus with his rock. They took the projector. They seemed delighted to have found it. And the films too, of course. I hope they watch them. Who knows what effect a dose of Chaplin might have on those horribly rigid minds.'

'It was the *Tokko*?'

'Oh, yes. All plain clothes and the sort of swagger that comes from not being answerable in the usual way. Not being required to explain or excuse anything.'

For half a minute Yuji joins him in a defeated silence then, roused by pangs of shame that he, a Japanese, is inescapably implicated in this desecration, this act of the horribly rigid minds, he asks, firmly, that he be allowed to put the house in order again.

'To clean up? I suppose we might do *something*. I can hardly leave it like this, eh? And I don't think I shall be seeing Hanako again.'

'They detained her?'

'No, no. In fact, I had the impression she was not at all surprised to see them. A question of loyalties, no doubt.'

They begin where they are, lifting the Buddha back to his niche by the door, furling the antique scrolls, setting the dragon pipes in their rack again. The books, as Yuji gathers them reverently from the floor, seem, in the trembling of their pages, to possess some knowledge of their recent treatment. From one of them, a Maison Gallimard edition of *Anna Karenina*, a piece of lilac paper flutters to the floor. When Yuji picks it up it's obviously a letter. He passes it to Feneon, who scans a few lines of the small precise handwriting and shakes his head.

'Not the one you were hoping for, I'm afraid. This is from a young woman I met before the war. The last war.' He holds the letter out between two fingers. 'Put her back with Anna and Vronsky. She's been in there so long they must all have become good friends by now.'

They are nearly two hours in the study. The salon, more spacious, less easy to ransack, is dealt with more quickly.

'Can you believe that they searched the stove?' says Feneon. 'Perhaps they expected to find the charred remains of secret documents. One of them even took a photograph of it. I'm pleased to report the stove maintained a heroic silence.'

When the last lamp is righted and the crystal fragments of a broken eau de vie glass have been swept onto a sheet of newspaper and carefully wrapped, they go to the bottom of the stairs.

'You won't have been up here before,' says Feneon. 'That painting is of Sézanne. The very street I was born in. This house here. You see? I looked through those windows as a child without the slightest idea there might be a place in the world called Japan.'

They go into his room. In the daylight it is less plain, less sparely furnished than it appeared the last time Yuji saw it. At the foot of the open wardrobe is a man-thick heap of shirts, and sprawled beside them, like a shot ghost, is the goose-grey smoking jacket.

'This they also photographed,' says Feneon, nodding to the bed. 'Really, when you think of it, it was the behaviour of lunatics.' With his sleeve he rubs at one of the brass orbs on the footboard as if to remove from it the smudge of a policeman's fingerprints, then he grimaces and presses at some stiffness in his neck. 'I'm too ancient for this kind of trouble,' he says. 'Let's do Alissa's room and then I'll investigate the kitchen. See if I can find us some lunch.'

They go to the end of the corridor. Feneon opens the door wide. The light in there, pouring through a mesh of fine lace, is softer, dimmer, paler. If, thinks Yuji, following the Frenchman inside, if he turns and looks at me now, will he not see everything, know everything? But Feneon does not turn. He is reaching over the bed, smoothing the bedding, the quilt of ivory satin.

There are clothes on the floor. Yuji is not sure if he should touch them, but fearing stillness, how it might betray him, he scoops up an armful of silks and linens, and briefly, as he inhales the scent his pressing releases, his behaviour of that night, of the following morning, of all the nights and mornings since, seems like the actions of a man impossible to respect or like, a small-natured man whose timidity has made him cruel.

'They wanted to take these,' says Feneon, crossing to the dressing table and tidying the photographs. 'I told them they would have to take me away with them. It seems they were not quite ready for that.'

He lifts one of the pictures and holds it out to Yuji. 'Recognise anyone?'

'Who could I recognise?'

'The child?'

'The face is so small . . .'

'It's Alissa! The girl holding her was one of our servants in Saigon. When we came to leave she was inconsolable. You would have thought she was losing one of her own.' He stares at the picture, then puts it back among the others. For a count of three, four seconds, he keeps his face averted. 'We're worn out,' he says, at last. '*Epuisé.*'

They go down to the kitchen, a room that seems not to have held much interest for the *Tokko*. Feneon finds two eggs and puts them in a pan to boil. Yuji slices a large *nashi* pear left ripening on the windowsill. 'And look,' says Feneon, 'half a loaf from the last decent bakery in Kanda. They bake for the Russian priests at the cathedral. I wonder what will become of *those* gentlemen.'

Rather than eat in the dining room, they sit at the little knife-scored table in the kitchen. They share a bottle of beer, clink glasses, though neither of them suggests a toast. When they have finished, Feneon sits back and wipes his lips, delicately, with the fat of his thumb.

'Now,' he says, 'it's time for you to leave, my friend. You have been very kind but I should not have let you stay so long. Is your bicycle at the front?'

Yuji nods.

'You can go through the garden. There's a gate behind the rose bush that leads into an alley. The gate is stiff but it works. The alley will take you back to the street. Don't wait around. Just ride home. You understand? I'll find some way of letting you know if I have to go away. We won't lose each other. And tell the rest of them. No visits, for everyone's safety, until this fever is over.'

They go to the kitchen door. Feneon pulls the bolts, opens the door cautiously and looks out.

'The gate is straight ahead. You see? And when we meet again I expect you to have written a poem or two.'

'I will try,' says Yuji, taking the other's proffered hand, feeling his own disappear into that large, dry grip.

'Shall I give your regards to Alissa?'

'Please.'

'Go quickly now. Be very careful.'

'And you, monsieur.'

Their hands part. Yuji, unsure if he is supposed to run or if running would simply draw attention to himself, begins to stride across the lawn. He does not look back, and as he passes the early afternoon shadows under the magnolia tree, he hears the sound of the kitchen door being shut again, shut and bolted.

13

He is squatting under the bulb in his room sewing a button onto a shirt. It's midnight. A week has passed since he went through the gate behind the rose bush, a week since he cycled home, wind tears and tears of shame in his eyes. A week in which he has been left to wonder if his rashness – that blind eagerness to demonstrate his loyalty – might not have brought much closer the day his own house, his own family, will be visited by 'the horribly rigid minds'. It is not hard to picture them, a gang in tight-fitting suits, chrysanthemum badges beneath the lapels of their jackets, rousting Mother from her room, harrying Father from his bed or his study. (And if he saw one lay a hand on Mother, grip her roughly, insult her perhaps, would he have the decency to attack that man?) He has even considered whether Kushida, knowing that his information would send him running down to Kanda, was setting a trap for him. Is that possible?

He is lost in these thoughts, biting the taut thread with his teeth, when he hears his name being called from the street. Once. Twice. A pause. Then a third time – a yowl like a cat on heat. He turns off the light, pads to the window. There are no cars out there, no crop-haired strangers under the lamps. Anyone at all? Did he dream that uncanny voice? Then he sees a movement, something crawling from the shadows outside Otaki's, a creature of some sort, certainly not a cat, more like a giant turtle dragging itself out of the sea. It moves towards the house, stops, looks up, a man now, a man suddenly, his face livid with the glare of the lamp. Then the voice again, that anguished cry.

At the bottom of the stairs, Miyo is sat erect in her bedding. No sign of Father yet, no Haruyo. He pushes on a pair of sandals, the first his fingers can find, and runs through the garden to the street. Kyoko is already out there, and behind her, at an embarrassed distance, Otaki, carrying the crutch and gabbling about how Mr Kitamura was most insistent, and really, what else could he do but keep serving him, a veteran after all, a distinguished veteran.

Saburo is lying, perfectly still, on his back, but his eyes are open, and when he sees Yuji he smiles. 'Comrade! Knew I could count on you. Knew *you* would come.'

He shakes off his wife, stretches up, clutches Yuji's hand (almost pulling him over), hauls himself onto his one and a half feet, breathes deeply, looks briefly victorious, and immediately collapses to the ground again. A second attempt is more successful. He wraps an arm round Yuji's neck, and the four of them, wedded to the drunken man's movements, teeter towards the old woman's gate. A dozen times Saburo stops to rage about the bastards who 'butchered him', or to ask, urgently, if Yuji remembers so-and-so from school, the kid with the big ears, or the one who cried a lot, or the one who, for half a sweet-bean cake, drank his own piss.

Grandma Kitamura is waiting for them with a lantern and a blanket. She tries to drape the blanket over Saburo's shoulders but he shrugs it off, irritably. 'Look,' he says to Yuji, touching the tabard he is wearing, the padded cotton waistcoat written over with what, by the lantern light, Yuji can now decipher as verses from the Lotus Sutra. 'Without this I would have been killed a hundred times. A thousand! "Oh, Buddha of sublime nature and unequalled power" . . . Go to bed, Granny. You' – he points at Kyoko – 'heat sake. We have a guest, in case you hadn't noticed. An old friend has called.'

'Would it be better to sleep now?' asks Yuji, softly. 'After all, we could talk in the morning. We—'

Saburo tightens his arm round Yuji's neck. He laughs. 'I can't hear a word you're saying.'

In a room at the back of the house, Kyoko puts out two sitting cushions, switches on the electric *kotatsu*, which immediately gives off a strange smell of burning. Yuji has not been in this room for years. The matting is frayed, the paper screens split and taped, the alcove, apart from an empty vase, bare.

Saburo sits, dragging Yuji with him. For a moment Saburo seems to lose consciousness, but then he looks up, shakes his head like a dazed boxer, and takes the unsmoked half of an army-ration cigarette from behind his ear. He gives Yuji the lighter, cups Yuji's hands in his own, and several times comes close to setting his eyelashes ablaze. In front of them, the damaged foot is on show, wrapped in a pinned sock. Kyoko brings in the sake. She pours, and puts the flask on the *kotatsu*. As she stands to leave she glances at Yuji, quickly shakes her head. He does not know what it means. A warning of some kind? (Get out as soon as you can!) Or is it to tell him that the bruise beside her eye, the greenish shadow the powder cannot entirely hide, is not there because Saburo has learnt anything of the game they have played these last months, his idle pursuit of her, her idle acceptance of it. Is that what she means?

The moment they are alone, Saburo begins to speak, and though he sways from the waist and the nicotine-bright fingers round the cigarette are not quite steady, his voice come from a place the alcohol has not touched. Cannot touch, perhaps.

'This,' he says, his forehead almost grazing Yuji's cheek, 'will happen to you. Don't bother fighting it. There's nothing you can do.'

'Do?'

'When you come back, they won't know you. They won't *want* to know you. They won't want to touch you.' He draws on the cigarette, holds the smoke down, then lets it seep past his gritted teeth. 'When I got my papers in '36, they were still training soldiers properly. January to May at the depot, and not just square-bashing. We were cobblers, tailors, armourers, cooks . . . I could strip down a Nambu and build it again in the time it would take you to eat a bowl of rice. A Japanese soldier had to know how to do everything! Fire a grenade-launcher? Yessir! Dig a latrine, read a map, march through the snow when you can't feel your feet? Yessir! These days they give them a uniform and pack them straight off on the boat. Half of them still seasick when they get to camp. Real specimens! Worse than you, Takano. City scum. Village idiots. Can't march, can't fight. It's left to us, NCOs, senior privates, to train them, and the only thing worth teaching them, the only thing we have *time* to teach them, is how to kill. Know how you do that? Eh? You get yourself a dozen Chink prisoners, line up the training squad, tell them if anyone looks away they'll get their teeth knocked in, then pull out the nearest prisoner and stick him in the belly with a bayonet. The army bayonet is the

Meiji type thirty. It is fifteen and a half inches long. Chinks are mostly skinny as you. Stick them right and you get eight, ten inches of steel out the other side. That's what we want to see, we say, though in fact we're usually trying not to piss ourselves laughing at the sight of their faces. Then the sergeant asks for a volunteer. And guess what? There's always someone who wants a go, some mama's boy who suddenly realises what he wants to do in life is jab a man in the guts. They all do it in the end, even the ones who look more scared than the Chinks they're sticking. The next day when you line them up, they're different. They've changed. There's no going back then. It's like . . .' He reaches out a weebling hand for his sake but the cup is too far away. He gives up.

'Now, taking heads,' he says, 'that needs a bit of skill. Use too much force and you'll make a mess of it, have them running all over the place like a chicken. Just keep it nice and calm, get the prisoner to kneel in front of you, pour a little water both sides of your blade, swish it off, lift the blade high, breathe out, breathe in . . . let it fall. Do it properly, you hardly feel the contact. Head pops off. Two big fountains of blood. Body tumbles into a hole. You wipe your blade, try not to look too pleased with yourself. Officers have the best swords, of course. Old family swords, or ones they've been given as graduation presents. Beautiful, some of them. They don't get knocked out of shape like an NCO's blade. You can keep chopping for as long as you've got strength in your arms. I knew a pair of captains, decent sorts really, family men, who had a competition to see how many heads they could take in an hour. When they'd finished, they had themselves photo-graphed standing by a mound of Chink heads, like it was some office golf tournament. You've heard of the "Three Alls", Takano?

Seize all, burn all, kill all. That's the army's motto. Seize all, burn all, kill all. And don't tell me it makes any difference who you were before – if you were educated or you could hardly write your own name. The educated ones can be the worst, like when I was up in Shunsi Province. What a shit-hole that is. Me and Yasumizo escorting a pair of Chinks to the hospital. No idea who they were. Big one might have been a communist, had that look about him. The other was probably just some peasant they pulled off the fields to make up the numbers. Anyway, we took them along to the hospital and when we got there they said we were in the wrong place. Have to go to the school next door, they said. Gave us a funny look. Well, we went over there. Just an ordinary middle school but they'd set up a kind of operating theatre in one of the classrooms with a sign on the door that said, "Training". The hospital director was there, a smug bastard called Nishimura, and a colonel from the medical service, and about six doctors, just arrived from the home islands by the look of them, all hoping to impress the brass. Anyway, we handed over our prisoners. The big Chink lay down on the bed without any trouble, but the other, the little one, he starts crying at the top of his lungs. "Ai-ai-ai-ai!" One orderly was pulling him, another pushing, but he was stronger than he looked and he knew what was coming. In the end it was the nurse who got him on the trolley. She could speak a few words of Chinese, and though she was only young she talked to him like she was his mama, patted his hand, nodded and smiled at him right until the moment one of the doctors rolled him over and gave him a jab in the spine. Tell you the truth, I'd have been happy to go then, have a smoke outside, but when you're a soldier no one cares what you want. You're not even a human being any more. Just a tool. Pick up, put down, throw away. So we stayed, me and

Yasumizo, in a corner of the classroom, scruffs from the infantry. "Now, then, gentlemen," says the colonel, "shall we start with the appendix?" I remember that. *Shall we start with the appendix?* Like he was ordering something at a restaurant. Well, those doctors must have been hungry 'cause they jumped to it. Ever seen an appendix? Doesn't look like much. Sort of thing you might use for fishing bait. Then they really got busy. Cut off the little peasant's arms, made a hole in the big Chink's throat. They were all chatting away, and when one of them made a mistake, got his nice white coat splashed, they all looked at each other and laughed. They cut off the Chinks' balls. I don't know what for. Science, I suppose. At the end of it the little peasant was good and dead but the other one was still breathing, a sort of "heh, heh, heh" noise. The colonel ordered one of the doctors to inject air into his heart but that didn't work so two of them tried to strangle him with a piece of string. I couldn't understand why they didn't just cut off his head. They'd cut off everything else and it wasn't like they didn't have enough knives in there. Then this old non-com medic, you know the type, bows and says, "Honourable doctors, if you inject him with anaesthesia, he'll die." So they do it and he dies and they all go off to wash their hands and have a drink while me and Yasumizo put what's left of our prisoners into a pit in the old playground. A big moon that night. The pit was as big as your garden. Stank like a tanning factory . . .'

From between his fingers the long-since-extinguished cigarette tumbles to the mat. He whispers something, some unintelligible protest, then at last falls silent, his weight pressing more and more heavily against Yuji's shoulder. After a minute the door slides open. The women come in. They have the bedding with them and swiftly, speechlessly, as though it has now a familiar routine, they lift the sleeping man and lie him in it. The old woman starts to undress him. Yuji follows Kyoko out of the room. She comes with him as far as the street gate. 'He's ill,' she says in a whisper. 'The wound keeps opening. Those things . . . Please, pay no attention.'

'You've heard them?'

'He's ill,' she says. 'And when he drinks . . .'

'You think they're not true?'

'True?'

'The stories?'

She shakes her head. 'I have to go in,' she says. 'I have to go in now.'

'You'll be needing this,' he says, taking the crutch from where Otaki has left it propped against the gate. He hands it to her as tenderly as he can, as though it was a spray of plum blossom. She thanks him, clutches it across her breasts, and scurries inside.

14

'What did he want?' asks Father, coming from his room and stopping Yuji at the top of the stairs the following morning.

'I don't know,' says Yuji. 'He was drunk.'

'I see,' says Father, 'Hmm.'

Yuji waits. Is that it? Can he go? He does not want to repeat what he has heard, to say (standing in the morning shadows at the top of the stairs) that their neighbour is an expert in decapitation, or that Japanese doctors in China behave like the criminally insane. Whatever Kyoko might wish to think he is sure the stories are true. Saburo hasn't the imagination to invent such things.

'He's brought it back with him,' says Father.

'What?'

'The war.'

'Yes.'

'I pity him.'

'Yes.'

'I never liked him, but even so.'

'Yes, even so.'

'To lose both parents while still a child. A hard beginning.'

'When you were in the army, Father . . .'

'It was 1913. There was no war.'

'I know. But what did you do?'

'Tried not to die of boredom.'

'That's all?'

'Studied when I could. Played a lot of *shogi*.'

'It wasn't so bad, then?'

'Stay on the right side of Kushida, Yuji. I'll do what I can.'

'Thank you.'

'Ishihara's group. Can they help you? I imagine they have better connections than I do. Now, at least.'

'You would approve of me accepting their help?'

Father starts down the stairs. 'I might,' he says over his shoulder, 'prefer it to having you howl in the street at night. Your mother certainly would.'

15

The money from Hideo Makiyama has dwindled to a handful of small change. The screenplay, which one day might bring him a hundred yen or more, is just a single sheet of paper with a single unfilmable scene about a boy flying to the heart of the sun. The last handout from Grandfather went on new boots for the coming winter. As for the banknotes Uncle Kensuke pressed into his hand at the station, he cannot account for them at all. Books? Beer?

It is time to see old Horikawa again, to sit at the window, look at trains and drink coffee. After his efforts to write 'something exalted, something delirious' he should have no difficulty scratching a few lines in praise of shipping companies or toothpaste. He sets off for Hibaya, cool early October sunshine on the back of his neck, but when he reaches the building and walks up the broken wax tiling of the stairs, the office door is shut and locked. There is no sign on it, no 'Back in an hour' or 'Closed for reasons of ill health'. He goes down to the repair shop, calls a greeting, steps inside. The shop is a nest, a densely packed hive of bicycles – new, old, wheels on, wheels off. They even hang from the ceiling, clusters of them suspended from hooks. He calls again, gets no reply. The concrete floor is dotted with flowers of oil. Behind a curtain at the back of the shop, an infant is wailing, methodically. He goes back upstairs, writes a note on a scrap of paper and slips it under the door, then, with nothing better to do, he eats under the railway line, an elbow-to-elbow place where every time a train rumbles overhead the surface of his broth breaks into delicate ripples.

After eating (and it's true what Kushida said, his appetite is better these days, he *is* healthier, so much so he has once or twice seriously considered taking up smoking), he walks to the park and squats on a grass bank beneath a maple tree to read the paper. The delegation who signed the pact in Berlin have arrived home. Prince Konoe and senior members of the government have expressed their gratitude. The Fifth Division has entered Hanoi. The people there have welcomed them as elder brothers, though in the photographs the people are just shapes in the margin, out of focus. The back page of the paper shows a woman modelling the new monpe trousers at the Matsuya department store. The trousers are a synthesis of fashion and the national will. They are elegant, perfectly modest, but leave the legs free for the physical labour all sections of society must now be prepared to take part in . . .

He folds the paper, discards it at the first bench he passes, and returns to the building. The office is still locked, and now, downstairs, the steel grille of the repair shop is shut and chained. Is there some local holiday? A neighbourhood *kami* of good profits, a Buddha of low taxes to be venerated? He looks at his watch. Almost half past three. On Tuesday afternoons the Montparnasse in Asakusa shows half-price double-bills of British, French or

American films. If he can get there in time, then the day will not have been wasted. He scribbles another note to Horikawa, hurries to the stop opposite the Imperial Theatre, takes a cross-town bus to the Kannon Temple, then jogs the 500 yards to the cinema.

'Make the most of it,' says Mr Suzuki, the manager of the Montparnasse, sitting in his white suit in the ticket booth. 'From now on I'm just showing *jidaigeki* pictures. Noble warriors, women with no eyebrows, lovely costumes . . .'

'Haven't you said that before?' asks Yuji, wheezing from his run, and looking past the manager's head at the posters for *Stagecoach* and *Pépé le Moko*.

'I mean it,' says the manager, snipping Yuji's ticket from the roll. 'This foreign stuff will get me shut down. Or worse. The next time you see me I'll have a samurai topknot. You'll think I'm one of the Forty-seven Ronin.'

In the little auditorium thirty, perhaps forty customers are waiting on seats of frayed green plush. A few couples, but mostly men on their own, amateurs of cinema – some in uniform – who find at the Montparnasse what the sushi *tsu* find at Kawashima's. Yuji takes a seat at the end of a row halfway back. There is a short wait while Suzuki moves from the ticket booth to the projection room (they can hear his footsteps, his weary tread on the stairs), then the newsreel begins – trumpets, eagles, a spinning globe. They stand for the Emperor, sit again, polish glasses, light cigarettes, and bend towards the screen, lean like divers at the edge of a glittering pool.

Three hours later, sated, they file outside, blinking in the blue and gold of early evening. Yuji loiters at the kerb, his atoms dispersed between the deserts of New Mexico and the labyrinth of the Kasbah. He is staring, with vacant intensity, at a board outside the confectionary shop on the other side of the narrow street. There is a painting on the board of the seasonal delicacy 'autumn comes to the treetops', and he is wondering what Ringo Kid – a man who gallops through treeless landscapes – might make of such a delicacy (would he buy some for a sweetheart?), when a customer, a woman, a slight figure in a blue and white kimono, comes out of the shop and stops directly opposite him.

'Mr Takano?'

'Mrs Yamaguchi!'

'What a surprise to see you here.'

Students on bicycles glide between them, then two taxis full of young geishas, *shamisen* cases on their laps. He crosses the street. She waits for him, neat as a doll, in her hands a box of sweets wrapped in paper decorated with autumn flowers – dahlias, amaranths.

'I was at the cinema,' says Yuji.

'The Montparnasse?'

'Yes.'

'What a nice way to spend the afternoon. What did you see?'

He tells her ('Gabin is a favourite of mine,' she says), and then, to defend himself against the charge no one has made, the accusation that he is the sort of young man who spends the day in cinemas instead of taking part in the physical labour even fashionable woman are preparing for, he gives an absurdly detailed reprise of his day – the failed search for Horikawa, his inability to find even the mechanic who would surely have been able to tell him where Horikawa was – an account she listens to intently and with just the faintest smile on her lips.

'And the dance school?' he asks, blushing and scowling at the paving stone between their feet.

She thanks him for his kind enquiry. It is not, she explains, a time favourable to an enterprise such as hers, but she has been able to keep a few of her older students, the professionals mostly. The others, one by one, have dropped away. She was particularly sorry not to have Mademoiselle Feneon any more.

'Alissa?'

'We have not seen her since the rainy season, though she wrote a most polite letter. I hope her ill health is no longer troubling her?'

'She's away,' says Yuji, quickly.

'In the country, perhaps?'

'Yes. In the country.'

'For a foreigner she danced very well.'

'She did?'

'Oh, yes. You should have seen her dancing "Snow". Really, a quite unexpected poise.'

'I have heard her play the piano. When she plays Chopin, it's as good as the radio.'

Mrs Yamaguchi nods, amused again. 'I hope you find your business acquaintance,' she says.

'My . . . ?'

'The man you were looking for?'

'Oh . . . yes. Thank you.'

She bows and moves away, pigeon-toed, her dancer's back straight as a board above the immaculately tied obi. Then she turns – sinks it seems – into one of the alleys that wind like waterless streams down towards the river.

A polite letter? Ill health? What else did the letter say? And if Alissa was ill, why had Feneon not spoken of it? What sort of illness? A serious one?

He recrosses the street. Outside the Montparnasse a small queue is forming for the evening showing. Suzuki is in his booth again, scissors and tickets at the ready. And something – the white of his suit, perhaps – brings unbidden to Yuji's mind the Hitomaro lines Alissa recited in the moonlit study: 'One morning like a bird she was gone in the white scarves of death.'

And then? Something about a child, who cries for her, who she left behind . . .

He looks towards the alley where Mrs Yamaguchi disappeared. If he ran, he might catch up with her, stop her, question her. What she doesn't know she will be able to guess, a woman like her. Who *else* can he ask now that Feneon's house is forbidden to him? He bites his lip, stares as though staring would bring her back, draw her to him. Then he looks down, walks to the wall beside the cinema, and quietly takes his place at the end of the queue.

PART THREE

Yuji in The Year of the Snake

鳥

I go out of the darkness
Onto a road of darkness
Lit only by the far-off
Moon on the edge of the mountains.

Izumi

1

Meetings of the local neighbourhood association are held in Otaki's noodle bar, a familiar space – gloomy, savoury, endearingly scuffed – where nobody's intimate domestic life need be exposed to the curiosity of his neighbours. There has not been a meeting since the irises were in flower. Then – at the firm request of the Home Ministry – associations from Okinawa to Hokkaido, gathered to discuss how they might contribute more to the national struggle, what they might cut back on, what they could do without, how, in this particular hour of destiny, they might, somehow, be better neighbours to each other.

This evening's meeting, twilight, the second week of November, is also at the exhortation of the ministry. A new guide has been issued, a booklet with the imperial standard on the cover, and inside, in numbered paragraphs, a list of the duties all loyal subjects must be ready to perform. Through the neighbourhood associations (the national defence women's groups, the Great Japan youth associations, the patriotic workers committees), every man and woman in the home islands will be welded into a single disciplined force. Everyone will have his place. Everyone will wait on the Emperor's word, ready, should the order come, for the 'smashing of the jewels' – the final sacrificial battle. There's a new slogan, the winning entry in a competition run by the *Asahi* newspaper. 'Abolish desire until victory!' Associations could, if they wished, shout this heartily at the conclusion of their meetings. Such behaviour, the booklet suggested, was in the interests of everyone.

Yuji, who has been delivering cigarettes to a beer hall in Shibuya with Mr Fujitomi and the blue Nissan, is the last to arrive. He nods his apologies to his neighbours, takes his place beside Father.

'You saw him today?' whispers Father.

'Yes.'

'And?'

'Sonoko says his appetite is improving.'

'And his movement?'

'Not yet.'

The men are ranged around a long low table at the back of the restaurant. Otaki, Itaki, Ozono, old Mr Kawabata, Mr Kiyama the wedding photographer, Father, Yuji. Saburo is at the top of the table, his crutch angled against the wall behind him. He is, apparently, in full uniform. He has a medal on his chest, the Wound Medal (Second Class). Of the others, three of them – Itaki, Otaki and Mr Kiyama – are in civil defence jackets. Behind the curtain, in the kitchen, Otaki's wife and sister are preparing refreshments for the end of the meeting. The only other woman present, kneeling in the obscurity by the door, is Grandma Kitamura.

'I suppose,' says Otaki, clearing his throat, 'we should make a start?' He glances at Father, the disgraced but still august professor of law, a man to whom the procedures of meetings must be almost second nature, but Father keeps his gaze on the tabletop.

'It's been a long time, hasn't it?' says Otaki, and laughs with embarrassment.

Yuji looks over at Saburo. Saburo is staring at him. Yuji looks away.

'It seems,' continues Otaki, doubtfully, 'we have to make some decisions?'

'An auspicious day for it,' says the wedding photographer.

'Indeed,' says Itaki, reverently inclining his head. 'The two-thousand-six-hundredth anniversary of the Empire!'

'Have you seen the pavilion outside the palace?' asks the photographer.

Yuji has seen it through the window of the Nissan. An immense and lavishly decorated tent, the centrepiece of the week's celebrations, radiant in the November sunshine. Crowds of police, crowds of soldiers . . .

'All the big ones will be there,' says the photographer. 'Prince Konoe, General Tojo, Admiral Nagano . . .'

'Imagine the food,' says Itaki, sighing. 'Though they say the Empress will never open her mouth in public.'

'I've heard that myself,' says the photographer. 'The thought of such modesty moved me greatly.' He straightens his back. His face takes on an expression of awed contemplation.

After a respectful interval (briefly disturbed by Mr Kawabata excusing himself and tottering away towards the toilet), Otaki holds up the ministry booklet. 'There's quite a lot in it,' he says. 'I was quite surprised.'

'The most important thing,' says Itaki, whose civil defence jacket is obviously home-dyed, and recently too, for some of the dye, a curious dun colour, has rubbed off on his wrists, 'is to elect a block captain. No?'

The wedding photographer nods vigorously. Yuji has heard nothing of this. A block captain? He scans his neighbours' faces, seeing, on at least three of them, the nervous smirks of schoolboy conspirators.

'When you think about,' says Otaki, 'it should be someone with experience.'

'I agree,' says Itaki. 'But someone with the *right* experience.' He looks at Saburo and grins.

'And a cool head,' says the photographer. 'Wouldn't that be important?'

'Certainly,' says Otaki, now, like the other two, casting shy glances at the lounging figure at the top of the table.

'Professor Takano,' drawls Saburo, watching the smoke of his cigarette flowing in slow blue waves from between his outstretched fingers, 'is the most educated man here . . .'

Father looks up. 'Quite impossible,' he says, addressing Otaki in a voice that invites no further discussion.

'Is it a position for a younger man?' asks Otaki, flustered.

'Perhaps you are right,' says Saburo. 'In which case, the professor's son would be a good candidate. Isn't it true,' he says, smiling at Yuji, 'that you're a few months younger than me?'

'It's true,' says Yuji. 'But I wonder if my experience is really suitable.'

'The difficulty,' answers Saburo, 'is knowing what your experience really is.'

The photographer giggles.

'His experience,' says Father, 'is more varied than you might imagine. How many of us here, for example, can speak another language, fluently, as Yuji does?'

'Is it Chinese?' asks Saburo, jutting his head forwards. 'Chinese is the language he'll need soon.'

Mr Kawabata returns from the toilet. 'Hardly a drop,' he mutters, knee joints cracking as he takes his place on the mat. 'And yet I felt I needed it.'

'But what about *you*?' asks Itaki, bowing and addressing Saburo as 'honourable soldier'.

'Wouldn't you consider it?' adds Otaki.

'We would really feel we had the right person,' says the photographer.

'Aren't you forgetting something?' asks Saburo, one finger tapping the Wound Medal.

'But you move around like a cat,' says Itaki.

'Really, it's remarkable,' says Kiyama.

'The truth,' says Saburo, 'is that my vote was going to be for Mr Ozono. He has made the greatest sacrifice. Shouldn't we show our appreciation of it by offering the position to him?'

Ozono blushes. 'Like the professor,' he says, 'it would be quite awkward, at this moment, to accept such a responsibility. If I still had Kenji to help in the shop, but . . .'

'You're the perfect choice,' says Itaki to Saburo. 'Don't you see?'

'I don't know,' says Saburo. 'There may be some people here who think I'm not up to it.'

'Eh? Everybody has the greatest confidence in you,' says Otaki, glancing eagerly around the table.

'Everybody?'

'Please,' says Itaki. 'You must let us insist.'

'It's embarrassing . . .' says Saburo. He waits. Is he counting off the seconds? Then he sighs as though some great burden is being lowered onto his shoulders. 'But if you are going to insist, what can I say except I will try to serve you and His Sacred Majesty with all my strength. Just as I did in China.'

'So you'll do it?' asks Otaki.

'Abolish victory until the final desire!' cries Mr Kawabata, his eyes tightly shut, his cheeks trembling with emotion.

Yuji looks over to the door. The old woman has leaned into the light so that it hangs in a yellow veil across her face. Seeing herself observed, she settles back on her haunches, steals her smile back into the shadows.

By eight thirty, swept along by a wave of satisfaction that the matter of the appointment (this irksome new post no honest tradesman could be expected to waste his time on) has been handled with the necessary deftness, all other business – saving deposits, sanitation, liaison with community councils, comfort bags for the troops – is dealt with easily. Otaki summons his wife. She comes in with a steaming earthenware pot of fat white udon noodles. The sister brings in the sake. They drink to the anniversary of the Empire, to the health of the imperial family, to the army, to the navy, to the homeland. They tilt back their heads and sing the neighbourhood association song ('A sharp tap, tap from the neighbourhood asso-ci-ation! When I opened the lattice gate, there was a fa-mi-liar face!') The photographer begins a story about a young couple he photographed the previous week in Shitaya, but no one, it seems, can understand whether the story is intended to be sentimental or lewd.

Father begins to push himself up from the mat. 'If you will excuse me . . .'

'Before we finish,' says Saburo, 'let me thank you again for your confidence in me.'

'Not at all,' says Otaki. 'It's we who must be grateful.'

'I am a soldier,' says Saburo. 'I think like a soldier.'

'That's exactly it,' says Itaki.

'Soldiers don't put off what needs to be done,' continues Saburo. 'They do it straight away.'

'Like photographers!' cries the photographer, his face blazing from the drink.

'So I have made a rota . . .'

'A rota?' asks Otaki, quietly.

'For fire-watching,' says Saburo. 'Other rotas will follow. I will post them on the gate of my house. Everyone will make it his duty to read them at least once a day. There can be no excuses.' He pauses to put on his cap, to carefully adjust it. 'The honour of taking the first watch I have awarded to the Takano family. It is now nine twenty. Deployment will commence at nine forty-five.' He uses the wall to gain his footing, takes the crutch and leaves with the old woman. The door slides shut. The chimes jangle. The men keep their eyes lowered. Otaki bares his teeth at the table, makes a kind of sucking noise. After a few moments his sister, very discreetly, begins collecting the dishes.

At nine fifty Yuji is in his greatcoat on the drying platform, a woollen muffler wrapped over his skull and knotted beneath his chin. On his right sleeve he wears the armband Saburo gave him at nine forty-five, a white band on which Kyoko or the old woman has embroidered the character for fire. He has also been issued with a wooden rattle and a whistle on a length of string. At ten o'clock Miyo brings him tea, then he is alone again. Father will relieve him at two o'clock but two o'clock is a long way off. He sniffs, dabs at his nose, punches some warmth into his arms. One by one, with a soft metallic sound, the big orange leaves of the gingko tree are falling. He starts to pace, then stops and creeps to the platform parapet. Something is moving down there. One of the cats? He leans over, squints. A torch beam bursts against his face.

'Don't let me catch you sleeping,' hisses Saburo, a voice without a body. 'Don't ever let me catch you sleeping!'

The light clicks off. For half a minute Yuji is blind, then the night patiently reassembles itself. The tree, the far-off flickering of 'Jintan Pills', the undulating roofs, the decorative rake of searchlights above the palace. And finally, untellable at first from the fragments of beam at the backs of his eyes, the stars in their vast garrisons, glistening in the brittle air.

2

In the heart of the Low City, a man is lying under the front of a blue van. Only his legs are visible, two stout legs and a pair of feet in split-toed canvas boots. A small crowd has gathered, the sort who will stop to watch two birds fighting over a worm. Yuji, raw-eyed after three shifts on the platform in the eight nights since the meeting at Otaki's, is kneeling at the side of the boots trying to decide whether he should mention the policeman who, at a policeman's leisurely pace, is making his way past the line of traffic behind the van. What do they have in the back today? Radio valves, two or three sacks of charcoal, some light bulbs, a case or two of Korean brandy . . . How interested would a policeman be in such things?

The legs are stirring. 'Give me a pull!'

Yuji grips the canvas heels, leans back his weight. A stocky, moon-faced, middle-aged man appears, Grandfather's neighbour, Mr Fujitomi.

'Try her now.'

In the cab, the ignition is a button on the floor. The first time Yuji tries it the engine rasps, sputters, dies. He tries again. This time it fires.

'Tough as tanks,' says Fujitomi, jumping up beside Yuji and using a sheet of newspaper to wipe the oil from his hands. 'You could drive one of these all the way to Moscow.' He swings shut the door. The policeman's face floats in the wing mirror. Fujitomi frowns. 'Let's go,' he says. 'The river. Nice and gently.'

After Grandfather's illness, that event in the middle of the night that had left him for a few hours paralysed and barely able to call for help ('It was,' said Sonoko, 'like the cawing of a bird'), Mr Fujitomi had made several neighbourly visits, each time bringing with him some little luxury – a half-dozen Californian lemons, a parcel of good tea or, on one occasion, a box of pharmaceuticals that Grandfather's doctor had assured them were no longer available – and on each visit he sat for an hour by Grandfather's head to listen, carefully, to the unintelligible sounds he made. On the third or fourth of these visits he found Yuji in the vegetable garden, prodding tentatively at the dry earth with one of Grandfather's hoes. He had laughed at him, told him the garden would take care of itself until the spring then – after a pause in which he seemed to study Yuji carefully, to weigh him up – added that his son, Tamotsu, had received his red paper a month ago and was now with the Thirty-fifth Regiment somewhere in central China.

'I hope he comes back soon,' said Yuji.

'You're supposed to offer your congratulations,' replied Fujitomi, 'but I too hope he comes home soon. Tell me something. You know how to drive?'

An hour later, on land at the back of Fujitomi's house, Yuji was at the wheel of the blue Nissan receiving his first driving lesson. Driving, so it turned out, was quite a pleasurable activity. It was not even that difficult, as long as all he had to avoid was a few trees.

'Tamotsu was my driver,' explained Fujitomi. 'And I have no other sons. Perhaps you could fill in for a while? Unless you have something better to do. There's money, of course. You won't be short.'

'You want me to drive for you?'

'Pick-ups and deliveries.'

'That's it?'

'Pick-ups and deliveries. No heavy work.'

There was one more afternoon driving circuits round the cedar trees, then early the following morning, a light mist on the road, they set off for the centre of Tokyo. Somehow – and even Fujitomi's imperturbability was tested – they survived the near-miss with the bus in Akasaka, the many near misses with angry cyclists, the terrifying moment when Yuji came within the width of a sandal from reversing into a canal in Kyobashi.

They picked up – sacks, boxes, sealed cases, crates, barrels. And they delivered – to hotels, to large houses, to the backs of businesses, to men who, looking somewhat like Mr Fujitomi, handed over grubby bundles of yen. Of these, at the end of the day, Yuji always received his share. By the first week of November, he could, had he wished it, have eaten at Kawashima's three nights a week. He could even have afforded the Snow Goose if there had only been someone to take there. He forgot about Horikawa, about scribbling for a living. He found it amusing, though slightly disconcerting, that money could be made so simply. Pick up, deliver. Pick up, deliver. No heavy work.

*   *   *

At the river (the engine has cut out twice more and twice more Fujitomi has crawled between the wheels), they cross at the Ryogoku Bridge. Their next collection is in Honjo, somewhere deep among its web of wires and chimney shadow. They pass temples, slums, little chaotic factories, then pull up beside a gate in a blackened wall. Yuji sounds the horn.

'Got a new boy?' asks the man who unlocks the gate.

'Helping while Tamotsu's across the water.'

'The Thirty-fifth, isn't it?' asks the man. 'Not a bad outfit. Long as he keeps his head down.'

Under his coat – a civilian coat of black and white twill – the man is in puttees, breeches, a tunic with five brass buttons down the front. So too are the men who load the van. It's not the first time in his new work that Yuji has seen this, and though Mr Fujitomi has offered no explanation, none, perhaps, is required. Rice, fuel, tobacco – even items like paper and soap – the army has them in abundance. All over the city there are depots, all over the country, soon, perhaps, all over Asia, each barracks, each camp, a new outlet, a fresh business. Is *this* what war is about? Not abstract concerns like racial destiny but the making of more and more money? A yen block to counter the dollar block, the sterling block? It is a view of things Yuji is not accustomed to, not yet. The soldiers, Mr Fujitomi, the likeable, practical men they meet in yards who snap open crates with a crowbar, who drag tarpaulins, who do impressive sums in their heads, seem part of a different system, a kind of parallel circuitry that has no more to do with sacrificial battles than it does, say, with poetry.

The last job (a customer for the Korean brandy) is finished an hour after dark. Half an hour later Yuji drops down from the Nissan outside Grandfather's gate. 'Give the old fellow my regards,' says Fujitomi, sliding across to the driver's seat. 'You're staying the night?'

'I have duties at home,' says Yuji.

'More of this fire-watching nonsense? Someone needs to sort that crank out.' He pulls the day's takings from the pocket of his coat, peels off the outermost note, passes it through the window. Yuji reaches up, takes the note between his fingers. There is something about the *feel* of this kind of money, money that does a job, that keeps itself busy. Some of the notes are worn soft as antique cotton. Crushed in the hand, they do not crease.

'Until tomorrow, then!'

'Until tomorrow.'

Grandfather is in the eight-mat room, a buttressing of small cushions around his hips, a slate-coloured blanket over his shoulders. Sonoko is beside him, holding a bowl of tea, or something medicinal perhaps. On the other side of the brazier, Father, looking both bored and anxious, is smoking a cigarette. When Yuji comes in, Grandfather says something, then says it again.

'Yes,' says Yuji, hoping he has made sense of those knotted sounds. 'It was good business today.'

Grandfather nods, smiles a lopsided smile.

Sonoko shuffles to the brazier, busies herself with the kettle.

'There's a train at quarter past,' says Father, dropping the end of his cigarette onto the coals. 'If we want to catch it, we should leave soon.' He sits up, kneels formally. 'Will you be all right?' he asks the old man. 'One us could probably stay if you wished it. And please remember the doctor will be here at nine tomorrow. He will want to take some blood. And please, give some consideration to my suggestion. The garden room in Hongo could be made most comfortable. It goes without saying that Sonoko would be welcome to accompany you.'

Grandfather is waving an arm, angrily. He is saying something angrily. Father blinks at him, confused for a moment. 'Noriko . . . ? Yes. Please do not concern yourself. I will take care of Noriko.'

'You want to do the first shift tonight?' asks Yuji as they follow the path through the garden.

'It would be better for you to have it,' says Father. 'And I'll come an hour earlier. Your rest is more necessary than mine.'

'I wouldn't say so.'

'Of course it is.'

'I'm only the driver.'

'Driving requires concentration.'

'I quite enjoy it.'

'You'll get to know the city.'

'Yes.'

'Fujitomi seems a decent sort. Though it may be he sails a little close to the wind . . .'

'It's just pick-ups, deliveries . . .'

They are passing the old rickshaw. In the dark under the tree it is almost invisible, the faintest gleam from the painted wheels.

'You think the story about the actor is true?' asks Yuji.

'What? Dragging him all the way to Kyoto? I used to think it wasn't. Now, well . . . perhaps he did it after all.'

'Yes, I think so too.'

'By the way,' says Father, 'before you came, he was trying to say something about *building* a rickshaw. And something about the Bank of Japan? I had no idea, but Sonoko seemed to think you would know what it was about.'

3

One Sunday every month, for as long as Yuji can remember, he and Father have sat in their nightrobes at the table in the Western room to eat a Western breakfast. Rice, fish, natto and green tea are exchanged for bread rolls and coffee, *kasutera* cakes, smoked ham, cheese cut from large, waxy blocks. Almost all of it was bought from the German delicatessen on the Ginza. Now, without any discussion between them, they have stopped going there. Was it the fall of France? The bombing of the English cities? The rumours (they are barely more than that, little muffled stories carried in the remnants of the liberal press) of what, under the smoke of war, might be happening to the European Jews? So they have lost the peppercorn salami, the Jarlsberg, the paper-thin slices of Black Forest ham. Even the last of the coffee, Lohmeyer's house blend, black as loam, has been abandoned, and today they are drinking another coffee, a lesser coffee, taken from a case with army markings in the back of the blue Nissan. There is no cause to complain, however. Having coffee at all makes them more fortunate than most, and *kasutera* cakes are still only ten sen a piece, sometimes less.

On the table, yesterday's newspaper lies open at a photograph, something quite artistic, of a soldier in silhouette, his arm flung back in readiness to hurl a grenade at the unseen enemy. Looking at it, Yuji thinks of Fumi Kihara and the giant match ('Do you need that more than he does?'). Father is reading the journal of the Japanese Archaeological Society ('Techniques for the Dating of Cultural Artefacts in Pre-Kofun-era Sites'). From somewhere in the garden, somewhere among the neatly etched shadows, comes the agitated twittering of sparrows.

'I wonder what it will be?' says Miyo, arriving from the street, her cheeks bright with cold.

'What what will be?' asks Yuji.

'The reason,' she says.

'The reason?'

'For going,' she says. 'The reason for going.'

Father lowers the journal, takes the cigarette from his mouth, and looks at her over the top of his glasses. 'What are you talking about?' he asks.

'The notice,' she says.

'On the Kitamuras' gate?' asks Father.

She nods.

'A new one?'

She nods.

'What does it say?'

'You have to go there at noon.'

'Today? Yuji, you better have a look.'

It's ten forty-five. Yuji finishes his coffee, dresses. The notice – this one in red ink – employs the same semi-official language as the others, and commands all members of the neighbourhood association and the women's defence group, to report to the block captain's house at twelve o'clock, Sunday, for a demonstration.

'Even soldiers get Sunday off,' mutters Itaki, reading the notice over Yuji's shoulder. 'At this rate we might as well all volunteer. Oh, by the way, Mrs Otaki says you can get sugar . . .'

'I'll ask,' says Yuji.

'And flour?'

'I'll ask.'

'We should have made you block captain,' says Itaki, turning back towards his shop. 'I said it all along.'

Promptly at noon they file into the Kitamura house, fifteen men and women, shuffling along the corridor of beaten earth behind Grandma Kitamura. Because the nature of the demonstration has remained a mystery, some of the neighbours are dressed formally as if for a visit to a government office, while others have put on overalls, boots, headscarves. They pass through the house and out into the garden. In the pond, under the dirty gold of its surface, Yuji glimpses the mottled back of a carp. Saburo and Kyoko are waiting at the bottom of the garden. Kyoko is wearing a pair of monpe trousers. They are not as elegant as those worn by the model in the newspaper. They make her legs look shorter, her hips broader.

Saburo is in a white military work tunic. He has a pickaxe over his shoulder. He starts shouting at them while they are still some distance off. He tells them they are on the front-line now, that they must develop the Yamamoto spirit, that the enemy could arrive at any time, right here, in Tokyo. 'That sky,' he bawls, pointing, 'could turn black with enemy planes. We have to get ready for that! We have to get ready *today*!' He glares at them, sucks in a

250

deep breath, steadies himself, throws down his crutch and raises the pickaxe. After a dozen swings he looks round at Kyoko. 'What are you waiting for?'

She starts to dig, tipping out with her shovel the ground he has broken. 'You, too, Granny,' says Saburo, roping together the two halves of an entrenching tool.

The neighbours neither move nor speak. The digging is very slow. After half an hour Mr Kawabata has to sit. An hour passes. The sweat drips from Saburo's nose. He swings and falls, gets up and swings again. Kyoko, in her baggy trousers, shovels dully, competently, as if through a dung heap on her father's farm. After two hours they stop. The old woman's face is violently flushed.

Saburo addresses them again. 'Trenches! Every household! Trenches to shelter in! Takano family, you have the biggest garden. You will set an example by digging the biggest trench. The deepest. Now go home. And remember, if you don't want to roast, you better dig!'

Yuji helps Mr Kawabata to stand. Mrs Kawabata, wearing her women's defence sash, is quietly weeping. 'We'll just have to roast,' she says, once they have reached the safety of the street. 'Old people like us won't have a chance anyway. Excuse me,' she says, 'for saying something improper, but I hope it happens soon. After all, it's not much to look forward to, is it?'

The neighbours, avoiding each other's eyes, turn away to their houses.

Up in the sewing room, mid-afternoon, a woollen jacket over his knees, Yuji is allowing himself to drift towards sleep. Now he has the fire-watching, the days in the blue van, sleep is something he would like to store up, to have a reserve of to set against a future scarcity, for it seems inevitable now that he and everyone else is entering a time when they will peer at the world through the smoke-glass of an inassuagable fatigue. He lets the book (*Les Fleurs du Mal*) slide from his grip, lets his chin drop towards his chest, sighs, and sees, in the lasts instants of consciousness – the first, perhaps, of dreaming – a sun-cleaned image of Kyoko shovelling the earth in her garden, while the young cat, the absurdly named Foreign Girl, limps over the grass towards him.

When he wakes, coming to suddenly in the twilit room with no sense of how long he has slept, he feels oddly calm, sober and calm, as if, in sleep, some old difficulty has found an unexpected resolution, though what difficulty, what resolution, he cannot tell himself. He is stretched there, willing the moment to go on a little longer, when he hears noises from outside, from the garden, and turns his head sharply towards the platform door. He listens for a second, then scrambles to his feet, opens the door, and goes onto the platform. Saburo is leaning over the fence (what is he standing on?). He is leaning over the fence and shouting at Father.

'You think I should come over and dig it for you? Are you afraid to get a blister on your hands? This is a final warning! If the trench is not started before nightfall . . .'

And father says something back, a low voice, a slow voice. Whatever it is he says it leaves Saburo speechless.

Yuji hurries down the stairs, slips at the turn, bounces down the last few steps, almost knocks over Miyo. He meets Father at the door of the Western room. 'Please excuse me,' he says. 'I ought to have started it. I will start immediately.'

He goes into the kitchen. Haruyo is steaming tofu for Mother's evening meal. The look he gives her, loaded with rage, visibly unsettles her. He takes the lean-to key from its peg beside the door and goes out to the narrow path (the tradesmen's path) that runs between the kitchen and the spindle hedge. He unlocks the lean-to. The air in there still tastes of summer, preserved somehow around the blades of tools, in the heat-warped wood of cobwebbed shelves. He chooses a mattock and walks through the garden holding it across his hips like a rifle. He should ask for Father's advice, of course, for his instructions, but he starts to dig near the old pine stump, hacking at the ground until, after ten minutes, the muscles in his back begin to spasm. He crouches, brow against the mattock's haft, cools off, then starts again, a slower, less angry rhythm that stops only when he can no longer clearly see his feet. If he is going to continue, he will need some light, and he is crossing the garden to fetch a lantern when Father summons him from the open door of the garden study. They go inside together.

'I was just fetching a lantern,' says Yuji.

'Listen to me,' says Father. He pauses. 'I have phoned Kensuke. I have told him of our situation. I have told him I am no longer certain of my ability to protect your mother. Her tranquillity.'

'You're going to the farm?'

'We will take the express on Wednesday.'

'Wednesday!'

'Tomorrow I will go to Setagaya. I will explain things.'

'And me?'

'You?'

'You wish me to remain here?'

'For us all to leave would draw . . . unnecessary attention.'

'I see.'

'I have an obligation to your mother.'

'Yes.'

'If we stayed. If something happened . . .'

'When will you return?'

'That will depend. Not, perhaps, until after the New Year. Do you need money?'

'No.'

'It may be easier for you when we have gone. I regret that we have not been able to help you more.'

'I have been a burden to you . . .' says Yuji, mechanically.

'You seem to be managing well enough these days.'

'With Mr Fujitomi?'

'You may end up a man of business, like your grandfather.'

'It seems unlikely.'

'Yes. Perhaps.'

'It's a long time since Mother travelled,' says Yuji.

'Yes,' says Father. 'Quite a long time.'

The window is a narrow rectangle a degree or so less utterly dark than the book-lined blackness of the study. Father has almost disappeared, can be seen only peripherally, as certain remote objects in the night sky are seen, by not looking at them directly. Again, they have come to the edge of a conversation, that long-postponed confessing that would begin – and either could begin it – with the words 'After Ryuichi . . .'. It might have freed them once (these two who have taken a certain pride in *not* speaking), but now, it seems, the time for it has passed. They have changed. They have been changed. Between them, the tilt of circumstance is quite different.

254

In the room the air is peppery against the lining of Yuji's nose. He sniffs, dabs his nostrils with a finger. 'The Wednesday express?' he asks. For all he can see of Father, he might as well be speaking to himself.

4

Yuji is in the first car with Mother and Father. Haruyo and Miyo and most of the luggage are in the car behind. As the cars arrived late (held up by some parade in Iidabashi) and loading them took longer than expected, Father is fidgeting with the shirt cuff above his watch and scowling at the back of the driver's head.

Yuji cannot take his eyes from Mother. How strange, how extraordinary to see her with the common light of day washing over her face! She smiles at him, but when the movement of the car jolts them in their seats she shuts her eyes as if in pain. She ought, thinks Yuji, to travel in a palanquin, or like an heirloom doll, wrapped in tissue paper inside a cedar box. How will she manage the train? And then another hour of driving, the twisting ascent to the farm on roads that at each sharp turn become rougher and narrower, more track than road? He is afraid for her, but feels too a flickering excitement, as though they were all setting off on a family outing, a trip to view the chrysanthemums at Dangozaka, a restaurant by the river. Even to the *kabuki* . . .

At the station, two elderly porters help them with the luggage, leading the way, puffing and calling briskly for room. The Kyoto train has almost finished boarding. At the windows, little parties, or single men or women are readying themselves for the awkward moment of farewell. The porters carry the cases inside. Father and Haruyo follow them up the steps. On the platform, Yuji and Miyo wait with Mother. Miyo is shaking with sobs. Mother murmurs to her, their heads close together, but the girl can neither look up nor reply.

Father climbs down from the train. 'There's not much time,' he says.

Mother takes his arm. She turns to Yuji. 'I will be thinking of you,' she says.

He nods. 'I will be thinking of you also.'

They look at each other, the ghost and her son, as if they were alone together. He hopes she cannot see the fear that has taken hold of him, the wild certainty that once she has stepped onto the train he will never see her again, that she will die (fade to nothing), or he will die (in some shell-hole in China). Father and Haruyo help her up the steps, almost carrying her. As soon as she is inside, the porters jump down and swing the door shut. A ragged ball of smoke rolls down the carriage roofs. A minute later the whole train shudders, rocks backwards, and begins, with the appearance of immense effort, to creep along the platform. Father struggles with the compartment window, forces it open. 'I will inform you of our arrival,' he says. Is that what he says? He can hardly be heard, hardly, in the sudden flow of steam, be seen. Yuji waves to him, then, in a gesture stolen from the cinema screen – *Hotel du Nord*? *The Citadel*? – he lifts his peach-bloom trilby from his head and holds it high until the last carriage is lost in the sunlight of midday and there are only the shining rails, narrowing and curving into the distance.

At the house, Miyo follows him like Asako's daughter. She looks at him with anxious, childish glances, while all around them the empty rooms give off some low electric hum of absence. They go from room to room. Surely, if they are patient, if they listen hard enough, they will hear a voice, the scrape of a wooden sole on the verandah.

He opens the doors to Mother's room. Everything in there – the sitting cushions, the red lacquer table in the alcove, the folding screen with its birds and willows, the not-quite-cold brazier – seems subtly unfamiliar, as though two hours' abandonment has remade them into not-quite-perfect replicas of themselves. From habit he looks for his brother, but the photograph and the cross have gone, leaving only their shadows on the sand-coloured wall.

He walks out of the room, slides shut the screens. He will not go in there again. He tells Miyo to put on warm clothes, clothes she can work in, then goes upstairs and changes into a pair of old trousers, an old pullover. She is waiting for him by the bottom of the stairs. He looks at her, manages a smile, and wonders what will become of her, how well she will survive these coming times. If his red paper arrives – and who is to say it will not come tonight? – she cannot remain in the house on her own. Would she want to go to Kyoto? Or back to her family in the north, the poverty of a home she has not seen in five years? If she wanted to stay in Tokyo, perhaps he could arrange something at the telephone exchange. The young girls there live together in dormitories. She would make friends. Be safe? Safe at least from Block Captain Kitamura.

He collects the tools from the lean-to and leads her down to the pine stump. They work, one behind the other, digging as if the sky might indeed, at any moment, grow dark with enemy planes. By dusk, their faces streaked with black sweat, they are stood to their thighs in a crooked mouth of raw soil. Yuji clambers out, reaches down a hand to Miyo. They sit on the ground, panting, feeling the cold steal into them as their sweat evaporates. She starts to cry again. He does not know what to say. He waits, fingering the blisters on his palms, until her sobs are quieter. 'Are you hungry?' he asks. She nods, wipes her nose on her wrist. They leave the tools in the trench, walk slowly through the garden to the unlit house.

5

The professor's absence is quickly noted, becomes for a week the favourite subject of local gossip, particularly the fact that his wife, an invalid, a woman barely seen in years, has gone with him, along with that frightening maid of hers. To veiled enquiries Yuji makes veiled replies. To Saburo's veiled taunts he says nothing.

The season's cold intensifies. He begins to dread the nights on the platform. There is no one now to relieve him at two a.m, no mumbled exchange before sinking down into a dreamless sleep. Miyo would take a turn if he asked her to but he cannot (those thin arms, thin legs) find it proper to make such a request. So the nights are his own, an interminable bridge of hours, of tedium, of cold.

For his duty, this first week in December, he has put on so many layers of clothing his moon-thrown shadow on the outside wall of Father's room is large as a bear's. He does not know what the time is – to look at his watch would mean exposing a strip of skin to the air – but he knows (his growing familiarity with stars, with grades of darkness) there are at least four or five hours before the first streaks of the dawn. Too tired even to yawn, he leans against one of the drying posts, listens to the calling of owls, and lets his gaze carry him over roofs and ghostly radio aerials to where the red eye of 'Jintan Pills' blinks on, blinks off, blinks on, blinks off. Why, tonight, does the sign bring such odd associations with it? Lilacs, light on silver cutlery, an arm swathed in white and yellow stripes.

He peers into the Kitamura garden, his eyes picking between the shadows, then goes on stiff legs to his room and starts, with only moonlight to help him, to search for the jacket he last wore that day of high summer in the Azabu Hills. He finds it between two others, hanging from the beading, then finds, in the left-hand pocket, the half-dozen little pills Dick Amazawa dropped there. He puts one on his tongue, hesitates, then adds another. All he has to wash them down with is a mouthful of the Korean brandy he keeps in a corner of the platform to stave off the worst of the cold. He drinks, swallows, shudders, resumes his watch.

After fifteen minutes the blood directly under the surface of his skin begins to simmer. Ten minutes after that he is grinding his teeth and shuffling restlessly across the slats of the platform deck. Should he have taken just one of the pills? A half? Too late now. If he has poisoned himself, then this is how he will end, a heap of clothes in which a man is hidden, his face to the stars. He rocks on the balls of his feet, observes, with some fascination, the mist of his own breath as it trails past his cheek. The night is ticking like a clock. The moon gives off a hiss of distant burning. The desire to lie down, to sleep, has been replaced by an equally urgent desire to explain himself to someone, to justify, to lay out his life in a great flood of words . . . Should he wake Miyo? Is it time for another pill? One more pill and his body might be shocked into poetry! He might even understand what Amazawa wants for the Unit, what

Ishihara's vision of the future is. Death as a religion? Violent death?

He is standing there, tense with the effort of keeping up with his own thoughts, when the noise, the racket at the edge of hearing he has been hoping would simply fade away, becomes, instead, more insistent. Wooden clappers. A drum. He listens, strains to hear, hears, understands, but cannot quite believe it. He is fire-watching and somewhere – or so the noises tell him – there is a fire. A real fire! He scans the 150 degrees of his view from the platform. Nothing there, nothing at all. What is the procedure now? What is he supposed to do? Call Saburo? Use his whistle? He has not, he realises, paid much attention to the scant instructions he has received, nor has he read the recently issued government manual – other than to glance at the title (*Stay and Fight!*) – a copy of which is under a pile of newspapers on the dresser downstairs.

He goes into the sewing room again, fills his arms with books, and carries them outside. At the back of the platform, the roof slopes to chest height. He builds a step out of dictionaries and novels and clambers up. He has never been on the roof before. The tiles grate and shift beneath his weight. He starts to climb (not a bear any more but a giant slug), writhing over the tiles, the bird droppings, the tufts of grass, the glittering moss, until his gloved hands grasp the ridge and he pulls himself up the final inches. He sees the fire immediately – a small cloud of pulsing orange light somewhere up by Watanabe's bathhouse – and in his excitement he lets go of the ridge and descends chaotically, losing three buttons from his coat and landing on the platform, winded but unhurt, on the cushion of his own back. He gropes around his neck for the whistle, lets off three short blasts, drops the whistle, and runs through the house.

'Fire by Watanabe's,' he says to Miyo as he pulls on a pair of boots.

'Fire by Watanabe's!' he calls to Saburo, who swings from his gate, bellowing orders. He commands Yuji to stop, Yuji cannot, the little pills will not let him. He mounts his bicycle. His legs seem immensely happy to be peddling. He weaves, stylishly, around all obstacles. 'Fire by Watanabe's bathhouse!' he calls to whoever he passes.

After ten minutes he smells it, a waft of smoke, sour, fungal. He slows. The way now is filling up with drowsy neighbours, bedrobes under winter coats. They wander about, leaderless. He leaves the bicycle against the shuttered window of a shop, and runs, part of a pack of running shadows, the length of a last street.

Already, at least a hundred people have gathered by the building, though the noise of them is buried under the rushing and crackle of the fire. Such is the confusion, the rapid shifting of light and dark, it takes Yuji several moments, standing on tiptoe and craning his neck, to realise that the fire is not by Watanabe's, it *is* Watanabe's. He lets out a sound, a moan of surprise and sorrow. 'Did they escape?' he shouts to the woman next to him. She doesn't hear him, or doesn't know. From a shattered window a flame shoots out, dies back, then leans from the window beside it, a lunatic in a yellow bed sheet.

Someone passes him a bucket. He passes it on, slopping water over his boots. Someone else sees his armband, the character for fire. The crowd opens a channel, lets him through, pushes him forward. Soon, he is close enough to feel the heat prickling the skin of his face. In the distance he can hear the swelling chant of a fire crew, then a group of men jog past, not firemen but soldiers, cloths tied round their faces. Immediately, unthinkingly, Yuji follows them, runs after them like a boy in a game. They go into the alley at the side of the bathhouse – the side that seeps smoke rather than flames – and climb a flight of rusted metal steps to a door at the level of the first floor. The door is locked. The soldier at the front bursts it open with his boot. On the other side, Mrs Watanabe is sprawled on the mat, her small white feet twitching. Two of the soldiers lift her and retreat towards the alley. The others, Yuji at the rear, start, on hands and knees, to go up the stairs. The smoke above their heads is black, clotted. The stairs are hot to the touch, even through gloves. On one of the steps a hole the size of a horse's eye has burnt away (or was it always there? A peephole?) and Yuji has a fire-lit glimpse of the women's baths below, the water crusted with ash.

At the entrance to the upper room the curtain is fringed with small flames. They duck beneath it, blunder on, crawl as far as the passage to the kitchen but can go no further. A single searing glance through narrowed eyes is enough to show that this is where it started, that old Watanabe, whatever is left of him, will be sifted from among the cinders of his rattan chair.

'Watch out!'

At the back of the kitchen something ignites, explodes with a shriek, burns with a bright green flame. Frightened now, awake at last to the danger, this peril he has so casually put himself in the path of, Yuji gets to his feet, intending, with held breath, to run for the top of the stairs, but as he turns he trips across the end of a table, scattering the tiles of a last mah-jong game. For a moment he is stunned, and when he raises his head he can no longer see the others. He calls out, drags his aching chest over the mats. The room, familiar to him from countless visits, has become a puzzle, a maze. Is *this* where it ends? Not in a shell-hole, but a bathhouse a mile from his home? He circles, squints crazily into the confused air, the flame-dark, then sees, an arm's-reach to the side of him, a smudge of khaki. He stretches for it, touches cloth, flesh. A smoke-blackened face looms towards his own. Two eyes widen, blink. Stare. Yuji stares back, the pair of them, for a long second neither can afford, frozen in mutual amazement. Then the face looks away, and together, burrowing under the smoke, they find the top of the stairs. The house is roaring like a sea. They slither down, side by side, coughing and retching. Odd events take place in Yuji's brain, leisurely imaginings, sequences, serenely lit, from boyhood (there, at the edge of the sea, is his brother gathering clams in a bucket, there is Grandfather standing in the low tide, his *yukata* gathered about his thighs . . .)

Against his cheek he feels a gust of air. *Cold* air. A voice shouts, 'One more here!' His shoulders are seized. A man, a fireman, a wonderful stranger, lifts him to his feet. Then more hands, more strong arms, an effortless progress through the crowd until he is set down, gently, on the far pavement, his back against a wall. A canteen of water is pushed towards him. He drinks, coughs furiously, splashes water into his eyes. His coat is buttonless now. Patches of it are smouldering. He grips his throbbing head, spits between his knees. It's several minutes before he feels well enough to look at the soldier beside him. A minute more before he has the wind to speak.

'It's you?' he asks. 'It's really you?' His voice is half an octave deeper. To his own ears he sounds like Father. 'I can't . . . It's so . . .' He drinks from the canteen again but coughs as he swallows and spews up the water. 'Poor Watanabe,' he says, at last. 'Think Mrs Watanabe made it?'

Junzo is wiping his face with the cloth that masked his mouth and nose. When he has finished he climbs to his feet, tugs a field cap from his belt and puts it on a scalp shaved so close it's hard to see any hair there at all.

'I wrote to you,' says Yuji, rising dizzily with the help of the wall. 'I even tried to visit. When you were in Kagurazaka . . . Did the girl tell you?'

Junzo is walking away. From behind he looks like a drunk pretending, very hard, to be sober. Yuji hobbles after him. The movement of one of his knees is sharply painful. He tugs at Junzo's elbow. 'What?' he asks. 'What?'

Junzo shakes him off. Yuji grabs at him again, is shaken off a second time. The third time Junzo swings round. The punch is not hard and the aim is clumsy but it sends them both sprawling onto the pavement. Breathless, awkward as a pair of deep-sea divers, they wrestle feebly by the heels of the crowd.

'Have you . . . lost . . . your mind?' gasps Yuji, pinned under the other's weight.

'Keep away from me,' hisses Junzo. 'Stay away from me!'

'What are you talking about? What—'

The crowd lets out a roar of excitement, surges back, breaks like surf over the pavement. The bathhouse roof is giving way. The flames roil up, unfurl themselves triumphantly. There's a noise like a volley of rifles, then the main beam, burnt through, sunders at its mid-point and flies into the house, sending up two swirling plumes of sparks. Almost at once the fire is calmer. The crowd advances. Yuji looks for Junzo, summons the breath to call his name, then sees him, his back, already half a street away. He sets off after him, walking as quickly as his damaged knee will allow. By the time he is close enough to speak they have left the fire and the crowd behind them.

'What is it? What have I done?'

Junzo neither slows nor answers. Yuji knows he will not be able to keep up much longer, that he will, in another eight or ten strides, fall behind and lose him. Whatever he is going to do he must do it now. He moves closer, and with a surge of force, an acceleration made up in equal parts of fear and anger and the feverish chemistry of Amazawa's pills, he hooks an arm round Junzo's neck and drops them both into the dust. It's a schoolboy throw, a schoolboy trick. He clings on, Junzo's throat in the crook of his elbow. In the playground, this is when the captured boy submits, becomes, in defeat, sullenly amenable, but Junzo, writhing one way then the other, is already managing to loosen Yuji's grip. He frees himself and with eyes tight shut strikes out at Yuji's padded body until a bout of coughing doubles him up and the fight is over. Yuji stands – this long night of falling and standing – dusts down his ruined coat, then leans and silently offers the wheezing Junzo his assistance. His hand is pushed away, though not with any vehemence.

'I saw you,' says Junzo, when he too is on his feet again.

'Saw me?'

'I saw you come out of the Snow Goose. I saw you get into the taxi.' His voice is toneless. A voice for reporting facts one is weary of living with. 'I saw you both.'

'Saw?'

'I was outside the billiard parlour.'

'We'd been . . . to the *kabuki*.'

'You left the house at dawn.'

'You saw me *then*?'

'A neighbour. The woman from the fan shop. Told Hanako.'

'And Hanako told you?'

A nod.

'Why would she tell you that?'

'Because I asked her.'

'When?'

'What does it matter? I already knew it all by then.'

'Knew?'

'That you had abandoned her.'

'Alissa?'

'If you had cared for her, if you had stayed at her side, I could have accepted it . . . her choosing you. I would have found a way of accepting it. I would even have tried to be happy for you. But you abandoned her. So I started hating you.'

'This is insanity,' says Yuji, a protest that comes out sounding like a question. He is beginning to flounder. Something is happening to him. He is being swept away. Everything is being swept away . . . 'Is she sick?' he asks, suddenly. 'I met her dance teacher in Asakusa. Mrs Yamaguchi. She said she'd had a letter.'

Junzo laughs. The laugh becomes a cough. He spits, swipes the drool from his lips. 'Sick? I don't think it's usually called a sickness. Can you really be as stupid as you sound?'

In the upstairs room of the house to the side of them, a light comes on. A shadow moves the other side of glass and paper. The seconds pass. The light goes off.

'She wanted to show me a picture,' whispers Yuji. 'She was explaining something.'

'You abandoned her.'

'She was trying to tell me . . . who she was.'

'And you abandoned her.'

'Please. Wait. You know where she is?'

A headshake.

'And Hanako?'

'No.'

'Who then?'

'Who?' Junzo's face lights up with a smile of utter misery. 'Who do you think?' He shivers. He has no coat, only his khaki tunic. 'You've always been blind,' he mutters, starting to shuffle away. There is no question of Yuji following him this time. He tries to remember where he left his bicycle. He remembers the pleasure of riding it. It seems to have been months ago.

'If you had said,' he calls, his voice loud as a dog's bark in the hush of the street, 'If you had said you loved her . . .' And though he cannot be certain at such a distance, cannot be sure through his bloodshot eyes, it seems that his friend, nearing the unlit corner, falters in his stride and stumbles against nothing.

6

He wakes with a taste of ash in his mouth, smoke and ash. Slowly, reluctantly, he opens his eyes to the light on the ceiling, then turns to where Miyo is kneeling beside him, a piece of sewing in her hands (the same piece she has pretended to be working at ever since Mother and Father left for Kyoto). When she sees him looking at her, she smiles excitedly.

'You're like a hero,' she says. 'Everyone knows about it. Even Mr Kitamura must be impressed!'

'Kitamura . . .' mumbles Yuji, then shuts his eyes again. He has aches, mysterious zones of pain, but no fever. He is not even particularly tired.

'The doctor is coming,' she whispers, leaning over him so close he can feel her breath on his face. 'The honourable doctor . . .' And immediately, as though he has been listening outside the door, waiting for his cue, Kushida appears. Glasses, moustache, leather bag. Large pale hands.

'So how is the young master of the house?' he asks, standing above the bed, the padded shoulders of his civil defence jacket outlined by the light coming through the platform door. 'It turns out you are the type who quite unexpectedly shows initiative. Even a sort of courage.'

'Do you know about the old woman?' asks Yuji. 'The bath-house-keeper's wife?'

Kushida makes a movement, a small gesture involving eyes, fingertips. A gesture to signal indifference. 'I don't believe,' he says, 'we should keep you away from the army much longer, do you? You should be storming an enemy machine-gun post rather than the local bathhouse. The public baths, by the way, are not at all hygienic. A tremendous source of contagion. If every bathhouse in the city burnt down we would be much the healthier for it.'

He bandages Yuji's swollen knee, dresses the burns on his left wrist, his left ear. 'Should I send the bill to your father? When can we expect to see the professor again?'

'You can send it to me,' says Yuji, sitting, then easing himself up from the mattress. 'Or if you prefer it I can pay you now. If you could wait downstairs? Miyo will bring you some tea.'

For the remainder of the day, of daylight, Yuji stays inside the house. When he moves he leans on a stick, a curious varnished black ornamental walking stick Father brought back from his tour of Europe and which for years – all the years of Yuji's life – has stood among the umbrellas in the pot in the vestibule. He has attacks of coughing, spits black phlegm, blows black mucus from his nose. How has he survived it all? What does his body want of him? He puts on the radio but after an hour could not have told anyone what he has been listening to. Saburo calls. Yuji has already instructed Miyo to say he is too unwell to receive visitors.

He drinks a cup of sake but finds, to his disappointment, he has no appetite for a second. At six o'clock he sends Miyo to Otaki's for noodles. They eat. She steals glances at him, looks of wonderment. Later, he bathes, sitting in the water with his leg raised to keep the bandages dry. After the bath he starts to shake. This gives him some comfort, some hope. Now, perhaps, he is about to fall ill, to lie dangerously ill for weeks, and then, of course, a long convalescence during which the world will simply right itself. What can be expected of a man too weak to hold a cup to his lips? He goes upstairs, crawls under his quilt, prepares to descend to the familiar confusion of fever, of the blood in riot, but the shivering stops. He cannot even sleep, cannot get close to it. He gets up, dresses, limps down the stairs and tells Miyo he is going out. She stares at him as if expecting news of another fire, then squats by the vestibule step to tie his laces. He waits, stands awhile, watching from the half-open door. He can hear Itaki in conversation with someone. When the voices cease he turns up his collar, pulls down the brim of his hat, and lurches to the gate.

It takes him forty minutes to reach the tram-stop. He's sweating. The pain in his knee has made him nauseous. On the tram he wonders if the other passengers, seeing him, his age, assume that his limp is a war wound. He gets down at the stop before the cathedral, walks under its immense shadow, then enters Feneon's garden by the gate behind the rose bush. The moonlight that lit his view from the platform last night now lies in a tangle of bones below the bare branches of the magnolia. From the house he can see no sign of life at all. He presses his face against a window – the only one unshuttered – and sees over the salon floor a thin stain of electric yellow that comes, must surely come, from beneath the study door. He taps on the glass, taps again more loudly, keeps tapping until the light suddenly swells and a figure appears, pauses, then comes cautiously forwards. Yuji lifts off his hat, shows himself, but it is not until the Frenchman's face is almost touching the glass on the other side that he recognises him, frowns, and points towards the kitchen door.

The moment Yuji is inside, Feneon slides home the bolts. The kitchen is several blocks of minimally variegated black. There is a smell of the food cooked earlier that evening. Grilled meat? Grilled chicken, perhaps.

They go to the study. The lamp with its green shade is the only source of light. On the big desk there are scattered sheets of writing paper, a fountain pen laid at the side of a half-written-over sheet.

'You've had an accident?' asks Feneon, leaning against a corner of the desk and looking at Yuji, at the black stick, the dressing on his ear.

'A fall,' says Yuji. 'My knee. It's not serious.'

'Sit,' says Feneon. He points to the armchair at the side of the desk. Yuji sits. He is not quite sure where to put the stick. In the end he holds it across the top of his thighs, gripping the wood in his fists. 'So,' says Feneon, 'what's this all about? I assume it must be important.'

Yuji nods. He has, in the few hours he has been at liberty to do so, forbidden himself to imagine the details of this moment. But now it has come he is seized by doubts. Is it possible he misunderstood what Junzo was saying? That Feneon will think he has gone mad? That the study door will open and there will be Alissa, unaltered? He plants the end of his stick on the floor, levers himself up. He has not misunderstood. The door will not open.

'I saw Junzo last night,' he says, addressing a cedilla of faded blue tapestry in the rug between them. 'He informed me of . . . a certain fact. It concerns your daughter.' He lifts his gaze. There is a not quite convincing expression of gentle bemusement on Feneon's face. 'Her situation,' says Yuji.

'Her situation?'

'Her difficult situation.'

'I see,' says Feneon. 'Yes. I see.' He rubs his knuckles softly over the burnished wood of the desk. 'Heaven knows how Junzo learnt about it. This city is even worse than Saigon for keeping secrets. I should have known it was pointless . . .' He shrugs. 'Though with half the world on fire and the other half about to catch, it begins to seem almost unimportant. What people think. What they know. I pity the poor child, arriving at such a moment.'

'The child?'

'Isn't that what you're talking about?'

'Yes.'

'You are enquiring as a friend, I suppose. Yes. It's quite proper . . . Well, let me assure you she is being well looked after. There is no need for any concern. As for her plans, what she intends to do *afterwards* . . .' He wafts the air. 'She is, as I'm sure you have noticed, a rather independent young woman.'

'I am glad she is well.'

'Oh, yes. Physically quite well.'

'And . . . the child's father?'

'What about him?'

'She has told you his name?'

For a moment it looks as if Feneon will refuse to answer his question. Then he moves his head, a sort of bridling. He shrugs again. 'She has not,' he says.

'Nothing?'

'Why? Are you thinking of challenging him? I doubt he's the sort of man who fights duels. That would require a certain sense of honour on his part.'

'But if he didn't know?'

'Know?'

'About the child.'

'You think that's likely? Anyway, it's the not-caring that matters. The not-caring one way or the other. I think we know the type of man who does that. There are names, are there not?'

'Names,' whispers Yuji. 'Yes . . .'

'You better sit down,' says Feneon, 'before you fall down. You don't look well at all. Shall I fetch you some water?'

'I just wanted to say,' says Yuji, switching now to the refuge, the audacity, of his own tongue, 'I just wanted to say that I am the child's father.'

'What?'

'The child's father.'

'Who? Who are you talking about?'

'I . . . Alissa . . . I am the father.'

There is a long pause, then a bark of laughter. 'You?'

They stare at each other. On Feneon's face there is a look of utter blankness. Then the blankness is replaced by a mask of astonishment. Not for an instant, not for a single instant, has Feneon imagined anything as impossible as Yuji being what he now claims to be. That much is clear. What is also clear, what has flashed from those grey eyes so plainly, so unguardedly, is the reason for such incredulity. Yuji is Japanese. He is a yellow man. A native. The daughter of a European gentleman might have such a person as a friend – it would almost be a mark of her breeding – but *more* than that?

'It was me,' repeats Yuji, tonelessly. Then, his face in a spasm, he shouts it in French. *'C'était moi! C'était moi! Je suis le coupable!'*

On the little finger of Feneon's right hand he wears a ring with a stone in it, a bevelled garnet of some sort, a semi-precious. It is this that opens Yuji's lip. He falls backwards, is caught by the chair, and sits there, dazed, watching spots of blood fall in dark irregular splashes onto his coat. After a moment he focuses on Feneon's hand holding out a handkerchief. He takes the handkerchief, presses it to his mouth. In the quiet between them the house moves through its repertory of small sounds, the fizzing of the lamp, the settling of boards.

'It's true?'

'Yes.'

'Not some idiotic fancy of yours?'

'Fancy?'

'One of your stupid ideas. Not true.'

'It's true,' says Yuji. 'It must be true.'

'*Must* be?'

'It's true.'

'It happened here?'

Yuji nods.

'Here in the house?'

'You were away.'

'So you sneaked in like a thief.'

'Yes,' says Yuji. 'Like a thief.'

'I used to keep a pistol in this desk,' says Feneon. 'You should be very happy that I no longer do.' He sits, seems momentarily lost, then pulls a clean sheet of paper towards him, unscrews the cap from the pen, writes three lines and tosses the paper onto the floor by Yuji's feet.

'Can you read it? It's where she is. In Yokohama. You will go there tomorrow or you will never see Alissa or myself again. It goes without saying that you would never be permitted to see the child.'

Yuji stands. He does not know if his lip has stopped bleeding. The handkerchief is heavily stained, probably ruined. He folds it, hiding as much of his blood as possible, then reaches out to leave it on the edge of the desk.

'No, no,' says Feneon, 'I don't want it back.'

7

The house whose address is scratched in large, angry letters on the piece of paper is a rambling foreign-style building on a quiet avenue high on the Yokohama Bluff. Brown shutters, a first-floor balcony with white wooden railings, a three-storey wooden tower, a small clock above its two upper windows like a mystical eye. On a board beside the porch a sign in English and Kanji reads, 'The Bullseye Piano Academy. Lessons by appointment only.' Across the windows of the ground floor, heavy, wine-red curtains have been drawn.

Yuji pulls the bell (a kind of stirrup on a chain), hears a remote jangling in the house's interior. He waits. No one comes. His heart is beating so hard that he has, after a minute, to turn away to catch his breath. He rings again. Another minute, then the door slowly opens and a face peeps out, young and blonde with dark eyes.

'You delivering?' she asks.

'Delivering?'

'We're not open for hours.'

'I was hoping to visit someone . . .'

'Do we know you?'

'Miss Feneon?'

'Who?'

'Alissa?'

'Everyone's in bed.'

'Ah. I'm sorry.'

She nibbles the edge of a painted fingernail, examines him, this handsome, somewhat battered young man, then steps out of sight and swings open the door. 'You can wait if you want. Miss Ogilvy will be down soon.'

The room he follows her into is large enough for a public dance. Certainly, shadowed by the curtains, it looks grand enough. She tugs a braided cord at the side of one of the windows, lets in enough of the morning to wake the mirrors and bring a glow to the gilded frames of the paintings – pictures of women beside pools of water, women in gowns on day beds, women combing out their hair. In the centre of the room is a billiard table, two cues laid side by side across one of its corners. There are no pianos.

'I'm Sandrine,' says the girl, sitting herself up on the ledge of the table. 'It's funny how you've both got sticks. You and Alissa.'

Her Japanese, though comprehensible, is thickly accented. She is wearing a robe of pale tangerine and on her feet a pair of yellow slippers that curl extravagantly at the toes.

'This is Miss Ogilvy's house?' asks Yuji.

She tilts her head. 'You don't know much, do you.'

'Are you a pupil here?'

'A pupil?'

'At the academy?'

'What academy?'

'The piano academy.'

279

'Oh.' She taps the curls of her slippers together, smiles at him. 'I'm very musical.'

She brings him, unrequested, a glass balloon of brandy. He has seen these glasses before but never drunk from one. For herself she has a smaller glass of something green, then perches again on the billiard table and tells Yuji about a great-uncle of hers who had both legs amputated in a war with the Austrians.

'That must be difficult for him,' says Yuji.

She laughs as though he has said something extremely funny, then immediately stops laughing and slides off the table.

'This is Alissa's friend,' she says to the woman silhouetted in the doorway.

The woman looks at Yuji, nods very slightly in response to his bow. 'Yes,' she says, 'I was warned to expect you.' She turns to Sandrine, addresses her in a language Yuji can only guess at. Russian, perhaps. Turkish, Farsi. The girl hangs her head, answers meekly, then hurries from the room, scuffing the leather soles of her slippers and leaving the little glass of green liquor behind her.

'I won't have them drinking in the morning,' says the woman. 'I would be grateful if you did not encourage it. They do not need much encouragement.'

Yuji apologises. It is, in the circumstances, easier to apologise.

'Can you speak English?' she asks.

He tells her he cannot.

'French, presumably?'

'Yes. Some.'

'I am Miss Ogilvy,' she says. 'I speak six languages, including, self-evidently, your own. By birth I am a citizen of the United States of America. Battle Creek in Michigan. It is a place you will not have heard of.'

'I would like to visit America,' says Yuji.

'Have you travelled at all? Have you ever been outside Japan?'

'Unfortunately,' says Yuji, picturing to himself the map in Horikawa's office, the black lines sealing the coasts, 'that has not been possible.'

'Yet I am informed you have pretensions to being a writer. A writer, even a Japanese one, must surely travel, if only for the stimulus of disappointment.' She scoops up a silent grey cat from the rug between her feet, strokes it with her wrist. She is taller than Yuji, thin, very upright. Her hair is of a kind that does not exist in Japan, fine and finely crinkled, brown, auburn, dyed. She is certainly old enough to be Sandrine's mother.

'Very well,' she says. 'Let us talk of the matter in hand. You are here to see Alissa.'

'Yes.'

'You are her friend.'

'Yes.'

'You are the one responsible for her condition.'

'I . . . Yes.'

'The baby, in Dr Saramago's estimate, will be born two weeks from today. On this occasion I happen to agree with him, though babies are not trains. They do not arrive according to a timetable.' She watches him with her small, brazen eyes. 'What do you know about babies, Mr Takano?'

'Know?'

'Do you, for example, like them?'

'Hmm. It's quite difficult to say.'

'I don't see it's difficult at all.'

'It's only . . . I have not met many.'

'Babies are everywhere. You do not need to be specifically

introduced to one. I wonder,' she says, 'if you have the stomach for this. Being afraid, of course, is not itself a disgrace. Your life is about to be altered in a manner you apparently did not expect it to be. You will be a father, and whatever arrangement you come to with Alissa, that will remain inescapably the case. The question, then, is this: are you sincere?'

'Sincere?'

'In your wish to be here. In your intention to behave with rather more practical decency than you seem to have felt necessary in the past. Nothing more, given the circumstances, can reasonably be expected of you. But neither can anything less.' She sets down the cat. Immediately it starts to wind itself round her narrow, stockinged ankles. 'I will give you a quarter of an hour to reflect. It is quite enough time to finish your refreshment and leave the house, if that is what you choose. If, however, you are still here when I return, then I will assume you wish me to understand you are indeed sincere. That we are to trust you.'

She wheels from him, walks out, followed by the prancing cat. For several seconds Yuji is as motionless as the women in the pictures, then he sets his glass balloon on the mantelpiece, limps to the billiard table, and spends the minutes granted him, precious minutes in which he ought to be grappling with the question of his sincerity (though the problem feels impervious to normal thought, almost mystical), rolling a billiard ball against one of the baize side-cushions. He does not hear her return. Her voice startles him.

'Very well,' she says. 'Shall we go up?'

*   *   *

282

Alissa's room is on the second floor at the end of the house furthest from the clock tower. It is slightly larger than her room in Kanda, its walls decorated with pink paper that light and time have faded to a blush. Opposite the door is a sash window looking towards the sea, where a pair of fishing boats, black shapes on the glittering swell, are making their patient progress from frame to painted frame.

Miss Ogilvy picks up a towel, a dirty cup. 'Do not,' she says to Alissa in briskly enunciated French, 'tire yourself out with talking.'

When she has gone, when the clip of her footfall has faded along the corridor, Yuji and Alissa are like shy children left by a well-meaning adult to become friends. At last, still stood by the door, Yuji looks up to where she is sitting in the floral armchair beside the window. She is wrapped in a rose-coloured gown, a fringe of flannel nightdress showing below the hem. Her hair, black as his own, is plaited and tied with a ribbon. She looks both exactly as he remembered her and entirely different, a change that is not simply the swollen abdomen on which she rests a small protective hand.

'Papa called last night,' she says. 'I don't know which of us he is more angry with. He said he hit you.'

'Not so hard.'

'It must have been hard if you need a walking stick.'

'That was something else. A fall.'

'He had no right to hit you.'

'Please. It is not important.'

'He had no right.'

Yuji nods, looks to the window. 'It's a nice view,' he says.

'Yes.'

'The sea . . .'

'Yes. It's restful.'

'Good.'

'They've been very kind to me,' she says. 'All of them. Miss Ogilvy especially.'

'Miss Ogilvy?'

'I know she can appear rather fierce at first. It's only because she has to keep everyone in order.'

'She told me I should travel.'

'That sounds like her.'

'And that I must not encourage her students to drink.'

'It was one of the girls?'

'Sandrine?'

'I expect she was encouraging you, wasn't she?'

'It seemed like that.'

From under the edge of the counterpane a seal-grey head appears, a black nose, two eyes sticky with sleep. Seeing Yuji, the animal sneezes and waddles over to him.

'She has to stay in here because of the cats,' says Alissa. 'Dr Saramago doesn't approve, but Miss Ogilvy says the Portuguese don't understand dogs. Horses but not dogs. She has opinions on every nationality you can think of. Lots on the Japanese, of course.' She gives Yuji a quick smile, then seeing how his attention returns again and again to her belly, the evidence of her belly, she says, 'I can't get used to it either. Being so . . . big.'

'It hurts you?'

'A little. At night, mostly. It depends on where the baby is.'

'Ah . . .' Yuji puts on a most serious face. He has no idea what she means. Where *can* it be? Sitting on the end of the bed?

'They move,' she says. 'They sleep, wake . . .'

'Is it sleeping now?'

'No. Awake, I think.' Then, after a pause, 'It's probably listening to us.'

She is teasing him, of course. Surely, she is teasing him, but the thought of a foetal witness to this scene, of a baby, his child, *theirs*, sitting the other side of her skin listening to everything . . . He searches her face for some hint of levity, but she is not smiling now. She is gazing at him intently, nakedly.

'Papa said Junzo told you.'

'Yes.'

'When?'

'Two nights ago.'

'Just two nights!'

'We met . . . by chance.'

She shakes her head, and for the first time a note of irritation enters her voice. 'A pity you couldn't have met by chance three months ago. There isn't much time now. Will they send him to China?'

'Probably.'

'And you?'

'I don't know. One day, I suppose.'

'This horrible war.'

'Yes.'

'I can't even bear to read a newspaper. I look at these' – she gestures to the little pile of magazines on the side-table – 'read about knitting and colic and what husbands like for supper.'

'I don't read as much as I used to,' says Yuji. 'I have become quite busy.'

'It's nice that you've come,' she says. 'I don't really know *why* you've come. Perhaps it doesn't matter.'

He opens his mouth. She silences him with a movement of her

hand. 'Don't explain,' she says. 'I'm not angry with you. I was at first. Then I was sad. Now all I want is for the baby to be safe. You see, it's really going to happen. It's not just an idea, something to amuse ourselves *talking* about. It's a real baby who's going to grow up, who's going to . . .' Her face creases. In Yuji something comes undone, some strapping of the heart. He would like to yell, let out a shout so loud the men on the fishing boats would hear him. He steps towards her, tries to crouch at her feet, but his knee is too sore, too stiff. He stands again, wincing.

She wipes her eyes, grins at him. 'Look at us,' she says, 'with our sticks.'

8

He visits every day, sometimes for an hour, sometimes for a whole morning or afternoon. They meet in her room or in the small dining room at the back of the house, or, on fine days, on the bench between the eucalyptus trees in the little salt-stunted garden. When she is not too tired and her ankles are not swollen, they walk in the winter sunshine, sticks in hand, Beatrice trotting contentedly at their heels. The awkwardness of the first encounter, of the second and the third, the confidences that awkwardness inspired, gives way to a gentle, mutual reticence. They talk together, easily, fluently, but sound, even to themselves, like strangers enjoying an unexpected friendship at a holiday resort. Little is said about the recent past, the three seasons since they knelt side by side in the dark to watch *Kasane*. Little is said about the life that sits or walks with them in her belly. And when, now and then, a silence between them fills with the weight of unspoken thoughts, there is always something to rescue them, some task, some antic of the dog, some intriguing or comical behaviour from one of Miss Ogilvy's 'girls'.

Of these, there are six, all foreigners: Sandrine, Rose, Kitty, Eva, Natasha, Mary. In the beginning, Yuji has difficulty telling them apart. All seem slightly blurred by strong perfume, and all, dressed in fabrics delicate as tissue paper, seem always to have just emerged from bed or bath. They are kind to him, treat him, he thinks, like a pet. He does not, after his second visit, expect to hear one of them play the piano.

That the academy might be an *unsuitable* place for a woman in Alissa's condition, a surprising place for Monsieur Feneon to be connected to, an altogether curious institution with a way of doing things that would – or so he guesses – not be much understood in the more traditional parts of the pleasure quarters . . . these are questions he turns over, with no great urgency, like loose change in his pocket. After all, there is no one to discuss it with, no one, yet, to be scandalised. And who is he – a person Feneon might have felt entitled to shoot – to raise so much as an eyebrow?

It is Rose (or perhaps Natasha) who tells Yuji, four days before the term Miss Ogilvy spoke of has expired, about the breaking of Alissa's waters. It is just after midday. The girl is helping him with his coat, tugging it clumsily off his shoulders in her excitement. 'Isn't it blissful?' she says. 'We were afraid you'd come too late.'

He waits in the empty billiard room, looking at the painted nymphs and the dimpled, slyly smiling wives of European aristo- crats, and wonders about this water they contain that breaks (like porcelain? Like a wave?).

After half an hour the door by the fireplace opens and Dr Saramago comes in. He is wearing a pearl-grey three-piece suit. He is fat and surprisingly young. He has been upstairs with Alissa. 'Not worrying,' he says, breezily. 'Baby later. Time for last sleep.' He laughs (as if out of a well of cooking oil in his throat), takes a fur coat from the back of a chair, pats Yuji's shoulder and leaves. A few minutes later Miss Ogilvy appears, crisp white apron, a dress with rolled sleeves, a rolled cigarette in her left hand.

'There are contractions,' she says, 'but true labour has yet to commence. You may go and see her.'

Alissa is in the bed. Her head, her narrow shoulders are raised on a heap of pillows. There is a fire in the grate, and since his visit the previous day a table has appeared at the end of the bed, a card table with towels on it, bundles of white gauze, a tin basin, a large pair of scissors. For two nauseating seconds Yuji remembers Saburo's story about the doctors in China. *Now, then, gentlemen, shall we start with the appendix?*

'Saramago,' he says, 'looks like an American gangster.'

She manages a smile. 'He's nice,' she says. 'He brings us little custard cakes to eat.'

Under the sheet, her body radiates a kind of imminence. The whole room is charged with it, a tension that has reached its perfection.

'I suppose it will be soon now,' he says.

'Yes,' she says. 'Will you be here?'

'Here?'

'At the house?'

'Yes. If you would like me to.'

'Yes,' she says, then shuts her eyes, clutches a corner of the sheet in her fist, moans. It is a sound she made the night they were together in her room in Kanda. She turns to Yuji, no attempt to hide the fear in her face. 'What if I can't do it?' she says. 'Saramago says he has things to help me. Miss Ogilvy says at my age it will be easy. But what if they're wrong?'

'They're not,' says Yuji, suddenly appalled at how little there is he can do for her. He steps up to the bed, reaches his fingertips to where the sheet is tented over her belly. 'Shall I fetch Miss Ogilvy?'

She nods. 'You don't need to love me,' she says as he opens the door. 'But you must love the child. Will you love the child?'

At three o'clock Dr Saramago returns. He smells of lunch, of China Town. He is upstairs for fifteen minutes, then comes down and leads Yuji to the billiard table. Yuji is good at billiards – he has had more time than most to practise it – but Saramago beats him easily.

'Next time, *shogi*,' says the doctor, grinning and carefully tying a little scarf around his throat. When asked about Alissa, about the baby, he makes an unrolling gesture with his right hand, something that might be readily understood in Porto or Lisbon but which tells Yuji nothing.

At six o'clock the doors are opened and the first of the evening's visitors arrive, a pair of naval officers, glamorous in caps and long military coats. Yuji is sent to wait in a room on the first floor of the tower. From the window he can see the lights of the neighbouring building. He buttons his jacket. There are radiators in the house, brass concertinas that gurgle and rattle like live things but give off very little useful heat, certainly not enough for the high-ceilinged rooms of the academy. He looks for something to read, finds in the bucket by the empty fireplace a newspaper from May 1938, reads a story about the fall of Swatow, then drops the paper on the boards and begins to pace. Behind a curtain in the far corner of the room is a painted door. He tries the handle. The door is not locked but leads only into a cupboard, its floor piled with women's shoes, women's boots. On a shelf at the back is a row of featureless wooden heads each with a coloured wig on it – black, blond, curly red – and from a hook below the shelf hangs a coil of buckled leather he mistakes at first for a horse's bridle.

In the billiard room, drunken voices sing along to the gramophone. (Is the music louder than usual tonight? Is there something the gentlemen should not be allowed to hear?) When it stops, Yuji dozes in a chair, wakes several times imagining his name has been called, then falls into a deeper sleep from which he is roused by someone standing over him with a lantern – Father, perhaps, come to tell him it's time for his watch on the platform.

'The electricity is off,' says Miss Ogilvy. 'The child was born by candlelight.'

He follows her, her lantern, up a flight of stairs and along the corridor. Nothing waking could have more perfectly the character of a dream. Not just the uncertain light ahead of him, or the dark figure whose shadow is so weirdly thrown on the corridor walls, but the sense that with each step on the worn carpet his old self, like something useless, something used and finished, is falling away, blowing from him like a dust, like fine ashes.

In the room the candles burn in little clusters. Three on the card table, three on the windowsill, five or six on the mantelpiece. All Miss Ogilvy's girls are there, one of them sitting on Saramago's expanse of pearl-grey lap. As Yuji arrives, they twitter with excitement, they rustle, then fall silent and turn adoringly to the propped-up figure of Alissa, the dark bundle lying at the opening of her nightgown.

Out of the hush – a hush that seems entirely theatrical – Alissa says, 'A little boy.'

'A little boy,' repeats Yuji. 'Yes.' Then, 'Thank you.'

Saramago erupts with laughter. Miss Ogilvy shoos the girls from the bed, prods Yuji, quite sharply, in the small of the back. He sits on the bed. The baby is wrapped in a towel, its face pressed against one of Alissa's breasts. It grunts as it sucks, groans like a dreaming dog. The girls, craning over the bed, sigh with pleasure. To Yuji the desperate sucking seems comical, slightly sinister.

'Look,' says Alissa, slipping the towel from the baby's head to reveal a half-dozen luxuriant wisps of slick black hair. Japanese hair? Western hair? Eurasian? With a finger – and how expert she is already, how much the mother – she draws her swollen nipple from the baby's mouth. 'Hold him,' she says. 'Take him.'

She shows him how to make a cradle of his arms, then leans forward and gently, very gently, rolls the baby from her arms to his. He feels its heat, the restless stretching of its body. There is something oddly dense about the weight of it, as if its life was rolled up tightly inside it like the sticky wing of an insect. It moves its dark-palmed hands, curls its feet, then rolls its face blindly towards his chest. A tip of tongue pokes out, touches the wool of his shirt. The eyes flutter in startlement. The ignorance of it! The utter helplessness! And this is his son? This *scrap*? It starts to squall. It becomes rage. Immediately he holds it out to Alissa, feels a moment of awe and resentment at how swiftly her presence soothes it.

Behind him, one of the girls comes in, bottles in her arms, dark green bells of champagne. Saramago opens them. Miss Ogilvy gives Yuji a glass. He turns to Alissa. She taps a fingernail against the rim of his glass. He drinks. Someone opens the window a little. There is the distant droning of an aircraft, of several aircraft. 'What on earth are they doing flying at this hour?' asks Miss Ogilvy. After a while the window is shut again.

9

Chains of coloured paper are hung in swags along the walls of the billiard room. A large Christmas tree is carried in by Yuji and the Chinese houseboy. The girls decorate it with the utmost seriousness. At the top they place a doll, a winged doll, an angel.

There are cards, lanterns – also a little carousel of brass reindeer, their movement powered by the heat of candles. When shown to the baby, he throws back his arms and squawks with excitement, though shown it a second time he seems indifferent.

He's too intelligent for such a toy,' says Feneon, grandly. 'Already he has escaped from Plato's cave.'

'What nonsense you talk,' says Miss Ogilvy, sponging a smear of regurgitated milk from the Frenchman's lapel.

In the six days since the birth Feneon has been a regular caller at the academy. The girls all seem to know him well, treat him like an indulgent father, are openly amused by Miss Ogilvy's rudeness to him.

To Yuji, Feneon has offered – with an ironic cocking of an eyebrow – his felicitations on the birth of a healthy son. If he is still angry with Yuji, he hides it well enough for them to speak to each other in civil tones, and for now at least the baby heals everything, distracts everyone, creates, in every room it lies in, a feeling of reverence, of incontinent hope.

At Miss Ogilvy's suggestion, Alissa and Yuji have named the child Emile. It would, she assured them, appeal to Feneon's vanity, it would mollify him, and though, on learning of it, Feneon protested, his delight was obvious. Emile. Baby Emile. Little Emile. When not in his mother's arms or on Feneon's knee, he is passed among the girls. Yuji, too, takes his turn, reluctantly at first, unable to free himself from the paralysing fear of dropping him, but as he grows in confidence he finds himself falling under the same fascination the others surrendered themselves to so eagerly. Shyly, then openly, he dots the child's brow with kisses, inhales the bready, powdery, new-animal scent of the warm black hair. At home, he notices his clothes have started to smell of the baby. Can anyone else smell it? His neighbours? Miyo?

'I presume your parents know nothing of all this,' says Feneon one evening, as they ride an empty carriage back into Tokyo together. 'The longer you leave it, the more difficult it will become. The more painful for them.'

Is he speaking from experience? How, Yuji would like to ask (and only in part to embarrass him), did you tell your parents about Alissa? Or were the thousands of miles between Sézanne and Saigon sufficient for the secret of a child, a lost mother, to be kept for ever? As for his own parents, what in his past dealings with them can reliably tell him how they will respond to the news of a bastard, half-caste grandson? Certainly he knows of cases where a son or daughter has been formally renounced, and for behaviour, for acts, far milder than his own might appear.

On the morning of Christmas Eve he tells Miyo he will be away for the night. He leaves her money to go to the New Year markets. He will be in Yokohama. She should go to the Otakis if she needs help. She nods. She does not ask him any questions, though there is something in the way she looks at him that makes it clear she has reached her own conclusion about nights away in Yokohama.

At midnight in the Bullseye Piano Academy the last visitors are guided – or waltzed, in the case of one beaming, red-faced old gentleman, the under-secretary of something – to the front door. The last taxi pulls away. The glasses and ashtrays and empty bottles of Monopole and Hennessy are carried to the kitchen.

When everything is in good order again, when the fire has been fed and poked into fresh life, they gather on the rug or draw up chairs, their palms held out to the flames. Emile is sprawled asleep on a blanket by Alissa's feet. Yuji kneels beside him. Natasha plays the guitar. They sing Christmas songs, Christmas carols. Most of these Yuji has never heard before, but one, '*Stille Nacht, Heilige Nacht*', is familiar to him. Mother – who must have been taught it by Grandfather Yakumo – used to sing it when he and Ryuichi were little boys, and because he has only ever heard it in her voice, he has always thought of it as somehow being a Japanese song, though now the foreigners are singing it, half joyfully, half sadly, he sees that it's theirs, that it comes out of their world.

After the singing, Feneon and Miss Ogilvy bring in the parcels that have lain so enticingly for days on the table in the back dining room. They spread them by the bottom of the tree. Rose – the youngest after Emile – reads out the names, reads out the doggerel that accompanies some of the names, and hands the parcel (with some ceremony, some giggling) to the recipient. Everybody has something. There are perfume bottles, ribbons, brooches, silken underwear. Alissa has a hat with a fox-fur brim, Yuji a tie with jagged orange stripes (a jazz tie!). For Emile, there are wooden toys and toys of tin, a pair of lamb's-wool booties, a Chinese-style jacket hardly bigger than a man's handkerchief.

'Shall we be able to do this next year?' asks Feneon, swirling the last of his brandy and letting his gaze rest on Alissa, on Emile.

'We are doing it *this* year,' says Miss Ogilvy. 'And that is what matters. A grandfather should be wise enough to know that.'

At bedtime – whatever time that is, three, four o'clock – Yuji has a mattress in the room where he waited the night Emile was born. ('You,' Miss Ogilvy informed him simply, 'are in the tower. You know where to go.') He lies there, slightly drunk, wondering if Alissa is upstairs listening for his footsteps or if, with the baby beside her, she is already fast asleep. What is he to her now? What is he *supposed* to be? Do the others all assume something? If they do, he wishes someone would tell him what it is. As for what he wants . . . He peers into the speckled dark of the room, moves his life around like the pieces of a puzzle, but just as the suspicion starts to grow in him that a life, his or anyone's, is not a puzzle at all but something quite different, something that does not admit of solutions, he is lying on his arm softly snoring and dreaming of Mother singing in a voice thin as wire, '*Schlaf in Himmlischer Ruh, schlafe in Himmlischer Ruh.*'

At mid-morning the house downstairs is deserted. Yuji takes a walk. He does not need his stick now. His knee has healed and the burns are no more than patches of raw new skin. When he comes back, he finds Sandrine and Mary turning the billiard table into a dining table. He helps them lift the heavy wooden lid, spread the spotless linen. The cats leap up, are chased off before they leave a trail of prints. In the kitchen, in swirls of steam, Miss Ogilvy, with two of the girls, is preparing dinner. ('You can't ask a Chinese to cook a Christmas dinner.') There is a roast duck, trays of sweet potatoes, a great saucepan of red cabbage. The pudding is a ball wrapped in muslin. Apparently it has to boil for hours.

It is dark again before everything is ready, the table set, the girls in their best clothes, the wine decanted. Miss Ogilvy takes photographs with her Leica and flashgun. Everyone together, then the girls in various demure poses by the mantelpiece. 'Now,' she says, 'the new family.' A chair is put out for Alissa and Emile. Yuji stands beside them. When Feneon is urged to join them he says he will, gladly, but first it should be just mother, father, son.

'As you wish,' says Miss Ogilvy, screwing a fresh bulb into the flashgun.

The baby is restless. Alissa settles him with a touch, then smiles up nervously at Yuji.

'At the camera, please!' calls Miss Ogilvy.

They turn to her, compose themselves. She lifts the gun. The light, white and chemical blue, is blinding, and for an instant it prints their shadows thickly on the far wall.

10

New Year is spent with Grandfather. Yuji travels to Setagaya with Miyo. Mr Fujitomi is there. He has brought his wife and sister with him. After eating, they go by taxi to a shrine next to the railway station, a small place compared with the one in Hongo, old, unfashionable. They take Grandfather's wheelchair. Yuji pushes it. How heavy the old man is, a dead weight, a dragging, dead weight.

Chief Priest Takashita comes out to welcome Grandfather personally. He presents him with a scroll on which a snake is drawn beside certain verses from *The Chronicle of Ancient Matters* petitioning good health.

They don't stay for long. Grandfather looks at Sonoko, who looks at Yuji, who turns the chair round. The taxi is waiting for them, the driver flicking through a magazine of fortune-telling.

At the house, the Fujitomis remain for a last flask of sake. Yuji sits with his secrets. Even Mr Fujitomi seems distracted. Has he heard anything from China? How long since the last letter? Grandfather is growling. His lower lip droops, trembles. When

Sonoko does not immediately translate for him, he tries to slap her leg.

'He says,' she says, 'Japan is finished.'

The others look politely interested. All day and all night the streets have been full of a fine white mist.

11

As soon as the holidays are over and the academy is open for business again, Alissa moves back to the house in Kanda. It is easier now, much easier for Yuji to visit. He can go for an hour in the morning, then meet Fujitomi in the Low City before returning to the house for another hour in the evening. He is pleased, yet he also understands that the move's indiscretion, its indifference to local scandal, means the hour of separation is not far away.

On the evening of 15 January, the day families gather to eat New Year gruel, he crosses the garden through a cold west wind to find Alissa and Emile asleep on the sofa in the salon. Feneon is sitting with his back to the stove, the dog on his lap, a newspaper spread across the table in front of him. He greets Yuji with a nod, and after folding away the paper, he fetches his chessboard from the study. In silence they make their opening moves, exchange pawns, clear the lines for more powerful pieces to enter the fray. It's Feneon's turn. After studying the board for a minute, he looks up at Yuji and says, 'I hope I can trust you to be discreet?'

A few months ago and the question would have felt slighting. Yuji would have brooded on it. Now it is merely part of the new honesty between them, the new *froideur*.

'I shall be leaving soon for Singapore. The British have a large garrison on the island and there's an English planter there, a man called Farrell, who I was able to help with some trouble in Saigon. He will, he assures me, now repay the favour. As soon as I have found a suitable house, I will send for Alissa and Emile. It should only be a matter of a few weeks, perhaps a month, but during that time they will be entirely in your care.'

There is no mention, no hint of the possibility of Yuji accompanying them. Is this how Feneon will free his daughter from her unfortunate connection? Or is it simply that Feneon, a practical man, understands as well as Yuji the impossibility of it? How, in better times, in Taisho times, a person like Professor Takano might go abroad, might even live there a season or two while he studied its ways, but now, for any young man – even one with a Class F exemption – to leave these islands without khaki on his back would be tantamount to desertion? He could never come home. He would have no home to come to.

'I will care for them,' says Yuji, quietly.

'Thank you,' says Feneon, using his bishop to knock over Yuji's knight. 'That's settled, then.'

The luggage – four trunks of battered tin, each with the markings of earlier journeys, the smudged chalk of a cabin number, a pasted-on, half-torn-off address in Bombay, Macau, Cholon – is sent to the Bullseye Academy and then, the day before the sailing, down to the docks to be loaded onto the *San Cristobal da Lisboa*. The

San Cristobal is bound for Shanghai. From there a second ship will take Feneon to Hong Kong, where a steamer of the Peninsular and Oriental Company will complete the journey to Singapore.

Alissa, Emile and Feneon have accompanied the trunks to the academy. Yuji joins them the morning of Feneon's departure. The weather, turbulent all week, has settled again and a phone call to the agents confirms the ship will sail at the appointed hour of three in the afternoon. They decide on an early lunch, but as soon as they sit down Alissa begins to weep like a child. She tries but cannot stop herself. Feneon takes her outside, returns five minutes later holding her hand. At the table, he tells tales of shipboard encounters, the Irish priest he once shared a cabin with on a crossing of the Arabian Sea, the Romanian countess who travelled with a wolf cub. Miss Ogilvy accuses him of invention, of being little better than a novelist, a *romancier*, but she has laughed along with the others.

The taxi comes at one.

'We'll say our goodbyes here,' says Feneon. 'No handkerchiefs waving from the quayside, please.'

The girls form a line. He embraces each in turn, embraces Miss Ogilvy, wipes the small tear from her cheek. He takes the baby in his arms, kisses him until he writhes in protest, then holds his daughter, strokes her hair, gently untangles himself. To Yuji he says, 'Did I ever apologise for hitting you?' He reaches into a pocket of his overcoat. 'This came to light while I was packing. I have no use for it now and perhaps it will make up for any unpleasantness between us.'

He kisses his daughter again, kisses his grandson, picks up Beatrice who, half demented with jealousy of the baby, will travel with him, and goes to the door. Through the window Yuji sees him getting into the car. The driver shuts the door. Feneon looks back at the house, smiles and turns away.

The girls immediately surround Alissa. They seem primed for dramas of this kind, of any kind. They are not reserved, not coolly secretive like the women in the paintings. Whatever they feel is played out on their faces without hesitation. Yuji moves away from them and looks at the envelope in his hand. There is a stamp with a lion on it, and an address written in ink faded to the colour of dried blood: '19 rue saint-Maur, Sézanne, France.' The paper is mottled, stained by time, by the immense journeys it has made. It is beautiful. He smiles at it. He almost prefers not to read it at all but to go on imagining it, the precious content, as if he was one of the old poets picturing the moon from behind drawn blinds. Then the thought seems idiotic, unworthy of such a gift, and he tugs the letter through the ragged lips of the envelope and tilts it towards the afternoon light.

For two minutes the handwriting is completely impenetrable. He begins to panic. To have it in his hands and not be able to read it! Unbearable! He starts again, scans each crabbed line as calmly, as methodically as he can. Single words appear – *silence . . . newspapers . . . money . . . dogs . . . God . . .* Then clusters of words – *I never find . . . half of Europe . . . into his fields . . . backs of carts . . .* Then at last, he has it. It speaks.

Harar, 4 February 1890

My dear Feneon,

Excuse my long silence. I never find anything interesting to say! Deserts full of stupid niggers, no roads, no mail, no travellers.

I haven't seen a French newspaper in weeks. For all I know half of Europe is dead with the pox. Well, so much the better – though naturally I hope a good Christian family like yours is spared!

My last caravan was a disaster. Did you hear of it? A year of incredible hardships and damn all to show except more creditors. Monsieur Ilg reproaches me for not giving the drivers sufficient provisions. He says he had to put the donkeys into his fields because they were covered in sores and too weak to continue. But is that really my fault? You know how things are here. Why should I be blamed?

As a result of all I have endured, the endless walking and riding in this damned country, I have varicose veins in my right leg that keep me awake all night. I've ordered some special stockings from Aden but I doubt they'll have them. I shall probably have to write to Mother and see if she can buy some in Vouziers. The silk ones are meant to be best, though the important thing is that there should be enough elastic in them. They also need to be long enough to give support to the whole leg and not just the knee, and they should be adjustable with some sort of lacing. In the meantime I shall have to struggle on as best I can, though the truth is I feel more like a dog tethered to the back of a cart than a human being. One day I'll stumble and some thoughtful bastard will cut me loose and leave me for the vultures. A charming prospect, don't you think?

Yours, with a feeble handshake,

A. Rimbaud

12

Miss Ogilvy offers Alissa her old pink bedroom at the academy. She will be safe there, and comfortable, until her father can send for her, but Alissa, with a smile, a shake of her head, leaves with Yuji and Emile for the early evening train to Tokyo. It's the slow train, the local. At each stop the carriage becomes more crowded. Alissa keeps her eyes lowered, holds the sleeping baby tightly in her arms. Yuji stands over them, gripping the ceiling strap. He is aware of people, women particularly, trying to get a clear view of the baby's face. One man, heavily drunk, looks as if he might pass a remark, but his courage fails him or he is too drunk to speak. He sits on the carriage floor, lets out a sigh as if of death, and falls asleep.

By the time the taxi drops them off in Kanda it has started to snow again. Alissa gives Yuji the house key. In the salon, he quickly cleans the ashes from the stove and builds a fire. When it catches, he swings shut the iron door, adjusts the vents, and feels a surge of primal satisfaction, the pleasure of bringing warmth where it is needed, of bringing it to those who have been *entrusted* to him.

'You really think he'll be all right?' asks Alissa, a question she has already put to Yuji four or five times since Feneon's departure. His words, for now, have the power to calm her, and this too gives him pleasure. 'He will,' he says, emphatically. She nods and busies herself with the baby.

They have brought a parcel of food with them from the academy, remains of the lunch no one had much appetite for. In the kitchen there are a last few bottles of wine. They open one, touch glasses. 'He was born out of a bottle of wine,' she says, blushing and looking down at the sleeping head by her thigh. They pick at the food, grow drowsy. A glance past the shutters into the garden shows the snow still falling heavily.

'You won't get home tonight,' she says. Yuji agrees. 'You could use Papa's room,' she adds, quickly. 'It's nicer than the spare room. There are blankets and sheets in the cupboard beside the kitchen.'

He tries to call Miyo but it seems the lines have been affected by the weather. All he can hear in the receiver is something like the whispering, the urgent whispering of phantom voices.

At ten Alissa goes upstairs with Emile. Yuji makes the bed in Feneon's room, puts out the light. The snow rubs its blunt fingers against the window. The city of millions is silent . . . Then the baby starts to wail, that sound Yuji is becoming so familiar with, that he seems to hear half a second before it begins. He sits up, willing it to stop, but it grows louder, an utterly intemperate sound, inhuman, like a giant cicada. Should he go in? Can he help? Would she *welcome* his help? He swings his legs to the edge of the bed but as his toes touch the floor the crying ceases, mid-phrase, leaving behind it a deep and brittle hush. He waits, then slowly lies his head on the bolster again, pulls up the blanket. He is tired but he knows that something in him will go on listening. Something in him will never stop listening now.

In the morning he tramps through the snow to the bakery, the one the Russian priests used to go to. There's a queue. There's always a queue now where food is sold. On his way back to the house, he is stopped by Ooka the bookseller. 'If the Frenchman left any nice books behind, why don't you bring them over to the stall? Nothing improper, of course, nothing unpatriotic, but there's still a market with the students for foreign stuff.'

Alissa eats half a loaf of dark bread, smothering the slices in jam. She drinks warm milk flavoured with cinnamon, and into the last glass breaks an egg, laughing at her own appetite. When she has finished, she passes Emile to Yuji and stretches out on the sofa. In less than a minute she's asleep. Yuji puts more wood on the stove, then sits on the rug opposite the sofa, the baby across his knees. Alissa is in her nightclothes still. The unbuttoned gown hangs open over the skin of one of her breasts. He stares at the edge, the seashell-pink rim of visible nipple, then looks away, frowns at the patterns in the rug and attempts to correct his thinking. Her breasts are for feeding the child. Their fullness is from the milk they carry. She is a mother (that object of universal veneration), a nursing mother, and yet the atmosphere around her, around her and the child, around all three of them, is drowsy and voluptuous and not at all what he might have imagined. He seems to be in a continuous state of mild arousal. Do *all* new fathers feel like this, everything sunk into the body? And what about the women? Was the 'ghost' an animal once, heavy as the one now sleeping with lips slightly parted on the sofa?

*   *   *

Day after day through the snowfalls of early February he makes his way down to Kanda. He sleeps in Feneon's room (the bed with the brass headboard, the springs that creak atonally every time he moves) more nights than he sleeps at home. He makes no effort to explain these absences to Miyo. He cannot tell her the truth – though he is longing to tell it to someone – and does not wish to make up stories. He pays her at least double what she was used to receiving from Father, and her duties now, a little cleaning, a little shopping, are almost non-existent, but each time he slides open the front door he half expects to find her gone, run off with the soy-seller's son, or taken service in some household where she will not be lonely or bored.

Once a week he fire-watches. When his name appears twice on the weekly roster, he simply ignores the second duty. Being afraid of Saburo is a habit he has fallen out of, quite suddenly, a luxury he no longer has the time for. When he does take his turn, he naps in the sewing room whenever it suits him, and on one of these twenty-minute sleeps, curled on the bedding with his overcoat pulled tightly about him, he dreams he has been left alone to care for the child. He is carrying him through Asakusa to the Mont-parnasse cinema. Ishihara is in there, and also – though Yuji only sees him from behind, the collar patches on his uniform, the shaved grey hair above the thickset neck – General Sugiyama. It's a Chaplin film, *The Orphan*. The general laughs uproariously. Ishihara twists in his seat. 'The future,' he says, blowing smoke into Yuji's face.

When Yuji leaves the cinema, Emile is so small he has to hold him in the palm of his hand like a frog. He goes into a restaurant, asks for a cup to put the child in. He is no bigger than a beetle now. A gang of soldiers arrives. They invite Yuji to drink with them. One, with movements both playful and threatening, makes a present of his bayonet. When they leave, Yuji looks for the cup, but there are cups everywhere, scores of them, spread over every table, all of them empty. He searches, his heart wrung by a terror not even the fire-dreams provoked. He has lost Emile! He has lost his son! (And what can he possibly tell Alissa?) There is an instant of deranged clarity in which, alone in the nightmare restaurant, he realises he must kill himself . . . then he comes to, making some grief-noise in his throat, and staggers onto the platform, gulps mouthfuls of cold dawn air until he comes to his senses, but the dream stays with him for days. Even when he holds Emile, feels the packed robustness of his body, he cannot quite pick out a last splinter of anxiety.

A telegram from Feneon. He is in Shanghai. He is well. He sends an embrace to his grandson. When Alissa shows it to Yuji, he reads it and passes it back without comment. She folds it, makes it small, then tucks it away in a pocket of the cardigan she is wearing. They look at the baby, play with the baby. When anything is in doubt, when the world threatens to force an entry, it is Emile they turn to, the power he has to root them in the present. His skin now has lost its look of long immersion and become smooth as a petal. The stump of umbilical cord that blackened and stank for a while has been shed to leave behind a clean, neat wound of separation. They lie him on the sofa, on the rug, on the bed. They examine him as though the human body was entirely new to them, their private discovery. One game, which entertains them for entire evenings, is to parcel out his features, divide them between Feneons and Takanos, between Orient and Occident. His eyes, in shape, are clearly Japanese, but their colour, hazel with gleams of new copper, comes from somewhere else. His mouth, his hands, the crown of his hair are, they agree, from the East. His nose, his feet, his skin tone, from the West. Yuji claims the child's back, Alissa his ears, particularly the lobes. It is only during the third or fourth time they play the game that Yuji realises Alissa is hoping to assemble, from the unnattributed fragments, a picture of Suzette. As for the fear, the unvoiced fear of the child being lame, there is nothing visible, nothing in the vigour with which he writhes his limbs, to suggest any cruel inheritance. He is, in his way, perfect.

They cook for each other, eat with gusto even the most un-promising results. They read aloud from what is left of Feneon's library: Turgenev, Chekhov, the stories of Maupassant. When they have finished the wine Yuji asks Mr Fujitomi where he can buy more, and is given the address of a house in Koshikawa, the mansion of some junior branch of a *zaibatsu* family where a servant, a retired sumo, leads Yuji down to a cellar lined with a thousand dusty green ends of bottles.

Fujitomi is the first person Yuji tells about Emile. They have spent half a day moving the contents of a failed shoe emporium from one end of the Low City to the other. Men's shoes, women's shoes, working boots, high fashion. Yuji picks out a pair of fleece-lined women's boots.

'You've someone in mind for those?' asks Fujitomi. 'I don't think they'll be missed.'

'There's a girl,' says Yuji, quietly.

'Pretty?'

'Yes.'

'Good for you.'

'A foreigner.'

'So your tastes run that way, do they?'

'I've known her a long time.'

'You'll know the size of her feet, then.'

'Yes.'

'Good for you.'

'We have a child.'

Silence. A beat of two. A beat of three.

'A *child*?'

'A baby boy.'

'You're kidding, right?'

'No.'

Fujitomi puts down the armful of rubber toilet slippers he is carrying, puffs out his cheeks, smoothes, with both hands, the skin of his scalp. 'A little boy?'

'Emile.'

'Em . . . ?'

'*Emile*. It's a French name.'

'French . . . You certainly know how to throw a surprise.'

'He was born before the New Year.'

'A Dragon boy?'

'Yes.'

'And the hour?'

'Ox, I think.'

'Highly auspicious.'

They laugh together.

'A little unofficial boy,' says Fujitomi, a sudden fleeting melancholy in his expression. 'A little international boy, well, well . . . Who else knows about this? Your father?'

Yuji shakes his head.

'You better start thinking what you're going to say. You won't be able to keep something like this quiet for long.'

'I know.'

'And the girl, the one who's going to be walking around in fleece-lined boots, what about her?'

'She will leave.'

'Leave?'

'Japan.'

'With the kid? *Em* . . . ?'

'Emile. Yes.'

'Where will they go?' He holds up a hand. 'No. Don't answer that. It's none of my business.' He grimaces. 'If you're asking for advice . . .'

'I'm not asking for advice,' says Yuji. 'I know there's nothing anyone can do.'

'Do? Oh, I wouldn't say *that*,' says Fujitomi, rummaging for a box. He finds one and packs the boots carefully inside. 'I hope she likes them,' he says. It is difficult to read the message in his eyes. Perhaps it is just difficult to take it seriously.

13

On 22 February a telegram arrives from Hong Kong. It is as brief, as portentous, as the one that preceded it. The same day, in Hongo, there is a letter for Yuji from Father. They have been snowed in for more than two weeks, though now a thaw will allow him to reach the store on the road below the farm where mail is accepted and sent on to the city. Mother has caught a chill but seems otherwise to find the mountain beneficial. On three occasions she has joined the family for the midday meal. As for himself, he has become quite the rustic, cutting wood, clearing snow off the roof, feeding the hens (those the foxes have not yet caught). What is Yuji's opinion of the situation in Setagaya? What are the doctors saying? He will, as soon as the weather permits, take the train to Tokyo.

Two days after the telegram and the letter, Emile develops a fever. One moment he is lying placidly in Alissa's lap, the next his limbs are rigid. He blinks, woken by some event deep in his body, then fires from his mouth a stream of creamy vomit. When it stops he howls. Alissa rocks him, gives him the breast his hands and mouth are fumbling for. Yuji cleans the vomit from the sofa, from the rug. Splashes of it have reached even the wall behind the table. He has just finished, is carrying the bucket back to the kitchen, when the baby, rolling his head from the nipple, is convulsed a second time.

What is an infant's grip on life? How tenacious? Can it slip away in an hour while his parents hover over him, ignorant and terrified?

A third attack, a fourth.

'There's a woman,' says Alissa, 'opposite the fan shop at the end of the street. She has children of her own. I know she sometimes looks after others . . .'

Her name is Kiyama. She follows Yuji through the evening blue of the snow. She asks no questions. She has not even taken off her apron. She comes into the house, bows to Alissa, and kneels on the floor. The child, panting on his mother's lap, lets the stranger handle him. She unpins his nappy and sniffs at it, gently palps the distended belly, looks over his skin for signs of something she evidently does not find.

'What a ni-ice little baby,' says the woman, sounding like a collector pleased to have found an unusual specimen so close to home.

'Is it serious?' asks Alissa. 'Should we call a doctor? Every time he's sick his whole body shakes . . .'

'You really speak Japanese!' says the woman, laughing and showing off her tobacco-stained teeth. 'How clever you must be. Don't worry about baby. Keep giving him your milk. You have a lot of milk?'

'I think so.'

'Keep him close to you, against your skin, like a little husband.' She laughs again and looks at Yuji. 'You have to sleep somewhere else tonight. Mother doesn't have strength for you too.'

As he thanks her at the door, he digs a five-yen note from his pocket. 'It's too much,' says the woman decisively. He takes out some change. In the end she accepts one yen and fifty sen, tucking the coins beneath her apron.

The vomiting continues but the intervals between each attack grow longer. Eventually, a few minutes before eleven, it stops. Alissa and the child sleep on the sofa, a single creature again as if Saramago's scissors had never put them apart. Yuji brings them a blanket from the spare room, then goes to the kitchen, rinses the cloths and hangs them to dry. Back in the salon, he puts wood into the stove, lets a little of the fragrant smoke spill out to cover the smell of sickness, yawns until he shudders, and sleeps in the armchair opposite the sofa, waking, moments later it seems, in a room packed with light, Alissa and Emile playing together on the floor. All sense of crisis has fled with the night. When he stirs, she looks at him, her face fresh as the morning.

'I'm going to cut your hair,' she says, grinning. 'It's starting to stick out over your ears. People will make comments.'

He goes out for food. The sun, already high, glints on melting ice and snow. He buys croquettes from the stand by the university, then, out of sheer good spirits, stays to talk with the vendor. Is business better in the cold weather?

'Better for the pocket,' says the man, 'but worse for the feet.'

'We were up all night with our son,' says Yuji. 'He gave us quite a fright, but this morning he's well.'

'That's how they are,' says the man. 'Your first?'

'Yes.'

'You'll get used to it,' he says. 'I've got five.' He gives Yuji an extra croquette, for free. 'Nothing like a croquette for keeping up your strength,' he says.

At the house, the bag of steaming food and two cups of *mugi-cha* make an instant party. The child who seemed so sick is now entirely restored. They look at him, wonderingly, and recount to each other the incidents of the night before, the vomiting, the visit, their own alarm, as a kind of comedy. How odd the woman was! And how absurd she should be so surprised by Alissa speaking Japanese! ('She must have seen me on the street for years.') Wiping the grease of the food from her fingers, she sits at the piano, plays Mozart, Bach, Debussy. Last of all she plays the Chopin.

'You remember it?' she asks.

He nods. The room is briefly filled with ghosts. She lowers the lid over the piano keys. After a while she says, 'Let's go outside.'

In the garden, they walk slow circles round the magnolia tree, Alissa in her fleece-lined boots, Emile with his red wool bonnet on, a Christmas present from Rose or Sandrine, or perhaps Natasha. Needing one hand for her stick, she holds the baby in the curve of the other arm, and when the arm is tired she passes him to Yuji.

'Wouldn't it be nice,' she says, as motes of snow, the first of a fresh fall, dance around them, 'if he could remember this.'

'The garden?' asks Yuji.

'And us,' she says. 'All together.'

Inside again, they read, doze, eat. In the warmth of the salon they are starting to have the intimacy of stabled animals. Dusk falls. From the street comes the scrape, scrape of someone shovel-ling snow. A woman calls her children in.

Alissa takes a bath. 'Do you want my water?' she asks, leaning, pink-faced, into the salon. So he lies in her water. The bath is enamelled iron, forged, perhaps – the scale is suggestive – by the same foundry that made the stove. He has not been in a bath like this before. His toes are on a level with his nose. The hardware of the taps has a nautical gleam, industrial, but if this is a good example of a foreign bath, then the foreigners have not quite understood. How reassuring that is! A weakness at last. He lies with his head on the cushion of curled iron. The water smells of roses. A bulb behind a half-globe of white glass burns unevenly, and below, over a wooden rack, a pair of stockings is hanging next to three squares of drying cotton, the baby's nappies.

'There are towels in the cupboard,' she calls through the door. 'And I put out one of Papa's old robes. It's a bit moth-eaten . . .'

He comes back into the salon wearing the robe. It's maroon and gold silk, the sort of garment he imagines an African princeling wearing, perhaps in a place like Harar. There are indeed moth-holes in it.

'Very nice,' she says, looking as if she might start to laugh.

'Is he feeding still?'

'No,' she says, glancing at the baby's head. 'He's asleep. Can you help me move him?'

Kneeling by her feet (roses, roses . . .), he takes the child's weight as she rolls him from her breast, then lifts him to the end of the sofa and lies him there. Though still asleep, the child pushes out his lips in some infant reflex of suckling.

'It must be good milk,' says Yuji. 'He even dreams of it.'

'I put a drop on my finger,' she says. 'I wanted to see what it tasted like.'

'And?'

'A little bit sweet. Would you like to try some?'

'Wouldn't I be stealing it from him?'

'Don't worry about that,' she says. 'Even when he feeds half the night I wake up with my breasts so full they ache. See how swollen they are even now?'

When his lips close round one of her nipples it stiffens against his tongue. He sucks but cannot at first make the milk come. He has forgotten how to. She touches his hair and with her other hand gently squeezes the base of her breast. 'There,' she says. 'Is it coming now?'

He slides his arms round her waist. His mind darkens with the old bliss. The milk comes surprisingly fast, warm as the skin it flows through and, as she told him, slightly sweet. He keeps some of it in his mouth, then lifts his head from her breast and lets the milk slide from his mouth into hers. She tenses, shivers, then bites his lip, nips it hard enough to bring a little blood away, just beside where her father cut him with his ring. He dabs it with his hand. 'Sorry,' she says, smiling and pushing a finger through one of the moth-holes in his gown. 'What a mess we're making of your beautiful face.'

For a week of winter nights, the child in a crib at the end of the bed, they are cautious lovers. She has, she confides, not quite recovered from the birth. She does not give him details. He is grateful. She leads him into other ways, things she heard about perhaps during her confinement at the Bullseye Piano Academy, those idle hours in the company of Miss Ogilvy's girls. When the baby wakes, they roll apart. For Yuji, there is something fascinating, something faintly unnerving, in the way she can, inside a few seconds, change the use, the aim of her body. One moment arched and hurrying after her pleasure, the next bent over the child, a mother entirely. And when the baby is soothed, she climbs up the bed with her appetite intact, as if all of it, nursing and lovemaking, were one continuous thought, one line of the brush.

*   *   *

Tokyo, 3 March: the Festival of Dolls. They dress up but go nowhere. Baby Emile has his arms threaded through the sleeves of his Chinese jacket. Alissa wears the rose kimono with the dark blue obi. Yuji, after much teasing, much prompting, also puts on a kimono, one of Father's, which he carries from the house in Hongo under the bemused gaze of Miyo. It is the first time he has worn a kimono since middle school, and looking at himself in the bathroom mirror at Kanda (with the pretty tiles all around it, silhouettes of courting couples in frocks and frock coats), he sees Father as a young man, clean-shaven and scowling. Sees Mother as a young man? But more than this – and beyond the fleeting irritation of realising that a person does not grow away from his parents but *towards* them – he sees a figure as Japanese as the Sumida river. This is the creature Feneon baulked at ('You . . . ?). The native Japanese out of his borrowed fashion and dressed again as he was intended. An exotic to them. A little exotic even to himself. He tugs at the obi, tugs at the heavy grey collar. He is not even sure he is wearing it correctly, that he has done everything he should, and yet, as he straightens his back and softens his shoulders, it begins to belong on him. He tries out a half-dozen different faces, turns left and right in front of the glass. It strikes him that he might make a passable actor. Then, less comfortably, comes the thought that he might, if he is not careful, end up as nothing, a being with no convincing identity at all, a stranger among strangers.

Alissa cooks the chicken Yuji paid excessively for at the butcher's in Shitaya. A scrawny carcass but fresh. They roast it, eat it with bowls of rice, a salad of grated cabbage. They drink wine, more than usual. Alissa teaches Yuji, thigh to thigh on the piano stool, the first two bars of the 'Moonlight' Sonata, then, singing her own accompaniment, shows him one of the dances she learnt at Mrs Yamaguchi's.

'You'll tire yourself out,' he says.

'What does that matter?' she asks, a sudden sharpness to her voice he does not respond to, that he pretends not to understand.

The moment passes but the day ends with a confused exchange of glances. She wants him to comfort her. He doesn't know how. In the morning he works with Fujitomi. There has been no snow for a week, and on the verges of some of the roads they pass in the blue van the flowers of the plum blossom show themselves tenderly against the darker world behind.

After lunch he goes back to Kanda. Alissa, her hair tied up in a cloth, is scrubbing the wooden boards of the hall. Yuji helps her to stand. Briefly, she rests her head against his chest, then sends him through to the salon where Emile is in a makeshift cradle of cushions on the sofa. Laboriously, the baby focuses on Yuji's face, frowns to find it is not the face he expects, but does not cry.

'I'll take him into the garden,' calls Yuji.

'Be sure to wrap him warmly,' she calls back.

In the garden, he walks on the newly uncovered grass, alone with his son. For now, out here, on what might be the first true day of spring, there is not, it seems, a single troubled thought in that small, fragrant head. Rested, fed, cleaned, the child is between appetites, and lies with his cheek against Yuji's arm, one hand drowsily fingering the air. What is he looking at? The pattern of the branches? A tail of cloud? Yuji talks to him. It is strange the things one says to an infant, the confidences, the declarations one drops into the wide, brown stare of such a child. How long will it last, that gaze unadorned as a dog's? Another year? Less than that? What will this face be in two or three years? What will he sound like? How will he *laugh*?

He is absorbed in this walking, this questioning, this careful circling of the tree, when he hears the doorbell. He has been expecting it, of course, privately counting off the days, so when he comes in to find Alissa in the salon, the unfolded telegram in her hand, his first emotion is relief. He waits, watching her, his fingers softly tapping a heartbeat on the baby's back.

'Papa,' she says.

'Yes.'

'He's there. He's found a house.'

'Yes.'

'He's sent for me.'

The baby stretches, grows impatient in Yuji's arms.

'I am to go to Miss Ogilvy's. She is arranging everything.'

'Miss Ogilvy?'

'Yes. The tickets. A ship.'

'When?'

'Soon.' The word barely audible. After a moment, and very gently, she takes the baby from him and steps back.

'Will you come to Yokohama with us?'

'Of course.'

'Papa says you should look after the keys.'

'Keys?'

'To the house.'

He nods. 'If I have to leave, I'll give them to Fujitomi.'

'Thank you.'

'And my uncle's address. I'll give you my uncle's address. The farm.'

'Yes.' She brushes her lips on the baby's head. 'It's been nice, though, hasn't it?'

He has hoped for another week, perhaps even two, but does not get them. After three days they are on the train to Yokohama, a pair of suitcases, far too big for the luggage rack, on the floor by their knees.

At the academy, their ringing is answered by Miss Ogilvy in person. They drag the cases inside. In the billiard room, the table is covered with a dust sheet and all the chairs have been herded to the corners of the room. The walls are bare. The women have been taken down, put away somewhere, but it is not until the household is all together in the dining room that Yuji finally understands that the academy is finished with. Miss Ogilvy and at least three of her girls will be going with Alissa to Singapore. The rest, presumably, will be taking other ships to other destinations. No one is staying.

'I have written to the President,' says Miss Ogilvy, helping herself to a crab's claw from one of the little boxes sent up from China Town. 'I have offered this house as a headquarters for the army of occupation.'

'The President?' asks Yuji, to whom these remarks seem to have been addressed.

'Of the United States,' says Miss Ogilvy. 'I seriously expect him to accept the offer.' She fixes him with the kind of penetrating stare her narrow face is peculiarly suited to producing. 'Unless,' she says, 'you think Japan will win the war.'

'What war?' asks Yuji, flummoxed. 'A war with the United States?'

She is sucking the meat from the claw. She nods.

'The imperial navy,' says Natasha, 'can't wait more than a few months. They won't have any oil left.'

'We were told that by an admiral,' says Sandrine. 'So we know what we're talking about.'

'You should learn English,' says Rose. 'When the Americans come, you can do business with them. Then Emile will have a rich daddy.'

An hour later, without a word to Yuji or any sign at all of what in these last days has been between them, Alissa goes up to bed with Emile. The others sit on at the table playing cards and drinking. One by one they drift off.

'Now you,' says Miss Ogilvy, when it's just her and Yuji left. 'There won't be much time in the morning. Go up and tell her how it will all be all right. Tell her you will see her again, that you will find a way. Tell her anything you think you can get her to believe.'

'I would go if I could,' says Yuji, quietly, furiously. 'Is it my fault things are like this?'

'In part,' says Miss Ogilvy. 'Though not entirely.'

In the bedroom, Alissa does not answer his whispered enquiry. She is lying with the baby's head tucked beneath her chin. He sits on the bed behind them, listening to the mingled rhythms of their breathing. Eventually he lies down. He does not undress or get under the covers. He has, he decides, already lost his briefly held right to such familiarity. Tomorrow – a few hours from now – they will separate, and it will not be for weeks or months but for years. It may, indeed, be for ever. That, in his heart, in the silence of his heart, is what he thinks it will be. For ever. The world will reach out for them, take them, hide them from each other. They will write at first, but soon it will not be safe to receive letters from Singapore because it will not be the postman who delivers them but the *Tokko*. And if she leaves Singapore? How will he ever know where they have gone? You can lose someone in Tokyo. What chance of finding a woman and a half-Japanese child in a world in ruins?

The cars are ordered for eleven o'clock. As the hour approaches, the girls hang round each other's necks, grow sentimental, rain kisses on Emile, his cheeks, his hands, his perfect feet. Yuji, the only man there, the only Japanese, waits on his own by the empty fireplace. At a quarter to the hour, Alissa, Emile in her arms, crosses the room and stands in front of him. She smiles. The smile tells him she too believes this is the last time they will see each other. It also tells him that this is a truth neither of them, as a matter of good style, of etiquette, of something else, perhaps, something more, will, even in these last minutes, hint at to each other. He has offered to go to the docks with her. The offer has been declined, firmly. The docks are full of police spies. It would be a quite unnecessary risk. And like her father (whose example she is clearly taking strength from), she does not like goodbyes to be drawn-out affairs.

'How happy he will be to see you,' says Yuji.

'Yes.'

'And Emile.'

'Yes.'

'Perhaps you will like Singapore.'

'The English are dull,' she says.

'Dull?'

'I don't know. I've only met a few.'

'Do you think he will learn to speak English there?'

'Papa?'

'Emile.'

'Yes. I suppose he might.'

There's a movement at the window. 'Coats on, girls!' calls Miss Ogilvy. 'The cars are here.'

'They're early,' says Yuji.

'And Japanese,' says Alissa, hurriedly. 'I'll see to that. And I'll tell him everything about you. I'll make him proud.'

The drivers come in. The smaller of the two turns down the corners of his mouth at the sight of so much luggage.

'I should help,' says Yuji.

'You stay with your family,' says Miss Ogilvy. And he stays, dumbly watching the bags being carried out, and now and then turning to meet Alissa's gaze. The timing is very delicate. He can, he thinks, do this for another minute or two. Five at most, no more. The last bag is collected, lashed precariously to the roof of a car.

Miss Ogilvy comes in, buttoning her coat. She looks slowly around the room, takes a large bunch of keys from her pocket. 'Are you ready?' she asks. They follow her out. Yuji carries Emile. When Alissa has sat herself in the back of the second car, when she has slid her stick beside her right leg, he leans down, and a little awkwardly, passes her the baby.

14

Forty-eight hours after the ship has sailed Yuji opens his eyes in a room he cannot remember having seen before. To the right, the direction he is facing, daylight seeps through a window of torn paper to show a pair of muslin sitting cushions, an old utility chest, a low table scattered with flasks and cups. He is not alone. From behind him comes the moist, arrhythmic rasp of snoring. He twists in the bedding, squints. A man is lying half a mat away. A large head, a pile of lank hair, an overcoat for a blanket. One arm is visible, one wrist. On the wrist is Yuji's watch. Yuji shuts his eyes, sleeps again. The next time he wakes there is a woman standing above him, prodding him with her foot.

'If you want to stay,' she says, 'you'll have to settle your bill first.'

He sits up, rubs his face, looks around.

'Your friend left an hour ago. Said you'd pay his share.'

He nods. He cannot speak yet. He is longing for some water.

'Quite a party you had,' says the woman, seeming, for the moment, to take pity on him. 'You must be joining up, eh?'

He nods again.

'You want some tea? I'll make you tea, but don't try to run off without paying. People who do that round here end up in the water.'

Round here? Round where?

She leaves, draws the door shut. Yuji, finding he is already fully dressed, shuffles on his knees to the window, forces it wide, and looks out over the smoking, crooked back lanes of China Town. A breeze carries smells of boiling, of frying, of bar latrines. He belches acid, wonders for a moment if he is going to faint.

'You've got it bad,' says the woman, coming in with his tea. 'Army life won't be as hard as all that. Just think how proud your mama will be. And the girls, they don't look twice at a man unless he's got a uniform on.'

She puts the bill under his cup. He finds, crumpled in different pockets, the money he needs. She counts it, counts the tip, raises the little plucked crescents of her eyebrows, and bows to him. 'They'll probably make you an officer,' she says. 'With your nice manners.'

The house is a bar with rooms, a low-grade assignation house. Downstairs, a girl is wiping a dirty cloth over a dirty table. Yuji mutters his goodbyes, trips over a hen at the door, gets out. He hopes he will not meet his 'friend' again, the self-professed artist who, at some hour in some bar the previous day (the New Moon? The Red Sleeve?) attached himself to Yuji, listened to his story, and later, presumably to compensate himself for attending so respectfully to the troubles of a drunken stranger, decided to steal Yuji's watch and hat.

He takes the first train for Tokyo, reads, with hallucinatory attention, a woman's magazine left behind on the seat ('Why

Mother-in-law Is Always Right'), then spends his last few sen on a tram from Tokyo Central to Hongo. In the vestibule, while he is shaking off his boots, Miyo appears.

'How fortunate!' she says, a delighted smile on her face. 'He only arrived an hour ago. Or two hours. But anyway, he was here when the man with the big car came. I wouldn't have known what to say. Have you lost your hat?'

He goes past her into the Western room. The screens to the Japanese room are open. Father is in there, kneeling by the alcove, carefully wrapping incense burners in sheets of tissue paper.

'Ah,' he says, catching sight of Yuji. 'Miyo didn't seem to know when you would be back.'

'Welcome home,' says Yuji. 'Please accept my apologies. I was not expecting you.'

'I telephoned two nights ago.'

'You did?'

'It doesn't matter. You're here now.'

'Are you well?'

'Thank you. Yes.'

'And Mother?'

'Surprisingly well. The parcel on the table is a gift from her. Cinnamon biscuits. Easter biscuits. A recipe of old Yakumo's.'

'Mother has been baking?'

'I should have taken her long ago. If I had realised how it would benefit her . . .'

Yuji looks at the parcel, touches it. He feels as though sake is seeping in a gum from his eyes, that he could, at any instant, become hysterical. He also feels quite calm. He picks up the envelope beside the parcel.

'A young man in a theatrical uniform delivered it,' says Father. 'If you had been here a little sooner, you would have met him.'

'There was a big car?'

'Apparently. Miyo saw it.'

'I think I have met him already.'

'A highly unpleasant type.'

'Yes. Shall I help you to wrap those?'

'I've nearly finished.'

Inside the envelope is an ivory card, a crest of some sort at the top, and below, in expensively printed calligraphy, an invitation to a private viewing of the Unit's inaugural film, *Blood and Silence*, to be shown at 3 p.m. the following Friday at the residence of Mr Kaoru Ishihara.

'I shall be going to Setagaya this evening,' says Father. 'When I spoke to Sonoko, she was not particularly encouraging.'

'No,' says Yuji. It is two weeks since he visited Grandfather. Did Sonoko mention that too?

'You'll be able to come, I hope?'

'Yes.'

'Then,' says Father, pushing himself to his feet, 'perhaps you might want to shave before we leave. And a fresh shirt . . . ?'

It's dusk when they set out, father and son, their gait almost indistinguishable as they pass the dark or softly lit houses of the street that for so many years has been their home. To the west, small flocks of birds flit across the sky. To the east, the moon is rising out of a chimney in Honjo.

'Have you had much trouble with Saburo?' asks Father.

'Not really,' says Yuji. 'Perhaps our mistake was to take him too seriously.'

'Your efforts at the bathhouse should keep him quiet for a while. I must congratulate you. I have already heard the story from Mrs Itaki and old Kawabata. It seems you saved the keeper's wife.'

'There were several of us,' says Yuji. 'And we could not save Watanabe.'

'A pity.'

'Yes.'

'Even so, you behaved correctly.'

'Dr Kushida says I'm ready for the army now.'

'I shall be seeing him tomorrow, or the next day.'

'I wonder,' says Yuji, 'if there is any point delaying the inevitable.'

'It will be hard to avoid it altogether,' says Father, 'but there is no need to embrace it before it becomes necessary.'

'I am hardly embracing it.'

'No,' says father, glancing across at him. 'Naturally.'

At the house in Setagaya, Sonoko, more nurse now than housekeeper, leads them to the little 'winter' room at the side of the house, where Grandfather is sitting beside a *kotatsu*. He looks up at his visitors, looks from one to the other. For a second Yuji is afraid he does not recognise them. Then he nods, croaks a welcome. Sonoko puts down sitting cushions. Would they like tea, or sake, perhaps? They ask for tea.

'Kensuke and Sawa send their regards,' says Father. 'Noriko, too, of course.' He pauses but there is no reply. Nothing.

'And Hiroshi has visited. Also Asako and the child.'

It's hard to say what the old man has heard, what he is attending to. Under the ridge of his grey brows, he seems to be staring inwards at some scene of disarray he cannot now ever turn away from.

'Hiroshi has finished his training. He will be posted soon. It could be anywhere. They are not informed until the last moment.'

Sonoko brings in the tea. Grandfather immediately turns to her, his eyes full of silent entreaty, as though he hoped she would send away these people who come to him with news of a world he has finished with. Father lights a cigarette. Good cigarettes are not easy to find any more. He draws on it thoughtfully, holds the smoke in his lungs for a second before letting it stream slowly through his nose. Grandfather says something to him. It's like the noise of a radio between stations, a growl of static in which words are hidden. He does not bother to repeat it. Father looks at Sonoko.

'He says you have learnt to sit up straight now.' There is the hint of a smile on her face.

Briefly, Father smiles too. 'Yes,' he says. 'The mountain has been a good teacher.'

The supper is invalid food, bland, easily chewed, easily swallowed. Conversation of any kind is so difficult it makes Father sweat. Yuji does not help him. The silence, interrupted only by the tap of the teapot on the lip of a cup, is easier to bear.

At nine thirty Sonoko informs them that it is time for Grandfather to retire. She stands and reaches down for him, slides an arm under his shoulder. 'Goodnight, Grandfather,' says Yuji. The old man flutters a hand at him, then turns, lets himself be led from the room, a lame ox led away by the farmer's wife. Twenty minutes later Sonoko returns.

'Does he sleep well?' asks Father.

'He sleeps,' she says, 'but when he wakes he is still tired.'

'Please inform us,' says Father, 'if you need more assistance.'
She thanks him.

In the eight-mat room, the lamp is lit, the bedding pulled from behind the fusuma doors, unrolled.

'You hardly spoke all evening,' says Father, taking off his jacket. 'Are you feeling unwell?'

'You too,' says Yuji, 'must be tired after your journey.'

'Yes. Travel is tiring.'

'Do you know how long you will be staying?'

'A week should be long enough.'

'Just a week?'

'With spring coming it's a busy time on the farm. Hiroshi's away, and the young fellow who used to help now and then has gone too. The more I can do, the more time Kensuke can spend in the dyeing barn. Even in these times there's quite a demand for his work . . . I'll visit again in a month or two. Much depends on what happens here. I hope you will keep us fully informed.'

Father takes his towel and leaves for the bathroom. Yuji, over-tired or not yet nearly tired enough, parts the doors of the model room and leans his face inside. The light from the lamp behind him gives the model an eerie, moonlit look. The threads of the satin river gleam. The tin tops of trams and taxis, the wire spars of a bridge, hold sparks, pale smears of light, while the rest, the labyrinth of little streets, the toy buildings with their toy-sized shadows, remain in darkness. (He cannot, for example, see the Bank of Japan.) Was there a moon the night before the earthquake? He doesn't know, though he must, at Uncle Kensuke's, have seen a moon rise or not. He tries to remember, to think of the mountain, of himself as a boy on the mountain, but his imagination offers him only what it has offered him all day, a white ship on a sea of living jade, a woman at the rail with a child in her arms.

'Is it finished?' asks Father, appearing at Yuji's shoulder his face smelling of the astringent brown soap Grandfather has long preferred.

'I don't know,' says Yuji. 'If he can't work on it any more, I suppose it is.'

'Don't you think Sonoko must have been doing most of it? I always thought so.'

Yuji slides the doors shut. He goes to the bathroom. When he returns, Father is in bed, unbuckling his watch.

'Have you lost yours?' he asks.

'It's at home,' says Yuji. He puts out the lamp. A night bird calls from the garden. The house settles.

'Miyo,' says Father, 'seemed in her own way to be hinting at something. I imagine she meant me to think you had found a new companion.'

For a moment Yuji is tempted to keep silent, to feign sleep. Then, speaking to the purple air above his head, he says, 'Yes.'

'Is it serious?'

'Perhaps.'

'That's good. The other was years ago.'

'Momoyo.'

'Yes. Well, no doubt you will tell us about her in your own time. Let us try to sleep now.'

15

The next morning Father stays at Setagaya, while Yuji, invent-
ing some appointment with Fujitomi, returns to Hongo. He
calls for Miyo. There is no answer. He goes onto the verandah and
looks down the garden – the gingko tree, the garden study, the
bamboo, the line of darker earth where he and Miyo dug the
trench. It's a garden that will need taking in hand soon. Spring
pruning, spring planting. The house, too, requires attention. There
is damp behind the dresser in the Western room, one of the beams
on the verandah needs splicing with new wood, some tiles (a result
of his climbing on them?) have fallen from the roof. It seems,
however, quite obvious to him that none of this will be done, not
by him, not, perhaps, by anyone.

He takes a bath, lies there staring at the drops of condensation
on the ceiling until the water is as chill as the air. *Wasn't he
sincere? Didn't he do everything that was expected of him?* Why,
then, this leaden sense of shame, this unsheddable feeling of
having, from the very beginning, imagined everything wrongly? No
wonder he cannot write poetry! *Dragonfly* had some of the honesty

of childhood in it, but since then, idle in his little sewing room, he has carefully misunderstood himself, made himself as much a ghost as Mother, a footless shade, babbling, ravenous to be thought clever, important, different. A shade who became a father. A father who has given up his son.

He does not spend the day. He moves its hours one by one, an idiot at an abacus. Night comes. It is almost comically threatening. He mutters the child's name until it sounds like a riddle. In Otaki's someone is singing. He does not recognise the voice. He lies down, a finger tracing the little ridges of the matting. He is thinking of the writer Akutagawa, his scraps of beautiful work, his misery, his taste for Veronal. (There are old bottles of it downstairs in Mother's room. She always had much more than she needed.) The thought is comforting, though slightly ridiculous. He is not Akutagawa. He is not Arthur Rimbaud dying of boredom and swollen veins in the desert. Nor is he Feneon or Uncle Kensuke or Father or Ryuichi. He is not Junzo. He is not Taro, or Professor Komada telling them that Proust slept in a cork-lined room. He is not Proust.

The singing stops. The list continues.

He will, he supposes, by morning, be left with *something*.

16

What should one wear to an afternoon of blood and silence? Something elegant? Something formal? Something of a military character? He chooses the suit that was his graduation gift from Father (and which Father must have intended him to wear on his first day in some school or office). White shirt, blue tie. He puts the box containing the ruby-headed pin in his jacket pocket, looks round for his watch, remembers, then goes down stairs.

As he steps into the street he sees Kyoko coming out of Itaki's. They cross beside her gateway.

'Be careful,' she says, not looking at him. 'He wishes to harm you.'

'He has always wished to harm me,' says Yuji. 'Did you not know?'

She goes in through her gate. He keeps walking. He is pleased, however, she has taken the trouble, the risk, however small, to warn him. Pleased that she is, in some way, a friend.

He eats in the Low City, a place by the water, then goes to the Mitsukoshi and buys a new watch, a Seiko, as much like his old watch as he can find. On a different floor in the same store, he buys a hat, plain brown, an austerity hat of the kind that will soberly express, in queues for the tram, queues for rice, meat, bread, sugar, charcoal, his devotion to the subjugation of China.

There is plenty of time. His watch, which the sales girl set for him with careful reference to her own, says ten past two. He flags a taxi outside the store, travels south to Azabu, gets out at the end of Ishihara's street, and walks, partly screened by the trees, until he is opposite the house. The car is there, bright as a new toy, but there is no sign of any guests, no prefatory commotion. He keeps walking, reaches the other end of the street, then comes slowly back on the same side. This time, as he approaches the house, he hears voices. One of them loud, good-humoured, a voice that knows it will not be contradicted. The other, Ota's, smooth, carefully subordinate. He stops and edges forward until he can see the flank of a ministry staff car, a uniformed driver at attention beside the open passenger door. He cannot see the men talking. Their voices fade into the garden. The driver drops his stance, swings shut the door of the car, and strolls round to lean against the warmth of the bonnet. For a second time, keeping to the sparse shadows of the trees, Yuji walks past the house. He tells himself he is waiting for a more opportune moment to make his entrance – it would not do to arrive so soon after such an important guest – but as he comes again to the junction with the main road he stands there like a man trying to remember the address of someone he has not visited in years, as if he doubted this clipped, respectful street could possibly be the one he wanted . . .

In his pocket, he touches the box with the pin inside. This, surely, is the moment to put it on, the moment to surrender himself to his protectors. With Ishihara there will be no forced marches in the snow. No beatings from drill instructors. No bayoneting of bound prisoners. He will be part of some troupe, semi-official, decorating the fringes of the regime, breathing, with their productions, a little life into the tiny souls of military planners. There will be cars and money. There will be pink-brown pills to banish sleep. There will be actresses whose age is hard to guess. There will be much excited talking about death, but little actual risk of it. Ishihara, perhaps, is the boy under the shutter he has looked for in so many dreams, the boy who will lift him to safety when the pillars of fire fall and the others are reduced to ashes.

He takes the box from his pocket. He is fiddling with the clasp, freeing it, when a taxi swings into the road from the direction of Roppongi and with a grinding of gears accelerates past him. He looks up, catches a brief clear view of Dick Amazawa, a glimpse of two others on the seat beside him.

Was he seen? Was he recognised? He is sure he was not. Amazawa, though looking out, was looking in, his big face blind to anything beyond the haze of his breath on the window. The time is ten past three. At exactly fourteen minutes past, the taxi returns. Yuji raises an arm, steps out.

'Shinjuku.'

'Shinjuku?'

The rear of the cab is blue with cigarette smoke but the smell of Fumi's perfume, a scent he remembers perfectly from their dance at the Don Juan, lingers in a sticky cloud of sherbet and honey.

They pull onto the main road, turn north. He cannot believe how simple it was (he who has had such trouble stopping taxis!). He twists, stares from the rear window at diminishing Azabu, holds his breath. It is not, of course, too late to tap the driver's shoulder, say he has forgotten something, has changed his mind. Apologise to Ota at the door, a low bow to Ishihara who will graciously excuse him, link arms and lead him over to the general. It is not too late, it is not too late . . . And then, plainly, it is. He breathes out, sits back, picks at the brown band of his new hat, and does not hear, until it is repeated for the third time, the driver's question.

'Whereabouts?'

In the days of Grandfather's youth, Shinjuku was little more than a way station on the road to the province of Kai, a place to find a bed for the night on visits to the city. Now, a short drive north from Azabu, it's modern Tokyo, its crowds as dense as any in Asakusa or the Ginza. He pays off the taxi outside the Hamada Cinema. There's a Mikio Naruse film playing.

'It's been on for twenty minutes,' say the girl with the tickets.

'It doesn't matter,' says Yuji, who's seen it before, twice.

The auditorium is almost empty. The film is melancholy, charming, restful. When he comes out – still on the steps of the cinema – he hears, above the ringing of trams and the rumble of passing trucks, the early evening chorus of birds.

He buys a skewer of gristly meat at a stall near the station, eats it while sitting on an upturned crate beside the stall (one of three that serve as the stall's restaurant). At some point he will have to make his way back across the city to Hongo. He will have to think about what he has *done* today, or undone. What he has broken. But for now he will fill out a little curl of time doing nothing anyone might imagine mattered, an hour that never needs to be accounted for. Who knows he's here? Who would think of looking for him in

Shinjuku? He chooses streets at random, stops under lanterns to listen to an accordion playing or a koto, then moves on, chooses again, this bright alley, this dark street. He wonders if he will find the Polar Bear Club, where Fumi worked, but realises it could have had a dozen different names since then, and would, anyway, have been shut for months by government order. He is becoming uncertain of his bearings, has, perhaps, strayed beyond the quarter's secret borders, when, turning one more corner, crossing a patch of green, then threading the gate of a little shrine, he finds himself on one of the new avenues, walking on a pavement washed by the light of a department store. The half-dark crowd swim by, brushing softly against each other. Yuji steps into the gutter to make room for a soldier walking with his wife and child, then hesitates, struck by something in the man's face. He looks back. The soldier has also stopped

'Excuse me,' says the soldier, taking off his cap, 'but were you a customer, perhaps?'

'A customer?'

'Maybe I fixed your bicycle?'

It takes a moment more, then Yuji suddenly recognises the little mechanic from the repair shop in Hibiya. 'So you're in the army now?'

'I trained in '37. I was surprised they left me alone as long as they did.'

'You've closed the shop?'

'I tried to find someone to run it while I was away but it's specialist work. My wife and the baby are going to live with my mother in Shiba.'

The woman is standing just behind the mechanic's shoulder, a child about a year old tied to her back in a shawl. She is much younger than her husband. She looks tired and slightly frightened.

'I'm sure your customers will not forget you,' says Yuji.

'Half of them are overseas themselves,' says the man. 'When I come home it'll be like starting again.'

'I used to do some work for Mr Horikawa,' says Yuji. 'He had an office above your workshop.'

'Of course. Every day he would look in and greet us. Nobody in the street had a bad word to say about him.'

'He's gone somewhere?'

'Gone?'

'Moved?'

'He's dead,' says the man.

'Horikawa?'

'It was even in the paper. I cut it out. If we were in the shop, I could find it for you. Popular Hibaya businessman in railway suicide. Something like that.'

'*Horikawa?*'

'With his son. The one who was a bit, you know, in the head . . .'

'Both of them? Both dead?'

'They went on to the line just the other side of the steel bridge. Waited there for the night train. It was a big funeral. Even the service of the forty-ninth day had a good turn-out. Or so I heard.'

The child, catching at her mother's hair, begins to whimper. The woman ignores it.

'When did it happen?' asks Yuji.

'The beginning of October? People say his heart was getting worse. That he was afraid of what would happen to his son if he couldn't care for him any more. His wife . . .' He sucks in his cheeks.

'Yes,' says Yuji.

'I'm sorry to be the one who brings bad news.'

'You weren't to know.'

'He's in the cemetery at Koishikawa if you want to pay your respects.'

'At Koishikawa?'

'They had a family plot.'

'Yes. I see. Thank you.'

'And if your bicycle needs fixing in, say, six months from now, maybe I'll be back in business.'

'I'll remember,' says Yuji. They nod to each other, continue on their way, the child's crying sounding in Yuji's head long after he could possibly still be hearing it.

17

O n the front door of the house in Kanda someone has nailed a large sheet of paper. On it is written (in calligraphy a child would be ashamed of) ABOLISH DESIRE UNTIL THE FINAL VICTORY!

For a few moments Yuji stands there with his bicycle, unsure what to do. Pass by? Pull it off? He cannot use the entrance through the garden. The kitchen door is bolted. And anyway, how would it help him now? It is too late for hiding. He leans his bicycle against the wall of the house. The sense of being observed from the buildings across the street is very strong. He takes the key from his pocket. As he opens the front door the paper flaps, shows, on its other side, an advertisement for tinned whale meat.

He stands in the blackness of the hallway, holds his breath, listens, then hurries through to the salon, opens the window and unlatches the shutters. Brilliant morning light cuts across the room.

He looks in the study, then all the rooms at the back of the house. All of it is secure, undisturbed, exactly as he and Alissa left it nine days ago (nine days!). Whoever nailed up the poster has not yet dared go any further than the door. Some neighbourhood patriot. Someone who imagines he has seen the enemy in his own street. Or was the poster discussed at a meeting of the local association? A warning, a punishment. Do they know his name? Where is Hanako now? Who does she talk to?

He goes upstairs, examines each room in turn until he comes to Alissa's. The curtains are part open (that, too, just as they left it). He sits on the stripped bed, then steps to the wardrobe and opens both its doors. Though she took all she could fit in the suitcases, pressed in, irritably, more and more, took most of her favourites, there are still eight or ten dresses hanging there, and in the rack of shelves beside the rail, blouses, shirts, rolled socks, camisoles. He touches the dresses, lets his fingers drift from one to the next. Most he cannot remember ever having seen her wear. Most smell only of the little embroidered pillows of lavender at the bottom of the wardrobe (*La vraie lavande de Provence*). A scarf – chiffon? – is steeped in some perfume of hers but this is not what he is looking for. He shuts the wardrobe, turns the little brass key. In the corner, in the space between the wardrobe and the wall, is a basket of plaited bamboo. He takes off the lid. It is a laundry basket, and crumpled at the bottom, overlooked or ignored, is one of her linen nightgowns. He lifts it out. It smells of her. It smells shockingly of the child. On the front are two small stains, creamy-yellow against the white, where her milk seeped from her, before or after a feed. He holds it up, examines it thoroughly, then takes off his clothes and pulls the gown over his head. It is tight across his upper back and shoulders but otherwise fits him quite comfortably. He curls on the bed, the rough ticking of the mattress. The room, the shadow light, hold him patiently. After an hour he gets up again, takes off the gown, puts on his clothes, goes downstairs, closes the shutter, re-crosses the salon, the dark hall, and leaves the house.

From Kanda he rides towards home, but when he reaches the main road above Yushima he turns left towards the cemetery. The guardian, an old man carrying a broom of bound twigs, guides Yuji to the Horikawa family plot. There are flowers there, white chrysanthemums, but they are not recent, their petals edged with brown, like rust. Behind the grave are wooden *sotoba* boards with Horikawa's Buddhist name and that of his son, who, in death, is named Righteous Serene Sincerity Boy. At the front, to the right of the grave, is a small box for business cards, the corner of a last card protruding a little from the slot.

Yuji has brought no flowers or incense with him. The guardian would probably have sold him some but the guardian has wandered away to where his presence is just the faint scratching of twigs on the path.

'I would have valued your advice,' says Yuji to the stone. 'You would have made me coffee on your spirit burner. We would have watched the trains and you would have told me what to do.' He bows, deeply, straightens his back, then leans down for the edge of card, the little white tongue poking from the box. 'With condolences, Yoichi Masuda, assistant to the vice president, West Japan Shipping Corp., Akita, Niigata, Hiroshima, Shiminoseki.' The address of Masuda's office is in Tokyo, the other side of Hibiya Park from Horikawa's. Yuji returns to the gate. He cannot hear the guardian's broom anymore, nor does there seem to be anyone else visiting the cemetery today, unless the two men standing under the cedar tree between the gate and the road are intending to go in. They have, however, nothing in their hands, and there is something slightly odd in the way the younger of the two glances at Yuji, then stares at the other man, in silence.

18

On the day of Father's departure they travel to the station by taxi, arriving there a few minutes after eleven. They have agreed to have coffee somewhere, a last conversation before the midday train renews their separation. 'There's a place across here,' says Yuji. 'It won't be as busy as the station.'

They cross the road, each of them carrying a suitcase. The café has not altered since Yuji was here with Taro. The mural of the temple, the photograph of Hitler and Mussolini, the waitresses in their berets. Even the record they are playing seems to be the same Italian song, in which the only word Yuji recognises is a drawn out 'amo-re, amo-re'.

They order coffee, are told there is no coffee, not this week, and order tea instead. There are not many other customers. A few couples, a few on their own reading newspapers and smoking.

'It's really starting to feel like spring,' says Father. 'It's years since I saw spring on the mountain. Perhaps, after all, you'll have an opportunity to visit?'

They have already, at home the previous evening, discussed those matters of a practical nature that need to be understood between them. Father and Mother will stay on at the farm for an unspecified period. In the meantime, if Yuji's red paper arrives (and Father's visit to Kushida produced no reassurances), then the house in Hongo will be shut down. Miyo will go to Setagaya to help Sonoko. Items of value – the books from the garden study, various old scrolls and lacquerware – can be stored somewhere safe, somewhere fireproof. Somewhere bombproof.

The waitress brings their tea. The clock on the wall behind Father's head says quarter past the hour.

'This is the first cold season I can remember,' says Father, 'that you have not been ill.'

'Yes.'

'It seems that the family is generally in better health these days.'

'Auntie Sawa?'

'Certainly no worse.'

Yuji nods. He feels he is carrying a small pistol in his hand which, beneath the table, he is pointing at Father's belly. He tells himself for the hundredth time that if he could face Feneon, say what he said to Feneon, then he can face Father. But Feneon – however Yuji sometimes chose to think of him – was not his father, whereas the man across the table, the bearded, still vigorous man tipping the ash from his cigarette into the mount Vesuvius ashtray, held him as a baby, taught him as a child, saw all his childish struggling towards the beginning of adulthood. All his subsequent failings.

'I hope,' says Father, 'it's not a crowded train.'

'No,' says Yuji.

'A crowded compartment, particularly when people are eating, makes the journey much more tiresome.'

'Perhaps you'll be fortunate?'

'Yes, perhaps.'

'What Miyo hinted at,' says Yuji, staring into the green depths of his tea, 'maybe it's more serious than I admitted.'

'You've admitted nothing,' says Father. 'Are you referring to your new friend?'

'Yes.'

'She is someone you wish the family to meet?'

'There are things that need to be explained,' says Yuji. 'There are aspects.'

'Aspects?'

'She is not Japanese.'

'A foreigner?'

'Yes.'

'I see.'

'Yes.'

'I wonder, could she be connected to the Feneons?'

'You *knew*?'

'I am guessing. How many foreigners are you acquainted with?'

'She is Monsieur Feneon's daughter.'

'And she has a name?'

'Alissa.'

'Alissa.'

'Yes.'

'I assume she lives in her father's house. Isn't that by the cathedral?'

Yuji nods. 'The house is empty now.'

'Empty?'

'They have left Japan.'

'The whole family?'

'It is only the two of them.'

'But the father and the daughter?'

'Yes.'

'They no longer felt safe here?'

'How could they?'

'I understand.'

'There is something else . . .'

'Yes?'

Yuji draws the photograph from the inside pocket of his jacket. It is one of those Miss Ogilvy made them sit for at Christmas. In the picture, Alissa's red jacket looks black. Emile is lying with his cheek against her upper arm. Alissa is smiling, shyly. Yuji finds his own expression impossible to read. Part of the fireplace is in view, and the front half of a grey cat. He passes the picture across the table. Father takes out his glasses, glances at his watch, then studies the picture. At last, removing his glasses, folding them, he gives the picture back.

'When was this taken?'

'Before the New Year.'

'Is it . . . this what it seems?'

'Yes.'

'And you have waited until now to tell me?'

'He was born in Yokohama. December the twenty-first. At night.'

'He?'

'His name is Emile.'

'Emile?'

'Like Zola.'

'You are telling me you have a son.'

'Yes.'

Father leans back in his chair. For Yuji, there is a moment of incongruous satisfaction in the way his words, his news, have felled the older man's mind. Then, moving his cup aside, he bows over the table, forehead almost touching the varnish. 'Please accept my apologies for not informing you sooner.'

'Sit up,' hisses father. 'You are drawing attention to us.'

Yuji sits up.

'It would . . .' begins Father, after a long pause filled by the idiotic, the half mad sighing of the music, 'it would have been courteous to . . . have chosen a moment when we could have . . . discussed this.' His voice is quiet. There is an edge of irritation, of bewilderment, but no anger. The old fierceness, that severity of character Yuji, as a boy, so dreaded to be the focus of, has not, it seems, returned from the mountain with him.

'I didn't know she was carrying a child.'

'What?'

'I didn't know until the end.'

'But it's yours?'

'Yes.'

'You're sure?'

'Yes.'

'I suppose . . . I suppose he has some of your features?'

'His eyes perhaps. His back . . .'

'His back?'

'Yes.'

'So you're a father.'

'Yes.'

'A father . . .' He shakes his head, lights another cigarette. 'Tomorrow, this conversation will seem like a dream.'

'Will you tell Mother?'

'I have no idea. What can I say to her? By the way, before I boarded the train Yuji informed me of something quite interesting.'

'I should have spoken sooner.'

'Of *course* you should.'

'You were away.'

'Please, do not make excuses.' For a few moments, looking past Yuji, Father gently rubs, with the tip of his thumb, the crease between his eyebrows. 'I am a grandfather,' he says at last.

'Yes.'

'Your mother is a grandmother.'

'Yes.'

'And he, this child, he is with his mother now?'

'Yes.'

'Alissa?'

'Yes.'

'They intend to return one day?'

'They still have a house.'

'In Kanda.'

'Yes.'

'And he is healthy.'

'Yes.'

'Emile.'

'Yes.'

'You could have chosen a name that's easier to pronounce.'

'If I have brought shame . . .'

'It's not a question of that. It's not . . . All that . . . With things as they are, I mean. We must think more practically.'

'Yes.'

'Do they sell sake in this place?'

'I don't think so.'

'A pity.'

Father reaches for the photograph, puts on his glasses again. 'I should like to have seen him. Once, at least.'

'Please, take it with you,' says Yuji.

'The photograph?'

'When you tell Mother, you could show it to her.'

'You have others?'

'No.'

'Then you must keep it.'

'Please take it.'

'You don't want it?'

'It's not that.'

'No?' They look at each other, study each other. The minute hand of the clock slides to ten to the hour.

'Your train,' says Yuji.

'The train? Mmm . . .'

Yuji pays. They cross the road in silence, enter the halls of the station.

'I'm near the engine, I think,' says Father, hurrying past the steel pillars at the side of the train as a guard follows behind them slamming doors.

'Here?'

'Three?'

'Yes.'

Father climbs the metal steps. Yuji swings up the cases.

'We cut it fine again,' says Father through the open window. 'Another minute . . .'

'Please give Mother my best wishes.'

'I will.'

'Thank her for the biscuits.'

'I will.'

'And Uncle Kensuke and Auntie Sawa . . .'

'All of them. Yes.'

A bell rings. A bell answers. The guard shouts a final warning.

'It may be a while,' says Yuji.

'You must do what is necessary,' calls Father. 'Ryuichi can take care of us now.' He opens a hand in farewell. Yuji, turning away, shields his eyes from the smoke.

19

While Miyo is out of the house watching, with the neighbourhood children, a show put on by a travelling entertainer (puppets in a shoebox theatre strapped to the back of a bicycle), Yuji telephones Mr Masuda. Masuda sounds as though he has just returned from a long lunch and is, perhaps, considering locking his door and sleeping for an hour, but his voice becomes more attentive when Yuji mentions Horikawa.

'You used to work for him?'

'I was the one who wrote the copy for your company last year. "The newest ships, the fastest routes . . ." '

' "Niigata Docks are truly a gateway to the world." I remember it. It had a good ring to it.'

'Thank you.'

'Mr Horikawa was a man I had a deep respect for. We sometimes played *shogi* together. Had things been different for him . . .'

'His circumstances . . .'

'Yes . . . It is very regrettable.'

'Yes.'

'But how is it I can help you, Mr Takano? Is this a business matter?'

20

The maid, a girl with large, drowsy eyes, the sleeves of her kimono tied up, a damp cloth in one hand, ushers Yuji into a room at the back of the house where a window at floor level admits a flow of even, shallow light. She puts out a sitting cushion for him beside the alcove. The scroll in the alcove is an ink drawing of a frog, a slightly mischievous-looking creature described with a half-dozen energetic lines. Something about this picture makes Yuji smile, and he is smiling still when Mrs Miyazaki comes in, bowing, chattering, her face puckered with embarrassment to find herself alone with such an educated young man, a published poet, a friend of her brilliant sons. Also, of course, someone who has seen her in consternation, who has seen her weep.

To calm her, he asks about the drawing of the frog.

'Junzo chose it,' she says, 'before he left. It was the one he liked best for springtime. It's only a copy of course. I think the original is in a museum in Kamakura. Or Nara? I'm sure *you* know where it is.'

'So he's gone?'

'It's nearly two weeks now. The Association of Patriotic Schoolgirls was at the station to wave them off. There were so many of them, all cheering so excitedly it was quite difficult for us to get close to the train and I was afraid we wouldn't find him. But then I heard his voice, calling me. We had his belt, you see. His thousand-stitch belt. Everyone in the street had sewed a stitch on it, lots of strangers too, though now with women waiting on every corner with needle and thread, it's a wonder anybody has the time to do anything else, don't you think?'

'He's gone to China?'

'He said they would be near a big river, though, of course, he wasn't allowed to tell me any more.'

'The Yangtze, perhaps.'

'Yes,' she says. 'Perhaps it was that one.'

'And Taro? There were two flags outside the house.'

'He's in Hanoi,' she says. 'They needed people who could speak French.'

'Translators.'

She nods. 'We were very honoured.'

'His French was always better than mine,' says Yuji.

'I'm sure that can't be true,' she says.

'I brought something for Junzo. I thought . . . I'd hoped he might still be here.'

'How kind of you,' she says, glancing at the package in Yuji's hands.

'It's just a book. Some French poems I had when I was at university. I tried to give it to him once before, when he volunteered . . . And there's a letter.'

'From you?'

'No. It's an old letter. Some of us thought it didn't even exist. But Junzo always believed in it.'

'So,' she says, trying not to look confused. 'It's an old one, then.'

Yuji puts the package on the mat and with both hands slides it towards Mrs Miyazaki's knees. Seeing the formality of his gesture, she accepts the package with as low a bow as the fullness of her waist, the tightness of her obi, permits. She touches the indigo cloth, Uncle Kensuke's 'test piece', in which the book and letter are wrapped. 'And this?' she asks.

'Yes,' says Yuji. 'It's all for him.'

For while she sits there, quiet as a flower. Her eyes have brimmed but the tears will not fall in front of him again.

'You are going away too?' she asks.

'Yes.'

'Then perhaps you will see him. You could give it to him yourself.'

'I am not going to China,' says Yuji.

'No?'

'Somewhere else.'

'Ah.' She nods, then bows again. 'On behalf of the Miyazaki family, please accept our congratulations. May you return safely one day.'

He thanks her. 'One day,' he says.

The door slides open. The maid, excusing herself through a stifled yawn, brings in the tea.

21

One more day for Fujitomi. One more day in the blue van. One more strip of soft money. When Yuji climbs from the van near a tram-stop in Nihombashi, he tells Fujitomi he is closing the house in Hongo.

'Then you'll need some help,' says Fujitomi, wiping the April warmth from his throat. 'Somewhere to store the valuables?'

Yuji nods.

'I've got a place up in Meguro Ward. Steel door. A ventilation grille even a mosquito would have trouble getting through. I've been putting some of my own stuff there . . .'

'Your own?'

'It's good to be prepared, eh? When do you need it?'

'Soon.'

'How soon?'

'Tomorrow afternoon?'

'As soon as that . . . Well, let's see. If I can leave those boxes of Shanghai eggs at the bakers in Monzen Nakacho and find somewhere for the golf balls, the van will be empty enough.'

'Thank you,' says Yuji. 'I'll be ready.'

They smile at each other through the open window. If, thinks Yuji, Fujitomi asks him a direct question now, if he asks him *the* direct question, then he will answer it, directly, but Fujitomi, long conditioned by that habitual restraint of curiosity required by the pick-up and delivery business, does not ask.

'I'll be there at half twelve,' he says. 'People will be busy with the midday meal. We'll have less of an audience.' He revs the engine, finds the gear at the third attempt. 'Looks like I shall have to do my own driving for a while,' he shouts, then grins, peers from the far window to watch the road, and moves the van, in a series of lurches, into the evening traffic.

When Yuji reaches home, two men walk into the house behind him. They do it so naturally – the air of people whose right to enter this or any house is beyond debate – that Yuji, turning to face them in the vestibule, is, at first, more impressed than alarmed, as if they have performed an interesting trick, a little theatrical coup. One man is several years older than the other. They are wearing smartly pressed but inexpensive suits, the same suits Yuji saw them in outside the cemetery.

'Surprised to see us?' asks the elder man.

'We know all about you,' says the younger, taking off his shoes and leaving them neatly beside the step.

'We're going to have a look around,' says the elder man. 'You don't mind, I hope?'

Miyo comes out of the kitchen. 'They want to look around,' says Yuji. She asks if she should serve tea.

'And something sweet,' says the elder man. 'I'm aching for something sweet.'

With Yuji walking between them, an arrangement they seem to fall into quite naturally, they go out to the verandah, put on garden slippers, and follow the curving path of worn and irregular slabs down to the garden study. Yuji opens the door. The study is chill and slightly damp. The elder man starts smoking. As he looks along the shelves he taps his ash into the palm of his hand, then scatters it on the wooden floor. The younger one has a camera. He photographs any book with a foreign title, photographs the photograph of Father with fellow students in a rowing boat on the Sumida, summer 1911. Also the picture beside it, Father and two unidentified foreigners, one a woman, all young, none quite in focus, in front of a statue in a park in London or Paris.

In the house, in the Western room, he takes a photograph of the wireless. In the Japanese room, it's the empty shelves beside the alcove that interest them.

They go up the stairs, open the storage cupboard, drag everything onto the landing, place in a pile – presumably for later confiscation – the jazz records, a bowler hat, a woman's felt cloche hat, several elaborately framed portraits of unsmiling ancestors Yuji could not have begun to identify. Then they go to Yuji's room. In here, locked inside a box of black and bronze tin, he has the telegram from Alissa ('Arrived Tuesday. All in good health. Emile eats everything.') He has Feneon's address in Singapore, a roll of 340 yen and a document authorising passage on the *Izu Dancer*, a cargo vessel chartered by the West Japan Shipping Corporation leaving Shiminoseki on the fifteenth bound for Tourane, Singkawang, Batavia. ('I'm in the rubber business now,' he told Masuda. 'And as you know, it's a crucial time for rubber.')

363

While the elder man searches through clothes, the younger lays out novels and books of poetry, arranges them first in a line and then in a square, as if it was important not just to present the evidence but to show it in a way that would be aesthetically pleasing.

'What are these?' asks the elder man, holding in his palm the last of Dick Amazawa's pills.

'I have headaches,' says Yuji.

'Shouldn't read so much,' says the younger man, who has now found the black and bronze box and is trying, with the pressure of his thumbs, to force up the lid. 'How does this open?' he asks.

'There's a key,' says Yuji.

'Find it.'

'It's just some money. Some savings.'

'Find it.'

The key is in Yuji's pocket. There is, he knows, not much sense in delaying the moment, but if he is about to be arrested, beaten, imprisoned, he would like a few seconds to prepare himself. Is it worth trying to run? He concentrates on not looking at the platform door. He would have only the smallest possible start on them, but if he could get outside, he could clamber down to the garden. Are they armed? Would they shoot at him? And where would he run to? Kanda? Setagaya? If they know all about him, they know about Kanda and Setagaya.

He pretends to be searching for the key among the clothes tangled on the floor. His mind, little by little, is assuming the blankness of surrender, of dumb capitulation. An hour ago he was free! Free to eat in Otaki's, free to ride his bicycle, free to make his plans. But already it seems hard to remember it, to recall exactly how that felt. He is about to start on some schoolboy story about having lost the key, or no, *given* it to someone, someone whose name he has unfortunately forgotten, when the elder man lets out a sharp grunt of surprise. Yuji turns to him. The man is holding the velvet-skinned case. The case is open. The pin, in its satin crease, gleams with the self-contained glamour of a weapon.

'This yours?'

'Yes.'

'You're sure?'

'Yes.'

'Where d'you get it?'

Yuji tells him.

The man stares at him, stares at the pin, runs his tongue along his teeth, glances at the younger man, looks back at the pin. 'You should have said,' he says, a high voice, a whine. 'Now you've let us embarrass ourselves. There was no need for that.'

'I'm sorry,' says Yuji.

'We've lost face.'

'I'm sorry.'

'You want us to help you put this back?' He gestures to the floor and, more generally, to the chaos on the landing.

'There's no need,' says Yuji.

'You should wear it,' says the man, shutting the case and giving it to Yuji. 'Save everyone a lot of trouble.'

'Yes,' says Yuji. 'Thank you.'

The younger man hangs his camera over his shoulder. He winks at Yuji. 'The key,' he says, 'it is in your pocket, right?'

22

He has a single tan suitcase with him. He is dressed plainly, the graduation suit again, the austerity hat. When he rose it was dark, when he left it was dark. Now, at six fifteen, the station's yellow lights are switched off and a crowd of men and women are streaming through the station doors. It is morning, officially.

He has drunk tea and eaten rice in the all-night food stall by the Station Hotel, but there is something wrong with his insides. An hour after the *Tokko* left he was racked with stomach cramps, followed by violent diarrhoea. It has been over a week now. The cramps have stopped but the diarrhoea remains troublesome, unpredictable.

He stands by a pillar, sits on a bench, studies, as discreetly as he can, what the others do, what is normal. He lines up to buy a newspaper. When he reaches the front of the queue, he becomes confused by the coins in his hand. The vendor is irritated. Time is money. Are there more policemen at the station this morning? More uniforms? Through the clustered speakers above his head a woman's voice, broken by amplification, is announcing the name and destination of a train. Part of the crowd peels away, advances in close formation. Yuji's gut grips tighter. He stops, shuts his eyes, breathes. All that has led to this moment is hidden from him. What was it? What made him think he could do this, could break through the black lines? Certainly, he is no longer guided by argument, by any of those justifications he muttered to himself for hours in the sewing room. All he has left now are skin memories. The ghostly weight of a child in his arms, a woman's hair on his face . . . How can that possibly be enough?

He picks up his case, drags it up the stairs, moves shoulder to shoulder with strangers, sees a train, sees a carriage number, starts to climb aboard, is stopped, shows his ticket. 'This one's for Hamamatsu,' says the guard, his face and voice quite unexpectedly friendly, solicitous even. He points the way. Yuji crosses under the line, surfaces, walks up beside another train. There's a board on the platform: 'Shiminoseki Express 0715.' It is not one of Kyoko's days, he knows this, but edging along the corridor, his case knocking against the calves of people leaning from the windows, he constantly expects to see her, to meet her startled gaze.

He finds his compartment. A man and woman are already there, people his parents' age. He nods to them, takes the seat opposite. Under his suit he is sweating, heavily. Does he look like a fugitive? Like one of the spies the association pamphlets urge citizens to be vigilant for? ('He will not reveal himself by his dress or manners. He will be cautious at all times.')

'You should put it up,' says the man, pointing to the luggage rack. Yuji lifts the case. If the lock failed now, some clothes would fall out, an oiled silk raincoat, a pair of straw sandals, a night-kimono, a towel, a pair of schoolboy's white gloves with stitching on the back and mother-of-pearl button at the wrist. He has a few books with him: Akutagawa, Soseki, Kafu. He has no foreign books. Nor in the end did he take his last copy of *Electric Dragonfly*, a little book that has always weighed too much. He has the photograph from the dresser in the Western room of Father and Mother on their wedding day, stiff as dolls. He has the pin. He has his money, his pass for the *Izu Dancer*. Also a letter, typed in the garden study, purporting to be from a rubber trader in Batavia inviting him to visit as soon as possible. It might, perhaps, fool someone.

Are they moving? No . . . Yes! They are moving, and for a moment he is thrown into confusion by his failure to notice it the instant it began. He turns to the window, grasps his knees, forces from his mind the memory of Miyo sobbing in the dark next to the vestibule step. As they pass through the marshalling yards they pick up speed. It's a beautiful morning, the sun, the pure spring sun, cresting the roofs of the Low City. He narrows his eyes and stares, wills himself to be a camera, to see and keep everything, but everything, the moment it appears, is swept away as though it was not really his to see any more. He sits back, opens the paper, hides behind the paper, looks at the senseless words, the senseless pictures.

'You're going all the way?' asks the man.

'All . . . ?' says Yuji, lowering the paper.

'To Shiminoseki?'

'Yes.'

'It's a long ride.'

'Yes.'

'We've been visiting family. We're from Hiroshima.'

Yuji nods.

The man looks at him, waiting. 'And you?' he asks.

'Me?' says Yuji, wondering if the carriage toilet is already occupied, if it is too soon to go and look. 'I'm from here.' He gestures to the window. 'I'm from Tokyo.'

Historical Note

On 9 and 10 March 1945, in an operation code-named Meeting House, more than three hundred B-29 Superfortresses from a base in the Mariana Islands made a low-level night attack over Tokyo. The raid began just after midnight and continued in waves for two and a half hours. Each plane was carrying up to eight tons of incendiary bombs. Film taken on the ground shows vast walls of fire moving uncontrollably in strong winds, while people, ant-like, scurry desperately for shelter. Estimates of casualties vary widely but it is likely that between eighty and a hundred thousand were killed that night, the majority from the old, densely populated wards near the river. By daybreak the Low City lay in ashes again.

The author would like to acknowledge the generous assistance of Beatrice Monti della Corte and the Santa Maddalena Foundation in Tuscany. Warmest thanks also to Etsuko Suda and Nanae Koimai for their advice on matters Japanese. All errors, as ever, are the sole responsibility of the author.